Cottage
on the
Hill

ALSO BY EMMA DAVIES

Emma Davies

Return to the Little Cottage on the Hill

bookouture

Published by Bookouture in 2018

An imprint of StoryFire Ltd.

Carmelite House
50 Victoria Embankment
London EC4Y 0DZ

www.bookouture.com

ISBN: 978-1-78681-503-3
eBook ISBN: 978-1-78681-502-6

Anam Cara – from the Celtic, meaning 'soul friend'

Chapter 1

Clara gave the room one final sweep and, with a satisfied nod, collected the duster and can of polish from the coffee table. The Gardener's Cottage was clean, welcoming and, most importantly, ready for their new booking. Their first guest, Isobel, had stayed with them for six weeks, and left only two days ago, but already Clara missed her, and her music. She had got used to hearing the sweet notes of her violin floating on the warm evening air. Isobel had stayed for the entire summer and, by the end of it, she had no longer seemed like a guest at all; she had become one of the team at Joy's Acre Farm.

Now that Tom had finished thatching the roof on the latest cottage to be renovated, it too was ready for occupancy and a family would be arriving tomorrow for a two-week stay. Clara glanced out of the window at the bright blue sky. What stories would their new guests bring with them, she wondered.

It was mid-morning, but already the day was beginning to warm up as she walked outside and into the huge garden that surrounded the cottages. The sharp, cold tang of autumn air she'd felt when she woke this morning had mellowed with the sunshine, but it would be back come the evening. It was a time of year that Clara adored, and she was looking forward to the new rhythms and routines that came to the garden with every new season. The summer had been extraordinarily hot, and it had been a battle to keep everything watered and growing well, but looking around her now, at the riot of blooms in every colour of the rainbow and the burgeoning produce in the vegetable beds, her efforts were being truly rewarded.

Clara picked her way down the path, mentally running through the numerous jobs she would need to attend to today. She would get to them all eventually, but first she needed to check in with Maddie to make sure that nothing more was needed to prepare for tomorrow, which was shaping up to be rather an eventful day…

A month or so ago, there had been great excitement when a documentary filmmaker called Adam Brooks had come to Joy's Acre looking for a location for a new series about rural businesses. The moment he had locked eyes on Joy's Acre he'd known he had found the place, and had called for his team to spend a couple of days filming material which would be aired later on next year. Yesterday though, Adam had been back in touch with a special request to return again, this time with a new proposition and someone else he wanted them to meet. They had no idea what was in store, but there was much to do to prepare for the visit.

The door to the Thatcher's Cottage was wide open and Clara could hear the drone of a vacuum cleaner coming from inside. She passed through into the kitchen and straight on into the living room where Maddie could be seen giving the colourful rug that covered most of the floor a rigorous once-over. Knowing that Maddie couldn't hear her, Clara smiled to herself as she crept forward and devilishly tapped Maddie on the shoulder from behind.

Maddie jumped a foot in the air, whirling around in shock. Seconds later, a wide grin spread across her face as she realised it was Clara.

'You ratbag!' she exclaimed, switching off the vacuum. 'You nearly gave me a heart attack – I should have you fired!'

Clara calmly tucked her mane of long blonde hair behind her ears and grinned back, sticking her tongue out for good measure.

'You and I both know Seth would just laugh. In fact, he'd be more likely to complain that he wasn't around to see the expression on your face!'

Maddie rolled her eyes. 'You know him too well,' she said.

And Clara did. She and Seth had been friends for years, long before everyone else had arrived at Joy's Acre. Back then, it had just been the two of them; Seth working to rebuild the derelict farmhouse and cottages he had inherited, and her trying to coerce the overgrown mess of a garden into shape. They were getting there, but everything had taken so long, and it was only when Maddie arrived earlier in the springtime that she had blown a breath of fresh air, not just through Seth's life, but through Joy's Acre itself. Now the former farm looked better than it ever had, and although renovations were still ongoing on two of the holiday cottages, the other two were beginning to bring in some much-needed income.

'So, come on,' she said. 'What's the news? Have you heard when they're coming yet?'

Maddie's face was a picture of excitement. 'No, I keep checking my phone every two minutes, but there's no word from Adam yet.'

'He must have said *something*?'

She shook her head. 'Nope, he's being very coy and won't tell me a thing. Only that he's bringing someone called Declan with him, and that we're all going to love him to bits…'

Clara pouted. 'Well I think that's very mean. It's not often you get a visit from a trendy TV producer – I think the least you can do is let a girl know when they're arriving so that she can put her lippy on…'

Maddie grinned. They both knew that it was highly unlikely Clara even owned any lipstick.

'Well, they're bound to arrive right at the wrong moment,' added Clara, 'but I don't suppose there's much we can do about that. Anyway, I left Trixie cooking up a storm in the main house, the Gardener's Cottage is all ready for later, and this place looks gorgeous, so what's there left to do?'

'Drink tea?' Maddie suggested as she looked around her. 'Come on, let's go and find Trixie. I reckon we've earned a break and, while we're at it we can make a list of any last little jobs.' She unplugged the Hoover from the wall and began to wind up the cord. 'It does look good, doesn't it?' she added, straightening up. 'I'm really pleased with it.'

'I think it's perfect,' Clara agreed, nodding. 'And the finishing touches are inspired.'

All of the cottages on Joy's Acre Farm were furnished in an authentic Victorian style, but made individual by the addition of items associated with a particular traditional craft, which also gave each of the cottages its name. They were currently standing in the newly finished Thatcher's Cottage and on the largest whitewashed wall in front of them was a huge salt dough bread sheaf and cornucopia that their first ever paying guest, Isobel, had made for them as a leaving gift. Woven corn dollies and other traditional wooden thatching equipment decorated the rest of the cottage. Clara thought it gave a warm, homely feel without being overly fussy, and now that this cottage would have its first guest arriving soon, no doubt they would find out if they had got things right.

Maddie stowed the Hoover in the cupboard under the stairs and gave the room one last look before turning to Clara.

'Right, let's go! With any luck, Trixie will have made something gooey and chocolatey to go with our cuppa.'

Clara groaned. She knew she wouldn't be able to resist Trixie's baking, even if it did mean she'd have to put in some extra-hard digging later on to compensate.

Once outside, she waved Maddie on. 'I'll catch you up,' she said. 'Let me just go and see if Tom wants a break yet.'

He'd been hard at it since eight that morning. No doubt he'd be desperate for a brew. Shielding her eyes against the sun, she squinted up at the roofline of the cottage next door where Tom was silhouetted against the light, his mess of pale blond hair like a halo around his head.

'Oi!' she shouted. 'Can you take a break from being a master thatcher extraordinaire and come and have a cup of tea?'

A good-looking face grinned back at her. 'Clara my dear,' he said in a false theatrical drawl. 'I am of course a master thatcher extraordinaire whatever activity I'm engaged in, so alas I cannot take a break from being that very thing... I can, however, cease my current industry on this roof to partake in a hot beverage. One moment...'

He sank the vicious-looking tool he was holding into the new area of thatch beside him, anchoring it in place, and reached behind his knees to unfasten the leather pads that protected his knees from the ladder as he worked. Shimmying down it, he was on the ground beside her in a matter of seconds.

'I thought you'd never ask, my mouth's as dry as a nun's—'

Clara swiftly held up her hand. 'Don't say it!' she warned, but her smile was warm as she linked her arm through Tom's.

'Good morning?' she asked.

'Yeah,' he replied, 'although I'm not sure why, but this roof is in a far worse state than the other two were. We had to take a lot more of the top layers off than we've done with the others, so it's going to take a wee bit longer, I'm afraid.' He wrinkled his nose at her. 'Don't say anything to Maddie though, not just yet. I'm hoping I can make up the time and she won't notice a thing.'

They couldn't rent out the cottage until Tom was finished on the roof, so he was always up against it to keep to the deadlines they had set. While the weather stayed fair it wasn't a problem, but a prolonged rainy spell could cause havoc…

'I won't,' she agreed. 'Besides, depending on what happens tomorrow, I think Maddie may well have her thoughts on other things. You'll be fine.'

They walked in silence the rest of the way to the main farmhouse, but almost as soon as they turned the corner into the yard they were enveloped by the most heavenly smell.

'If that's elevenses, I shall be a very happy bunny…'

Clara grinned. 'If that's elevenses, I fear for my waistline…' She gave Tom a sideways glance. 'So, how is Isobel…?' She let the sentence dangle with just a hint of suggestion.

'She's fine, thanks.' Tom carried on walking, dropping her arm as they reached the door and chivalrously indicating that Clara should go first.

The door was never locked, and she reached for the door handle, making as if to turn it, but stopping at the last moment.

'If you really think *fine, thanks* is a suitable response, then you're going to have to wait a very long time for your cake…' Clara rolled her eyes. 'You're not getting past me until you spill the beans, so come on, tell me.'

Tom's eyes flashed with amusement. 'Funny,' he said, 'a few weeks ago you took every opportunity to shut me up if I so much as mentioned my love life, now you want *details*? Whatever has got into you?'

'Heavens, that cake smells good, doesn't it? I wonder what it is? It could be lemon drizzle, or that wonderful chocolate, cherry and almond one she made last week… of course, she might even have made your favourite, Victoria sponge…'

Tom groaned. 'Okay, okay, I give in…' He grinned. 'Isobel is officially the best thing that's ever happened to me, and I am happier than a pig in clover.'

'See, that wasn't so hard, was it?'

'Moreover, she's really back in her stride and composing beautiful music like a thing possessed, *and* she's already been asked to play a couple more gigs with the string quartet she helped out a few weeks ago. So, what with that and my mate Ginger's insistence that she continue to perform with the band, she's over the moon and more than happy to just let things play out.'

'Quite literally…' Clara's face was lit with a warm smile. 'I am so pleased for you, Tom, really…'

He blushed. 'I know. Who would have thought that so much could have happened in such a short space of time?'

'Perhaps it was meant to be?' she replied, finally turning the door handle. 'And the story's not over yet…'

The delicious smell became even stronger as they walked through the door – the unmistakeable aroma of cinnamon.

'Oh, dear Lord, she's made pastries…'

Trixie was indeed just drizzling icing over a batch of cinnamon whirls which sat in the centre of the huge pine table in the kitchen. She looked up and grinned as they entered.

'Morning!'

Trixie had been busy; alongside the rows and rows of golden pastries on the table were several freshly baked loaves of bread, laid out in a neat row to cool.

'Maddie's just gone to check her emails… *again*, but the kettle's on. Won't be a tick.'

She finished what she was doing and turned her back on them to place the bowl she had been using beside the sink.

'Don't *even* think about it!' she said sharply, without turning around. Tom froze, his arm outstretched to sample a delicious treat.

He withdrew his hand swiftly, throwing Clara a sheepish look. 'How does she know?' he whispered. And Clara just shrugged.

'I have eyes in the back of my head, and a highly developed sixth sense for pilfering…' Trixie turned around and winked at Clara. 'There's also the fact that your reputation precedes you.'

She poured hot water from the kettle into the waiting teapot, and placed it on the table, beside a collection of mugs and a stack of plates.

'Is Seth joining us?' asked Trixie.

Clara was about to comment that she had no idea, when Maddie walked back into the room and pulled a face.

'Not just yet,' she said. 'He's gone to see a certain lady landowner named Agatha…'

'Ooh, ouch,' replied Clara.

Trixie took up one of the laden plates and removed two of the cinnamon swirls. 'Then I'd better save these for when he gets back,' she remarked. 'He'll be needing them.'

Maddie gave her a grateful smile. 'I expect so, thanks, Trixie. I doubt he'll be in a sunny mood when he gets back. She doesn't usually have that effect on him, as well we know.'

'Is this to do with the blacksmith who's arriving later?' asked Clara. 'She's taking part in the competition, isn't she?'

Maddie nodded. 'Yes, her name is Megan, and I believe so. I suspect you and Tom already know this, but the competition is held every three years, and according to Seth, Agatha has always hosted it. She'll have an impossibly long list of jobs that want doing if I know her…' She straightened up. 'Anyway, enough talk of Agatha, I really don't want to think about her today, not when I've just had an email from Adam!'

Her expression changed in an instant, as she exchanged an excited grin with Clara and the others.

Trixie quickly handed round the plates, waving at the pastries so that everyone knew to start digging in. 'Come on then, when's he coming?'

'At ten tomorrow morning.' Maddie sat back in her chair. 'Which is the most horrendous timing of course, seeing as the Carter family are due at eleven, but we'll have to make it work somehow.' She leaned into her next words. 'Apparently Declan is *very* excited at the prospect of meeting us all, but you and Clara in particular…'

Trixie snorted. 'I bet he isn't!'

'Well, that's what the man said. I'm only repeating it.'

Clara giggled. 'Go on, Maddie. What else did Adam say?'

'Only that he'd be able to give us a bit more information as to where they're at with the documentary.' She paused for a moment. 'The editing is coming along nicely. Although they don't yet have anything they can show us, it won't be long. He mentioned there could be a possibility they will need to pop back for a few more shots, but tomorrow will be all about this other chap, Declan. He wants to see some examples of produce from the garden, specifically anything which Trixie can use to make something delicious in the kitchen … but we're not to go to any trouble.'

Clara stared at Maddie and then at Trixie, whose eyes were already on her.

'Oh my God,' she said. 'Not go to any trouble… Are you *mad*?'

There was a loud screech of chair leg against floor as Trixie jumped up and snatched up a notebook from beside the kettle.

'Damn, that won't do,' she said to no one in particular. 'I was just going to make a quiche for lunch tomorrow because I figured that if they'd been travelling, the Carter family wouldn't fancy anything too heavy, but that's *so* boring…' She sucked at her lip. 'Clara, what have we got in the garden that's absolutely gorgeous at the moment?'

Clara mentally walked through the beds she'd been working on. 'Well, the first of the red cabbages look nigh on perfect, and there are some gorgeous squashes now too. No, wait.' She waggled her fingers at Trixie. 'Swiss chard, that's what you should use. It looks so pretty right now. I've still got late raspberries too if you want something sweet? They make divine puddings, don't they?'

Trixie narrowed her eyes, thinking, as Clara groaned. 'I've got a million and one things to do. How on earth am I going to have the grounds looking perfect by *tomorrow?*'

Maddie laid a hand on Clara's arm. 'Who said it had to be perfect? Don't torture yourself,' she said, eyeing Trixie as well. 'Neither of you. If there's anything urgent that needs doing Tom and I can help, can't we, Tom? And Seth will be back later this afternoon. Besides, everything is ready for the Carters, and Megan won't be here until teatime, so that's only one meal for her, Trixie. The rest of us can make do with whatever.' She reached for the teapot and began to pour for them all. 'Let's just relax, have a cup of tea and make a list.'

Clara exchanged a knowing look with Tom. Maddie's lists were infamous, but where would they all be without them?

Chapter 2

Megan opened one eye and looked round her. She had no idea what the time was but, unfortunately, the morning seemed to have arrived. She nestled her head back down into the soft pillow. After what she'd been used to this past year, this bed felt like a slice of heaven and, given the exhausting journey she'd had yesterday, she would just as happily have slept inside a cardboard box.

She lifted an arm and felt around on the bedside table for her watch, bringing it close to her face and peering at it. It was only seven o'clock. Why on earth, on the one morning that she had the opportunity for a lie-in, did she have to wake at her normal time? She replaced her watch and resolutely buried her head back into the pillow. There was no way she was getting up yet.

Three minutes later, she flung back the covers with a sigh and stood up. It was no good, she was wide awake now. She looked around the airy room feeling a rising sense of excitement. It had been pitch-black when she'd arrived last night and although Seth, the owner of the cottages, had been very welcoming, their torch-led procession through the garden had done nothing to give her any sense of where she was. Even her bedroom looked very different in the daylight.

She crossed to the window, drawing aside the curtains slightly to peek through, and then flinging them wide as she caught a glimpse of what was beyond. She'd had no idea that the view was like this from up here. It was incredible. She had grown up in Summersmeade, the village she could see in the distance, but the road up to the farm was so thickly lined with trees that you never had any sense of how open it was once you reached the top. She knew the estate was here of course, everyone did, and in the winter when the trees were bare you could see the main house from the village road, but never had she been in a position to view the valley from this stunning perspective.

Looking down, she realised that there was a gate in the boundary wall behind the cottage that led directly into the fields below. It was all the invitation she needed. Turning from the window, she grabbed her holdall from the floor where she'd unceremoniously dumped it last night. She could get the rest of her things from the car later, but this bag held all she needed for now. Hauling it onto the bed, she rummaged around, pulling out a tee shirt, leggings and a pair of running shoes. A couple of minutes later, she was ready. A quick half-hour run around the field and she would come back and have a proper explore. She hastily tied up her hair into a ponytail and took off down the stairs, out the door, and into the morning.

As she slipped through the gate, she realised she hadn't had a chance to feel nervous about the competition yet, or even about seeing Liam again. Her journey yesterday had been so fraught that she hadn't had room in her head for much else, but now, as she picked her way past the crop of brambles at the field's edge, she could feel the faint stirrings of anxiety about what the day had in store for her. It wasn't just nerves churning her stomach, she was excited too; she had waited a long time for this moment. She took a deep breath and tried to let the thoughts slide from her head as she broke into a run. It was a beautiful morning, too good to waste fretting about what was to come. For now, she would just enjoy the present.

The air was still cool, but the blue of the sky promised riches to come and, although it would be a while yet before the countryside showed off in full autumnal glory, the fields were already golden from weeks of summer sun and the leaves around her just beginning to take on the burnished colours of the season. Megan lengthened her stride, feeling the energy surge through her legs as she began to find her rhythm.

She realised her error only as she turned the bottom corner of the field; she had instinctively run forwards, down the hill, but now that she was running along its length at the bottom, she realised that the final leg of her run would be uphill all the way. It had been a while since she'd been running on the local hills and she was quite out of practice. Still, she had a perfect view of the cottage she would call home for the next few weeks, and the other matching holiday-lets she'd briefly spied between the trees when she'd left. She had the whole morning before she was due at the forge, so there was plenty of time to explore.

Digging deep, she turned for home, her legs powering her up the slope. It was a lot steeper than it looked. About three-quarters of the way up the burning in her legs was becoming uncomfortable. It would have been easy to slow her pace the rest of the way, or even walk, but despite her laboured breathing Megan wasn't about to give up. She sucked air into her lungs and picked up her pace. It was second nature for her to push herself and she had faith in her body. You never knew what you were capable of until you tried.

Exalted and exhausted, she arrived back where she'd started at the top of the hill, puffing hard but already feeling the buzz of oxygen flowing back into the muscles of her legs now that she had stopped. She waited a few more moments, taking in one final sweep of the view before turning and making her way back through the gate. This time, however, instead of turning towards the cottage, she carried on walking out into the gardens she had seen earlier, making her way towards a bench she had spied in the middle of a neat lawn. She crashed down onto it, bending to rest her elbows on her knees, her hands loosely clasped in front of her. She hung forwards, head down, eyes closed, and waited for her breathing to slow. A trickle of sweat ran down the end of her nose and she puffed at it to blow it away.

'Good morning...'

Startled, Megan looked up sharply.

'Sorry, I didn't mean to make you jump.'

A slender figure was standing beside her, a friendly face smiling a greeting. 'It's a beautiful morning, isn't it? Where did you go, across the fields?'

Megan wiped the sweat away from her face and nodded. 'Down the fields actually, and then back up again – that was the problem.' She paused for moment. 'Sorry, I'll get my breath back in a minute.'

'At least you've got some left. I'd be on oxygen by now if I'd just done what you've done. I'm Clara, by the way.'

'Megan.' She nodded. 'Are you staying here too?'

The woman smiled. 'No, I work here. I'm the gardener.' She stuck out a welly-encased leg as proof. 'Just trying to get a bit ahead. We've got rather a busy day lined up.'

Megan straightened up even further now that her breathing had eased, and for the first time began to take in what was around her. She puffed out her cheeks.

'Oh, that's better. I haven't run on hills for a while. I'm seriously out of practice. I can't believe I grew up nearby and I never knew that all this was here; it's a beautiful spot.' She pointed at the nearest flower bed. 'My mum's a keen gardener too, I bet she'd love this; so much colour.'

'I think it's probably my favourite time of year. The chrysanthemums are such show-offs, aren't they, but they do look amazing.' Clara squinted against the sun. 'How long is it since you've been back this way?'

'A couple of years. I've been up in Lancashire, finishing my training, and getting a bit of experience under my belt.'

Clara nodded. 'Of course, you're a blacksmith, aren't you? Maddie did say.'

'Yes, although I'm hoping to specialise in the more artistic side of things. I'm taking part in the competition up at Summersmeade Hall.' She glanced at her watch. 'In fact, I probably ought to go and get myself sorted out. I promised I'd go and see my parents before everything kicks off, and I got here so late yesterday there was no time.' She pulled a face. 'Pile-up on the M6,' she added. 'I spent most of the day breathing in other people's exhaust fumes while sitting in queues of traffic.'

She received a sympathetic look. 'Still, the event doesn't start properly until tomorrow. You've got plenty of time.' She stood back slightly as Megan got to her feet. 'I'll send Trixie over in a bit with your breakfast, she's the cook here. Would half an hour or so be okay?'

Megan was suddenly desperate for a drink. 'Perfect,' she said.

★

It was a strange feeling driving back through the village, not because she had been away for a long time, but because on every other occasion she had returned home it had been just that, a return to the house she had grown up in as a child. Now, however, her eldest brother had moved back in with his wife and two small children, meaning there was no longer any room for Megan to stay with her parents.

She couldn't blame them. It was supposed to be only a temporary measure until they got themselves sorted out again, but her brother's business had failed quite spectacularly and, until they had paid off their considerable debts, they were going nowhere.

Nestled on the passenger seat of the car was the most beautiful bouquet; deep reds, burnt oranges and bright yellow blooms, all of her mum's favourite colours. Trixie had brought them across to her along with breakfast and, even if she wasn't quite where she wanted to be, Megan couldn't fault her stay at Joy's Acre so far. Perhaps it had been the best option after all.

Still, there was no time to dwell on that now. She had just turned into the small lane beside the church, swinging up the winding driveway of the former rectory. If she knew her mum, the curtain would have been twitching for the last half-hour or so awaiting her arrival.

Just as she had expected, her mother was out of the door before Megan had even turned off the ignition, waiting impatiently at the side of the car for her daughter to clamber out, her eyes shining.

'Aw, Mum!' Megan cried as she threw her arms around her, pleased that her mother looked and felt just the same as she had the last time she had hugged her. Her mum was a very young-at-heart woman in her mid-sixties, but she was also supposed to have retired. It worried Megan that having two boisterous grandchildren under her roof might have begun to take its toll, but her arms felt just as strong as ever. As she drew back she could already see her dad over her mother's shoulder, hovering by the front door.

'How's my favourite daughter then?' he called as she collected the flowers from the car. It was a running joke; she only had brothers.

She laughed. 'Good…! Glad to be back.'

He gave her a look that was usually the prerogative of her mother. A look that asked if she was eating enough, sleeping enough, and was happy and contented. She went forward to hug him too.

'And I'm honestly fine. So there's no need to look at me like that.'

'Sure you haven't lost any weight?' It was her mum this time.

'Positive. I eat like horse, Mum.'

'Yes, but you must burn off so many calories hefting great lumps of iron around all day.'

'And I stuff my face with chocolate in between, so there's no danger of me fading away to nothing.'

Her mum buried her face in the flowers. 'I'll put these in some water, come on in, love.'

The house smelled, as it always did, of the orange blossom perfume her mum wore and a faint trace of wood smoke from the fire in the study which had never drawn properly, but which her father still insisted on lighting. She felt her nerves begin to settle as she started to relax, following her father down the hallway and into the living room. A pile of toys had been tidied away into a corner of the room, but other than that, it looked to Megan as if nothing had changed since she'd last been home.

'I'm sorry about yesterday,' she started. 'It all went a bit pear-shaped in the end.'

'A horrible journey, but at least you weren't one of those caught up in the accident. My chicken pie can be made again, but you can't.' Her mum frowned. 'So, don't you worry about that. Besides, we can have a meal together on another night.'

'I know, Mum, but once the competition's under way it will be harder. I might not be finishing until late. And now that they've announced there's a huge commission to fight for as well, I'm going to be busier than ever.' She pulled a face. 'All supposing I get through, of course. If I don't, I'll be eating with you every night.'

'Now what kind of talk is that?'

'Dad, I'm five-foot-five, and a woman.'

'And?'

'Clearly not your average blacksmith. If the judges are the bunch of old fogeys they usually are, I'll have no chance.'

'You have just as much chance as any of the others, Megan, and don't forget, *I* know just how good you are. Besides which, it isn't just the competition judges deciding the final round is it? The National Trust people will have their say too. The chance to win a commission to design a new gate for them is not something they're going to give away lightly. They have a reputation to uphold, and their decision will have to satisfy a whole variety of interested parties. They'll need to award on merit and merit only. Imagine the furore if they didn't?'

Megan screwed up her face. 'That just makes it worse, Dad. The stakes are so much higher that usual; we all have far more to lose.'

'Or win, Megan. Or win,' he said.

'Yes, well, let's just wait and see, shall we?' said her mum, tutting; no doubt anxious to turn the conversation away from any 'unpleasantness'. 'No point in thinking the worst now, is there? Now, first things first, let me go and put these beautiful blooms somewhere cool, get us all a drink and then I want to hear all your news.' She looked at Megan over the top of the flowers. 'And you can start with that young man of yours…'

'Mum, it's not really like that,' Megan protested a few minutes later when her mother had seen to the flowers. 'Liam's not going back on a promise, because we never agreed to it in the first place.'

'Except that everyone knew you would move in with him, one day. For goodness' sake, you've practically been engaged since you were in primary school.'

Megan tipped her head to one side. 'Perhaps that's just it though; everyone expects it, but that doesn't mean it's the right thing to do.

Moving in together would be a big step for us, and we have to be sure it's what we both want.'

'Carol…' Her dad's note of warning sounded from the corner of the room.

'I know, Bob, I'm not having a go.' She softened her look at Megan with a smile. 'I just want you to be happy, love, that's all. And I suppose that seeing as you've been away for so long, I just thought you and Liam would want to spend as much time together as possible. Coming back for the competition seemed to be the perfect opportunity.'

'I am happy, Mum. And it might be the perfect opportunity, but actually I agree with Liam. This competition is going to be hard – physically and mentally. I'm going to be tired, dirty, and stressed and none of these things are a great way to pick up a long-distance relationship where the people involved haven't seen each other for over two months. In fact, it could make for an absolute disaster. Liam and I are still going to see each other, but staying up at Joy's Acre, at least for the time being, just gives us a bit more space to acclimatise.'

Her mum sat back in her chair and picked up a cup of tea from the table beside her. 'Okay, but just as long as you're sure.'

Megan gave a hearty smile and breathed a slight sigh of relief; that was the first hurdle successfully negotiated. She'd known her mum would be very vocal on the subject of her and Liam moving in together, or *not* moving in together as it turned out, but at least it seemed as if she had managed to persuade her that everything was okay. Now all she had to do was convince herself.

Chapter 3

They had all agreed that the very worst thing they could do today was make too much of a fuss; so no welcome party, and no standing in a stiff line at the gates waiting to shake hands. Maddie was going to wait in the house to greet Adam and Declan when they arrived and everybody else, including Clara, was to go about their business as normal. Then, depending on how things played out, they would be called upon when needed.

So that's how Clara found herself standing in the middle of a flower bed pretending to look busy. Tom was up on the roof of the cottage behind her doing the same, no doubt, and Trixie would be cooling her heels in the kitchen. It was hard to know what to do. The compost heaps all needed some attention and she really needed to earth up the second bed of potatoes, but both of these jobs were dirty ones, and it would be just her luck to be called upon to greet their visitors with a huge streak of mud across one cheek.

There was also the small matter of a family of new guests who were due to arrive shortly, traffic dependent. Clara was on standby to welcome them to Joy's Acre and show them to their accommodation. She crossed over to the bench where she had left her secateurs earlier and began to wander the paths, deadheading as she went, filling the pockets of her smock with her clippings. She checked her watch and moved on.

Moments later, as she glanced up, she saw Trixie making a wild dash across the garden. She was obviously trying to be discreet – under normal circumstances if Trixie was running that fast, her movement would be accompanied by excited shrieking. Today, she was making do with exaggerated arm movements designed to attract Clara's attention, but they shouted urgency just as surely as if she had yelled at the top of her voice. Clara did wonder whether Trixie would actually be able to stop once she reached her, and was just preparing for impact when she skidded to a halt, and stood grinning and panting in front of her like a lunatic.

'Hello,' said Clara, laughing. 'Did you want something, Trixie?'

'Oh, very funny,' panted her friend. 'I can't bloody speak now.' She heaved in a breath, fanning her face. 'You might want to come to the kitchen,' she said eventually.

'*Really?*'

Trixie stuck out her tongue. 'Don't then… but you'll never find out quite how gorgeous Declan is if you don't…' Her eyes twinkled. 'Actually, he's not really my type. Red hair for one, and I could never go out with someone who has hair that colour, not when mine's bright pink – it would clash dreadfully – but he has this whole… *thing* going on. I don't know what you'd call it, but it's *mighty* impressive.'

Well now she was intrigued. Clara had to admit that she hadn't come across many mighty impressive men in her past before.

'So what's going on then? I thought we were all supposed to stay out of the way?'

'Well yes, so did I, but we've been summoned…'

Clara grinned. Trixie's face was a picture. 'Right, well I'll go and root out Tom then, shall I?'

But Trixie shook her head. 'No,' she said, 'it's just us – you and me.' She tugged at her arm. 'Come on, I can't wait to hear what they want to talk to us about!' And with that she took off, dragging Clara with her.

'Wait,' she spluttered, trying to slow her down. 'I can't run like you can, hold on!' It would have been much easier if she hadn't been laughing so much. 'And mind the hair, it's really not—'

Trixie stopped suddenly, as they rounded the corner of the house, and came face to face with Maddie and her guests. 'Oops,' she said.

Clara almost cannoned into the back of her, one hand on her head trying to keep her bun in place which was listing alarmingly to one side.

She registered Adam's warm smile in front of her. He looked like he always did: relaxed, genial, his curly grey hair and trendy glasses lending his smart workwear a more casual look, but still very much in control.

'Clara, it's so lovely to see you again.'

He moved forward to kiss her, and she tentatively let go of her hair, feeling her bun slip to one side and settle in an unsteady heap above one ear. She pulled a sheepish expression.

'It's good to see you too,' she replied truthfully, leaning toward him and offering her cheek. They had almost made contact when he suddenly changed direction, rejecting the cheek she had offered in case he dislodged her hair even further and instead switching sides. It made for an awkward clash somewhere in the middle. She felt herself flush red with embarrassment. She must look like she'd been dragged through a hedge backwards.

Reluctantly, she turned her attention to their other guest.

'Clara, this is Declan Connolly,' said Adam, grinning.

Clara had expected a shock of bright carroty hair, but Declan was altogether... softer. In fact, everything about him looked gentle and warm. His hair was more of a reddish blond, and he stood tall and slender, relaxed in a navy linen suit, rumpled but still very much a suit. He wasn't what she had envisioned at all. And just as she was processing the information, trying to decide whether she liked the look of him or not, the pin that was the only thing standing between her hair being up or being down finally gave way and her hair cascaded around her, right down to her waist.

It wasn't really the kind of thing you could just ignore, seeing as she now had hair covering most of her face. She tried to give Trixie a *look what you've done now* stare, but even that didn't really work. Instead she flipped her head, tucked, smoothed and flattened as best she could and stood, mortified, but smiling, as she tried to scoop it all back up into its rightful place again.

'No, don't, leave it down...'

Her hands fluttered back down to her sides.

'You have beautiful hair...' She looked at the man who had just spoken, so quietly she almost hadn't heard him. A soft Irish brogue and eyes like jade. 'Hello, Clara.' She took the hand that was outstretched. 'I've heard so much about you.'

She looked at Maddie, panic-stricken.

Fortunately, Maddie simply smiled and came forward, touching her arm lightly. 'We've just been talking with Declan about the gardens here, Clara. In fact, we were on our way out to see you when Trixie, er... delivered you.'

Beside her Trixie tried to stifle a snort of laughter, not quite succeeding.

'Perhaps I should explain,' said Adam. 'Declan is the head of the production company who commissioned the documentary series from me in which Joy's Acre features—'

'And I'm intrigued,' added Declan. 'I've seen some of the material that Adam has shot and it caught my eye, the gardens and cookery aspects of it particularly. I thought I should come and take a closer look for myself.'

'We thought perhaps you might like to give Declan a tour,' said Maddie, although there was no suggestion that Clara had any choice in the matter.

Declan stepped forward eagerly, almost turning his back on everyone else. 'That's my fault, I'm afraid. I don't have a huge amount of time available today, so I'd prefer to get straight down to things if I can. Would that be all right with you, Clara?' His look was very direct. 'I've been hugely impressed by what I've seen from Adam, but there's nothing like seeing the gardens through the eyes of the person who created them.' He looked at her for a moment, smiling, before indicating the path ahead of them. 'Shall we?' he added. 'Let's walk and you can tell me about your garden, Clara.'

She might as well have been talking about flying to the moon for all she could remember of the first ten minutes or so of the conversation. But gradually, listening to Declan's interested questions and insightful replies, she began to relax.

'We really didn't have that much to go on when we first arrived,' she continued. 'Joy, the artist who once lived here, sadly didn't leave us many of her paintings. In fact, there are only four that we know of in existence, but even so they're still the best record we have of what the gardens looked like back then.'

'And the farm is named after her, is that right?'

'Yes, her name was Joy Davenport. Her husband bought the farm and named it after her in a grand declaration of love. That's the Victorians for you.' She gestured across to the cottage where Megan was staying. 'I read up on everything I could get my hands on about Victorian garden design, and so the gardens which surround each cottage are as authentic as I've been able to get them.'

'And what self-respecting Victorian estate didn't have a walled garden? Producing food headed straight for the kitchen.'

Clara nodded. 'Well, yes indeed. Although this is where I have to claim a little artistic licence. The design of the garden does incorporate many traditional features, but I'm afraid that now it's rather more aligned with what everyone here likes to eat.'

Declan looked around him, his hands still stuffed casually in the pockets of his trousers. Then, removing them, he put his fingers to his lips and narrowed his eyes before suddenly spinning around.

'Right, Trixie, where are you?' He beckoned her over. 'Go and stand over there a minute, next to Clara.' Trixie did as she was told, elbowing Clara gently in the ribs, an amused smirk on her face.

The silence stretched out as he regarded them both for a minute, clearly thinking hard. About what though, Clara was none the wiser and his scrutiny was beginning to make her a little uncomfortable. She felt as if she was being assessed for market. Trixie was right, he certainly had a 'thing' going on, but what you'd call it she had no idea.

His gaze flicked to his right. 'Okay, here's what I want you to do.' He moved until he was standing on the edge of the vegetable bed closest to him. 'If I'm not much mistaken, these are potatoes, yes?' He didn't wait for a response. 'So, Clara, I want an explanation of what you're growing here. Any jobs you've done, what you're about to do, that kind of thing. Don't think about it too much, just go with what comes out of your head... Right, go.'

She stared at him for a moment, aware that Adam too had come to stand a little closer. Maddie gave her a tentative smile, although it was obvious she hadn't a clue what was going on either.

'Just whatever comes to you is fine.' Declan gave her a beaming smile; she really rather wished he hadn't.

'Well, these are my spuds. What we call main crop potatoes, a bit of an exactly-what-it-says-on-the-tin description, because it's what we eat after we've munched our way through all the lovely new potatoes. They've been in the ground since April and are pretty much ready to be harvested now. If I leave them in for too much longer the slugs will be dining out, and these are too good, I'm afraid.' She looked up at Declan. 'Would you like me to dig a couple of potatoes up for you to see?'

He nodded, but said nothing further.

There was always a fork sunk into her potato beds somewhere, and it took her only a few seconds to retrieve it. She knew the earth would be soft and yielding, and a firm boot slid the tines into the ground just where she wanted them. Moments later a pile of knobbly, mud-encrusted potatoes lay on the ground.

'They've taken a bucket-load of watering this year, because of the really hot summer we had, but they're a good size, and, look, a beautiful colour too.' She picked one up and rubbed away the soil to reveal the skin. 'They're called Pink Firs, quite a traditional variety, but apart from looking very pretty, they taste amazing.' She licked her lips; she was running out of things to say. 'Apart from watering, the only other thing you have to remember with these guys is that they're a bit shy and like to keep covered up. Just like we get sunburnt shoulders if we're not careful, spuds like the soil heaped up around them for the same reason. Only whereas we tend to go pink in the sun, they go green...'

Before she could think of anything else, Declan suddenly leaned forward and took the potato from her hand.

'Catch,' he said, grinning at Trixie and, after a second or two, tossed it over to her. 'Right, now Clara's grown it, what are you going to do with it, Trixie?'

Clara felt relief flood through her. She was off the hook, for now. And Trixie was much better at this type of thing than she was. As an ex-barmaid, she could talk about pretty much anything and everything...

Trixie rubbed some more of the soil off the potato. 'It's the colour that's so wonderful about these, and it's true what they say, we really do eat with our eyes. I always try to preserve colour and texture where I can, so I'd definitely crush these, just gently, with a fork after boiling them in their skins. Then simply roast them off with some olive oil, garlic and herbs. Lemon juice is amazing too, with a few shallots, and if you're feeling adventurous sprinkle a healthy serving of parmesan over the top. Crispy, soft, *and* gooey all at the same time, what's not to like?'

Declan looked across at Adam. 'Are you hungry yet?' he asked, a twinkle in his eye. He turned back to look at first Clara and then Trixie.

'Right, shall we have a little chat? Adam, I think I've got everything I need, if you're ready...?'

Adam nodded. 'Is Seth here today, Maddie? Or close by?'

She gave him a puzzled look. 'No, he's next door. As in the estate. Not actually that close, I'm afraid, and pretty busy I would imagine. Did you need to speak to him, I can try and get him on the phone?'

Declan and Adam exchanged looks. 'It's not absolutely necessary right at this moment,' said Declan, 'but I think we will need to have a chat pretty soon. For now, perhaps we could all go and sit down somewhere?'

Clara caught Trixie's eye and grinned. Whatever had just taken place in the last few minutes it looked as if they were about to find out.

'The kitchen is probably best,' suggested Maddie. 'I know it's not quite time for elevenses yet, but even so a pot of coffee and some of Trixie's toffee apple cake might be nice.' She glanced up to the roofline of the cottage on her left. 'Besides, we have some guests due to arrive any minute. And I'm not sure that having us all standing out here is quite the reception we had in mind for them. If you can excuse me for just a moment, I'll go and have a word with Tom. I'm sure he won't mind playing the role of welcoming committee.'

On Maddie's cue, Clara stepped forward. 'I'll take you back round to the house,' she said as evenly as possible, although her heart was still going like the clappers at the thought of what was coming next.

'Perhaps I should explain,' began Adam as soon as they were all settled.

A pot of coffee was indeed standing on the table in front of them, as was an entire cake, nestling on a plate, but as yet no one had wanted to be the first to make a move. Even Adam looked a little nervous; only Declan appeared completely relaxed.

'All of you know that when I first came to Joy's Acre it was with the intention of filming a documentary as part of a series I'd been commissioned to make, and you now know that Declan is the head of the production company that will air the programmes next year, in fact, he owns it. What you might not be aware is that his company also make a whole host of other programmes aimed at the lifestyle market.' He looked at everyone over the top of his glasses. 'And I probably don't need to tell you how buoyant a market that is right now.' He grinned at them all in turn. 'Perhaps I ought to let Declan step in here…'

Oh, they were smooth, thought Clara – a well-oiled double act, definitely graduates of charm school, but she liked Adam, and filming pieces for the documentary with him had been huge fun.

Declan had been sitting back in his chair, long legs stretched out in front of him, and apart from the beginnings of a smile, he hadn't moved the whole time Adam was speaking. Now though, he sat up straight, and pulled his chair closer to the table, leaning in, with his arms folded in front of him. His look was very direct.

'I've worked with Adam over a number of years now, and I'll be totally honest, I meet a lot of people, and in my business not all of them are nice. Working in media can be tough. You're only as good as your last set of ratings, and it's a pretty cut-throat world at times. I come across a lot of people who have set a course straight for the top and they'll tell you whatever you want to hear in an effort to get there. I'm happy to say, Adam is not one of those people. I trust his judgement, and so when he told me he had found something special, I believed him.' He suddenly broke into a wide grin. 'That's a compliment by the way, you can all stop looking so serious!'

He surveyed them all in turn.

'I tell you what, let's have a bit of this cake, and we can talk while we eat, otherwise I feel a bit like we're all back in school.' He pushed the cake towards Trixie. 'Come on, you can divvy it up, no being stingy now, and Maddie, why don't you pour the coffee?'

Clara used the opportunity to sneak a few glances at Declan while he was busy accepting plates and mugs. He wasn't what you might call conventionally handsome, but his colouring, particularly the paleness of his eyebrows and lashes, gave his face an openness that Clara liked. He smiled at her, and she looked away.

'Right, so… as Adam said, the lifestyle sector of programme-making is very buoyant, but it's very transient too; fickle, if you like. You would think that we've all seen enough houses being renovated, food being cooked and gardens being dug up to last us a lifetime, but strangely enough viewers still can't seem to get enough of them. However, what is very evident is that people get bored with the same format all the time and so we're constantly looking for original ways to deliver. And that's where you guys come in.' He took an enormous mouthful of cake, and chewed for a moment, smiling at the same time.

'Wonderful…' he said, looking at Trixie, finishing his mouthful and then resuming where he'd left off. 'There's a real focus at the moment on the importance of the simple things in life,' he stopped to pull a face, 'except I don't know whether you've noticed, but often what is meant to be a simple way of living is still hugely materialistic and aspirational, but in a much less shove-it-down-your-throat kind of way. So, let's strip it all back to basics and present something which still appeals to lovers of cookery and gardening programmes, but in a very organic way… exactly in the way in fact that you two demonstrated outside.'

He nodded at Maddie, and then looked across at Adam before grinning back at them. 'What I want is to make a series of programmes, where we literally take the produce from the garden, walk fifteen steps and have it transformed into a mouth-watering meal. And, Clara and Trixie, I'd like you two to present it.'

Chapter 4

'I wondered whether or not I should dye my hair?'

Clara looked up from the tray she was carrying. 'I thought you did dye it, Trixie... or are you trying to tell me that bright pink is your natural colour?'

Trixie slid her a sideways glance. 'Very funny. No, I meant dye it a more normal colour, maybe brown?'

Clara studied her. 'What's your natural colour?'

'Sort of mousey? I think. I'm not sure I can remember any more. But I could go darker... or lighter?'

'Nope,' said Clara, after a minute. 'The pink is what makes you, you. It's part of your character.'

'But you don't think people might think I'm a bit... I dunno... trashy?'

'People, as in who?' Clara frowned. 'Oh, I get it. People as in the massed televisual audience who will be tuning in every week to see TV's two newest stars...'

Trixie blushed. 'Well I can't help thinking about it. Haven't you been?'

'Trying not to actually,' replied Clara. 'The whole thing terrifies me.'

'Why? You heard what Declan said. You're a natural. I think he's a pretty smart guy. There's no way he would have suggested it if he didn't think we were up to it.'

'Hmm… His opinion, not mine.' She put the tray of glasses she was carrying down onto the table. 'Anyway, I don't know why we're even having this conversation. Nothing has been agreed as yet. And as for your hair, anybody who would want you to change it just to appear on television doesn't know you very well.' She looked her up and down. 'Or maybe they do. Maybe you're exactly what they do want. An antidote to all the long-haired, big-smiled, airbrushed…' She stopped in case she said something rude. 'Perhaps it's time for someone with pink hair, who wears sparkly boots and doesn't give a… to take centre-stage for a change.'

Trixie grinned. 'I thought we weren't going to talk about it,' she said. 'Come on, let's get the rest of the stuff laid out and then we can have a bit of a breather.'

Between them they made several trips, carrying extra glasses, crockery, chairs, tablecloths and cutlery backwards and forwards between the house and the long trestle tables that they had already set up outside. Given the warm forecast for the day, it had been suggested yesterday that a picnic be held that evening in honour of the arrival of their new guests. It was something they had done with their first guest, and it was a lovely informal way to break the ice. The guests didn't have to come of course, but everyone hoped they would. It seemed to set a nice tone for their visit.

Maddie had disappeared to welcome the Carter family as soon as Adam and Declan had gone, leaving Trixie and Clara to make a very belated start on lunch preparations. Now they had spent the rest of the afternoon, not only cooking up some treats for that evening, but also, much to Trixie's annoyance, baking some extra cakes which Seth had asked her to provide for the blacksmithing competition.

'It's very nice to be asked, but I do wish Seth had thought to check with me first before agreeing. Great timing, it's not.' Trixie was leaning up against the sink, her hands wrapped around a very welcome mug of tea.

Clara looked up from the table. 'Well, you know why, don't you? It's because Agatha asked – demanded probably, if I know her – and he couldn't say no.'

Trixie sighed. 'What is it with those two anyway? I thought they were related.'

'They are, but Summersmeade Hall has been in Agatha's family for years, and when her husband died, leaving Joy's Acre to his grand-daughter, Jen, it was so that she and Seth could come to live there and renovate the farm. When Jen died, Seth made a promise that he would honour Jen's wishes for the farm but, well, then it all went a bit pear-shaped. We all know it was because Seth couldn't cope with his grief, but Agatha still seems to think that he's betrayed her memory somehow. In fact, I'm not so sure that Agatha doesn't actually blame Seth for Jen's death, crazy though that sounds. It's only since Maddie's arrival that work here has got going again, but that hasn't been without its problems, as you know. I think that now things have improved so dramatically, Seth's trying to build a few bridges, but Agatha doesn't exactly make it easy for him.'

'Which is why he's helping out with the blacksmithing competition this time around. Ah, I get it now…' She drank a mouthful of tea. 'It doesn't excuse him volunteering my services to make all the refreshments though. I've got enough to do.'

'I know,' Clara commiserated, 'but I'll always help, you know that.'

Trixie stared into the bottom of her mug. 'Right, where did we get up to?'

★

Maddie had been dispatched to talk to Seth at some point during the afternoon, so news from Declan's visit wasn't a complete surprise. Even so, he still looked a little shell-shocked on his return to the farm. He and Maddie were standing in the garden, chatting quietly and looking up at the big barn that stood to one side of garden. Next to it stood the three cottages that Tom was currently re-thatching; the first in the row, the Thatcher's Cottage, was already finished and was where the Carter family were staying. Clara wandered across to Seth and Maddie, a huge bunch of flowers in her hand.

'No prizes for guessing what you're thinking,' she said.

Seth looked sheepish. 'I can't pretend that an injection of cash wouldn't help sort this place out – it would – but I have no idea what we'd be talking about financially, or whether it's the right thing for everyone concerned either. The barn isn't going anywhere, but I did make a promise to you and Trixie, and I'm well aware that it's going to take some time to come good on it.'

'I'm perfectly happy where I am, Seth. And so is Trixie as far as I know. Accommodation for us in the barn is the ideal, and it will happen one day, but one thing at a time.' She lifted the flowers to her nose. 'And right now, I've some finishing touches to attend to. These are for the tables tonight.' She was about to turn away when Maddie took her arm.

'I know we're going to talk about this later, Clara, all of us together, but off the record, what do you think about Declan's idea?'

Clara faltered. 'Well it's bit of shock I guess, I didn't really—'

'Only I'm getting the feeling that you're not all that keen. Or have I got that wrong?' Maddie looked at her, concern written across her face. 'You helped me so much when I first came here, sticking up for me, believing in me. I'd like to do the same for you... if I need to.'

Clara bit her lip. 'And you always said it was me who was the perceptive one…' She smiled. 'I'm not honestly sure what I think at the moment, Maddie. It all came a bit out of the blue… but being on TV and all that would entail, I'm really not sure I'm cut out for all that. I'm just a gardener… at heart I think that's all I am.'

Seth frowned at her. 'You're never *just* anything, Clara. Joy's Acre wouldn't work without you, I hope you know that. And however much I'd love to get the barn finished, that makes no difference to our final decision, so don't you go thinking that it does.' He gave her a knowing look. 'Besides, they have to do their screen test thingy first, don't they? They might decide that they just couldn't possibly live with the shape of your nose.'

Clara stuck out her tongue. 'Pig,' she said, laughing. There was no need for any reply. Clara knew full well that he was only teasing.

'Right, I just need to go and see a man about a roof and I'll be with you. No doubt you and Trixie have prepared enough food for the entire village?'

'Of course,' replied Clara. 'Would you have it any other way?'

She fell into step with Maddie as Seth turned away to go and speak with Tom.

'What do you think, Maddie?' she asked as they walked along the path back into the main part of the garden. 'Do you think we should do this? It can't be every day that something like this comes along?'

Maddie stopped for a moment, searching her face. 'No, it can't be. But you could say the same thing about lightning, and that doesn't make it a good thing.'

★

The Carter family were obviously suffering from the demands of having a young family. Emily was perhaps in her late twenties, her husband Luke a little older by Clara's reckoning, and both wore the exhausted expressions caused by too many disturbed nights and an almost constant anxiety. Their children, two girls, only just over a year apart in age, were very lively toddlers.

'Oh, this is heaven,' said Emily, sitting down at the long table, one of the girls balanced on her lap. 'Not having to think about cooking… It's the very worst thing when you've had a busy day. It just about finishes me off.'

'Well, we thought that the evening was too lovely to waste, so I hope you don't mind having something so informal tonight.'

Maddie was circling the table pouring drinks. As usual, the table was heaped with food.

'No, it's lovely.' Emily looked at her husband. 'Actually, it's one of the reasons why we chose to come here… Holidays are a bit of a nightmare with the girls. Hotels want you to eat at just the wrong time and, while self-catering is great for us, it is a bit like a busman's holiday. Having our meals cooked for us will be amazing.'

Trixie blushed. 'Well I hope so. That's the plan anyway.'

'Right, I think I've introduced everyone,' added Maddie, 'so help yourselves and tuck in, there's a mountain of food to get through. I should add for Megan's benefit that there's one person missing at the moment, and that's Tom, our thatcher.' She turned slightly to smile at Emily. 'You met him earlier when you arrived, I know, but he's currently up on the roof somewhere, I think, taking advantage of the light evenings while he can. I'm not sure whether you've come across him yet, Megan, and, in any case, he's going to join us later, but you can't miss him. He's blond, blue-eyed and gorgeous… and—'

'Don't let him hear you say that, for goodness' sake,' quipped Clara. 'We'll never hear the last of it.'

'*And*... I was going to say, very helpful. So shout if you need anything.'

Megan smiled, looking a little awkward.

'So what are you planning to do while you're here?' asked Clara, turning to Luke. 'I realise I'm biased, but you've picked a lovely spot.'

He picked up a piece of chicken, nodding. 'Explore, hopefully,' he said. 'Step off the hamster wheel for a couple of weeks and get out in the fresh air. Now the school summer holidays are over, it should be nice and quiet everywhere.'

Seth nodded. 'Mind you, it never really gets that busy up on the hills, but there are some great places to walk, and plenty of great places to visit with the children.'

'There are some leaflets in the cottage,' added Maddie. 'I hope you found them okay?'

Emily smiled. 'Oh, yes, we've already made a list.' She uncurled her daughter's fingers from the tablecloth, picking up some slices of apple to entice her with.

'And if you get stuck, there's always the blacksmithing competition going on at the estate next door.' Seth looked at the girls. 'I wouldn't recommend you getting too hands-on, but on the judging days there's always demonstrations of things going on as well. They usually have the local farrier up with his shire horses, making horseshoes – folks get to take them home after if you fancy one for the mantelpiece.' He turned to Megan, who was absentmindedly picking at a piece of pizza. 'First day tomorrow, Megan, isn't that right?'

She looked up, startled. 'Oh... yes. The competition is a local tradition. I actually grew up in the village, so I know all about it, and now that I'm supposedly all grown up too, I get to take part this year instead of just watching.'

'In fact, you might even be the youngest competitor,' said Seth.

'I'm the only woman,' replied Megan. 'I know that much. And to kick off tomorrow we're making a set of fireside tools. It's a timed, live competition, and this first round is an elimination round, so anyone not up to scratch goes home.'

'Ouch,' muttered Clara. 'That's a bit brutal.'

'It's okay though,' replied Seth. 'I checked, she's paid up for the full three weeks.'

Maddie shot Seth an exaggerated look. But it was okay, Megan was smiling.

'I'm here to see family too... and friends, so when I do go out of the competition I'll have plenty of time to catch up.'

'No chance of that,' said Clara. 'Not when you're staying at Joy's Acre. Joy might be long since dead and buried, but her creative spirit lives on...' She broke off, looking at the Carters. 'Not literally, you understand, but creative endeavours do seem to flourish here for some reason. So you're going straight to the top, Megan, no doubt about it.'

'Right,' she said. 'Well... that's good.' And with that she picked up her glass, looking slightly more relaxed than before.

The chatter continued for a few more minutes before Clara spied Maddie giving Seth a surreptitious nudge. He cleared his throat.

'Um...' he began, unwilling to break up the conversations around the table. 'Sorry, but before I forget, there's something I just wanted to mention to everyone while you're all together. Only, we have some visitors coming to Joy's Acre on Tuesday next week and, although I don't think they'll cause too much of a disruption, they will be out and about in the garden, so I thought I ought to mention it.'

He looked hesitantly at Clara. 'You probably won't be aware, but we had a film crew here a few weeks back, shooting for a documentary they're making about rural businesses. Joy's Acre was lucky enough to be picked to take part and the show will be aired next summer. However, it seems we rather caught the eye of another TV producer, and… well, the upshot of it is that they'd like to make a series featuring Clara and Trixie here.' He paused while the reaction rippled around the table.

'To be honest, I don't know that much about it,' Seth went on. 'The producer rather sprang it on us this morning, and we're not even certain it's something we want to do, but they'll be here anyway, on Tuesday. I think the idea is to do some kind of screen test, so if you're around and spot a camera pointing in your direction, probably best to duck.'

*

'I think that went okay,' said Maddie after dinner, once all the guests had dispersed. 'No one looked too put out at the news, and it will be quite nice if they came to watch, it might make things slightly more relaxed?' She looked at Clara for confirmation, but seeing that she wasn't going to get any, took another sip of her drink. 'We should go and get Tom,' she added to no one in particular.

'I'll go,' said Seth, getting up from the table.

'Odd that he didn't appear for dinner,' said Clara. 'That's not like him.'

Maddie frowned. 'Maybe he just got carried away working. Besides, there's plenty of food left. He can have some now.'

They sat in silence, Trixie fiddling with a piece of tin foil which had been used to wrap some of the food. She folded it over and over until she had made a long strip.

It wasn't late but the evening was just beginning to cool, and Clara slipped her arms into the cardigan that was hanging on the back of her chair. She looked up at the sound of the two men approaching.

'Well you need a break anyway, regardless of that. Come and have something to eat.' Seth's voice was soft but clear on the night air. Tom's muttered response, however, was lost against the backdrop of birdsong.

He plonked himself down on the seat next to Clara, his eyes roaming the table. 'Blimey, you could have saved me some of your Victoria sponge, Trixie,' he said.

'Well you knew where it was… You know what it's like around here, the quick or the dead.'

Tom opened his mouth to say something and then thought better of it. 'Yeah, well some of us had work to be getting on with.'

Clara exchanged a glance with Trixie. It was unusual for Tom not to pick up on any banter that was going. He was probably just tired, hungry too perhaps. She slid a few of the plates and dishes down the table towards him so that he could help himself.

'Long day though, Tom,' she said. 'We probably should have peeled you off the roof earlier. I expect you could do with the break.' She lifted the jug of lemonade up towards him, and he nodded at her unspoken offer.

'Have you had a good day?' she asked, placing a full glass down in front of him.

He smiled suddenly at the concern in her voice. 'Sorry, Clara. Ignore me. I'm just tired, and a bit grumpy.' He looked around the table. 'Did you all have a good day schmoozing with the TV people?'

Clara closed her eyes as she realised she hadn't seen Tom all day. No wonder he was being less than his usual genial self.

Maddie's hand flew to her mouth. 'Oh, Tom, I'm so sorry... I didn't think. We finished later than I thought this morning, and then I had to go and say hello to the Carters, and go and find Seth and...' She grimaced. 'Someone should have come and told you though...'

'Yeah, well Trixie filled me in slightly when she brought me a sandwich at lunch. But it would have been nice to have been involved in discussions.'

'Tom, nothing's been discussed as yet, not really. That's one of the reasons why we thought tonight's meal would be a good idea. Give us an opportunity to let everyone have their say.' Seth ran a hand through his dark curls. 'I don't know any details yet, mate, none of us do. It was all a bit of a surprise this morning, but it's clear that we need a lot more information before we commit to anything.'

Tom gave Trixie a searching look. 'But I thought...'

She blushed. 'I'm sorry. That was me letting my mouth run away with me. I was excited, and you know what I'm like, I babble incessantly.'

'So, you're not definitely making this series then?'

Maddie leaned forward. 'I really don't know, Tom. The producer and crew are coming on Tuesday to do some screen tests. We'll have an opportunity then to find out the exact details of what's being proposed. I guess, for now, what we need to know is how everybody feels about what could well be the best opportunity we've ever had, but which will also undoubtedly be a huge intrusion as well.'

'Yeah, there's more work involved on this re-thatch than any of the other cottages. I can't afford to lose time running around after people like I have today, just because you're all busy doing other stuff, things you don't normally do. At the end of the day it's going to be me who gets it in the neck when this cottage isn't finished on schedule. You need to think about the knock-on effects.'

'Which is exactly why we need to have this conversation,' said Seth. 'I'm very conscious of all these things, but I'm also interested to hear what Trixie and Clara have to say, seeing as it involves them the most. And yet, so far, neither of them has said anything…'

Clara was aware of Trixie watching her, but she didn't want to be the one to speak first. Tom was obviously utterly irritated by the whole thing. In fact, she couldn't remember a time when he had seemed so grumpy. She was beginning to feel rather uncomfortable.

Trixie pushed her strip of tin foil to one side. 'Well, I think it's bloody amazing, even if no one else does. For goodness' sake, this is television we're talking about. A one-off documentary is one thing, but this is something else entirely. A chance to really put Joy's Acre firmly on the map. Everybody will want to come here and see what we're about.' She sat back and waited for everyone's reaction, suddenly bursting out laughing. 'And come on, who doesn't want to be on TV?'

Clara grinned. It was just like Trixie to speak her mind but, although she often spoke with a bluntness which could be misunderstood, you always knew that she meant well. It was just the way she was. She also had an uncanny ability to voice the things no one else was prepared to say. The tension around the table popped like a balloon.

'Well you do, obviously!' Clara laughed. 'But that's because you can talk to people, and aren't shy and awkward like I am.'

'Clara, you have beautiful blue eyes, a mane of golden hair and a sylph-like figure. The cameras are going to love you. I'm short, a bit on the dumpy side and have all the grace of a sack of potatoes…'

The two women smiled at one another.

'It is a bit exciting,' acknowledged Clara. 'But the thought still terrifies me, I'm not going to lie. And Tom's right; we mustn't let our proper work suffer.' She paused for a moment. 'So what do we do?'

Seth looked around the table. 'I think there's only one thing we can do, and that's wait and see. We need more information to be able to make a proper decision and, until Tuesday is out of the way, we simply won't have it. So let's clear this lot away and switch off for a bit. Tomorrow will be another busy day.'

Clara nodded and got to her feet, smiling at Tom, who was holding his still laden plate, reluctant to let it go. It seemed the most sensible thing to do. She was very aware, however, that although Trixie was trying hard to hide it, she was about to burst with excitement.

Chapter 5

Megan had only ever taken part in one other competition before, and that was nothing like on the scale of this one. She had been a spectator at this event several times in the past, but under the rules of the competition all entrants were allowed one visit to the site to familiarise themselves the day before things began in earnest. Megan had made sure she took advantage of it. It was as much about sizing up the competition as it was about finding your way around. No one wanted to miss the opportunity to gain any slight advantage over the others they could. Her visit had simultaneously managed to calm her nerves and send her anxiety rocketing. She had hardly slept a wink, and now, all too soon, the first day of the competition had arrived.

Things were already beginning to hot up – and not just around the forges, which were fired up and glowing nicely. The Hall wasn't open to visitors yet, but all the competitors and judges had arrived. She was trying to remain focused, but it was hard when she kept getting constantly interrupted by people, none of whom was Liam. She couldn't believe she still hadn't seen him yet, but he had promised her that he would be here today. She looked up eagerly again at the sound of footsteps, but her heart sank when she saw who it was.

'I heard you were taking part this year. Long time, no see, Meggie.'

She gritted her teeth at the mention of the childhood name he knew she hated. 'Julian,' she said. 'And you, back again, I see.'

'It will be just like old times; the two of us working together again.'

He hadn't changed a bit. Still the same thick blond hair, gelled into a quiff, the same overly large and very white teeth, and a mouth which curled around an all-too-familiar sneer.

Megan glared at him, her hands on her hips. 'We never worked together, Julian, and this is nothing like the old times. You were apprentice to my dad back then just the same as I was; a trainee, even if you did think you were superior to me. You might be three years older than I am, but times have changed and now we're both qualified. So, despite your assurances when we were younger that I would never make the grade, as you can see I proved you wrong.'

'You did.' He grinned at her. 'And here we both are; older, wiser... much better... in my case, anyway. I've three years' more experience than you, Meggie, and I reckon my chances are good this time. The competition isn't up to much.'

Megan looked around her. There were many faces she recognised, and others she knew by reputation. His comment was arrogant, but she knew he was just trying to wind her up. She held his look until he had the grace to look away.

'We'll see,' she said. 'But your bullying tactics are not going to make one ounce of difference to how I perform in this competition, Julian, or my determination to prove you wrong once and for all.' She gave him one final withering glance. 'May the best blacksmith win.'

'Yeah,' he said. 'May the best *man* win.'

She waited until he had walked away before turning back to what she was doing. *Damn.* He was so infuriating. Why did she always let him get to her? She lifted her head and took a deep breath. She had things to prepare and she was not going to let Julian Bamford take up any more room in her head.

Summersmeade Hall was unusual in that it still retained its own working forge and stables, unlike other houses of a similar size and stature from its era. The wide, open forecourt made a perfect setting for the competition, and with the addition of a couple of marquees for the judges and refreshments, it provided the competitors and public with everything they might need.

Megan was pleased to see that she had been given a space in the original forge, along with one other blacksmith. It made no real difference, but there was something familiar about the space and she much preferred the original red-brick chimney with its furnace to the modern mobile forges that had been brought in to accommodate all the competitors. She had already set out all her tools, and with a glance at her watch she checked them over one last time. There was only half an hour to go.

'Well now, aren't you a sight for sore eyes...'

She whirled around. 'Liam!' They looked at one another for just a second before the gap closed between them and she was in his arms. Everything about him felt so warm and familiar that she let herself relax into his embrace.

'Oh, I've missed you,' he said. 'And you look amazing.'

She pulled away, looking down at her old dungarees and worn tee shirt. 'Time really does make the heart grow fonder, doesn't it? Anybody would think we hadn't seen one another in years!'

'I know, but it seems ages since you were last home, and well...' He paused to kiss her nose. 'The last couple of months have felt like an eternity.'

'I've missed you too,' she said.

It was the truth; she did miss him dreadfully when she was away. She was so used to turning around and him always being there that she couldn't imagine her life any other way. The problem was that now she wasn't entirely sure Liam still felt the same. After all, what other reason could there be for his suggesting that she stayed at Joy's Acre on this visit, and not with him?

In a way she understood it. Liam was self-employed and he worked long hours, often in the evenings. She would be on her own for much of the time. But she and Liam had grown up together; they had been virtually inseparable as children, then on into adolescence, and now that they were older there was a heavy expectation that they would take their relationship to the next level. In fact, it seemed that each time they saw each other, the pressure to do so increased even more.

Despite what he said, perhaps Liam wasn't ready for the commitment after all, and didn't know how to tell her. The thought made her feel shy and awkward, but today was not the day to be dwelling on such things, so she mustered a smile.

'I wasn't sure if you were going to be able to get here today? Or at least not until later?'

'Well, there have to be some perks for working for yourself. No, I made sure I kept the day free. I wouldn't have missed this for the world.'

Megan took his hands, leaning up against him. 'Thank you,' she said softly. 'Julian has already been sniffing around, being his usual obnoxious self and trying to make me feel inadequate.'

'And you're better than him.'

She looked up. 'We don't know that, Liam, I haven't seen his work in a long time and—'

He smiled. 'I actually meant, better as in, you know, not being an arrogant bully...' He stroked her hair. 'That chip on your shoulder

doesn't get any smaller, does it? Listen, I know he gets to you, and
that he made your life a misery when you were younger, but you are
here in your own right now, Megan, don't give him the satisfaction.'

'I know…'

He pulled her in closer. 'Now give me a kiss and go and get yourself
sorted. I'll be here, all day…'

★

'Ladies and gentlemen, welcome to the sixth Summersmeade Blacksmithing Competition. As usual, I'd like to thank Agatha Wainwright
for very generously providing us with the most marvellous of facilities
again, and Seth Thomas for his invaluable help in organising the
set-up here today. For those of you who haven't been before, the rules
are the same as they are on every occasion, and very straightforward.
The competition is based on an elimination process, with the bottom
three scoring blacksmiths at the end of each round being asked to leave,
until only three remain. These three will go through to the final. The
scoring criteria for each round will be published at the start of each day's
competition, with aggregate scores being used to determine who goes
out each week. As you may be aware, there has been a slight change to
proceedings this year with competitors having the opportunity to win
a commission from the National Trust as part of the prize. Therefore
those going though to the final will have one week to work on their
submission and the eventual winner will be judged, not only on their
overall scores during the coming weeks, but on their design piece which
they will present on the final day.'

A ripple of anticipation went around the crowd.

'And so, without further ado, let's kick off this year's competition
with round one! Competitors will have three hours to complete a fireside

set, comprising of a pair of tongs, a shovel and a poker. Marks will be given for balance and proportion, quality of finish, technical skill and originality of design. Gentlemen… and lady… your time starts, now!'

Megan dipped her head in acknowledgement of the cheering and shouts of encouragement and walked back into the forge. As the only woman in the competition, she was clearly something of a curiosity, and seemed to be attracting slightly more attention than the other competitors, for the moment anyway. Their encouragement was lovely, but Megan was determined to produce work that would have them rooting for her to win simply because she was the best blacksmith, and not solely on account of her gender. She shook her head, trying to clear these thoughts away. She had work to do.

Making a fireside set was easy; it was something that all apprentice blacksmiths learned how to do, and an experienced blacksmith could do it in their sleep. But therein lay its danger; it was easy to become complacent, and there was a world of difference between a good set and a bad set. Megan had made dozens of them in the past, but today she was approaching the task as if she had never made one before in her life.

It was tempting to concentrate mainly on the design, to create something which would make it stand out from the other entries, but without enough attention to the balance and weighting of the pieces they would be next to useless, and there was every chance that the finish would suffer as a result too. Megan would be keeping hers simple, elegant and functional, but her pieces must be perfect. She took her apron from a hook on the wall, tied it around herself, and picked up the first length of iron.

For the next hour or so, Megan was aware of nothing save for the beating of metal against metal. The air rang with the sound of it as her hammer rose and fell, coaxing the molten iron into new shapes. Orange sparks rose around her as she twisted and turned the metal against her anvil, working quickly until the rosy hue paled to battleship grey and she had to thrust the piece back into the fire to heat once more. The air stank with the tang of coal and hot metal, but Megan loved it. To her, it felt like coming home.

She was aware of glances from the other blacksmith with whom she was sharing the forge, but she ignored him. She didn't want to know what he was thinking; there would be time enough for that later, and nothing should detract her from the task in hand. Neither did she want to compare her own work with that of the others; she had to have absolute faith in what she was doing.

After an hour she had nearly completed the tongs, perhaps the most difficult element of the set as the sinuous curve of both the handle and the tong itself had to be perfectly symmetrical on either side. She straightened up, looking at it critically, but she had done well. It was a good start, and the curling vine embellishment around the handle was neat and beautifully tapered. She damped down the excitement that always rose in her stomach whenever she saw a piece coming together. She had a long way to go yet.

People were milling about on the periphery of the forge while she worked. Stopping for a few minutes to see what she was about, before moving on to the next competitor and, although Megan never engaged with any of them, she was painfully aware that they were there. After a while, however, she noticed that a couple had been watching her for quite some time, and as she returned to the anvil the next time after heating her poker, she glanced up casually, surprised to see that it was Seth and Clara.

She mouthed hello, not really wanting to talk, but also well aware that holding a conversation would be very difficult against the background noise. Clara gave her a thumbs up and smiled, and she felt herself relax a little. It would be good to have another woman to chat to when all this was over. She grinned back, raising her hammer in a little salute before bending her head once more and getting back to work.

*

The final hour flew past without Megan even noticing, and she used every minute of her allotted time to polish and perfect her pieces. But now the time was up and she could do no more. She blew out her cheeks, suddenly feeling the heat, and knowing that her face and neck would be covered in black smuts, but really not caring. She undid the strings on her leather apron and walked slowly to hang it back up until another day, using the time to centre herself and settle her nerves. Now she would be required to carry her work over to the judges' marquee, and for the first time place it among that of the other blacksmiths, something which would draw inevitable comparisons.

She ducked her head under the marquee's guy ropes and scanned the inside of the tent. A row of tables lined the perimeter, and she could see that several blacksmiths had already laid out their work. She began to check the tables in turn for the one which held a card with her name on it.

'Would you like a hand with that, love? Heavy, aren't they?'

She looked up to see Julian grinning at her from the far end of a table she had just stopped by. She ignored him and lifted her set so that it sat squarely in her allotted place. She adjusted the hang of the tongs, and stepped back to give her work a final once-over, catching the eye of one of the judges who was standing nearby to survey the proceedings. She gave a nervous smile, but his face remained impassive.

Julian was staring openly at her, and it was obvious that she was the subject of his conversation with the man standing next to him. There was no way she was going to hang around and become included in it – it would be only a matter of time before he made his way over to jeer at her. She was just about to turn away when she heard a voice in her ear.

'Just ignore them. Proof that Neanderthals are still very much alive and kicking.'

She looked up, startled to see a face almost covered with a big brown bushy beard, looking, not at her, but at the table, and more specifically at her entry.

'And I never said that, obviously.'

Her eyes flew to the lanyard around the man's neck. He was one of the judges.

'I am, however, pleased to see that you're very much giving them a run for their money…' His eyes were still averted.

'And I guess you never said that either,' she murmured.

There was no reply, but as the man moved past her, he looked up and caught her eye for just a split second before moving away. She stared after him, unsure what to make of his words, but a small smile played across her face. With a final look at her work, she left the marquee and went in search of the refreshment tent.

She spotted Clara first, standing behind a table that had obviously once been laden with cakes, but which now looked like a plague of locusts had passed over it.

Clara smiled a greeting. 'I bet you're starving.'

It was just gone two o'clock and Megan's stomach had been growling for the past hour, at least. She looked down at the paltry offerings still left on the table.

'I wasn't sure what you liked, so I saved you a bit of a variety. I hope that's okay?' Clara bent down and produced a plate from a box at her feet with at least six different slices of cake on it. 'Can't have our favourite contestant going without, plus there have to be some perks to staying with us.' She placed it down on the table.

Megan grinned. 'Oh, I could kiss you,' she said, touched at the thought. 'Thank you so much. They don't usually have cakes at this competition, so I was pinning all my hopes on the burger van.'

Clara wrinkled her nose.

'I know,' said Megan. 'That's what I thought.' She looked at the choices in front of her, picking up a muffin. 'A bit daft really, you've obviously done very well.'

'Hmm, much to Trixie's delight *and* dismay. I had to send out for emergency supplies mid-way through proceedings, and the poor girl is baking like a thing possessed. It's great for business though. I'm amazed it's never been done before.'

Megan grimaced. 'Yeah, well, somehow cakes don't seem to fit the image for grimy blacksmiths, do they? I mean, it's not the same as your Sunday afternoon cricket tea, is it?'

'No, I suppose not. Barmy though.' Clara looked round her. 'How have you found things today though, has it gone well? It must be hard for you being—'

'The only woman?'

'Oh… well I was about to say one of the youngest here…'

Megan looked down at her half-eaten muffin. 'Sorry,' she muttered. 'Ignore me. I tend to get on my soapbox a bit every now and again.'

'No, don't apologise,' said Clara. 'I hadn't really thought about it, I'm a bit naive like that. Do you get much comment then? From men, I mean. I expect most women think it's great what you do.'

'It's weird actually…' Megan paused for a moment, thinking. 'When I was at college no one batted an eyelid. There weren't many women on the course but there were a few of us, and the subject never even came up. Since then I've been lucky enough to get a job working for a company up in Lancashire, and the team are great, but the customers… I mean, I'm young, five-foot-not-very-much, and a woman as well, I'm an easy target. And you'd be surprised, it's mostly men who comment, but I've had some really choice remarks from women too. One farmer's wife even asked me if I felt awkward taking a job away from a local man.'

Clara's eyes widened. 'No!… That's ridiculous.'

Megan shrugged. 'It happens, and I try hard not to let it get to me, but unfortunately I have one or two thorns in my side who take great delight in undermining me at every step of the way. One of them is here today actually.'

Clara raised her eyebrows.

'A guy called Julian. Big hair, big teeth, walks around like he owns the place.'

'No, sorry. It's not ringing any bells, but I've seen lot of people today.'

'Don't worry. It's not like I expect you to spike his cake or anything. And most people are really nice, they judge my work on its merits. The crowd is good here today too, and very encouraging…' She bit her lip. 'I just have to hope that I do okay, and not let anyone down.'

Clara's smile was warm. 'You can only do your best, that way there's no question of letting anyone down, especially not yourself.'

Megan nodded, biting into her muffin, and then quickly taking another mouthful. Heavens they were good. She grinned as she spotted Liam coming towards her with Seth. They were deep in conversation.

'Brilliant, Megan… just brilliant.' Liam was grinning from ear to ear, and she leant forward to receive his kiss. 'There's no way you're going home today, your set is streaks ahead of the others.'

'Nothing like a bit of bias, is there?' she commented, but her smile matched his. 'I can see you've met Seth, Liam, and this is Clara, who's the gardener over at Joy's Acre, and obviously today in charge of some mighty fine cakes.'

They shook hands.

'I think your entry looked very impressive from where I was standing too,' put in Seth. 'Not only aesthetically very pleasing, but the finish looked next to perfect as well.'

'Not too… girly?'

Seth considered her question. 'No… I wouldn't say so. Elegant, yes, and possibly more refined in design than some of the others which were distinctly heavier and more masculine looking, but I'm not sure you could ever describe something made out of iron as "girly".'

'The standard looked good, Megan, but you're right up there, honestly, don't you think?'

Megan pulled a face at Liam. 'I don't know, I haven't looked at any of the others. I can't. Not until it's all over. Then I'll look and see what was scored higher, and try to work out why.'

Liam put his arm around her and pulled her in close. 'What are you like?' he muttered, kissing her nose. 'When are you ever going to start believing in yourself?'

★

The deliberation of the judges took just over an hour, and so it was three o'clock before word went around that the competitors' scores were available. Megan felt sick, the nerves beginning to churn her stomach. Please dear God, let her not have to go home today. She couldn't bear it.

Clutching Liam's hand, they walked back into the judging tent. Beside each of the displayed fireside sets a piece of paper had been pinned, and it was all Megan could do to restrain herself from running across the marquee. On the bottom of the paper there would be a number – a score out of eighty which represented the total marks awarded to each competitor. On its own it was worthy of scrutiny, but it was how it compared against all the other marks that was of real importance. And for that, she would have to wait a little longer.

She was aware that Liam had stood back slightly so that she had space to view her result, but, as it was, the minute she saw that the first digit of her score was a seven, she reached back quickly for his hand again. It was going to be okay, surely it was enough? She glanced at the columns on the sheet, scarcely taking in the detail, but noticing that she had scored her highest marks for technical skill and the quality of finish. She allowed herself a small smile. She would take it all in fully in a little while, but for now she was desperate to hear confirmation of the places.

The noise around her was rising, and it took the head judge several minutes before he could gain everyone's attention. Once the room had quietened a little he started to speak and the remaining voices fell silent. Her jaw was clenched together in anticipation as she wished he would just get on with it.

As was tradition, the names of those who had not made the grade were never read out. Instead a list was called out of those competitors who would be going through. If you were on the list, you were in, it was as simple as that.

Her heart was in her mouth as the roll call of names began.

'… John Woodard… Brian Ellis… Peter Fielding… Julian Bamford…'

Well I might have known he'd get through.

'… Jason Moorland… Craig Somerville…'

Come on…

'Ben Ford… Harry Wightwick… Luke Greenwood…'

That's it, I'm going home.

'James Elton… Nigel Parry…'

Shit.

'And finally, Megan Forrester…'

Chapter 6

It wasn't a bit how Clara imagined it would be. To start with, there were a lot fewer people than she'd expected, and as she watched them all climb out of the van, sporting jeans, trainers and faded tee shirts, she began to feel a little less nervous. The film crew were just ordinary people, doing a job, like her, and as she and Trixie stood in the kitchen brewing what would probably be the first of many rounds of tea, she began to feel that she might, just possibly, get through this.

Tuesday had been a very long time coming. They had been working flat-out, of course. The blacksmithing competition on Saturday had taken up a huge chunk of time, and Clara hadn't had much time to think about anything else. Sunday she'd spent at home, trying to tame her own garden, but Monday had dragged on and on. And every time her attention wandered from the task in hand, a little voice would whisper about the very thing she was trying so hard to forget.

'Are you okay?'

Clara looked at Trixie and swallowed. 'I think so, you?'

'Terrified.'

'Then why are we even doing this, Trixie?'

She pursed her lips together. 'Because some stupid idiot thought it would be a good idea...'

Clara came forward to give her a hug. 'And you do realise I'm going to remind you of that every chance I get, don't you?'

'Yeah, me and my big mouth...'

She suddenly looked up as Declan's tall figure crossed in front of the kitchen window with Seth in tow. She groaned. 'Oh God...'

Seconds later they were in the kitchen.

'Morning, ladies, are we both okay?'

Could that man get any more relaxed-looking? Clara gave a nervous smile. 'I have absolutely no idea.'

'Great stuff, and yourself, Trixie?'

She straightened her tee shirt. 'Probably,' she said.

Declan just grinned at them both, nodding. 'Right, well...' He eyed the tray of tea things on the table. 'Let's grab a hold of that, shall we, and go and meet the guys and talk tactics. Everyone thinks better with a cup of tea.'

He stood by the doorway waiting for them to pass. 'After you,' he said.

Clara trailed after Trixie, holding a plate of cookies. It really was the most perfect day outside. There had been a bright full moon the night before, and the clearest of skies had brought a drop in temperature and a sweeping morning mist that clung to the fields. Now the sun had risen fully, the last of the smoky wisps of white mist were parting to reveal a landscape still bursting with colour. It was the light that Clara loved at this time of year; so much less harsh than the stark brightness of mid-summer – softer and more golden – and the garden glowed with it.

Maddie was already there and chatting to the three others that Declan had brought with him, two men and a woman. Various bits of equipment sat on the trestle table beside them, among them a large camera. Clara tried hard not to stare at it as she placed the plate of biscuits down. Beside her, Trixie lowered the tray, rattling the crockery together and wincing at Clara.

'I was convinced I was going to drop that,' she whispered. 'But there's no way I can be "mother", my hands are shaking far too much. I'll look like a complete prat.'

Clara was sympathetic. She doubted she would be able to either, her own hands were doing the same.

'Right, folks,' announced Declan. 'Introductions. Maddie you've met, and this is Clara and Trixie,' he indicated them both in turn. 'And so, to my right is Ed, the cameraman, who will make you all look gorgeous, Billy, who is on the sound boom and will make you all sound gorgeous, and Samantha, who wields a make-up brush like no one else I know, and will also make you all look gorgeous.' He laughed at his own joke, but no one minded. 'So, let's all get a cuppa and then we can have a chat about how this whole thing is going to work. Guys, just help yourselves.'

It was by far the easiest thing, and Clara wondered whether it had been a deliberate move on Declan's part. He seemed to be particularly good at putting people at ease. His team were obviously used to looking after themselves and needed no second invitation, falling on the biscuits with undisguised glee.

'I take it you got my notes?' continued Declan, once everyone was settled. 'The key thing is that we marry both the cookery and gardening aspects together so that they make sense. I want viewers to see a continuous connection between the ground and the kitchen, so the action shots we see must be relevant to each other. We can use lots of careful editing to show this to best effect… So, for example, if we see Clara digging in the soil with a fork we would then switch to a shot where it looks as if Trixie is digging into some food she's made with a fork… Does that make sense?'

Heads were nodding.

'Which is why I asked you for some ideas. You two know best what's going to translate well from one to the other, look great in the garden, but also have terrific plate appeal.' He looked between Clara and Trixie. 'Now don't panic if you haven't thought of anything. Today is just about taking some test shots, looking at camera angles, that kind of thing. We'll be big on making this place look fantastic on TV, which won't be hard at all, but we need to be sure that we can get the right atmosphere across. If you've come up with something we can use today, great. If not, there'll be plenty of time.'

Clara swallowed. 'Well, we did come up with one thing we thought would work…'

Declan's smile beamed its full force at her from across the table.

'Just that everyone thinks of strawberries as a summer thing, which they are, mainly, but they don't get that way by themselves. I grow new plants from runners so that at this time of year I can plant them out and we'll get an even bigger crop next year. Putting them in now will mean they get well established, and it's a job I'd already lined up to do over the next few days anyway. I thought I could talk about how you do this. And of course this year's plants are also still fruiting well, so we thought Trixie could make something very simple, but that makes them into something a bit special…'

'Go on…'

'I add balsamic vinegar and sugar to them,' continued Trixie, 'that's it. It sounds revolting, but believe me it tastes amazing, and the colour is beautiful. Once you've added the ingredients, you leave them to steep for a while and it develops into the most wonderful syrup. You can then ladle the strawberries onto ice cream, or serve them on their own with cream. Even spoon them all over the top of a plain sponge cake.

The syrup seeps down, you see…' She checked to see the expression on Declan's face. 'My favourite though is to put the strawberries with meringues, either crushed like Eton Mess, or whole like on a pavlova. You can't go wrong really.'

Declan looked at his team. 'See, I told you they were good. That all sounds perfect, just the sort of thing we were looking for.' He nodded at Trixie. 'We'll rig up an outdoor kitchen, not today, but you'd have a small cooker and a hob to use. It's important that we get action shots of you actually cooking, literally the minute Clara has brought you something from the garden.' He grinned at her. 'That is, of course, assuming that you make your own meringues and they're not bought in from Tesco.'

Trixie stuck out her tongue. Clara smiled; she would never have had the nerve to do something like that, but that was where her friend's personality shone through.

★

An hour later and they were good to go. Declan's notes had also included some suggestions on the best things to wear. He stressed that it was to be their choice, but what would work best were clothes with simple lines and bright colours which would enhance the overall impression they were trying to give. Jeans were fine – anything they were comfortable working in. The one stipulation he had made was that for the majority of the shots Clara should wear her hair up, and it was this aspect that was just receiving the finishing touches now. Samantha was keen that it stayed put and didn't wobble during the shots – she had obviously got the measure of it perfectly.

She had already given Clara a light dusting of make-up, wanting the look to be fresh and natural, exactly how someone who spent all their time outdoors might appear. It was something that Clara never bothered with. She couldn't see the point for exactly that same reason; she *did* spend pretty much all her time outside and the flowers and vegetables didn't mind what she looked like. Besides, Clara was comfortable in her own skin, it was just the way she was. Samantha, however, was adamant that a little make-up was needed, just for the camera, which had a way of draining the skin tone if you weren't careful.

Clara had already gathered together all the things she would need to plant her new strawberries, and she really couldn't put things off any longer.

'The camera will film you continuously, Clara,' said Declan. 'So don't worry about stopping or starting. Just perform the routines you would do normally and we'll take care of what images we want to see. It's all in the edit, as they say. I may stop you from time to time and ask you to repeat something, but otherwise just carry on. Is that okay?'

Clara nodded.

'The only thing I do want you to do is to stop each time you have an instruction to say and, if you can, deliver it to the camera, or part of it at least. We'll probably use a mixture of live speech and voiceovers for the finished article but it won't matter one jot today, we'll just go for it. So, just like you did on my first visit, simply chat away as you would do normally, using words that come naturally to you. Easier said than done, I know, but try and speak like you usually do.'

'Well, I'll try... I'm not actually sure I'll be able to speak at all.'

'It will take you a few minutes to relax into it, but don't worry, we're used to that. If you think of the camera as a friend that you're trying to explain something to, it might help. A one-sided conversation admittedly, but see how you go.'

She looked up and caught Maddie's eye. She was standing on the path to one side, Seth beside her. He was beaming a smile in her direction, but Maddie looked so serious by comparison. Maddie then gave a slight nod and her expression changed to one of sympathy and understanding, perhaps thinking back to the time when she was new to Joy's Acre and had felt so like a fish out of water herself. It had been Clara who had befriended her then, believed in her, and now it was Maddie's turn to do the same for her. The memory passed between them, a reminder of a special bond they would always share.

Clara's stomach was still churning though and, despite everyone's obvious support she really wasn't sure she could do this. It was madness, surely? She didn't do things like this; she was a gardener for heaven's sake, not a TV star. Taking a very deep breath, she summoned every ounce of nerve she could lay her hands on and took up her place beside the strawberries.

Kneeling down, she selected a new plant which had already established itself from a runner and tried to find a comfortable pose. She looked up at Declan, swallowing briefly and trying to clear her throat surreptitiously. *Please, please, please, let's get this over with.*

'Right, Clara... and we're rolling, so whenever you're ready...'

She fluffed the first couple of lines, not surprisingly. The words had been in her head all morning, repeating themselves over and over like a mantra, but although she got them out eventually, they weren't in quite the right order. She felt like she was speaking a foreign language. Declan simply laughed.

'Brilliant! Right, now we've got that out the way, you'll be fine. Take it away, Clara!'

And she did. Miraculously, the words she needed popped into her head and came straight out of her mouth and, once she got over the initial weirdness of looking into a camera, she realised that she was back in her garden, doing the thing she loved best, and it was this feeling that carried her onwards. Her hands cupped the small leaves of the plant at her feet.

'So, these strawberry plants are several years old now, and while they've cropped well for us this summer, they will become less productive as the years go by. Luckily for us though, strawberries are nothing if not generous.' She pointed to a green stem, trailing across the ground.

'These are runners, the strawberry plant's natural way of providing more plants—'

'Clara, can I just stop you there for a moment?' It was Declan again. She looked up, surprised.

'That was great, but we're losing what you're saying. You've got to remember that you're not here by yourself, so anything you say has to be delivered upwards towards the camera and not directed towards the ground. Could you just start that bit again, please?'

Clara's mind was a complete blank. She couldn't even remember what she'd just said! And what did he mean, deliver it upwards? How could she look down so she could see what she was doing, and up at the same time? She stared at him.

'It's fine, just say that line again.' He smiled and nodded. It was meant to be reassuring, but she wondered what was behind his benign expression. This probably wasn't going at all the way he wanted.

'I can't remember what I was going to say…' She bit her lip.

Declan turned around, looking for help.

'These are runners…' supplied Maddie, coming forward. 'You were talking about strawberries being generous…'

Clara nodded, hugely grateful. She re-ran the phrase in her head, shuffling her position slightly.

'These are runners, the strawberry plant's way of providing more plants for free; so do make the most of this natural freebie. After all, it would seem rude not to, wouldn't it?' Her hand traced the runner back to the main plant. She stopped and looked up. 'However, in the first couple of years of the plant's life, these runners should be cut off – they take a lot of energy for the plant to produce and rather than have that energy go into making runners, what we want is for the plant to produce more fruit instead. By cutting them off, from just where they emerge, you'll give the plant the best chance of doing that.'

'Clara, this is wonderful… Could we see some of the fruit? There looks to be a good few strawberries just behind you.'

Startled, she looked across at Declan. 'Oh… right…'

'And don't look at me…'

She looked across again. 'No… Right… Oh God, I've done it again, sorry…'

He grinned at her again, nodding.

She gathered herself again and shuffled backwards. 'So, if you can remember to do that for the first couple of years, this is what you'll get: the most gorgeous, plump, and sweet strawberries that are far tastier than anything you'll buy in the shops.' She pulled off a couple of the strawberries from the plant, wiped a small piece of straw from the underside of one of them and bit it in half, grinning. 'Absolutely beautiful.' She swallowed quickly. *What on earth had she done that for?* Now she probably had juice running down her chin. She drew in another breath. *Look up,* she reminded herself.

'So, now that our plants are well established and we want the runners to grow, it's very easy to turn them into new plants. In the summer, say around mid-July, if you look closely at the end of the runners you'll probably be able to see tiny roots already forming. To get these to root simply peg down this runner, either directly into the soil, or like I've done, into pots sunk into the ground.' She pulled out one of her hairpins from the ground surrounding the runner. 'And if you've got hair like mine, you'll have a never-ending supply of these anyway…' She looked up and smiled, but there was no reaction. *Should she carry on?*

'After that, just let Mother Nature take its course. After six weeks or so, you should see that the runner you've pegged has become a small plant, all by itself.' She ran her fingers over the tiny leaves on the new plant by her feet. 'Just like this one… And now you've got two choices. You can either leave the plant where it is to grow on, or you can dig up the pot and replant it somewhere else, into a new space straight away or to overwinter in a greenhouse if you have one.'

She fished in the pocket of her smock and took out a pair of secateurs. 'Either way, just cut the new plant free from its parent and you're good to go.' She made a quick cut through the runner. 'In our case, we've got a new bed ready and waiting for these, so that in another couple of years when these existing strawberry plants are past their best and not producing much, we can dig up this whole bed and use it for another crop, but we'll still have a new bed of strawberries which by then will be cropping well anyway. If you grow more plants from runners every three to four years you'll always have a good supply of healthy plants, and more importantly, these beauties.' She pulled the husk from the half-eaten strawberry and popped the rest in her mouth.

'Of course, you don't need bags of room, either, just scale up or down according to what space you have. Even use pots or planters, if you prefer; the principle will be just the same…'

She drew to a halt, not wanting to look at Declan, but running out of things to say. The next step would be to actually dig the plant up and move it to its new home, but she wasn't sure whether she should do that or not.

An exuberant round of applause rang out. 'Clara, that was brilliant!'

All of a sudden there was movement and noise as everything around Clara came back to life. Trixie was still clapping, her face split by a massive grin, but now the others had joined in too and, as she stood up, Declan came across and before she even realised what was happening had pulled her into a hug. She had just a moment to take in the strong warm tug of his arms, his towering height and the faint lemony smell of his aftershave before he pulled away again, leaving her feeling quite breathless. It was a long time since anyone outside of Joy's Acre had hugged her.

'Clara, that *was* brilliant. Well done!'

She flushed bright red and covered her mouth with her hand. 'Oh my goodness,' she said. 'I've never done anything like that before.'

'But how did it feel?' Declan wanted to know. 'Good?'

'Yes… no, it was awful. I don't know… weird, it was definitely weird. And I didn't know whether to stop but I've kind of finished this bit and I couldn't think of anything else to say.'

'It was a great place to stop. I think if we need any more then we can set up again by the other bed and have you plant some things up.' He held out his hand to help Clara back onto the path. 'Right now, I think you should have a breather, and then Trixie, if you could just take a look and make sure you have everything you need, we'll be ready to go with you a few minutes. Obviously we won't be making the meringues today, but you can still talk us through the other things, and show us some of the possibilities you've already discussed.'

Trixie nodded, her eyes shiny with excitement.

He looked across to Samantha, who was standing by ready to give Trixie a quick fix. 'I'd like to see Clara picking some strawberries first of all, and then take them straight across to Trixie to carry on with. But let's see Clara's hair down for this one, I think, don't you?'

Chapter 7

'Would you like a hand?'

Clara looked up to see Megan standing by the path.

'I'm no gardener, but I think I recognise a weed when I see one.' She squinted up at the sky. 'It's been a beautiful day, hasn't it? And I've been stuck inside for far too long.' She placed both hands into the small of her back and arched her spine backwards.

'It's not a great idea if you've got backache,' said Clara, 'but I never say no to help, if you think you're up to it.'

Megan smiled. 'I'm fine. Just a bit stiff, that's all. I've been bent over the table most of the day, working, and am in desperate need of some fresh air.'

Clara was standing in the garden of the cottage which Tom was currently re-thatching. In truth she probably shouldn't be out here, she felt more tired than she could remember being in a long while, and for Clara that wasn't good news. She was four years post-op from a bone marrow transplant and while her leukaemia was a thing of the past, she did need to look after herself. But, she was doing what she always did when her head was filled with unwanted thoughts; and this afternoon, tired or not, she was determined to keep going.

'I'm afraid it all wants digging over,' said Clara. 'It's very much what you'd call a work in progress.'

'No problem,' replied Megan. 'Have you got another fork?' She walked over to where Clara pointed and took up a position at the opposite end of the bed from her. 'I'm pretty good at digging,' she added. 'Arm muscles like Popeye.'

'Oh, of course!' said Clara, laughing. 'You must have. Well, in that case, I expect you to have dug over the whole bed by teatime. There's some spare gloves here too if you want them,' she added, taking them across.

Megan stopped to put them on and then plunged the fork into the soil. 'Am I just turning it over, taking out the weeds, that kind of thing?'

'Yes please, that would be wonderful. I need to think about getting some stuff in here so that the plants can get themselves established before the winter comes in, but we're heading into the worst part of the year. The garden won't really come into its own until next year, so I think the best I can hope for is some nice flowering shrubs, good leaf colour and neat and tidy.'

'And no weeds.'

'Exactly!' Clara bent down to pull a fat worm from the tines of her fork. 'Sorry, mister,' she said. 'I might not have speared you, but my little robin friend is pretty quick off the mark. I'd say run for your life, but… you know…'

'Wriggle for your life?'

'He's going to have to…'

There was silence for a few moments while the girls carried on digging.

'So what have you been working on?' asked Clara. 'Something for the competition?'

'Hmm. Just thrashing some ideas around at the moment. The announcement that there was a commission to fight for this time came as a bit of a shock. A fabulous shock, but there isn't a huge amount of time to be honest, and certainly not as much as I'd like. It's a big undertaking, and the planning stage is going to be crucial.'

'Is that not usual then?'

Megan took off a glove and scratched her nose. 'No, never... not as far as I can remember anyway. No one even knew about it until after the closing date had passed for submission of our entry forms – the organisers sent us a letter informing us afterwards. The prize is usually just a few hundred pounds and an engraved shield, so people tend to enter for the glory rather than anything they stand to win. Even so, it's a very established competition around here, well known within the industry. Winning it is a very good endorsement for the future.'

'So winning it and then gaining an impressive commission as well must be huge.'

'Bloody enormous... and just think of the cachet of designing something that's going to be used on a National Trust property, where thousands of people are going to see it. Never mind the twenty K...'

Clara leant on her fork for a moment. 'Something like that would pretty much set you up for life...' She could see the spark of desire in Megan's eyes. 'From your point of view though I guess it was a good job that none of you knew about the commission before you entered. Just think how much attention it would have attracted. The competition would have been swamped with entries.'

Megan nodded. 'I don't think the organisers could have coped. It was just as much of a surprise to them as well apparently. The head judge said the National Trust had approached them only fairly recently; some bigwig from high up lives not far from here I gather and, as they were just about to embark on a commissioning exercise for the new gate, suggested they use the competition to do just that. I suppose it makes sense. They've reserved the right not to use any of the final designs, but from their point of view it makes their task so much easier.' She bent down to lift some weeds clear of the ground. 'With my cynical head on of course, I suspect that they're getting the gate for a bargain, but who bloody cares? I certainly don't.'

Clara watched for a moment as Megan thrust her fork back into the soil. She was nothing if not determined. 'This means a lot to you, doesn't it?' she said.

Megan straightened. 'Oh yes…' Her words were borne on a sigh. 'I can't begin to tell you, Clara. Winning a commission like that, having money like that, it's all I've ever dreamed of. I could open my own forge, start my own business…' She clenched her jaw. 'I'm just not sure how I'm ever going to win, that's all.'

'But you did so well on Saturday.'

'I did well enough.' Megan's eyes met hers. 'But this, this is something else. What's required for the final is…' She stared about her, searching for the right words. 'I just think that maybe it's bigger than me.' Her foot was back on top of the fork.

'I see,' said Clara, recognising her condition. 'Which is why you're out here digging like a thing possessed.'

There was a long sigh. 'I was going to go for a run but then I saw you could do with some help and thought better of it. Sometimes you don't want to be alone with your thoughts, do you?'

'No, sometimes you don't,' said Clara quietly. 'But I do know one thing…'

Megan looked up.

'That we never truly know what we're capable of until we're faced with losing the thing we love. Then, I think we really find out what we're made of.'

They both fell silent after that. Megan gave a curt nod and if anything picked up her pace even more. It was amazing how quickly the work progressed with two of them working away and, after another hour or so, it was nearly done. Clara had only been joking when she said that she wanted the bed finished by teatime, but surprisingly that's exactly what had happened.

'Blimey, remind me to give you a shout next time I want some hard grafting done,' said Clara, grinning. 'I can't believe how much we got done!'

'Girl power,' replied Megan succinctly. 'But that was great, thank you, just what I needed.'

Clara stared at her, amused. 'I think you might be just a tiny bit weird,' she said. 'But bizarrely I know exactly what you mean.' She looked at her watch. 'Would you like to come over to the main house for some tea? We usually stop around now.'

Megan thought for a moment. 'I'd quite like that,' she replied, 'but you know, I think I need to get back to my design. I'm in the right frame of mind now, and all of a sudden my ideas seem quite a lot clearer.'

'Then I'm glad, but thank you, Megan. My own head feels much clearer now too. Plus, my workload has just halved!'

She began to take off her gloves as Megan did the same. 'You will come and ask if you need any help with anything, won't you?'

'Oh, I will, don't worry.' She stuck the fork back into the soil. 'I'll just leave this here, shall I?' She picked her way back onto the main path. 'Thanks, Clara, I'll see you soon,' she added, waving.

Clara watched her go, waving her own goodbye. She had taken an instant liking to the plucky blacksmith, who, whether you acknowledged it or not, was trying to make her way in what was very definitely a man's world. Winning the competition could change her life and although Clara had had only a quick opportunity to view the entrants' work on Saturday, from what she had seen of Megan's, it had compared very favourably with the others'. She must make a point of chatting to Seth about it, to see what he thought. It would be wonderful if Megan was in with a realistic chance of winning.

There had been a time in Clara's own life, just four short years ago, when she had stared death in the face and beaten it. Up until that time she had lived, as many people did, without much thought for either the world she lived in, or indeed her place within it. Since that time she had thought of nothing else.

She understood how it happened, and she would never be critical of anybody else's choices, but it had shocked her how easy it was to be complacent. How you could move through the years seemingly happy when in fact you had never taken the time to even find out what made you happy. Truly happy, that is, not the kind of happy that you get from buying a new pair of shoes, or eating a meal at a nice restaurant, but the kind of all-pervasive joy you feel when walking in the moonlight, seeing the world lit by a silvery glow, so peaceful and calm. Or when standing on the shoreline feeling impossibly small in an impossibly big world, understanding how tiny you are, and yet there you are still, existing against all the odds; a small, essential part of an infinite universe.

Talking with Megan had reminded Clara of this. How, after she had been given a second chance at life, she had made a pact with herself to never do anything which took her away from what made her happy, from those things which were as important to her as breathing. It was the reason she was a gardener, the reason why she had come to Joy's Acre, and it was also, importantly, why she had stayed.

Even before Maddie and Trixie had arrived, when it was just her and Seth, Joy's Acre had always had the most wonderful atmosphere. It was a place where things could be nurtured, where they had space to grow, ideas as well as living things. And whatever happened here, you always seemed to be protected from the harsh realities of the real world. It was a place where old-fashioned values still stood, where there was always plenty of time for the things that mattered, and where you could forget about the mad rush of the often uncaring and ruthless world outside. A TV crew with its brash commercialism and bright lights would surely chase away those things, and Clara didn't think she could bear it.

And then there was her own involvement in the project; showing off didn't come easy to her, and however hard the others tried to convince her otherwise, that wasn't the sort of person she wanted to become. That wasn't the sort of person she wanted any of them to become. She couldn't just go along it. She would have to tell everyone how she felt. With these thoughts firmly in her head she wandered through the garden and around to the main house.

Trixie was kneading bread. Pounding the dough back and forth to the beat of the latest Taylor Swift song which was blaring out of the radio on the side. She laughed as she saw Clara come into the kitchen, holding up her sticky hands and pulling a face as she motioned at how helpless she was. Clara quickly crossed to the radio and turned the volume down.

'No loaf gets out alive, eh?' she said. 'I think I've just been doing the same thing in the garden.'

Trixie beamed. 'I know. I'm so excited I needed something to do which would get rid of my nervous energy. I was going to make some pastries for breakfast tomorrow, but then I thought they'd probably be as tough as old boots. Bread making is much more the thing.'

Clara faltered a little, thrown by the expression on Trixie's face. It was in such stark contrast to the way she was feeling; while it was true that her emotions were in turmoil, excitement had played no part in them.

'Is Maddie around? Or Seth?'

Trixie glanced at her watch. 'Due back any minute I should think. They just popped out for something...' She gave Clara a cheeky grin. 'Anyway, I'm quite pleased they're not here right now, otherwise I would have had to rein it in a bit, and actually...'

She picked up a tea towel from the table and hastily wiped her hands. 'Yippedee-bloody-doodah!' She screwed up her face. 'Oh, Clara, I'm so excited. Wasn't it brilliant? Weren't you brilliant? In fact, weren't *we* brilliant? Declan would be mad not to sign us up on the spot. And I think he was really pleased too. He made all the right noises, didn't he? And Samantha mentioned that it's really easy to tell when he's not happy about something, but that in her opinion it all went really well. He'll put together a proposal or something, Seth said, but he didn't think that would take him long, and...' She trailed off when she realised that Clara wasn't jumping around to quite the extent that she was.

'What's the matter? Aren't you excited?'

Clara took in her flushed expression, and eyes which were shiny bright with emotion. She had no choice but to flash back a grin.

'Oh I am excited... Just not as excited as you...'

Trixie burst out laughing. 'I know, I'm sorry. I'm such a loon. Don't worry, I will calm down. Eventually.' She narrowed her eyes. 'And I know what your problem is – you're far too modest for words. You don't think you were any good, do you?'

Clara didn't have the heart to tell her that that was the least of her concerns.

'But you needn't worry, because you absolutely nailed it, Clara, in fact more than that...' A slow smile crept up her face. 'I'd even go so far as to say that Declan was *very* taken with you, if you get my meaning... wink, wink...'

Now that *was* news to Clara. She blushed. 'What?' It was getting worse by the minute. 'No, I don't think so. He's just friendly, that's all. I bet he's like that with everyone. After all, it is his job – he has to put people at ease, doesn't he?'

There was another cheeky grin. 'If you say so,' replied Trixie. 'But, like I said, you're far too modest... But it's okay, he's really not my type. For starters he's at least three foot taller than me, and I'm not really a fan of ginger... It suits him... I mean, he's quite good-looking and everything, just not for me.'

Clara was lost for words, something which Trixie rarely was.

'And not for me either, Trixie. Honestly, what are you like? The poor man. Plus, we know nothing about him. He's very probably married or has a girlfriend at the least—'

'No, he doesn't actually.'

'How do you know that?' Clara spluttered.

'Because we got talking, you know... about things...'

Clara shook her head, amused. 'Only you could find out stuff like that in a heartbeat. For goodness' sake, I bet you even got his inside leg measurement.'

'Thirty-four.'

'You're kidding me? Trixie, that's impossible, that's—' She stopped as she registered the look on Trixie's face, and then blushed.

'I'm so gullible,' she groaned.

Trixie laughed. 'I reckon it is thirty-four though. I mean, he's six-foot-something easily.'

'Maybe, but that still doesn't change the fact that it's of no consequence to me whether he's married, divorced, widowed, single, straight, gay, or living with eight cats. He's here to do a job, and so am I.'

'You sure about that? I think you're protesting just a teeny bit too much…'

'Trixie! Yes… I'm absolutely positive.'

'Positive about what?' asked Maddie, coming into the kitchen.

Clara spun around and then looked at Trixie's grinning face. 'Don't you dare,' she warned. She turned back to Maddie. 'Just ignore her, she's being… mischievous.'

Maddie rolled her eyes. 'Oh, she's not going on about Declan again, is she? Don't worry, Clara, I've already heard it all.' She winked at Trixie. 'Although it did cross my mind as well… Anyone could see how taken Declan was with you.'

For some reason Clara's heart was thumping in her chest. She opened her mouth to say something and then changed her mind. It would only make them worse. Instead she fixed Trixie with as stern an expression as she could muster.

'I was going to ask you if you needed a hand with making dinner, but I'm not sure I want to now.'

Trixie's hand flew to her mouth. 'Oh God, the chicken!' She raced across the kitchen and fiddled with the dials on the big range cooker, checking her watch. 'Ah, well… might be a little later than planned, that's all.' She came back to stand before them. 'It's all gone a bit out the window this afternoon, hasn't it? I haven't been able to think straight.'

Maddie just smiled. 'That might be just about to get worse, I'm afraid. Seth is on his way back with some champagne.'

'Champagne, what for?' asked Clara.

'Well, it's kind of traditional, isn't it? When you're celebrating…'

Clara looked between them, feeling her heart sink a little. She had expected Trixie's exuberance, but this was all beginning to sound too much like a done deal for her liking. Were they not even going to have the opportunity to talk about what had happened earlier today? She needed to be able to tell them how she was feeling. She gave a tentative smile.

'A bit early for that, isn't it?' she said.

'Well, it's five o'clock somewhere.' Maddie laughed, and looked pointedly at the clock, which was already showing half past.

'I didn't really mean the time,' continued Clara. 'I mean in general… too early in the grand scheme of things to be drinking champagne, when we don't even know what's happening yet.'

Maddie looked a little nervous. 'No, I know, but it just felt like a nice thing to do. Seth will be here in a minute so we can have a proper chat.'

Trixie had turned her attention back to the dough on the table. She scooped it up and dropped it into a waiting bowl with a heavy thud, draping a clean tea towel over it, then carried it to stand on the work surface beside the cooker.

'I'll get cleared up,' she said.

Clara felt awful. The atmosphere in the kitchen had completely changed and it was all her fault. She hadn't meant to put a dampener on things, but she wasn't sure how she could say the things she wanted to without that happening. She looked at Trixie. Or even whether she should say them at all…

Trixie was such a good friend. Without her, Clara would never have achieved the things she had, and their business at the farmers' market was going from strength to strength. The cookbook they had been producing was in the final stages of preparation, and they had ideas for so much more here at Joy's Acre. In many ways they were like chalk and cheese – perhaps the reason they got on so well – and Clara could see that for Trixie the chance to appear on television was a dream come true. She would be the first to say that people like her didn't get chances like that, and maybe she was right. So how could Clara possibly take that away from her? There must be a way to do this and for them both to be happy. With a final look at her friend's face, Clara realised that, whatever it took, she would just have to find it.

'I'll give you a hand,' she said, brightening her face into a wide smile. 'And then I'll go and see if I can find any champagne glasses. Otherwise we might well be drinking it from a pint glass!'

Trixie looked up and grinned. 'I'd be quite happy drinking it out of the bottle but perhaps that's not quite the image I should be trying to cultivate.'

Clara nudged her with her hip. 'Not now you're going to be a mega famous TV star, no.'

It did the trick. The tension lifted and Trixie turned up the radio a little, singing along, mouthing at her and Maddie until they both joined in as well. It was how Seth found them moments later.

'Not sure we'll be needing this,' he joked. 'You lot look pretty merry already.'

Tom was hot on his heels. 'All the more for me then, and I haven't even done anything, so I'm not sure I deserve it.'

'You're part of Joy's Acre, Tom. Of course you deserve it,' said Maddie. 'Besides, it's important that all of us discuss the implications of Declan's visit.'

'Not much to discuss, is there?' he replied. 'By the sounds of it, Trixie and Clara have it in the bag.' He winked at Clara. 'Although I'm surprised at you, flirting like that…'

'I did not!' she shot back.

'She didn't have to,' put in Trixie. 'I mean, Declan was already there…'

'Yes, so I hear…'

'For goodness' sake, you've been on the roof all day,' Clara said, exasperated. 'How on earth do you know about that?' She stopped herself. 'Not that there's anything to know about, but even so.'

Tom just tapped the side of his nose. 'I have my sources,' he said.

And Clara could guess exactly what those were.

Seth moved across and turned off the radio. 'Right, folks, come and sit down before we get too carried away.' He put the bottle of champagne down on the table. 'I need to fill you in on some of what you won't have heard, and then in all seriousness, we do need to discuss things properly. There's a lot at stake.'

Chapter 8

Megan opened the door to Liam's house and let herself in. It was curious being here without him and, although she had his permission, she still felt a little awkward about being in his private space.

A part of her acknowledged that, if things had gone more according to plan, it wouldn't just be his space, but hers as well. It also occurred to her that this was the perfect opportunity to have a good snoop around now that Liam was at work and she had the place to herself but, tempting though that was, she knew she wouldn't. What if she found something she didn't like? She and Liam had been apart for weeks at a time and she really had no idea what he did with his free time, the same way he had no idea what she did with hers. But they had to trust one another, didn't they? Otherwise, where would they be?

So, instead of dwelling on her insecurities, she walked through into the lounge to the little study area Liam had set up and put down her things on the desk. First of all, she needed a big mug of coffee, and then she needed to do some research. She turned on the computer and, while waiting for it to boot up, went to put the kettle on.

The next round of the competition, to be held this Saturday, wasn't one she could prepare for. They would be required to replicate sets of four given pieces of metal work. Most likely a horseshoe, a scroll, a twist of some sort and then a more elaborate piece such as a wall sconce. They would need to copy each piece, usually between four to six times, and as always, within a given timescale. Deviation from the original design wasn't permitted and the finished articles had to be identical. It was all down to what happened on the day, and so there was nothing that Megan could do to prepare in advance. Today therefore, she would be turning her attention to the monumental task of designing and creating a gate for a local stately home.

She had been pleased with the initial drawings she had done the day before and, after spending some time outside digging with Clara, she had returned to her design anew looking at it with fresh eyes. It was then, however, that she had realised that she might have been barking up completely the wrong tree.

As soon as she had started to sketch out her ideas for the design, she had naturally focused on not just the things she thought she was good at, but also elements which would show off her skills to their best advantage. Marrying these two starting points together, she had come up with a design that she'd thought could work and had even begun to embellish it, but now she realised, with horror, that she knew nothing about the place where the gate would eventually be installed. It wasn't just the historical aspect of the site which concerned her, but also the physicality of the setting. Without viewing it, how could she possibly know whether her design would marry with its surroundings? However, with the property currently not open until the weekend, Sunday would be leaving things rather too late and she would lose the opportunity of several more days' work. A spot of Internet digging would have to suffice for the time being.

It was difficult to know exactly what the judges would be looking for. The information they had been given specified only the physical size of the gate. Interpretation beyond that would be left open to the competitors to decide but, despite the openness of the brief, Megan was certain that the judges from the National Trust already knew what they wanted; it just remained to be seen whether anyone came close. The existing gate was beautiful, and given the Trust's reputation for expert repair and restoration of its properties and their contents, she had to wonder whether they wanted an almost exact replica of what had already done them proud for years, or whether they were prepared for a more visionary approach. For her sake, she hoped it was the latter but it wouldn't do to discount the heritage angle, and somehow she had to find a balance between both.

As she sipped her coffee, she looked through page after page of images from the Internet, most of them from National Trust properties but some from rather grand private houses. There were beautiful designs; some plain, some elaborate, the ultra-modern designs and the very traditional, but none of them showed Megan anything truly inspiring, and she sat back in the chair feeling defeated.

Another hour later and she was feeling thoroughly despondent. After Googling the property's history and looking at various pictures of artefacts, she had a rudimentary knowledge of the place, but it was all so flat and lifeless. Simply a list of names and dates and places, repeated over and over, on each of the sites she looked at, and all of which could be found by anybody after a few minutes of searching. It was therefore information that the other competitors probably already had, and she'd be willing to bet that several of them would be basing their designs around the historical data. She tapped her pen against her teeth. What she needed was something that fitted seamlessly in with the surroundings of the property but which also, in a unique way, spoke of its very essence.

She threw down the pen on the table and stared at the screen, pulling her ponytail repeatedly through one hand as she sat deep in thought. It was a soothing motion, something she had done since she was young and studying for her exams. Now she did it subconsciously whenever she was feeling stressed, and it did seem to help. It allowed her brain to freewheel, and she often had no real sensation of thinking about anything much until, suddenly, an idea coalesced, or a single thought made itself known to her. The images of the property in question had been scrolling past her eyes for the last few minutes, almost without her seeing them, until, eyes narrowing, she realised that she was peering at one of them more closely. Her hand had stilled on the computer mouse and she sat up a little straighter, as thoughts rushed through her head.

The gardens at the property were one of its most highly prized features and reminded her of Joy's Acre, albeit on a much grander scale. Clara had designed the gardens to have multiple focal points, so that it didn't matter from which direction you looked, there was always a framed vista of some sort. It was a technique that the Victorians had also put to good use and, although the gardens that Megan was looking at were much older, the same principles seemed to apply. She clicked on the image that had grabbed her attention and viewed it full-sized. *I wonder…* she thought to herself.

Minimising the open programs on the computer, Megan looked to see what photo-editing software Liam had installed and was pleased to see a program she could work with. Within moments she had copied the photo and opened it back up again, this time within the new program so that she could begin to alter it.

The photo showed the gate that was already in situ at the property, the same one that whoever won the competition would be lucky enough to replace, and the image had been taken from the path as if you were just about to push open the gate and go through. From such an angle the details of the garden through the gate were clear to see.

Fortunately, the photograph had been taken on a bright day, and was full of colour, and with a few deft clicks, Megan was able to begin 'removing' the gate from the photo altogether. It was painstaking work, and although it didn't need to be perfect, she wanted to get the result as good as she could. It would prove to be of huge benefit in the long run. Working solidly, it took well over an hour before she was happy with the finished result. She sat back, looking at her work critically before giving a satisfied nod and printing two pictures off; one before her alterations, and one after.

She carried them over to the dining area, laying them down on the table. Pulling her sketch book towards her she sat for quite some time, letting the images and ideas burble through her head. And then, with a mounting sense of excitement, she began to draw.

It was exactly how Liam found her hours later when he popped home after his morning appointments. By then, she had covered the table in page after page of designs, and one or two balled-up pieces of paper. The wrapper from a bar of chocolate lay discarded to one side. She nearly jumped out of her skin when his voice sounded from the doorway.

'Flipping 'eck, Liam, you nearly frightened the life out of me. Don't creep up on people like that!'

He grinned, and turned on his heel, going to stand by the front door, where he made a grand show of flinging it wide. He stepped outside and then back into the hallway.

'Hi, honey, I'm home,' he called, holding his door keys up and rattling them vigorously.

'Oh, very funny.'

'I actually think I said your name three times before you realised anyone was speaking to you,' said Liam. 'I might have to buy a mega-phone just to be on the safe side.'

He crossed over to the table where she was still sitting and kissed her cheek.

'I don't suppose you've had anything to eat, have you?' he said, checking his watch. 'It's nearly two o'clock.'

Now that he mentioned it, Megan was ravenous. She shook her head.

'I got a bit engrossed,' she said, stating the obvious, 'but I didn't want to, you know, go fishing around in your kitchen.'

He took hold of her hands, pulling her to her feet. 'What are you like?' He sighed. 'I told you to just make yourself at home, and help yourself to whatever you wanted.'

'I know... but it felt a bit... weird, I suppose. Because you weren't here. Anyway, I did make myself a cup of coffee.'

'No, well, I get that, I suppose. I'd probably feel the same in someone else's house.' He eyed her mug where any remnants of liquid had long since dried up.

'I tell you what,' he said. 'It's still a beautiful day out there, why don't we pop out for something to eat? I haven't got any more appointments now until this evening.'

Megan looked at her work. She had made good progress with it, but she still wasn't finished. She was about to say she'd rather not, when another idea came to her. 'Could we go for a drive instead? And maybe grab something on the way?'

He looked puzzled. 'Sure, if you want to...' And then the penny dropped. 'Oh, I get it.' He leaned over and picked up one of the photos. 'Is this where we're going?' he asked. 'And where would that be, exactly?'

Megan grinned. 'Not far,' she replied, picking up her coat and handbag from the chair beside her. 'I'll tell you on the way.'

★

'I don't know how you do it,' muttered Liam with a scornful look at the carrier bag she was holding.

They were sitting in the car park of the local supermarket as Megan unpacked a pork pie, some Hula Hoops and a family-sized bag of Maltesers from the carrier on her lap. She passed him an egg and cress sandwich.

'What?' she said, grinning. 'I work it off.' She wasn't the slightest bit worried about her extremely unhealthy food. 'Are you sure that's all you wanted?' She smiled at the look on Liam's face. Their makeshift lunch was obviously not quite what he had in mind. 'I'll make us a proper dinner later, I promise.'

He peeled the wrapper from his sandwich and took a reluctant bite. 'Right, come on then. I still haven't the faintest idea where it is we're going.'

'Powis Castle,' said Megan, crunching on a crisp. 'It isn't open, but that doesn't matter, it's just the outside I want to get at. I need to take some photos if I can.'

Liam nodded. 'This is to do with the competition, I'm guessing. The commission?'

'Hmm. I've had the most brilliant idea, but there's only so much I can do at home. I need to be there to see whether what I've got in mind will work.'

'Right, we'd best get going then.' He took another bite of his sandwich, pulled a face and returned it to its wrapper, thrusting the whole lot back at Megan. 'I'll pass if you don't mind,' he said, turning the car key in the ignition. Moments later they pulled out onto the road.

It was another ten minutes before Megan spoke again. This was partly down to the fact that she was still eating, but also partly because she was trying to decide how best to broach a subject which had been constantly on her mind for the last few days. With the competition in full swing it wasn't the best timing, but she had to know where she stood, particularly as she hadn't felt all that comfortable in Liam's house this morning.

She let the Malteser in her mouth dissolve and then swallowed. 'I thought your lounge looked really nice,' she said as an opener.

Liam gave her a sideways glance from the driver's seat. 'I haven't done much,' he said. 'Besides unpack. I haven't really had the time.'

'No, but you can't expect to do everything at once, can you? It's still a nice room. And I didn't go outside or anything, but what I could see of the garden through the kitchen window looked lovely.'

'My grandma was a keen gardener, I think. Not so great at interior decor though…' He let the sentence hang.

Megan thought back to their previous conversations on the subject. 'It's just a little dated, that's all. And you have to expect that, given her age. I don't suppose you're that keen to wallpaper and paint when you're in your seventies, are you? Besides, it could be a lot worse.'

'Oh, definitely. And I think the period features will look really nice once they're made a feature of again.'

She nodded, even though he probably couldn't see her. 'I can't believe it's been six months already since you moved in. Crikey, it will be Christmas soon…'

'I know! You'll have to help me choose the tree,' he said, risking a turn of his head to look at her. He was grinning.

Megan felt the atmosphere ease a little. 'One so big it will fill that whole corner and no one will be able to see the TV?'

'Of course, that's a given… but then there's never anything on anyway so that won't matter…'

'I thought I might—'

'I wondered if—'

They both started to speak at the same time, and Megan laughed. 'Go on,' she said. 'You first.'

Liam slid a hand from the steering wheel and ran it through his hair. 'I wondered if you might be home then?' he asked. 'For good, I mean. Or even if you've had a chance to think about what you might do after the competition?'

Megan's stomach gave a little flip. She had been waiting a long time to talk about this, and now that the opportunity had arrived she was incredibly nervous. Liam's welcome home had been lovely but the fact of the matter was that, despite her use of his house today, he was living there and she was staying at Joy's Acre. There was no guarantee he wanted the things she did longer term and, right now, she just couldn't read how he was feeling.

She smiled and tried to make her voice sound relaxed. 'Well, it all rather depends on how well I do, of course. If I won… oh God, I can't even think about that, it would make such a difference to everything… to us… Even if I did well I think it would stand me in good stead to find work locally… and I guess that's where I am right now.' She paused and reached across to give Liam's hand a squeeze, reassurance for herself as much as anything. 'I don't want to work away from home any more, Liam, I want to come home.'

For a moment she thought she'd said the wrong thing. Liam seemed to be concentrating hard on the road, and she couldn't discern any particular expression on his face. But then she became aware that the car was slowing and, with a flick of the wheel, Liam steered quickly into a passing space at the side of the road.

As soon as the car had reached a stop he pulled on the handbrake and turned to her.

'I had a feeling today was going to be a good day,' he murmured just seconds before his lips met hers.

In an instant, the distance between them melted away and a feeling of utter relief swept over her. It had never been like this before in all the times that Megan had returned home after a period away. Usually, it felt like time had stood still and she just picked up from where she had left off, but ever since she first let Liam know when she would be home this time, things had seemed somehow awkward between them. It was almost as if the weight of expectation on them was too great for them to extricate themselves. They were both getting older. Liam had a house now. Her training was coming to an end. All these things seemed to be shining a huge spotlight on their future together, and for some reason they had seemed incapable of talking about it.

'I thought you'd gone off me,' admitted Megan, finally voicing her fears.

'I thought you were going to tell me you weren't coming back,' replied Liam.

Both of them blushed as they grinned stupidly at one another, hands still clasped together, straining at their seat belts.

'For goodness' sake, what are we like?' said Megan.

'As bad as one another?' suggested Liam, with a rueful smile. 'I'd convinced myself that you'd got another boyfriend, some big beefy blacksmith who could bend metal with his bare hands... I wouldn't stand a chance.'

Megan shuddered. 'Oh, no, thank you very much. I couldn't think of anything worse.'

'Some slim-hipped Adonis then?'

'No, you muppet...' She touched her lips to his. 'Just you.'

Liam looked at the road ahead and then back to Megan. 'Well, we just need to make sure that you win this competition then, don't we, so that you can come back to me all the sooner.' He paused to put the car into gear and then, without another word, drove off.

Chapter 9

It had taken Clara an unusually long time to get to sleep; physical tiredness from long days in the garden together with her naturally buoyant mood ensured that she rarely had trouble sleeping, but last night had proved to be the exception.

This morning, however, she was determined to put her thoughts behind her. The decision had been made and under the circumstances it was the only thing they could do. They would await Declan's proposal and, if it was acceptable, move forward from there. The logic was unquestionable, and Clara's personal feelings would adjust in time; they would have to, for Trixie's sake. Besides, there was little point in trying to think about it today. She would have enough on her hands dealing with Agatha, particularly if she was in one of her contrary moods, but perhaps that was for the best. The less time she had to dwell on things the better.

Manoeuvring her car through the archway into the rear courtyard of the Hall, she was pleased to see Seth had already arrived. It would mean she wouldn't have to run the gauntlet of small talk with Agatha on her own. Climbing from her car, she could already hear voices coming from the other side of the wall and, fixing a smile on her face, she went through the gate to join them.

'Yes, I'm sure she'll be here any minute, Agatha. You know Clara as well as I do, and she's never late.' There was a slightly impatient tone to Seth's voice that indicated to Clara just what kind of a morning he'd had, but mindful of his wish to put things between him and Agatha on a better footing, she was anxious not to make things any worse.

She found Seth sitting on the bench just inside the wall, a mug cradled in his hands. What was even more surprising was that Agatha was sitting beside him, and in front of her, resting on an upturned plant pot, was a tray of tea things.

'Good morning,' she said as brightly as she could. 'How are you, Agatha?'

She braced herself for the inevitable reply. She always asked after Agatha's health and she always regretted doing so.

'Old,' came the reply. 'And sitting out here waiting for you isn't doing my bones any good either.'

Clara shot Seth a nervous glance, but he looked surprisingly relaxed.

'Now now, Agatha. That's not very nice, is it? Not when Clara has come to help.'

The old lady looked away.

'Yes, well, if I wasn't quite so frail I'd have done the job myself.'

Clara smiled to herself. Agatha had the constitution of an ox.

'But you can't, and Clara is the expert here, let's not forget that. You want the grounds to look lovely for the competition and she's the person to transform that whole area for you. So, shall we go and have a look at the plants?'

Agatha rose and almost managed a gracious smile. 'I've had some things delivered, Clara, which are resting in the greenhouse. I'm afraid I have no idea whether they will be suitable – I had to leave things up to my supplier – but they are traditional varieties, I believe. Perhaps you would be kind enough to let me know if they are not to your taste. There are also several bags of potting compost, but more can be delivered should you require them.' She began to walk away in the direction of the house. 'I shall leave you to get on but you may fetch me when you're done so that I may check on your work. Perhaps you could also return the tray of tea things to the kitchen.'

Clara closed her mouth, which had fallen open. She stared at Seth, waiting before Agatha was finally out of earshot before speaking.

'What on earth is going on? For Agatha, that was almost polite.'

Seth just grinned. 'You wait until you see what's in the greenhouse.'

'But I've got a boot-load of stuff in the car. Agatha has never provided plants before.'

'I know.' Seth got to his feet, and took her arm. 'She was actually quite anxious about the choice and whether you would like them or not. I think it might be called trying to make amends. But whatever it is, let's just be grateful. It's going to make our lives so much easier, not to mention pleasant. Come on, and I'll fill you in.'

He led her across the garden and to the vast greenhouse that spanned the far end.

'Providing refreshments is not the only thing that's changed about the blacksmithing competition this year. It would seem that the local population has been very complimentary about the way in which things have been organised this time around, and have been very vocal on the subject. Agatha has been forced to listen to countless glowing references, not only about me, but also about the wonderful food and produce that has been flowing out of Joy's Acre. I knew you and Trixie were a hit at the local farmers' market, but I didn't realise you had quite as many fans as you do. Apparently Agatha has been told time and again how delighted she must be, and it would seem that she has decided there may be some merit to our little business after all.'

'No…' Clara was disbelieving.

Seth grinned. 'Oh yes… Agatha delights in playing the lady of the manor, as you know, and it seems she's quite enjoying all this attention. I suggest we make the most of it while it lasts.'

'Ah, and that would explain her new-found interest in having the place looking tip-top.'

'I suggested putting out all the troughs and planters when we first began to discuss arrangements for the competition, and Agatha dismissed the idea in her usual forthright manner. She said the place would be full of blacksmiths for heaven's sake, why on earth would they want to look at flowers? Now it would seem she's in love with the idea.' He gave her a wry look. 'And of course, very grateful to you for agreeing to come and plant up everything.'

Clara would have made some derogatory comment had it not been for the fact that she had just spotted the laden benches inside the greenhouse. She hurried to the door.

'Crikey, Seth, how much does she think there is to plant? There's probably three times as much as I need here.' She walked forward. 'Mind you, she's picked some beautiful varieties, or rather the nursery has. I'm spoilt for choice.' She glanced at her watch. 'Right, come on then, let's get these troughs and whatnot shifted, and I'll get cracking. Once I've checked where Agatha wants them, will you be all right to pop back later and help me set them into place?'

'No problem. I've got to come back anyway to fix her front door. The lock appears to have slipped.'

She followed him through to the far end of the greenhouse to a separate store room which was stuffed full of all manner of stone pots and tubs, many of them unused for years, and far too heavy for her to lift by herself. It took quite a while to sort through them and select a dozen or so to use.

'Are you sure you're okay with this today, Clara?' Seth straightened up, giving her a searching look. 'You look unusually tired.'

She mirrored his stance, giving him an equally direct look. 'Perfectly,' she said. 'So no fussing. I didn't sleep particularly well so maybe that's why. Too much excitement, I expect.' She knew better than to try and pull the wool over Seth's eyes completely, he would see through her ruse in seconds. But she didn't have to give him the whole truth.

'It *was* quite a day,' he replied. 'I think everyone was feeling it by the end of the day, and the champagne pretty much finished everyone off. A good day though?'

'Scary, and nerve-wracking, but Declan and his team seem nice people. I'm sure they'll be great to work with… if we get the chance, that is.'

'I don't suppose it will take Declan long to put together his proposal,' he said. 'I think he's quite certain about what he wants, and from what he said quite certain that he's found it. There are no guarantees of course, but…' He trailed off, still searching her face.

'Clara, you and I have been friends for too long to be anything less than honest with each other,' he continued. 'And I realise it would have been hard yesterday with us all together, with all the banter about Declan and with Trixie being… rather excited, shall we say. But there's just you and me now… You would say, wouldn't you, if you weren't happy about the prospect of this TV series going ahead?'

'Of course I would,' she said straight away. 'It's important that we all agree on this, but it's far too good an opportunity to miss, Seth.' She swallowed, thinking carefully about her next words. 'I'll be the first to admit that I probably have the most reservations out of all of us, but I think that's just me, because I'm not a particularly confident person. And I worry about the changes that all this might bring to Joy's Acre, but I'm not telling you anything you don't already know. The chance to get the barn finished and fully kitted out is too important to let slip through our fingers and if the money from the TV series can do that, then who am I to argue.'

'Well, strictly speaking it's yours and Trixie's money…'

She shook her head. 'No, we agreed. The needs of the many outweigh the needs of the few. There's no question of either of us accepting this personally. It's for the farm, no argument.'

His eyes held hers for a few more seconds before he looked away, satisfied. Clara let out the breath she'd been holding as slowly as she could so that Seth wouldn't notice it. She hadn't lied to him. She had been as truthful as she could, anything less would have aroused suspicion, but it still didn't change how she felt inside. She owed too much to Seth and to Trixie, in fact to everyone at Joy's Acre, to let her thoughts prejudice the amazing opportunity they had just been given. But nothing could get rid of the sinking sensation she felt every time she thought of what the next few weeks would bring, or her very real fear that nothing would ever be the same again…

After Seth left, Clara wandered around the back of the house to the courtyard where she had arrived earlier, and through to the other side to where the stables and the competition area lay. Looking at it with a critical eye, she made her own decisions about where the planters should be added, and although Agatha might have different ideas, at least it gave her a place to start from.

Back in the greenhouse, armed with this information, she worked steadily for the next couple of hours. It was warm under the glass and this and the very fact that Clara had her hands plunged into soil were enough to allow her mood to lift and settle. She was doing what she loved best, how could she feel anything else?

The selection of plants at her disposal was very pleasing, and she spent quite some time sorting through them before beginning to pot them up into their new homes. She wanted different effects for different areas of the space available. Some planters needed to be full of colour, but would not necessarily need to be long-lasting. Other planters needed single showy specimens, while some needed to have a mix of plants of differing colours, textures and sizes and could hopefully be reused elsewhere once the competition was over. They would overwinter, providing interest and decoration for many months to come. The possibilities were endless, and it was Clara's skill in selecting the right plant for the right occasion that would make all the difference.

Fully immersed in her work, it came as quite a surprise when Agatha suddenly appeared beside her. She hadn't even heard her approach, and visibly started.

'Goodness, how beautiful these are, Clara.' The elderly lady was holding a mug of tea, a wistful expression on her face.

Clara looked down and smiled at her handiwork. 'Thank you,' she said. 'It's not that often I get to choose from such an array of gorgeous plants. I feel rather spoilt.'

Agatha put the mug down on the bench beside Clara and looked around. 'It's been a long time since I did any proper gardening, and I seem to have rather over-catered, as it were. Perhaps whatever is left might be found a home at Joy's Acre?'

'Oh, I couldn't possibly do that,' replied Clara, surprised. It hadn't been that long ago when Agatha had angrily withdrawn her funding of the renovations at the farm over a squabble with Seth. 'But I'd be happy to plant whatever is left here, either in these gardens, or elsewhere if you'd prefer...'

'I will have a think, and decide what seems most suitable.' Her face was wearing its habitual stern expression, but as Clara watched it softened a little. 'It will be good to see some colour here again, some life... Rather a lot of years have gone by since the Hall looked at its best. Perhaps too long.' She stared at the garden through the greenhouse windows. It was tired and overgrown.

Clara ran her fingers through the foliage of a particularly vivid Japanese maple. 'Most of these shrubs will go on and on, right through the winter. And the chrysanthemums will flower for weeks yet. They'll make a huge difference, and if you like I can pop back from time to time to keep an eye on them. I made sure that I planted them so that as one thing comes to an end another is just beginning to come into its own. And now they're in containers, they'll pretty much look after themselves until the spring.'

'I think you've done a wonderful job. The competition seems to be going wonderfully well this year, and Seth has been such a huge help in making it so. It was his suggestion actually to spruce the place up a bit.' She eyed Clara over the top of her glasses. 'I expect he told you. However, I didn't listen to start with.' She pursed her lips. 'I can see now that I was wrong.'

Clara didn't know quite what to say. What Agatha said was true but to agree with her did seem rather like rubbing salt in the wound. Whatever she had said in the past, however she had acted, Clara could feel her reaching out, and she couldn't help but respond. It was in her very nature to care for things. She stretched a hand towards the mug Agatha had brought with her.

'Is this for me?'

Agatha nodded.

'Thank you. I'm parched actually. It's such a beautiful day, but very warm in here. Shall we go and sit outside for a minute?'

There was a bench not far from the greenhouse. Cleverly placed to catch the sun, it rested against a brick wall beside a gnarled and lichen-covered apple tree. Clara could feel the radiated warmth from the wall against her back as she sat down and turned her face to the sun. She waited a moment until Agatha had joined her.

'I don't think I've ever seen any pictures of the Hall,' she said. 'In its heyday, I mean, but there must be some, surely?'

'I have drawers full of them,' replied Agatha. 'But it's been years since I even thought to bring them out. There's no one else to look at them but me now, and although my memory is not what it was, there are some things which never fade.'

Clara nodded, staring out across the garden to the area beyond where the stables lay. She'd just had a sudden thought, and it was probably a mad idea, but there was only one way to find out.

'I would love to see them,' she said. 'And I bet I'm not the only one. The next round of the competition is not until Saturday, that's two whole days away yet. Why don't we get some of the photos together and make a display of them? We could put them onto boards and stand them in the end stable as it's not being used for the competition. I'm sure people would be interested to see what the Hall looked like back then.'

Agatha stared at her, obviously shocked. She looked down at her hands. 'Why would you even do that for me?' she asked quietly.

The question surprised her. 'Because I think it would mean a lot to you,' Clara answered truthfully. 'You've lived here a very long time, Agatha, and things change; it's inevitable. I've never found anyone yet who could stop the passage of time, but sometimes it's nice to bring the past with us into the future. Joy's Acre is the perfect example of that. And I know other people would like to see it too.'

'We used to hold the fete here, did you know that? Every year. It was the highlight of the village calendar. My husband started it, the year after we moved here, more as a garden party really, to welcome our friends and neighbours, but over time it grew. All the local school children came. It was quite magical.'

Clara couldn't conceive of an Agatha who would welcome noisy children to her home. How times had changed.

'I had no idea,' she said. 'But it must have been very special. And I'm sure there are still plenty of people around who would remember it. I don't suppose you would have any photos of that either, would you? Or even past blacksmithing competitions. I expect you've seen a fair few of those as well.'

Agatha smiled, her blue eyes twinkling. 'I do believe I have,' she said. 'Do you really think people would be interested?'

Clara drank her tea. 'I think they'd be fascinated.' She gave a satisfied nod. 'I tell you what, Agatha. I'm nearly done here, and then until Seth gets back to help me put the planters into position, there's nothing else I can do. Why don't I come across to the house in a bit, and I can help you sort through the photos? We can pick the best ones together.'

Chapter 10

In all the time Clara had been at Joy's Acre, she had never set foot inside the house where Agatha lived. She had been summoned imperiously with Seth on numerous occasions to see to the hedge or mend some of the fencing up at the Hall, but never been invited into what she had always seen as Agatha's inner sanctum. Something had changed today, and although Clara had no idea why Agatha seemed to be behaving so differently, she was certainly intrigued.

As soon as she finished planting up the last remaining pots she washed the worst of the mud off her hands at the outside tap and dried them on her apron but, even so, she grimaced as she raised a hand to knock on the back door. At least her boots weren't muddy.

Agatha answered almost straight away, practically pulling on her arm in her haste to get Clara inside.

'Come through, I've managed to pull out some of the old albums, but I think the rest might be in the hall cupboard.'

Clara stepped into a long flagstone passageway. 'Is there somewhere I can wash my hands, Agatha?' she asked. 'I'd hate to dirty your photos.'

They turned off the corridor into what was still a very old-fashioned scullery. It didn't look like it had altered in years.

'In here is best,' said Agatha. 'There's soap and an old towel. It's where I used to wash Bailey's feet after walks.'

Clara had no idea who Bailey was – a dog, she presumed, although in all the time she had known her, Clara had never seen Agatha with one. A ceramic water bowl lay on the floor. Clean, but a trifle dusty. She washed her hands as swiftly as possible.

The hall cupboard turned out to be an enormous oak dresser, a monstrosity that must have been fifteen-foot long, and at least eight-foot high. It spanned one whole side of the hallway, but oddly didn't look overly big in the impressive tiled space. On instruction, Clara opened a series of cupboard doors towards one end and, amid piles of papers, hats, gloves, scarves, old newspapers and a box of unopened Christmas crackers, Clara located at least a dozen old photograph albums and pulled them out onto the floor.

'We'll go in the drawing room,' said Agatha, leading the way, and Clara had to smile. She was still being bossed about, but at least it was with a considerably gentler tone than she was used to.

Clara picked up a stack of the albums and followed her, almost gasping out loud at the loveliness of the room she walked into. Situated at the front of the house, it was lit by a series of floor-to-ceiling windows draped in heavy gold and cream crewel-work curtains. A burnished mahogany floor stretched away from her, centred on which, and facing each other, were a pair of matching sofas, separated by a heavy rug. An ornate fireplace stood to their left.

At the far end of the room was a long table underneath another window and it was on this that Clara placed the albums. There were several there already. It would appear that she had rather a long afternoon ahead of her, but Clara couldn't wait to see what lay inside them. Imagine what Seth would say when she told him.

'Shall I make us some more tea while you bring in the rest of the albums?' asked Agatha, watching with satisfaction. 'I have some custard creams as well if you're partial to those.'

Like most things in Agatha's life, the photograph albums were well ordered. All dated, they fell into three distinct groups: photographs of the fete, the blacksmithing competition and general life at the Hall. Selecting the first of these, from the early 1970s, it was immediately clear to Clara that Agatha and her husband had been lavish hosts. Page after page showed the Hall transformed for elegant dinners, extravagant parties and grand family gatherings. The fashions may have been questionable but the hospitality provided was certainly not.

'You all look like you had the most amazing fun,' remarked Clara, tracing a finger over the photos. 'These pictures of Christmas time are wonderful. I'm from a very small family myself – we never had get-togethers like these, and I always wished we did; brothers, sisters, uncles, aunts, nieces, nephews, all joining together.'

Agatha sighed. 'I remember it being incredibly hard work, but yes… you're right, it was fun too.' She pulled a bright blue album towards her. 'I used to love the summer parties the most. We would open the doors into the garden and let the party spill over onto the terraces. You young things would frown at it now, but I distinctly recall the smell of cigarette smoke wafting in on a warm summer's evening, mixing with the heady scent of the wallflowers and stocks from the borders. It was quite the most wonderful thing.' She flipped over a few pages. 'And all the dresses. Such bright colours and patterns, as if they were trying to outdo the flowers – and some of them did, I can assure you. Hideous now of course, but back then, all the rage.'

Clara looked to where she was pointing, to the photograph of the stone steps leading from the very room she was sitting in now, down to a manicured sweep of lawns; the terraces massed with blooms of every variety, huge roses trailing from the walls of the house, their heavy heads hanging down. She could almost smell the perfume.

She would have continued looking had Agatha not closed the book suddenly, reaching for another from the pile with a broad smile on her face.

'I must show you this,' she said. 'It was a night I don't think I'll ever forget.' She was opening the pages of a red book this time. 'New Year's Eve on the night we started a new millennium. It seemed the whole world had been waiting with bated breath, and as the clocks struck, the sky was lit over and over again by more fireworks than I think I've ever seen in my life before. And look…' She tapped at a picture on the page.

It showed a young girl wearing a silver dress and shoes. Her golden hair was lit by the fireworks over her head, and she smiled shyly into the camera, champagne glass in hand.

'You remind me of her,' said Agatha softly. 'The hair of course, but you have her quietness, her calm.'

Clara peered at the image. 'Who is she?'

Agatha's smile was tinged with sadness. 'My granddaughter,' she said.

'That's Jen?' Clara stared at the photo. 'Oh my goodness, Agatha, she was beautiful…' She swallowed, unsure what to say next.

'And it was on that night she first met Seth.' Agatha looked up at her. 'It was pure chance of course. Seth had been staying with relatives over Christmas at one of the holiday cottages in the village. My husband got talking to them in the pub on Christmas Eve and invited them to the party. He invited everyone, I seem to recall, and most of them turned up. But it didn't matter. Jennifer and Seth went their separate ways after that night, and didn't meet again until years later. She never spoke of it to me, and I always wondered if they even remembered they had met before.'

Clara put her hand to her throat. 'But you can ask him now. Oh, you must! That's such a beautiful story. It's like they were always meant to be together.'

'And yet they had so little time. How can that possibly be fair?'

'It's not, but you know Agatha, the one thing I do know is that Jen was happy.' She laid her hand over the old lady's. 'I don't know all the details of their life together, but Jen loved Joy's Acre, she was full of hopes and dreams, in the first flush of life as a newlywed with Seth. How much better is it that, however short her life, at least she had all those things? And she shared them with someone who loved her very much.'

Agatha was silent for a moment, her blue eyes resting briefly on Jen's photo before turning back to Clara. 'You've always seemed like a very sensible, and indeed, astute young lady,' she said. 'So might I now ask you something? A little personal...'

She didn't even need to ask; Clara was way ahead of her. She took a deep breath.

'No, I don't think you've been altogether fair in your treatment of Seth...' she said, answering Agatha's unspoken question. She held up her hand. 'But,' she added quickly, softening her voice, 'I understand why, perfectly. You were both grieving, shocked and angry at Jen's death, and all you could see was that Seth had somehow failed your granddaughter. And then I arrived... What else were you to think?'

Agatha hung her head. 'I'm so ashamed to admit it, but it's true. I convinced myself that he'd brought you here to fill Jen's place, even though I knew the circumstances of your meeting meant that could never be the case. But I believed it just the same.'

'It must have been a terrible thing for you...' Clara faltered for a second. 'I never really realised either how similar we looked, not until just now when I saw her photo... but you know how Seth and I met, Agatha. When he became my bone marrow donor he had no idea who I was. I wasn't even a name on a piece of paper, that's how careful they are to protect everyone involved. It wasn't until two years after my transplant that Seth was allowed to find out more, and that was only because I gave him permission to.'

She ran her fingers over the photo again. 'What I said earlier about it seemingly being fate that had brought Seth and Jen together, what if the same is true now? For all of us at Joy's Acre, me... Maddie too...'

She let the sentence dangle, knowing how badly Agatha had treated Maddie when she had first arrived. 'Seth couldn't fulfil Jen's wishes for the farm on his own, Agatha, he wasn't able to, but he saved my life, and now, in turn, I've been able to save Jen's garden, to finish the work she started. It's the same for Maddie. You brought her in to wield a big stick over Seth and get him to move forwards with the renovations of the farm, but instead of coercing him into doing it, she gave him a reason to *want* to. He is happier than I've seen him in ages... and I think Jen would have been happy too. She'd certainly approve of all this.' She indicated the photo albums strewn over the table.

'Do you know, I think she would,' agreed Agatha. 'She always said that memories were not things that should be treated like precious ornaments, rarely touched and allowed to gather dust, but that's exactly what I've done. I've as much failed her memory as I once believed Seth had done.' Agatha lifted her chin. 'But no longer. You're quite right of course; I've behaved appallingly to Maddie, to all of you, and it's time to set that right.'

She pulled another album towards her, this time one containing photos of the fetes.

'It's high time I dusted all these off. Now, let's have a look and see which ones we think we should put on display.'

A slight brusqueness had returned to Agatha's voice, signalling the end of the recent topic of discussion, but Clara was in no doubt how difficult it would have been for Agatha to admit those things to herself, let alone anyone else. It was actually a huge compliment that she had chosen Clara to hear them, and with a smile she returned her attention to the task in hand.

It proved incredibly difficult to single out which pictures to use. There were so many which captured the gardens looking exquisite, or the joyful celebrations of the summer fete. Even the blacksmithing competition had been the showcase for a great deal of talent, and it was hard to pick examples that were any better than the rest.

Eventually though, amid tea, several custard creams, and light-hearted conversation, she and Agatha had collected together a batch of photos which gave a brilliant insight into life at the Hall over the last few decades.

'I think these are something to be immensely proud of, Agatha, and they will look wonderful displayed. I'm not sure how we'll do it yet, but I'm certain we can get them up in time for the next round of competition at the weekend. I wouldn't mind betting there will be lots of smiles on faces when people see them. I should imagine a good many of the villagers will have fond memories of these times too.'

'I hope so,' said Agatha, nodding. 'They were good years.' She pushed the pile of photos towards Clara. 'Perhaps it's just the change in seasons,' she continued, 'the inexorable move towards another winter, or seeing one more blacksmithing competition take place, but all these reminders of time passing have rather been playing on my mind just lately.' She looked a little embarrassed. 'Thank you, Clara.'

'No, thank *you*,' she replied, smiling warmly. 'I'd never have had the opportunity to see the Hall in all her glory otherwise. It's been fascinating, and now that we've made a start with all the new planters, I'd be very happy to continue looking after them. I'm sure there will be some other things I could attend to as well… if you would like me to, that is?' She had absolutely no idea how she would find the time to do any of these things, but that wasn't the point.

'My dear, I'd be delighted.'

Clara glanced at her watch. 'Shall we go and have a look and see where you'd like everything to go? Seth should be back shortly, and then we can move them into position for you.'

As it was, they met Seth just coming along the path to the back door.

'Perfect timing,' he said.

'Isn't it?' replied Agatha, beaming. 'And have you seen the wonderful planters Clara has put together? They'll transform the place.' She motioned to Seth to walk on ahead. 'Come along then, let's go and make the Hall look beautiful again.'

Seth's expression in the face of Agatha's enthusiasm was a picture, but Clara could do no more than simply grin at him. It wasn't until they were alone for a moment in the greenhouse that he was able to give her another wayward glance.

'What on earth is wrong with Agatha?' he asked. 'She's like a dog with two tails. And you look considerably better than you did this morning as well.'

Clara stopped mid-tracks and looked at Seth, surprised. She had forgotten all about her earlier anxiety.

'Let's just say that Agatha and I have passed a very pleasant morning, and I do feel better, thank you.'

She received a puzzled look.

'I'll tell you about it later,' she said, spying Agatha coming through the garden to meet them. 'It's rather a long story.'

Chapter 11

Forty minutes later and Clara was back in her car heading for the nearest town. She really didn't have the time to be doing this, but neither did she have time to waste. She just hoped that her plan to involve Maddie in getting Agatha's display ready was a good one.

It only took ten minutes or so to arrive at her destination, and she headed for the art supplies shop which she hoped would have what she was looking for. It had occurred to her that the easiest way to display the photos might be to fix them to some large artists' canvases. They were lightweight, could be hung easily, and a whole series of them would look very effective displayed on the walls around the competition area.

Walking along the High Street, she stopped as she always did to look in the florist's window. The gardens at Joy's Acre were so full of flowers that she seldom had need to buy anything from the shop, but the window displays were always enticing and Clara couldn't resist. She often found inspiration for new colour combinations or unusual ideas for flower arrangements, and now that the cottages at the farm were open for business, she liked to provide them with fresh blooms when she could.

This afternoon there was a particularly interesting combination of heathers and ornamental cabbages in the window. She was still mulling over what shrubs to put in the garden of the cottage she and Megan had dug over the other day, so she popped inside to get the names of the varieties in question and check the prices.

The place was always busy. Rather cleverly the owners had installed a small tearoom into a space at the rear of the shop and most of the customers browsed the goods either on their way to, or from, having a cup of tea. She paid them no notice and continued looking around until she overheard a voice that she recognised.

'I don't really mind the cost,' said Declan, 'and I've never seen roses this deep in colour before. They'd be perfect. She only has a birthday once a year and I want her present to be really special.'

Clara tried hard to concentrate on the row of heathers she was looking at, but Declan's voice and his sudden burst of laughter seemed to be the only things she could hear.

'… But do they say I love you?' he asked the assistant. 'Rather than I'm sorry, or I'm guilty?' He laughed again. 'Is there even such a thing as guilty flowers?' Clara couldn't hear the florist's reply. 'So you'd be made up if you received them…?' This time she did hear the emphatic *yes* in reply. 'Then, these it is. That's perfect, thanks.'

She risked a slight downwards glance behind her, and was dismayed to see a pair of feet heading in her direction. If she was going to be able to leave without being noticed, it would have to be now.

'Clara?'

Her heart sank.

'Declan, hello. Sorry, I was miles away,' she lied.

'This must be an occupational hazard for you, I would imagine.'

She gave a slight smile. 'Yes, it's true enough. I can never pass a florist's shop without being nosy.' She needed to know what he was doing there. 'You're a long way from home?' she added.

'Yes, busy morning. Just getting some background location shots of the area, which is stunning by the way. I didn't know Shropshire at all well before Tuesday, but now we've been here a couple of days we've been able to take a lot more in. You live in a very beautiful part of the country.'

She nodded, although it hardly seemed a fitting response.

'Sadly, I've got to get back home tonight; I've a rather special birthday to attend, but I've got time to grab a coffee if you're free? It would be great to have a chat.'

As her stomach did a little flip she realised that her anxiety of that morning had returned. But as she wracked her brain for a suitable reply, it was also apparent that she wasn't sure what was causing it now – thoughts of the TV show, or Declan himself. His eyes were a unique green colour, that was for certain, and the way he was smiling at her seemed…

She thrust the thoughts aside, chastising herself for being so ridiculous. Just because everyone at Joy's Acre had teased her about his fancying her, didn't make it so. In fact, Trixie must have got her information wrong, after all. He might have told her that he didn't have a wife or girlfriend… Her train of thought crashed to a halt as she realised something else. *The cheeky so and so…* Moments ago he'd been buying flowers for someone special and now he was flirting with her. She tutted.

'I don't think that's very wise, do you? In fact, I'm not sure how you could even ask me.'

His head shot up, but she was determined to make the point.

'I'm not sure that whoever you bought those beautiful roses for would approve, do you?' She ignored his attempts to speak. 'So, I don't think I'll be having coffee with you, thanks very much.' And with that she fled the shop.

It wasn't until she was almost at the art supply shop that something else occurred to her, and her cheeks immediately coloured red. *Clara Campbell*, she said to herself sternly, *you are not disappointed, so you can get that notion out of your head straight away.*

★

'So come on then,' said Seth, once the dinner things had been tidied away. 'Let's have a look at these photos. I'm dying to know the reason for Agatha's sudden change in behaviour. She's been almost civil to me for weeks and then today it's as if both Clara and I have the sun shining out of our—'

'Yes, thank you, Seth,' said Maddie. 'We get the picture. It does seem strange though, considering how she's been in the past.'

Clara smiled sympathetically. Maddie in particular had been on the receiving end of Agatha's vicious tongue, not long after she arrived. In fact, she had almost left Joy's Acre because of it. What made it even more ironic, though, was that it was this very thing that had proved to be the turnaround in their fortunes, and Maddie's relationship with Seth.

'I felt a bit sorry for her actually. She seemed a bit… lost somehow, reminiscing about the old times – when her husband was alive and when it was obvious she had lots of people around her. I think she's been lonely the last few years.'

'She didn't need to be,' remarked Seth. 'But you can only push people away so many times before they actually stay away.'

'People usually have a reason for doing so though,' said Clara, trying to be as diplomatic as possible. 'And she did admit that she'd treated you and Maddie badly. She was so pleased when I suggested putting up a display of the photos, I think it's her way of trying to reconnect with the village, and rebuild some bridges maybe.' She looked across at Maddie. 'With both of you as well.'

She began to spread out some of the photos on the table. 'I don't know what's triggered the change in her but something has. She talked a bit about the blacksmithing competition, how seeing it come around again had made her think about the passing of the years. Perhaps she's just feeling her age.'

Seth picked up a picture of the Hall, deep in snow. 'Crikey, I remember this. It was the year we first moved here, so it would have been not long after Agatha's husband died. The drifts were so bad we couldn't get down the lane to the village for four days. It took Davy from the farm at the bottom of the hill that long to dig the road out with his tractor, and I've never been so pleased to see someone in all my life. Jen and I joked that if it was going to be like that every winter we'd sooner not stay.' He looked up, colouring slightly, but Maddie just smiled. She took the photo from him.

'It's beautiful though,' she said. 'How could you not have fallen in love with the place? It was like something from a fairy tale.' She picked up another photo, again of the house but this time taken in high summer. Wisteria hung in elegant swathes across the back of the house. 'Imagine the smell,' she said.

Maddie looked back at Seth, but he was staring into the distance, lost in thought. She waved a hand in front of his face.

'Sorry,' he said, breaking into a smile. 'But I've just had a thought. Excuse me for a minute.' And with that he left the room.

Clara glanced at Maddie, but if she had been affected by the mention of Jen's name she gave no sign of it.

'So, what's the plan with these then, Clara?' she asked.

'Well that's where I'm hoping you might be able to help me,' she replied, briefly describing what she had in mind. 'I'm not good at things like that, but you could make the display look fantastic. If I did it, it would just look like a bunch of photos stuck on a board, whereas with your help we might make it look quite professional. I got the feeling from Agatha that she was keen to make the place look as good as possible, especially since we've already gone to the trouble of adding all the planters.'

This time it was Maddie's turn to stare into space, obviously deep in thought.

'It might also help you,' added Clara, 'if Agatha knew you had helped to put the display together, I mean. It might go some of the way to mend the differences between you… if you want to, that is.'

Maddie suddenly smiled at Clara. 'I'm tempted to say no – recompense for all the trouble she put me through when I first arrived – but I won't of course… In fact—' She broke off for a moment, thinking some more. 'I'm intrigued by the notion of the fete actually. I wonder…' She looked at Clara, eyes sparkling.

Clara grinned. 'Maddie Porter,' she said. 'You don't ever stop, do you? I can see exactly what you're thinking… Not content with having a documentary and prospective TV series to help put Joy's Acre on the map, you're now thinking we should resurrect the annual village fete, aren't you, with us running it?'

Maddie had the grace to blush. 'But wouldn't it be brilliant? And from what you've said I think Agatha might love the idea.'

'And how on earth will we find the time to do that as well? We're going to find it increasingly hard to cope with the workload as it is, never mind organising something like that too.'

'But that's the beauty of it,' replied Maddie. 'It's quite likely we may need to employ some more people soon, particularly as we move into next year. What better way to get the support of the village than by asking them to help us stage the fete?'

'What fete?' asked Seth, coming back into the room. He was carrying a leather-bound notebook.

Clara groaned. 'No, please don't tell him, Maddie. Otherwise he's going to think it's a great idea too, I just know it.'

Seth looked between the two of them, a slow smile spreading across his face. 'Sorry, Clara, I thought we should get the fete up and running again the minute I saw the photos.' He positively beamed at Maddie and it warmed Clara's heart to see the look that passed between them.

'I've also realised just why Agatha has suddenly seemed to be turning over a new leaf. Or at least discovered a possible cause of it.' He placed the notebook down on the table and opened the front cover. Clara could see that it was a diary.

'This was Jen's,' he said. 'From the year she died. Last Saturday would have been her thirty-fifth birthday—' He stopped when he caught sight of the expression on Clara's face.

She felt awful. How could she possibly have forgotten? But Seth just gave her a gentle smile.

'It's fine, Clara. Really... Maddie and I, well we...' And then he stopped again. 'We raised a glass to her,' he continued. 'And I just suddenly remembered that her and Agatha's birthdays were quite close together. I've just checked and, in fact, they're exactly a week apart. This coming Saturday will be Agatha's *eightieth* birthday.'

'Oh my goodness!' exclaimed Clara. 'Well that rather explains things... Oh, poor Agatha. She's obviously feeling her mortality.'

Seth nodded. 'We should do something, shouldn't we? Have some sort of celebration?'

'At the blacksmithing competition?' jumped in Clara. 'That would be perfect, particularly given the display we're putting together. I'm sure we could get her birthday announced during the proceedings, and then maybe ask everyone to join in singing "Happy Birthday" or something, and have a piece of cake. It needn't be something that takes a massive amount of organising.'

'Good,' said Maddie. 'Because I can't see how we'd manage that otherwise. We could ask Trixie about making a special cake but she might kill us, given that she's already going to be baking for the refreshments.'

Seth smiled. 'Hmm, true, but at least we could organise some flowers. What do you think? That wouldn't take much.'

'Yes, well just as long as you don't ask me to do it,' said Clara, pulling a face. 'I'm not going back to the florist's any time soon.'

Maddie raised an eyebrow. 'Oh? Do tell. What happened? Did you have an altercation over the agapanthus?'

'No, not quite… If you must know I bumped into Declan in there this afternoon.' She turned to Seth, frowning. 'Did you know he was still in the area?'

He didn't quite meet her eyes. 'I had an email from him, yes. He mentioned they might stick around for a couple of days, to get a bit of background footage, and I—'

'Never mind about that,' cut in Maddie. 'What happened with Declan?'

Clara could feel her face growing hot. 'Well it wasn't my fault. I wasn't the one behaving badly…'

'What happened, Clara?' repeated Seth, concerned now, whether for her sake or because of the possibility of there being a problem with the TV show, Clara couldn't tell.

'Cheeky so-and-so asked me to have a coffee with him, that's what.' Clara pouted, remembering their exchange.

Maddie suppressed a giggle. 'Well, there's hardly a law against that. Besides, it was obvious he liked you when he was here…'

'That's not the point,' protested Clara. 'I'd just had to listen to him order flowers… and not just any old flowers. He went to great pains to ensure they were the type that say "I love you". He even quizzed the sales assistant to make sure they would be suitable. And then in the next breath he asks me out.'

'Clara, he asked you for a coffee, not out on a date. It's hardly the same thing… I expect he just thought it would be a good opportunity to have a chat about his ideas for the show.'

'Oh…' Clara could feel her cheeks growing even hotter, and she dipped her head in embarrassment at the memory of their argument. Although, strictly speaking, it hadn't been an argument – she had railed against his suggestion and he'd been unable to get a word in edgeways. 'Yes, I suppose you're right.' It was quite possible that she had overreacted…

'Oh dear,' she said, biting her lip. 'I think I've just made a complete idiot of myself.'

Chapter 12

'I want to know how on earth you managed to do all this without Agatha even noticing,' said Maddie, looking around her. 'That woman never misses a thing.'

'We lied.' Clara laughed. 'There was no other way around it. Seth told her that the committee needed to undertake a health and safety inspection of the competition area, and as such no one was allowed near it. Then, while she was out the way, Trixie and I blew up balloons until we thought we were going to pass out and… ta-dah!' She looked up at the ceiling of the stable area which was massed with colour. 'I reckon it looks pretty good, don't you?'

'Brilliant! And having the display up today as well makes it even more special. Agatha will be chuffed to bits.'

It was the second Saturday of the competition, Agatha's eightieth birthday, and the competition area at the Hall had been transformed. Not only were Clara's planters in place adding life and colour, but she had also created some stunning floral arrangements to place in the marquees. They were originally going to stand just by the entrances, but the wind had picked up a little overnight and had threatened to topple them. Still, they made a welcome addition wherever they were placed.

As discussed, the end stable of the row of forges had been transformed into a mini museum of life at the Hall over the last several decades. With Maddie's expert help, the huge boards Clara had bought had been covered with photos, and interspersed with other memorabilia that Agatha had unearthed. She had also provided captions for the some of the photos, and now that the boards had been hung on the walls in chronological order, they provided a wonderful snapshot into the past. Adding balloons and a huge birthday banner to the room were brilliant finishing touches, and Clara was thrilled with the result.

The first competitors were already beginning to arrive and get set up for the day and Clara checked her watch.

'Crikey, I need to get back and help Trixie bring the cakes over or she'll never speak to me again.' She grimaced at Maddie. 'She was a bit stressed this morning.'

'I'm not surprised. She's a victim of her own success in a way, which is a massive compliment, but doesn't get the work done any quicker, does it? It's certainly going to be a busy few weeks.' She glanced around her. 'I'll come back with you if you like, Seth can keep an eye on things here.'

★

Megan stood back to survey her work critically. It was so important that she got things off on the right footing. The competition had started a little earlier today as it would do with each successive round, but if she wasn't careful she could still end up very short on time.

A scuffle of leaves blew across the entrance to the forge and she glanced out at the sky. So far, the Indian summer they had been enjoying had shown no signs of coming to an end, but today there was a definite keenness to the wind and a few ominous dark clouds were rolling in from the west. It wasn't the only unwelcome thing heading her way; she frowned as she saw Julian bounding towards her, a mug in his hand.

'What do you want?' she asked bluntly.

'Well that's a lovely greeting, I must say. I only came to see how you were getting on, there's no need to be so rude. It's been ages since we had a chat.'

'Julian, I haven't got time for this, and neither have you, despite the impression you're trying to give. So unless you do actually want something, could we save the inane small talk until later.'

He sipped reflectively at his mug, pointedly staring over her shoulder at the forge behind her.

'You really are never going to give this up, are you? I'd have thought by now you'd have got bored of pretending to be a blacksmith just to prove to me how very capable you are. It doesn't impress me, you know.'

Despite the heat emanating from the forge behind her, a surge of fire flooded through her. She took a deep, steadying breath.

'I think that might just be the most arrogant thing you've ever said, Julian. You're priceless, you know that? Why on earth would I want to impress you, I don't even like you. And for your information, the only person I'm doing this for is me.' She looked up as Clara came into the forge, offering her a weak smile.

'So, I'll say it again, Julian. Was there anything you wanted? Because if not, I'm sure you have things you need to be doing.'

She stood back as Clara very deliberately stepped between them, and passed a mug of tea to Megan.

Julian gave Clara a lazy smile. 'No, nothing I wanted, but just let me know if you need a hand with your gate, won't you? They're awfully big, are you sure you'll manage?'

'You have an awfully big mouth, are you sure you can manage that?' Megan glared at him. 'Only it seems to be running away with you.'

He rolled his eyes dramatically at Clara. 'I was only trying to offer assistance.'

'No you weren't, Julian, you were trying to belittle me, same as you always do. There are loads of other competitors here today, and not one of them will ask me that question apart from you.'

'They'll be thinking it though,' he replied. 'Even if none of them are man enough to say it to your face, whereas I genuinely came to offer you help. For goodness' sake, Megan, you really do need help getting that chip off your shoulder.'

Megan's stance didn't alter as she stared him down. He was a good foot taller than her, and ironically, though his mouth may well have been of normal size, he had the most enormous teeth. Coupled with his slicked-back blond hair, she had a sudden mental image of him in a navy blazer propping up a bar somewhere, chatting up the nearest girl. He looked slightly out of place amid the rather grimy ramshackle atmosphere of the forge, and she had a sudden urge to giggle.

Clara flashed Julian a huge but insincere smile which dropped from her face a second later as she turned her back on him and rolled her eyes at Megan. She placed the mug down on a work bench at the back of the room, returning to stand at her side.

Megan flapped her hands in Julian's general direction as if trying to shoo a dumb animal out of her way. 'Go on,' she said, 'off you pop, there's a good boy.'

Julian opened his mouth to speak again and then closed it. 'We'll see,' he said finally, turning on his heels to leave.

Megan just shrugged. 'I'm quaking in my boots,' she called after his back, before turning to Clara. 'What a loathsome bucket of slime,' she said, grinning.

'Well that's one way of putting it,' Clara agreed. 'What an obnoxious man.' She paused to watch him walk back to his own area. 'What was all that about anyway?'

'Oh, just Julian throwing his weight around, which is something he likes to do whenever he gets the opportunity.'

'You obviously know one another?'

'Too well.' Megan nodded, the end of her ponytail swishing against her shoulders. 'We were both apprentices to my dad at the same time, for a little while anyway. I was in my first year, while Julian was in his last. He used to tell me then that I was only playing at blacksmithing, and that when I grew up I'd have to get a proper job for a girl.'

'What a charmer...'

'The sad thing is, his work is very good and I'd actually love to tell him, if he could only learn how to act like a decent human being. I don't mind losing a competition to someone whose work is better than mine, but not to some arrogant bully who thinks he's entitled just because his dad owns half the next-door village.'

'Oh, well that makes sense. He looks as if he comes from money,' replied Clara, and then she frowned. 'Anyway, who said you're going to lose?'

'Me, if I don't get a move on.' She pulled a face. 'Sorry, Clara. Thanks for the tea, but I really need to make a start. I'll catch up with you later, if that's okay?'

Clara smiled her assent. 'Good luck,' she urged. 'I'll save you some cake.'

Megan waved a goodbye and then turned back to the forge. She knew exactly why Julian had come in here. She would need all her concentration for today's round and she was damned if she'd give him the satisfaction of having that broken by his arrogant sniping. The trouble was, his words were hard to ignore and if she wasn't careful that's exactly what would happen. She took a deep breath and a mouthful of tea and flexed her fingers. Then she got to work.

★

By the time Clara got back to the refreshment tent, Trixie and Maddie were already busy serving drinks to the first of the spectators, but Trixie was anxious to get away.

'The Carters would like to take a picnic out with them this morning, and I've less than an hour to get it ready for them. I haven't given it nearly as much thought as I would have liked. At least they won't be back until late tonight which gives me a little more time, but I've still got Agatha's cake to decorate, don't forget.'

Maddie held out her hand for her apron. 'Go,' she said. 'And don't worry, they're not going to do the honours with the cake until lunch, so you've plenty of time.'

Trixie pulled out her phone to check the time. 'Glad you think so,' she said, but then she smiled, looking at the trestle table in front of them which was already covered with an array of cakes, muffins and gooey slices. 'And if you could try not to sell this lot, I'd be very grateful. Tell folks they're really not all that nice or something.' And with that she thrust her apron into Maddie's hand and took off across the marquee.

Maddie stared after her. 'Oh dear,' she said. 'Maybe we should wait and not sell the cakes until a bit later. What do you think?'

Clara eyed three burly men who were obviously heading purposefully in their direction. 'I'm not sure we're going to be given the choice,' she replied, smiling a greeting at the first to make eye contact with her. 'Can you serve them, Maddie? I'll go and get Seth.'

It took a while to root him out, but eventually she spotted him deep in the corner of the stable where the exhibition was. He was talking to four people, and Agatha, who was standing beside him, was chatting to at least another six. She hovered awkwardly, wondering whether she could interrupt, but Agatha was clearly delighted to be the centre of attention and, after a few moments more hopping on the spot, she turned to go.

She was halfway across the courtyard when she heard her name being called and turned back. Seth was standing at the edge of the stable, waving at her.

'I saw you loitering, is everything all right?' he asked as soon as she had reached him.

She gave a quick nod. 'Fine, except that there's even more people here than last week. I had no idea it got this busy, and at the rate we're already serving people with refreshments, we're going to run out of everything pretty soon. I was going to ask you to come and help Maddie so that I could go and give Trixie a hand, but...' She glanced at the crowd of people still inside the stable. 'It looks like you might be a bit busy too.'

'I know. Agatha's having the time of her life talking over old times with some of the villagers, but I don't think we realised quite how interested people were going to be in the history of this place.' He looked concerned. 'I'm kind of loath to leave her,' he added. 'She is *eighty* after all. I've got a horrible feeling if I don't keep an eye on her, she'll either keel over or will disappear and I'll find her giving guided tours of the Hall to all and sundry.' He looked past Clara out across the courtyard. 'Do you think you'll manage? I'd give Tom a call to come and lend a hand except that he's at a gig today.'

Clara grimaced. 'I guess we'll have to,' she said, but then grinned. 'It's great though, isn't it? All of this, I mean. I'm thrilled for Agatha. It really feels as if things are coming to life again, and we'll be okay, we always are.' She gave him a reassuring smile. 'And don't worry about the birthday cake; between us, Maddie and I will make sure that it arrives on time.'

'Thanks Clara, I'll come over, if I can... when I can.'

She rolled her sleeves up on the way back to the marquee. For the next half an hour or so, Clara thought they might be all right after all, as the numbers in the tent had thinned out a little on her return, but at the stroke of eleven they found themselves knee-deep in customers again. They served solidly, dishing out just as much cake as tea and coffee and, with every slice that went out, Clara's anxiety rose another notch. She handed back her latest customer their change before switching her attention to the next in line with a smile.

'Yes please?' she said automatically, looking up.

'I'll have whatever you recommend.'

She hadn't really been paying attention to the people she was serving, simply nodding and smiling or quickly passing the time of day with those villagers she knew, but Declan was probably the last person she'd expected to see, and her body reacted automatically. A horrendous rush of colour shot up her neck. She stared at him, the vivid memory of their last conversation rendering her speechless.

'Declan, hello!' Maddie, it would seem, had no such reticence. 'I had no idea you would be coming here today.'

'It would appear I'm unable to keep away.' He grinned. 'There must be something about this place.' He gestured at the table. 'All made by Trixie's fair hand, I hope?'

Clara managed a nod. He was smiling at her, waiting for a response. *For goodness' sake, you're a grown woman not a hormonal teenager. Pull yourself together.*

'They're all good, I'm not sure what you'd prefer?'

'And popular too, by the look of things…'

They were, and Clara, seeing the queue of people behind Declan, began mentally totting up how many cakes were left. She flashed Maddie an anxious look.

'I'll go with one of the muffins, I think. I seem to remember how good they were from the last time.'

Clara picked one up and handed it to him. And about time too – how long did it take to choose a cake, for heaven's sake!

He beamed a smile at her and then tossed his money into the tin that was on the table.

'Keep the change,' he said, moving around to their side of the table. 'It's brilliant this, isn't it? A quintessential British village event. I love them. A lady from the post office told me about it, otherwise I would have had no idea it was on.'

Clara ignored him and continued to serve the next customer.

'This is my first competition too,' replied Maddie. 'It's only held every three years, you see. From what I can gather it's usually just a local event but, as you can see, once Joy's Acre decides to get involved, things just… spiral.' She grinned. 'The competition spans several weeks, but we weren't anywhere near this busy last week; I think word has spread.' She handed Clara's customer a cup of tea. 'So how come you are here, anyway? Despite what you say, I'm sure there are any number of things which should be keeping you away.'

He held up a hand. 'Guilty as charged,' he said. 'I'm usually a bit of a workaholic, but I promised myself I'd take a few days off this last week. Besides, I never knew what a gorgeous place Shropshire was, and it seemed too good an opportunity to miss – getting a bit of local colour on the one hand and some well-earned R&R on the other.'

'So are you staying through until Tuesday then?' Maddie asked, looking pointedly at Clara.

He bit into his muffin with a nod. 'A small bed and breakfast just the other side of the village. I'm being spoiled rotten.'

'I bet you are,' replied Maddie, obviously finding it very amusing. 'Well, let us know if you get stuck for ideas of things to do, I'm sure we can help with suggestions, can't we, Clara?'

Clara was about to make some non-committal noise when she saw a sudden change in Maddie's expression. It was one she had come to know well over the preceding months, and was usually followed by one of her 'bright' ideas. She braced herself.

'I've just had the most brilliant thought,' she said, with a satisfied grin at Clara. She turned to Declan. 'Were you being truthful when you said you wanted to get immersed in local colour? Only, I'm just wondering *how* immersed,' she said.

Clara could feel herself begin to visibly shrink.

Declan looked a little surprised but parried the question. 'Up to the elbows?' he quipped. 'Why, what did you have in mind?'

Maddie was already undoing her pinafore. 'I need to get back to Joy's Acre,' she said, 'or we aren't going to have anything left to sell. It's too busy at the moment to leave Clara on her own, but you could step in, couldn't you? A man of your talents could help hold the fort, I'm sure.'

Clara's eyes widened, horrified. She tried mouthing *No* at Maddie but her effort was cut short by Declan's smiling face.

'Not something I've ever done before,' he admitted. 'But I'm prepared to give it a go. I'm sure Clara can show me the ropes.'

She could indeed, and where to hang himself... or Maddie for that matter. She knew exactly what her friend was up to, and they would be having words later. The trouble was that, for now, there was nothing she could do about it. She couldn't be rude to Declan, and one of them *did* need to get back to the farm. She took a deep breath. And smiled.

'It's a doddle,' she said, holding out her hand for Maddie's pink flowery apron. 'But rules are rules. You have to put this on first,' she said, biting back her grin. Seeing him wear it would almost make it worth it. Almost.

'No problem,' he said, his face expressionless. 'I can channel my feminine side.' He pulled the apron over his head and tied it around his back, the strings only just reaching. He smoothed it down. 'What do you think? Gorgeous... or do I look like I need locking up?'

Oh, gorgeous definitely...

'Fantastic,' declared Maddie. 'Right, well I'll catch you two later. Have fun!' And with that she disappeared before either of them could say anything else.

Despite herself, Clara was desperately trying to keep a straight face. 'Right well, there's the price list... there's the tea, coffee, milk, sugar and hot water in the urn, and...' she looked up, '... there's the customers.'

'If I get through this do I automatically become an honorary member of the Women's Institute?'

She smiled then. 'No, I'm afraid not. You just get to die a better person, knowing that you have served cake to the best of your ability. That, and you got the chance to rock a cerise pink pinny for the afternoon. Not many people get to say that about their lives.'

His eyes crinkled at hers. 'I consider myself honoured.' And then he turned to the next person in the queue. 'Sir, what would you like... and please don't say a date...'

Clara giggled as she reached for a slice of lemon drizzle cake, and that was all either of them said for the next ten minutes or so.

It was a companionable silence though and, although Clara was still very aware of the occasion when they'd last met, she was inclined, for now, to say nothing. It would only spoil things. What she hadn't bargained for, however, was for Declan to be thinking the same thing, only without the reticence. His comment caught her off guard.

'I think I owe you a huge apology,' he said, during a slight lull in proceedings. 'For the last time we met? It was only after you'd gone that I realised how it must have looked…'

'When I stormed out, you mean?'

He looked at her. 'It was much more gracious than that,' he said generously. 'And you were right, to challenge me like that… I should have explained myself, only I was momentarily lost for words…'

'I'm not surprised, I did rather jump down your throat.'

'I didn't actually mean that,' he said, giving an odd smile, hesitant perhaps. 'You won't even be aware of it, but you were standing in front of several buckets of huge hydrangea heads, and with the sun shining from the window behind you, well…' He tipped his head at her. 'I would have painted it if I could.'

'Oh…'

'So now I feel doubly bound to explain myself,' he continued, 'because I think you got entirely the wrong idea about the flowers and I'm very keen to put that right. My *mother* was delighted with them…'

'Oh,' said Clara again, turning pink. 'I had a feeling I'd behaved like a complete and utter idiot, and it would seem I was right.' She gave a sheepish smile. 'Not my finest hour.'

'On the contrary,' replied Declan. 'A very fine five minutes from where I was standing. And, under the circumstances, entirely understandable. I'm also quite pleased you're the kind of girl who thinks it highly inappropriate to be buying a loved one flowers one minute and flirting with someone else the next.'

Clara smiled, and then she realised what he had said. '*Were* you flirting?'

'God, yes,' came the quick reply.

'I see…' *What on earth did she say now?* She looked down at the table. 'Well, in that case we could grab that cup of coffee now…' She grinned. 'Although could you please take off that apron for a minute? I really can't take you seriously.'

Chapter 13

'For she's a jolly good fe-e-llow... and so say all of us!'

The gathered crowd broke into spontaneous applause, led by Seth, who had just taken possession of Agatha's huge birthday cake from Maddie and was doing his best to get it safely to the table without dropping it.

Maddie had only reappeared some ten minutes earlier and had just offloaded another batch of cakes with a warning that one or two of them were still warm. Now they were all gathered in the refreshment tent waiting to toast the birthday girl before the last couple of hours of the competition and the judging.

'Speech!' shouted someone from the crowd.

Clara didn't think she had ever seen Agatha lost for words. The last time she had seen her, the old lady had been enjoying herself immensely, chatting with the villagers, reminiscing about old times, clearly delighted to be the centre of attention. Now, she looked genuinely moved about the fuss being made over her, and was finding it hard to speak at all.

After a few moments she held up her hand, composed once more.

'Goodness,' she said. 'I am being spoilt today, and to think that a few weeks ago I was dreading my birthday.' She paused to look fondly at everyone around her. 'They're not much fun when you get to my age, you know... Too many people that you will never see again, too many things that will never happen again, and altogether too many endings and not nearly enough beginnings…' She waggled her fingers at Clara, beckoning her forward. She took a step closer.

'Which is why,' she continued, 'I'm very happy to see new life being breathed into old traditions by these three very special people here, and this competition is a wonderful example. I've had such fun this morning thinking about all the wonderful times that we've seen at the Hall and I couldn't have done that without them. So, while I'm very touched by all your birthday good wishes, I'd also like you to help me thank Seth and Maddie and Clara, and everyone else at Joy's Acre, not only for everything here today but also for showing me that not everything comes to an end.'

There was a spontaneous round of applause and, like Maddie and Seth, Clara blushed a little at having been thrown into the spotlight, especially because, beside her, Declan was clapping loudest of all. Despite the embarrassment, however, Clara was chuffed to bits at how happy Agatha was. It really hadn't taken much to achieve what they had today, but the difference it had made to her was immeasurable. It was a huge indication of how much things had changed over recent weeks.

It would have been impossible for Trixie to make a cake big enough for everyone to have a piece, but Maddie and Clara set about cutting it up into as many portions as possible, and if nothing else it would help eke out the rest of the cakes. Of course, they gave Agatha the biggest slice, and Seth, taking her plate, linked arms and steered her gently away from the crowds.

'Right, young lady,' he said. 'That's quite enough excitement for one day. A cup of tea and some peace and quiet will be just the thing to go with that cake, and then I think a bit of rest wouldn't go amiss. What do you think?'

'She reminds me of a woman I know from our village,' remarked Declan, watching her leave. 'Still going strong at ninety-two, and a tongue on her like you wouldn't believe.'

'Sounds like Agatha all right,' replied Maddie. 'But to give her her dues, I never realised before a few days ago how much she has done for the village in the past. Or if the reaction from the villagers to this lot has been anything to go by, quite how much she's held in high esteem.'

'It's such a brilliant example of what local communities should be all about. The Hall at its centre, big events that everyone can get involved with. I just love this stuff. And, it's exactly what I was looking for when I talked about local colour earlier. So, the fact that Joy's Acre is involved in the whole competition now is just perfect. People love stuff like this.'

Clara gave him a sideways glance. 'I assume we're talking TV audiences?' she asked, amused. 'Don't you ever stop? Not everything is a media opportunity, you know.'

'I get very excitable,' he replied, looking sheepish.

He had removed the flowery apron, underneath which were a pair of jeans and a white linen shirt. He looked anything but excitable. He looked cool, calm… what had Trixie called it? A thing? Yes, there was definitely a thing going on… She looked away.

'Now that it's calmed down a bit in here, I wondered if we might go and see the competitors? That was kind of the reason why I came along today…'

Clara was about to reply when Maddie beat her to it. 'Yes, go on. I can hold the fort here for a bit, and now that Agatha is going for a rest I can always call on Seth if I get stuck.'

Clara hesitated, looking at Declan and then back at Maddie. 'I ought to get back and give Trixie a hand,' she said. 'I did promise I would this morning, and she'll still have dinner to cook, don't forget.'

But Maddie waved an airy hand. 'Everything was perfectly under control when I left, Clara. We won't need any more cakes here now, so I'm sure she'll be fine. Go and give Declan the guided tour. You can introduce him to Megan.'

'Megan?'

'She's one of the competitors,' replied Maddie. 'And also one of our guests, so it's quite possible you might come across her at Joy's Acre. If you needed any more testimonies, well, she could be quite a good person to interview…' She trailed off with a cheeky grin, knowing full well that Declan had seen through her incredibly poorly disguised marketing ploy.

'I'll bear it in mind,' he said, smiling before turning to Clara. 'Shall we?' he asked.

'I think we better had,' muttered Clara, 'or I'll never hear the last of it… Megan is very good though, they all are. Come and see what you think.'

She filled Declan in on the background to the competition as they walked across the courtyard, shivering slightly at the sudden change in temperature now that they were away from the stuffy marquee.

'I think this is the first year Megan has entered. She's very young, but it's an amazing opportunity for whoever wins.'

'It sounds it,' agreed Declan. 'But the chance to gain a commission like that must really put the pressure on though.'

Clara nodded. 'You haven't seen Megan yet. I don't think there are many people who get the better of her, and as for the competitors here, she's certainly going to give them a run for their money. She's cool as a cucumber.'

★

'I haven't mislaid it, Liam. It's not here, simple as that. And don't you dare say I can't count.' Megan glared at him, still holding a metal rod, glowing white hot at its tip. She looked up as Clara walked into the forge accompanied by another man.

'Is everything okay?' asked Clara, stepping forward.

Megan gave a tight smile, placing the metal on top of the anvil and starting to beat it rhythmically.

'I'll let Liam explain, seeing as he has all the answers,' she said, still directing all her concentration on her work in progress. She really didn't have time for all this.

'One of Megan's pieces had gone missing,' said Liam. 'A two-ended scroll, one of the hardest components to make.'

'Except that it hasn't "gone missing", has it?' she hissed without looking up. 'Someone's pinched it, and I reckon we can all guess who…'

'Megan,' shushed Liam. 'You can't go around saying stuff like that… or if you're going to say it, at least keep your voice down.'

She lifted the beaten metal and looked at it with a critical eye before turning to Clara. 'I had everything laid out on the table at the back, with just my horseshoes left to make. I went in for a drink and something to eat and when I came back out one of the scrolls was missing. Liam seems to think that I've simply mislaid it, or that I've forgotten how to count but, as I'm really not that stupid, what other explanation can there be, Clara, except that it's been pinched? You were here earlier; you know how foul Julian was. I wouldn't put anything past that man.'

She saw Clara look across to the table in question, where she knew that everything looked in perfect order; all the pieces laid out in rows, straight, symmetrical, nothing lying where it shouldn't. Her expression wasn't hard to read.

Megan rolled her eyes. 'Right, well I can see you don't believe me either, so don't bother saying anything.'

'It's not that,' Clara protested. She opened her mouth to say something and then shut it again. 'Just… well, do you really think Julian would have done such a thing? It would have been pretty difficult with all these people around.'

'I know that,' replied Megan, getting crosser by the minute. 'But I wouldn't have said anything if I didn't think it was him, would I?' She paused for a moment, trying to work out what Clara was thinking. 'Oh, for goodness' sake…'

The man beside her took a sudden step forward, holding out his hand.

'Oh, gosh… sorry,' stuttered Clara. 'I haven't introduced you… Megan, this is Declan. He's been working on the filming project over at Joy's Acre that we mentioned and is just visiting today. I brought him over to see how you were getting on.'

Megan looked him up and down. She didn't wish to be rude and took his offered hand, but it didn't change anything. She wasn't about to be mollified by anybody, not when she was so certain what had happened. To her surprise though he simply nodded at her in understanding.

'So, where does this leave you, Megan?' he said. 'Is there anything you can do about it?'

She shook her head. 'No, not without proof, which of course I don't have… I'll just have to make a replacement. What other choice is there?'

He nodded again. 'That doesn't seem right though,' he said. 'Do you even have time to do that?'

'Barely…' She spoke through gritted teeth, taking the rod back to the forge and thrusting it into the bed of coals. 'And I haven't got time to have a debate about it now, so can we save this until later?'

If she didn't get a move on she really wouldn't have any hope of finishing. Whatever she felt on the matter would have to wait, for now at least.

'I'm sorry,' she added, trying to soften her last words a little. 'I really do have to…' She let her sentence trail off, biting her lip.

From the corner of her eye she saw Declan take Clara's arm, and she drew in a slow steadying breath.

'Perhaps we should all leave you to it,' he said.

'Liam?'

There was a pause as Liam looked from her to Clara to Declan and back again. She pasted on an encouraging smile. 'I'll see you later, okay?'

He nodded reluctantly. 'Only if you're sure…'

She widened her smile. 'I'll be fine… honestly.'

It took another second or two before he realised that there was no point in his staying, and he came forward to kiss her. 'You can do this, Megan, you know you can.'

She nodded and waved, trying to keep the look of relief from her face as the three of them left the forge. There was a second when it could have gone either way – when she could have given into the frustration and hurt that even Liam hadn't taken what she was saying seriously and sunk to the floor in floods of tears – but her anger got the upper hand. She thrust the iron rod even further into the heat of the forge and clenched her jaw together, thinking only of the task ahead of her. Bastard. She'd show him.

*

Declan's hand lay solicitously in the small of her back as he ushered Clara away from the forge, standing back a little to let Liam leave first.

She caught his eye as he did so, giving him a sympathetic smile as they followed him out to stand a little way away from the stable area.

'I'm sorry… Megan's rather stressed, as you could see.'

'Goodness, don't apologise,' replied Clara. 'This is a huge thing for Megan, I'm not surprised she's upset. What an awful thing to happen.'

'She does seem very certain that the piece has gone missing though,' said Declan. 'Isn't there something we can do? Someone we can speak to?'

Clara was surprised to see Liam hesitate just a fraction too long.

'Don't you think this *has* got anything to do with Julian then?' she asked. 'Only, he *was* being a nuisance early this morning when I brought teas around for everyone.'

'Was he?' asked Liam, eyes narrowing. 'Why, what did he say?'

'Not a lot. Megan very gracefully threw him out, but he did make stupid comments about her being a woman and not being able to lift the gate they're making for the final round.'

Liam's mouth settled into a thin line.

'She more than held her own though,' added Clara.

'That's what worries me,' he said. 'It's not that I don't believe Megan. Julian is an obnoxious little worm of the very worst kind, but the trouble is that he's learnt what buttons to push, and boy does he push them.'

'And every time he does, Megan jumps…' supplied Clara. 'Hmm, she mentioned they have history. But, even so. If one of her pieces *has* gone missing, that's serious. That's not just teasing, however biting it might be.'

'It is…' He stopped, looking worried. 'And this is the most horrendous thing to say, but as much as I dislike Julian myself, I'm not sure even he'd stoop this low.'

He looked really uncomfortable and Clara felt for him, he was in such a difficult position.

'I mean, I'd do anything to support Megan, and I hope she knows that… But at the moment she's so uptight about Julian, what she can't seem to see is that if we make a complaint, or an accusation of any kind, without proof… well, Megan might as well write herself out of the competition today. At best she could end up looking very stupid, but worst case scenario, she could find herself accused of trying to subvert the competition.'

Declan nodded. 'And I would imagine that with competitions like these there's a great deal of honour involved, an unwritten code of conduct, if you like. They don't normally like people to rock the boat.'

'But that's so unfair!' protested Clara. 'I understand what you're saying, Liam. I don't know Megan anything like as well as you do, but it's obvious she's very conscious of her size and her gender when it comes to the art of blacksmithing. Perhaps that could cause her to overreact, or lead her to jump to conclusions, but what if she's right? If someone *is* cheating, it shouldn't be ignored.'

Liam nodded. 'I know,' he said, looking dejected. 'And as far as doing anything about it, I'm damned if I do, and damned if I don't.' He looked back towards the forge. 'But the most important thing right now is that Megan completes this round of the competition, and moves forward to the next. So, I suggest we stay out of her way for now. Perversely, being in a bad mood might help her get finished on time.'

Clara gave him a sympathetic smile. 'And you can pick up the pieces later?'

'Something like that…'

She looked back at Declan. 'We'll go and have a wander, shall we?' she said. 'And leave you to it. If you get the chance, wish Megan luck, we'll all be rooting for her.'

'I will.'

They left Liam hovering and made their way back towards the other forges. The air was still loud with the ringing chime of metal being struck.

'Which one is Julian?' asked Declan, trying to see past the other people watching the competition.

Clara craned her head. 'Second from the end,' she said. 'You can't miss him. He looks like a dentist.'

Declan raised an eyebrow. 'Nothing like being innocent before being proved guilty, is there?'

'What? I'm just saying… he does look like a dentist. Not that there's anything wrong with dentists per se, it's just that…' She trailed off.

'I know.' He gave her a warm smile. 'You have that wonderfully protective look on your face. I get exactly what you mean.'

Clara laid her hands on her cheeks, feeling them colour again.

'I'll go and have a nose about, shall I? I've never met the man, so I can pretend to be an idiot spectator and see if he's in the mood to talk.' He grinned. 'Actually, I won't have to pretend… but you never know, he might let something drop.'

'Declan, you don't have to do that.' She was touched that he would even think of doing such a thing.

'No, I know I don't, but I'm trying to impress someone, and I figured this might earn me a few brownie points.'

'And wearing a flowery apron all afternoon didn't?' she parried, slightly embarrassed by her bold response.

'Oh, thank heaven,' he said. 'I thought for a minute it had all been for nothing.'

His look was teasing, his green eyes dancing in a sudden beam of sunshine that slanted across the courtyard, and suddenly Clara had no idea what to say. She had a feeling this conversation was leading somewhere, but she wasn't at all sure how to get there, or even if she wanted to go… yet.

She cleared her throat. 'I'd better pop back to see how Maddie is getting on. Shall I meet you back in the marquee?'

★

'What do you think?' asked Clara a little while later.

They were standing in the judging tent having done the rounds of all the entries. The results were due to be announced in a few minutes.

Declan pulled a face. 'I'm not an expert, but the standard looked high to me. There was only one entrant who I could see was lacking something, and that was pretty obvious because one of the scrolls wasn't finished.'

'But what did you think about Megan's work?'

Neither she, nor Liam, were anywhere to be seen, but Clara hoped that she wasn't going to miss the announcement.

'I thought she'd nailed it, if that's not an appalling choice of words. Her work looked very uniform, and I really couldn't spot any difference from one piece to the next, especially the twists, and they must be incredibly difficult. The only thing I noticed was that two of her horseshoes weren't finished as well as the other four, but I'm guessing that's where she ran out of time. The most important thing was that the scrolls all looked identical. I think she deliberately left the horseshoes until last because they're the easiest element to make. But I have no idea how they're scored.'

Declan grimaced. 'I expect we're about to find out.'

Seth had wandered over to meet them. He nodded a greeting. 'It's okay, Megan is outside with Liam and Maddie. Megan is convinced she's going home of course, but Maddie has plied her with several pieces of cake, on the basis that if nothing else helps, that might.'

'It can't make things any worse…' agreed Clara.

'I gather you had a chat with Julian, Declan. I don't suppose he gave anything away, did he?'

Declan sighed. 'Unfortunately, he was very open, quite personable in fact. Granted, he looks like a prize prat, but I don't think he's a blacksmith for any reason other than that he enjoys his work. That much was obvious. And I have to say, his work looked very good.'

Clara shifted her weight from one foot to the other. 'Even Megan would agree with you there. She said to me this morning that she'd really like to respect his work, but the only thing that prevented her from doing so was his attitude. I don't think there's any doubt he's good at what he does.' She lowered her voice. 'The question is whether he's a cheat.'

'Or someone else is,' added Seth.

They stood in silence looking at one another, as the hum of conversation around the room grew louder in response to the level of anticipation. Clara checked her watch and then all at once the room fell silent as the judges made their way back into the marquee. As she looked up she spotted Maddie slipping into the back of the tent. She hurried over, a worried look on her face.

'Megan won't come in,' she said. 'Liam's trying to talk her into it, but she's adamant. Says she won't give Julian the satisfaction of seeing her go out.'

Clara nodded, grim determination on her face.

She leaned in towards Seth. 'I'm going to go and find her. Whatever happens, she should be here for this.'

Seth nodded, looking equally concerned.

Clara exited the tent, looking skyward as the first fat drops of rain began to fall, blown across the grass by a sudden gust of wind. She hurried across the courtyard towards the forges – not that she had any real idea where Megan might be, but that seemed to be the safest bet. Raised voices could be heard before she was even halfway across.

'You're twisting my words, Megan, I said no such thing!'

'You didn't need to. Go on, search the bloody place if you think you're going to find it. A huge lump of metal doesn't just fall off the bench without anyone noticing, let alone roll into a darkened corner never to be seen again.'

She couldn't catch what came next.

'Well, it's obvious you don't believe me.'

'And you don't believe me either. God, Megan, you're impossible when you're in this kind of mood.' There was a groan of frustration. 'Look, at least come across to the tent for the judging.'

Clara took a few steps forward into the silence, close enough so that Megan, who was facing outward, could see her. Her hands were on her hips.

'They're just about to start,' she said tentatively. 'I thought I should come and tell you.'

'Thanks, Clara.' The hands moved from Megan's hips as she folded her arms in front of her. 'Not that there's much point really.'

'Then Julian has as good as won.'

Liam's voice was soft but there was no mistaking the force of his words.

'He's right, Megan,' Clara said. 'We have no proof that Julian took your missing scroll, but if he did, that's bad enough without letting him have power over you as well. If you allow him to make you feel like a loser, then you will have lost… whatever happens.'

'But—'

'Go back to the marquee with your head held high, because when you go through to the next round, despite what happened today, it will be the biggest kick in the teeth for him. He'll be able to see that you can stand up to him, no matter what, and that you won't be bettered by him.'

Megan was at least listening now, but she was still not convinced. 'And if I go out?'

'Then he will still see someone proud and capable of their place in the competition, but someone who has lost only because of *his* actions, not through any lack of skill on your part. And that makes you better than him.'

Liam held out his arm for Megan to take. 'Shall we?' he said. And with a gentle smile Megan began to remove her apron.

The judging had already started by the time they returned.

'… And the standard set seemed almost impossible to be bettered, but today we have seen some truly excellent examples of workmanship. Before we go on to give the results of today's judging, I'd just like to award one or two commendations to individuals whose efforts today are of special note. The first of these goes to… Jason Moorland, whose examples of basket twisting have set an incredibly high standard.'

There was a spontaneous round of applause.

'And the second point of note goes to Megan Forrester, whose penny scrolls have also shown superlative skill.'

Megan cupped her hand around her mouth and leaned close to Clara. 'That's it, I'm going home. They always do that before you go out; big you up, so you don't feel so bad.'

Liam snaked his arm around her waist, pulling her closer to him with a tug. 'Shhh,' he said, shaking his head gently. 'What are you like?'

The judge waited for the applause to die down.

Clara smiled reassuringly at Megan and then turned back to face front, where she could also keep an eye on Julian, who was standing to her left. Twice he had looked over, and twice she had held his look until he glanced away. She set her mouth in a hard line.

'And so, we come inevitably to the final marks for today's competition. As before these marks have been awarded under four different categories, slightly different than before, given that today the competitors had to copy designs already given to them. Marks therefore have been awarded for technical skill, quality of finish, and how closely they were able to match all of their pieces to the original design. We've also awarded points for the number of items completed, or rather the use and management of time.'

He paused to look around the room. 'I make the distinction because, unusually, *all* of our entrants managed to finish. This has not been the case in other years, and would normally make our task in judging this round considerably easier; not so today... so thanks, guys...'

He stopped again to allow the titter of polite amusement to ripple around the room. 'The individual mark sheets for each competitor will be found next to their work, should anyone wish to scrutinise these. So without further ado, the nine entrants through to the next round are...'

The judge began to read out the list, his voice ringing loud in the near silent room. Clara held her breath, and began to count, her eyes on Julian the whole time. The names meant nothing to her, bar one, and when she heard it, she saw a moment of thunder cross Julian's face that disappeared as quickly as it had come, but Clara had seen it. More importantly, Julian knew that she had.

Beside her, Megan collapsed into Liam's arms, her eyes closed but with the biggest grin on her face. Seth had two fingers in his mouth and his piercing whistle joined the other calls and whoops from around the room amid the general applause. This was what Megan needed to hear; the real appreciation and support for her work, that was based on nothing but her skill as an artist.

There was a sudden pause as the judge stopped speaking, and the voice inside Clara's head that was still counting stopped with it. Eight names had been read out, only eight.

'So these competitors are all safely through to the next round, but as I mentioned before, the judging for this round has proved to be particularly difficult and has resulted in an unprecedented tie between two of our blacksmiths. These are Julian Bamford and Luke Greenwood—'

A swoop of noise erupted around the room.

The judge held up his hand. 'However...' He struggled to make himself heard. 'However... the rules of the competition are quite clear, in that aggregate scoring from all rounds must be used to determine elimination from the competition, in which case...' He held up his hand again. 'Ladies and gentlemen, please... in which case the aggregate scores mean that the last person through to the next round is... Julian Bamford.'

Megan looked up, straight ahead and grinned, giving a small nod. Then she took Liam's hand and walked from the tent without looking back.

Chapter 14

'I could do with a serious makeover today,' said Clara, pulling at the skin around her eyes. 'I don't think I slept a wink last night.'

'Oh?' Trixie looked up from where she was washing dishes at the sink. 'Too busy thinking about Declan?'

Clara stuck out her tongue. 'No,' she retorted. 'Sheer terror.' She moved across to Trixie, nudging her with her hip. 'Come on, let me finish these. You go and jump in the shower.'

Trixie was already peeling off the yellow washing-up gloves. 'I will, if you don't mind. Can't let my audience down, can I?' She grinned as she got to the door, before pulling her mouth into a sexy pout. 'Got to make myself look beautiful…'

'Aren't you nervous at all?' asked Clara.

'What of? Impending fame and fortune? No way… bring it on!' she replied, flouncing out of the door.

Clara laughed, picking up the gloves, and feeling rather relieved. Trixie seemed to be back to her normal sunny self. Perhaps it was just that she had managed to get some rest yesterday and recover from the frenetic activity of Saturday. It had been a busy day for them all, but Clara hadn't realised quite how much Trixie had had to contend with during the day until they had all returned home from the black-smithing competition. They were all tired but at least in good spirits;

Trixie's mood, on the other hand, could only have been described as approaching boiling point.

And as for Clara's mood, well that was something she had been trying to decide on ever since Saturday. Despite her immediate dismissal of Trixie's comment about Declan just now, in truth he had never been far from her thoughts. She looked up as she heard a car door slam from across the yard, and her stomach gave a little kick. He was early; she might have known.

I'll see you at ten, he had said, and here it was only just gone nine. What on earth was she going to do with him for a whole hour? She quickly peeled off the gloves again and shot down the hallway into the office, where Maddie was already at work, trying to type while eating a piece of toast at the same time.

'Declan's here already,' she blurted out, 'but I can't look after him, I have stuff to get ready.'

Maddie merely smiled at the panic on Clara's face. 'Shoo,' she said. 'Out the back door, quick.' She got to her feet, picking up her plate. 'I'll see if he wants breakfast.' She gave Clara a swift wink as she passed her, and tapped the side of her nose. 'Mum's the word,' she said.

Clara stared after her, about to retaliate when she realised that if she really didn't want to be seen then she wouldn't have long to make herself scarce. She left the room as quickly as she had entered it, and a few moments later she was in the garden, where she breathed a sigh of relief.

There were things she needed to do before the filming started, there were always things to do, but… She walked the path that took her into the central space, pulling her fleece a little more tightly around her against the cool of the morning. She made for the bench, and sat down with a sigh before taking a long calming breath. Someone had started a bonfire somewhere, one of her favourite smells of the autumn, and she breathed in its smoky scent, feeling happy to be in her favourite space in the whole world. In fact, the garden was Clara's whole world, and she rarely wished to be anywhere else. She closed her eyes and let her thoughts drift outward, clearing a space in her mind until there was just her and nothing else except the deep connection she felt with the living things around her.

A few moments later she became aware that a shadow had fallen over her, and she swiftly opened her eyes, taking a second to adjust to the change in light. A familiar face looked down on her.

'If you're trying to hide you need to find a better place…'

'Morning, Tom.' She smiled. 'I'm not hiding, I'm just… having a few minutes to myself.'

'Oh, right… only Maddie said you were hiding.' He plonked himself down on the bench beside her. 'But it's okay, you'll be quite safe for a few minutes. Trixie has Declan holed up in the kitchen and is batting her eyelashes at him.'

'Good.' She stared out across the garden.

'Bit keen, is he?' She and Tom had been friends for a long time.

She sighed. 'No, it's not that, it's just… He's been lovely actually, good company.' She thought for a moment how best to explain. 'But I'm not very good with change. It's taken me a long time to get to where I am now, and I don't want to lose what I have.' She looked at his relaxed pose beside her. 'That probably sounds stupid.'

Tom looked at her, his blue eyes taking in every detail, checking what he knew to be her default settings and measuring what he now saw against it.

'Not coming from you, it doesn't.' He nudged her gently with his shoulder. 'Although… now of course I have seen the light as far as my own personal relationships go, I'm fully qualified to dispense irritatingly smug advice and say that you shouldn't miss out on the opportunity of something wonderful because you're worried that things might change. It's quite possible that they could change into something even better.'

'You appear to now also be highly qualified in stating the obvious as well,' muttered Clara, although she was smiling. 'But it's been a while since I thought about anybody in a… romantic way… I suppose I'm feeling a bit unsure of myself, that's all. And, of course, Declan isn't just some bloke, is he? He just happens to be the TV producer of a show he's keen to get off the ground, and that, frankly, is still terrifying.'

'One thing at a time, Clara, one thing at a time.' Tom rubbed his hands together briskly, as a sudden gust of wind sent leaves chasing down the path. 'What is it you've always said? *You can't rush time in a garden…* Sounds like good advice to me.'

Clara glanced up. 'It looks like we might be in for a spot of rain anyway, and that might slow things right down.'

'In more than one way unfortunately.' He pulled his phone from his pocket, and tapped at it a couple of times, before handing it across to her. 'Check out the weather forecast. By the end of the week we could be in trouble.'

The message on the screen was clear: several days of heavy rain.

'Is that going to cause you problems?'

Tom took back the phone and tapped it against his chin. 'Hard to tell. Thatching in light rain isn't usually too much of a problem, just quite unpleasant. Thatching in a downpour, however – not advisable. And definitely not in the case of the cottage I'm working on now. I think I mentioned we had to remove far more of the old thatch with this one than on the other cottages. Not only does that mean that a greater depth of new thatch needs to be laid, but also that the roof itself hasn't got a huge amount of protection during the process. And water landing on it will just pour through into the rooms below. The roof will have to be covered with tarpaulin until the rain passes – no question.'

'Which could put you massively behind schedule?'

'Potentially, yes. There are other jobs I can be getting on with – preparatory work, so that once we hit a dry spell again I can crack on apace, but we're heading into the wrong end of the year, weather-wise.' He got to his feet. 'Still, I'm not going to panic just yet... and you mustn't either.' He gave her a stern look. 'Promise?'

She smiled back. 'Promise,' she replied, wondering whether it was too late to cross her fingers. The sudden sound of laughter coming from around the corner of the house told her that it was.

'I think that's your cue,' said Tom, with a warm smile. 'Go on. It'll be fine. Go and hear what the big man has to say.' He held out his hand to pull her up from the bench, and she accepted it gladly. It didn't do to stop for too long; she was inordinately tired.

★

Over the course of Saturday, in between serving tea and cake, she and Declan had talked about a whole host of subjects. From music – they had similar tastes – to football – he loved it, she hated it. Then there were books – they were both avid readers, although his tastes lay toward the more literary end of the market. Food, of course – he couldn't abide fish and she wasn't great with anything that had a shell. But the one thing they had not spoken about at all was the proposal for the TV series and, in her ignorance, she had assumed that this was the case for them all.

It very soon became obvious, however, that Seth had been in receipt of Declan's proposal before the weekend, and while everyone else had collapsed in a heap come Saturday night, worn out by the day's events,

Seth had met with Declan at a local hostelry and thrashed out the terms of a deal which they were both happy with. All that now remained was for Clara and Trixie to give their consent.

They were sitting at the more spacious table in the dining room this time, with Declan's laptop set up at one end so that everyone could see it with relative ease. And they were all there, Tom as well, dragged back down from the roof.

'Of course, these are just preliminary shots,' said Declan. 'There's not much in terms of editing gone on, but even so you'll be able to see very clearly, at least I hope you will, what has got us all so excited.'

He clicked a couple of buttons and a picture appeared in the centre of the screen, followed by a sudden booming noise and then a flickering of images before the picture settled down and the clip started playing.

Clara let out a nervous giggle as her head and shoulders filled the screen. She was looking away from the camera, self-conscious and flustered, obviously listening to some directions from Declan, but then she turned back towards the camera and smiled. It was a perfectly framed shot, but Clara was transfixed. The face staring back at her was unrecognisable: honey blonde hair piled on her head, deep blue eyes and a wide curving mouth. It couldn't possibly be her.

She was aware that several heads in the room had swivelled to look at her, and Tom let out a low whistle. It was difficult to know what to think. She had never seen herself like that before; it wasn't at all like looking in a mirror.

'It doesn't even look like me,' she said, biting her lip. 'Where did all those freckles come from?'

'Freckles?' asked Trixie. 'What freckles?'

Clara leaned forward, peering at the screen. 'On my nose, there are *hundreds* of them.'

Trixie snorted. 'About three,' she said. 'And all they do is make your peaches and cream complexion look even more adorable.'

'Yeah, right…'

'Actually, Clara,' said Tom. 'She is right. You look beautiful.'

She frowned, turning back to continue watching as her on-screen self began to describe what she was doing with the strawberry runners. Clara saw very clearly the moment when she lost herself, when she forgot about the camera and allowed her love of her garden and her passion to come spilling out. She felt her tension began to ease a little. At least she sounded as if she knew what she was talking about. She had been afraid that she'd sounded like a complete idiot.

Her section lasted for about ten minutes, during which time there was absolute silence in the room. This changed the minute the camera switched to Trixie when there was a collective gasp. The contrast couldn't have been any more apparent. While Clara had appeared calm and serene, with an assured, almost hypnotic way of speaking, Trixie was a fiery ball of enthusiastic energy. With her bright pink hair glowing in the sun and ruby red lips chattering away, she fizzed her way through the recipe she was describing; funny, vibrant and charming all at the same time.

The video cut off abruptly, leaving behind an astounded silence that stretched out as everyone struggled for what to say. Unsurprisingly, it was Trixie who spoke first.

'They even managed to make my bum look normal size, I can't believe it.'

Tom rolled his eyes, laughing. 'Oh, Trixie, trust you!'

'What?' she said. 'It's a valid comment, I was terrified it was going to look huge.'

Declan leaned forward, his eyes sparkling. 'Well, as you can see it didn't, and I hope you agree that you both looked wonderful, in different ways, but the contrast is what makes it work so well.' He looked across at Seth and gave a slight nod. 'I sincerely hope you ladies are going to say yes to me.'

The room fell silent again as Clara and Trixie looked at one another. They were chalk and cheese, but never had their obvious differences worked so well together – what they had just seen had been proof enough. Trixie's eyes were shining, it was obvious how she felt, and for the first time since this whole idea had first been mooted, Clara almost began to believe that it might actually work. She hadn't looked nearly as bad on screen as she thought she would, and Trixie had been brilliant. She was made for something like this and, despite Clara's misgivings, there was no way that she could stand in her way. She didn't think she could live with herself if she did. She drew in a deep breath.

'It's a yes from me,' she whispered.

'Bloody hell!' shrieked Trixie. 'It's a yes from me too!'

Declan extended his hand to both of them. 'I am so very, very glad you said that.' He grinned. 'Because I've already booked the crew for tomorrow!'

'Someone put the kettle on!' yelled Seth.

The room erupted with a flurry of movement as everyone got up simultaneously, laughing and hugging. Clara felt Declan's arms go around her before she even knew what was happening. His voice was soft in her ear.

'And are you going to say yes to me too?'

Clara stared at him, confused.

'Dinner? Tonight?'

She burst out laughing. 'Yes, why not?'

Chapter 15

It was a casual dinner date. At least, that's what Declan had said. Nothing heavy, just a chance to get to know one another a bit better. In a relaxed setting. With a bite of something to eat. Except that for Clara it might as well have been a meal out in the poshest restaurant imaginable.

Declan had left Joy's Acre soon after their meeting and so for much of the day it had been business as usual. Autumn was just as busy a time for her in the garden as the summer and there were plenty of jobs that needed doing: crops to harvest; others to be planted to allow them time to settle in before winter; large areas to be cleared and put to bed. Clara had also helped Trixie to prepare lunch and dinner for everyone as usual and so the day had passed quickly, albeit with a slightly more exuberant atmosphere than usual. However, now it was early evening and she was back at home, tying herself in knots trying to get ready.

She couldn't remember the last time she had been on a date, something which very much belonged to her old life; the one she'd had before she became ill. It was strange the way her life had become categorised into two halves but, in a way, she supposed it was inevitable. She'd been young, free and single before her illness, with a happy go lucky attitude to life, but nothing made you re-evaluate the things you cared about more than the threat of having them taken away from you. Things had got pretty intense between her and Seth during her recovery, but it quickly became clear they were just good friends, and so any thoughts of love had been pushed to the back of her mind and she had resolved to keep them there until she was fully recovered. Despite her misgivings about things changing so fast at Joy's Acre, she couldn't deny that Declan had caught her eye and perhaps this in itself was enough of a sign that the time had come to allow this area of her life to blossom once more. But she'd be lying if she said it didn't terrify her.

Clara knew it wouldn't do to turn herself into a painted and primped version of herself – Declan would see through that in a moment – but she did want to look as if she had at least made an effort. Her wardrobe choices were fairly limited but, by the time she had laid out nearly every single item of clothing she possessed, it certainly didn't look that way. She'd thought scenes like this only happened in films, but now, faced with the reality of finding something to wear, she found herself laughing at the irony.

In the end, she settled for a white linen smock patterned with small yellow flowers and green leaves. It was her all over, but slightly smarter than what she would usually wear. Paired with a pair of her favourite jeans, clean this time rather than covered in mud, she felt comfortable. She kept her make-up light, but couldn't help grinning to herself as she softly curled her hair, entirely for Declan's benefit.

An hour later, and they were on their way to the pub in Declan's car; dark blue, sleek and very fast. In just half an hour they were seated in a quiet corner of the bar each sipping from a glass of local cider.

'I was recommended this place by my landlady at the B&B,' said Declan. 'Apparently it's not as popular as some places locally because the manager has all the charm of a plank of wood – her words, not mine – but his chef is the dog's bollocks.'

Clara snorted into her drink, laughing. 'She didn't really say that, did she?'

'No word of a lie. She certainly has a wonderful turn of phrase, but her breakfasts are truly worth getting out of bed for, so I can make allowances. I might have the vegetarian option this evening though, just in case there is any chance of canine wotsits being served.'

'Oh no…' Clara put her hand over her mouth at the thought. She picked up the menu from the table. 'If there's meatballs on here, I'm going home…'

Declan picked up his own menu, his eyes lit with amusement. They really were very attractive, Clara thought to herself.

He cleared his throat. 'Can I just say, Clara, how lovely it is to be here with you…' He winced as the last words were delivered. 'For the love of God…' He shook his head. 'I'm sorry, Clara, I don't usually do this and I—'

She laid a hand on his sleeve. 'Me neither.' She smiled. 'And it's nice to be here…'

He let out a breath, lowering the menu. 'Thank you. That was only going to get worse…' He ran a hand through his hair. 'However appallingly it was delivered, the sentiment was honest at least.'

Clara smiled. 'And there's me thinking you had the gift of the blarney.' She searched his face for a moment. 'Or at least you usually do, when you're at work, I mean. You didn't strike me as the type that would get tongue-tied in these sorts of situations.' And she broadened her smile. 'It's rather endearing, actually.'

'Is it?' He held her look. 'Thank God.'

'I'm intrigued though,' she continued. 'There's the whole…' She blushed suddenly as she wondered how best to put it. 'Trixie says you have a "thing" going on, and well, I… probably agree with her.' She groaned. 'And you have this amazing job that must attract women like bees to a honey pot, then there's the way you dress, like your clothes are a second skin, there's the car and yet…' She ground to a halt. 'You're just as rubbish at this as I am. How come?'

He actually blushed. 'Usual story, I suppose,' he replied. 'All work and no play… My job takes me all over the country. I live out of a suitcase most weeks, I get home once in a blue moon and I spend my days being endlessly polite and patient and charming… not all the time…' He smirked. 'I can be mean and moody too. Seriously though, I'm nearly forty, and it's all a bit jading… Most of the people I meet are shallow wannabes, and some days I'd give my right arm for a bit of intelligent conversation. I don't really have time for relationships.' He stopped suddenly. 'No, that's not strictly true. I haven't made time for relationships, because I haven't wanted to.'

The words 'until now' hung unspoken in the air between them, Clara swallowed.

'So, where's home when you're not living out of a suitcase?' she asked.

'Originally? A small village about twenty miles from Dublin in County Kildare. Racehorse country. Just me, my ma and da, three brothers and a sister.' He smiled at the amusement on her face as he suddenly launched into a thick Irish brogue. 'I know. There's only one of my brothers living at home now, but when we all get home together, jeez… that's some craic, I tell you.'

'And how about now?'

'A tiny two-bedroom, overpriced terrace in Camden. Although not for long, hopefully.'

Clara gave a low whistle. 'Are you looking to move then?'

'In celebration of my advancing years,' he said, nodding. 'Yeah, time to quit London and put down some roots, I reckon.'

She was about to ask him where when he picked up his menu again. 'Anyway, we didn't come here to talk about me,' he said.

'I did,' she bounced back.

He grinned. 'Why don't we order, and then I can stop boring you rigid and you can tell me all about you.'

Clara already knew what she wanted to order. 'I'll have the risotto please,' she said straight away, always a sucker for the gooey, creamy rice dish.

Declan got to his feet. 'Right, well, I'll go and see just how much of a plank the manager really is. Can I get you another drink as well?'

She shook her head. Drinking was a rarity for her, any more than one drink – particularly of the local cider – and she would be under the table.

'No thanks, but if we could maybe have a jug of water with the food that would be great.' *Gently does it, Clara.*

It was obvious why he had stopped the conversation, and in a way, Clara was grateful. Putting down roots was pretty much the same thing as settling down, and probably not something it was wise to talk about on a first date. Although, if she were honest with herself, this had stopped feeling like a first date after about the first five minutes. Declan was one of the easiest people to talk to she had ever met, and despite his aura of success and sophistication, it was pleasing to find that underneath it all he had just the same vulnerabilities as she had. A sudden image of him wearing that ridiculous apron on the Saturday before popped into her head, and she smiled at the memory.

He returned to their table a couple of minutes later. On a Monday night in October the pub wasn't particularly busy so with any luck the food wouldn't take too long either; she was starving.

'Are all your brothers and sister in the film-making industry as well, or is it just you?' she asked as soon as he was seated.

'Hardly. My dad's a racehorse trainer, and two of my brothers followed in the family business, breeding and training horses, but the other is a sheep farmer in Wicklow. My sister lives in Portugal with her husband where they run a small hotel.'

'And you weren't tempted by either horses or sheep then?'

'No.' He laughed. 'I'm allergic to horses for one thing. And terrified of them too, which of course the family find hysterically funny.'

He waggled a finger at her. 'But, come on, enough about me. Tell me about your family. You're obviously not a local lass either.'

She smiled. 'Well, I come from the smallest family imaginable,' she said. 'I have a brother, who's married with a three-year-old daughter. My mum is an only child and my dad has a sister who is married with no children either. So, even when we all get together, we hardly fill a room.'

'Imagine how quiet that must be,' replied Declan. 'It's still a shock when I go home and we're all en masse; it takes a few days to acclimatise to the sheer volume that everyone has to talk at to make themselves heard.' He paused for a moment. 'I wouldn't have it any other way though. My family's big, rowdy, raucous and chaotic, but, 'tis grand, as they say.'

He took another mouthful of his drink. 'And have you always been a gardener?' he asked. 'It looks as if it's something you've done your whole life; born under a mulberry bush and all that.'

'Well I don't know about that, but no, for a very long time I was a medical secretary. Extremely boring and not very well paid. But at least the Latin terminology came in handy when I began to develop green fingers. It started off as a hobby and then… well, it's a long story, but you could say I got bitten by the bug.'

'And you've been at Joy's Acre for quite a while now?'

Clara thought for a moment. 'Coming up four years. Seth didn't seem to mind that I didn't know what I was really doing when I first arrived, but...'

She trailed off, wondering how much to say. None of it was a secret as such, but Clara was a private person by nature and the problems of her past weren't something she was used to sharing. Declan was still smiling at her, one forearm resting casually on the table as he leaned slightly towards her. His face was open, interested. She shifted slightly in her chair.

'Well, we were helping each other out, I guess. I don't suppose Seth will mind my telling you, but he first came to Joy's Acre with his wife. She was Agatha's granddaughter but she sadly died not all that long after they were married, and Seth's attempts to continue with the farm's renovation fell by the wayside rather. I'd got myself into a bit of a pickle as well and so I agreed to come and help.'

'So you really have played a major part in transforming Joy's Acre.'

'Well I...' She smiled at Declan's nodding head. 'Yes, I suppose I have. The gardens at least. Seth gave me free rein to do whatever I wanted and it gave me something to get my teeth into just at the time I needed it most. Maybe that's why I love it so much.'

'It shows.' His finger was tracing the edge of a beer mat, and he grinned at her rolling of her eyes. 'What? It does. You look... like you're a part of the garden itself. When you're there, it's like you lose yourself... in a good way... like you're at one with everything.' He pulled a face. 'How's that for a cheesy line?'

She laughed. 'It's not an easy thing to describe, is it? But bizarrely, your description, corny though it might be, was pretty much spot on. That is how it feels to me too.'

'It's what the camera loves about you. It comes across when you're speaking.'

'Oh…' She blushed, looking down at the table. She hadn't imagined that they would talk about the filming.

Almost immediately he reached his hand out across the table. 'I'm sorry, Clara, I promised myself I wasn't going to talk shop; force of habit, I'm afraid.'

'Good, because I shall ignore you if you do.' She held his look. It wasn't just that she was uncomfortable talking about this aspect of herself, but also because Declan was the last person with whom she wanted to discuss how she was really feeling about the show.

He was studying her face and she wished she hadn't spoken her last sentence with quite as much emphasis as she had. She tried to smile and look relaxed, and all of a sudden Declan laughed.

'Remind me never to get in your bad books,' he said. 'That was quite some stare.' He cocked his head to one side. 'But I can see how much Joy's Acre means to you, Clara and, before I change the subject, can I just say that I do understand how the prospect of the filming must be making you feel. It's already clear to me that you and Trixie are very different from one another. For me, that's what makes your partnership special, and I would guess the reason why you're such good friends. But, because I understand that, I can guess your warning alarm bells are beginning to chime…' He held up a hand as she began to protest. 'So, I just want to say that I promise I will do my utmost to make sure that nothing changes as a result of the filming. How's that?'

Clara smiled gently, and dipped her head slightly, but she said nothing.

Declan laughed again. 'Okay, okay, I'll stop now.' He took another sip of his drink. 'So, let me see, changing the subject… what was your favourite book as a child? Smooth, or crunchy peanut butter? And where do you stand on the whole pronunciation of "scone" versus "scon" debate…?'

Chapter 16

'You've got to be kidding me.'

Clara looked up at Trixie's words. From her vantage point in the kitchen Trixie had a clear line of sight across the yard in front of the house to where the farm's vehicles were parked. A dark green van had just pulled off the lane, followed by another. It was eight in the morning; Clara was cleaning mushrooms and Trixie was peeling potatoes in an effort to get ahead for later. Laid out on the counter top by her side were the ingredients for a hearty cooked breakfast.

As she rose from the table, Clara could already see another van negotiating the turn and pulling into the now crowded parking area. She looked at Trixie.

'They can't be arriving yet, surely? Declan said they wouldn't be shooting until nearer lunchtime.'

'Well, unless three vans just happened to have become lost and have stopped to ask for directions, I would say that they have.'

Clara had joined her, standing at the sink looking out of the kitchen window. Even as she watched she recognised Samantha, the make-up lady, clambering from one of the vehicles.

'I'll go and get Maddie,' she replied, an anxious look on her face.

By the time she returned to the kitchen with both Seth and Maddie in tow, a small crowd of people were standing in the parking area, stretching stiff legs and looking around at the setting for their latest job.

'Well, they can't bloody park like that for a start,' muttered Maddie. 'Tom will be here any minute, and if any of our guests want to go out today, they're well and truly blocked in.' She looked pointedly at Seth, but she didn't have to, he was already heading out of the door.

Trixie looked utterly panic-stricken. 'Please tell me I haven't got to cater for that lot as well?'

'No, of course not.' Maddie's reply came quickly but as she turned her head away slightly, Clara could see by the look in her eyes that she wasn't entirely convinced. 'I'll go and see what I can find out,' she added, following in Seth's footsteps.

Trixie arched her eyebrows at Clara. 'That's a yes then,' she said. She stared at the food in front of her, and then, sighing, picked up the kettle and began to fill it.

'Don't worry, I'll sort the drinks,' said Clara. 'So that you can concentrate on the breakfast. That lot out there will just have to wait.'

'What, even Declan?'

Clara stuck out her tongue. 'Yes, even Declan.'

So far this morning the subject of Clara's date hadn't been broached, and Clara certainly wasn't about to bring it up. Given Trixie's ability to lower the tone of any conversation, she knew exactly what she would be in for when she did. Her head was still trying to process the events of last night and she wasn't sure she could cope with being teased to death as well. To her surprise, though, Trixie made no further comment.

'What time does everyone want to eat?' she asked.

'Around nine-ish,' replied Trixie. 'At least our guests both want breakfast at roughly the same time. Although the Carters have said they'd be happy to have it a bit before if it was ready. I think they plan on going out soon after. The rest of us... will have to wait and see.'

Clara stared out the window to where Seth could be seen waving his arms around directing traffic. Nobody would be going anywhere until the vans were shifted. She returned to the table to finish the mushrooms.

'Right, these will be done shortly, then what's next?'

Trixie pulled a face. 'I don't suppose you fancy stringing the beans, do you?'

After the summer glut, some days it felt like she could string beans in her sleep, but this was pretty much the last of the harvest now, destined for the freezer, so Clara said nothing and just nodded.

It was a relief when Maddie, Seth and the crew, including Declan, walked past the kitchen window and carried on around the side of the house and into the gardens. It would have been a nightmare to have them all in the kitchen. Clara counted numbers as they filed past. Several of them she recognised – Declan of course, and Samantha, plus Ed and Billy who had been before – but this time there were three others, which made seven extra folks on site. She made no comment, but knew that Trixie, who was now slicing tomatoes in half, would have just done exactly the same thing.

There was no sign of anyone for at least fifteen minutes, but then the back door slammed at the other end of the house and both women exchanged glances. Trixie turned back to the cooker. Footsteps could be heard echoing up the hall, and it was too much to think that they would simply stop by the study door and not come as far as the kitchen. Trixie was still resolutely cooking breakfast, so it was Clara who looked up as Maddie came into the room.

'So, what's the damage then?' asked Trixie, finally turning around, a pair of metal tongs in her hand.

'I'll bloody kill him,' muttered Maddie. 'Honest to God, Trixie, I tried my best to stop him before he even got started, but he and Declan were doing this massive male bonding thing and I couldn't get anywhere near him to say anything without being overheard. I tried looking daggers at him as well, but even that made no difference.'

'What did Seth say, Maddie?'

She flashed Clara a helpless look. 'He offered them all bacon sandwiches… I'm sorry, Trixie. I did say that you were in the middle of cooking our guests' breakfast and that I wasn't sure you would have enough to cater for everyone, but…'

'We can't possibly say no now that Seth has opened his big mouth.' Trixie's mouth was set in a hard line.

'No, I don't think we can.'

There was silence for a moment apart from the sound of bacon sizzling. The smell of it was making Clara drool, but she thrust aside her own hunger.

'Do we even have enough bacon?' asked Maddie.

'Yeah, I have enough bacon,' replied Trixie, reaching into the deep drawer beside the cooker and removing another large pan. 'But that's hardly the point, is it.'

She crossed to the larder on the far side of the kitchen and returned with a fresh loaf of bread. She plonked it down on the table, and then, retrieving a bread knife and chopping board from the counter, set them beside it. 'Perhaps one of you could slice that,' she said, returning to the cooker, one hand flicking the kettle on to boil as she passed.

Maddie picked up the bread knife with a look at Clara.

'I'll get the teapots,' she replied, getting up.

★

To Clara's untrained eye it looked as if everyone had been standing around all morning. According to Declan, they were still planning to start filming around half eleven, but before then there were a number of things to be done. Except that Clara couldn't see much actually being accomplished. Granted, quite a large number of bits of equipment were now lying about the place, together with a cookery area, very much 'dressed' for the occasion but, each time she checked to see what was happening, apart from several heads bent together, that was pretty much it.

It was hard to know what to do. Clara would normally go straight out to the garden after helping Trixie with breakfast, provided there was nothing else to be prepared for the farmers' markets they attended. Today though, the garden felt rather off-limits, and there was also the added complication that whatever she did would result in her becoming muddy or dishevelled in some way. Nobody had told her that she shouldn't carry on with her work as normal, but it felt awkward and so, after pottering around in a desultory fashion for a bit, she rather reluctantly made her way back to the kitchen.

On a normal day, if just Trixie was at work in there, the radio would be on, or failing that, music of some kind played from her iPod. Today though, there was silence. The kitchen wasn't empty, however; Trixie was busy at the table kneading bread. They always joked that it was the perfect task if you were angry or stressed: the stretching, pulling, and sometimes pounding of the dough that was required was brilliant for venting frustrations, and after this morning, Clara wasn't at all surprised to find Trixie doing just that. She just hoped her mood had improved as a result.

Clara didn't blame her; Seth had been made to apologise for landing so much extra work on her plate, and at a time when she could ill afford it, but it hadn't taken away the fact that the work still had to be done. Of course, Trixie had managed it with seeming ease, and with her and Maddie ferrying food back and forth, the breakfasts had been delivered on time, with seven rounds of bacon sandwiches delivered shortly afterward. After that, with all the bread gone, Tom had to make do with two toasted crusts covered in beans and Maddie, Clara and Trixie, all ravenous by then, had to settle for cereal. Seth, feeling guilty, had foregone breakfast altogether, even though he had a hard day's work ahead of him with renovations to the barn. It was fine, but it had set the day off to a bad start, and Clara had felt the tension keenly.

Trixie looked up as she entered the kitchen. 'It's probably bad how much pleasure I've derived from tearing him limb from limb,' she said, indicating the bread as she pushed the heel of her hand into it hard. 'If this were a voodoo doll, Seth would be in serious trouble by now.'

'Who says he isn't?' replied Clara, trying to work out whether Trixie really was in a better frame of mind. The comment was light-hearted but her expression was still stony. 'I don't think you're going to have to worry about Seth doing that again any time soon; Maddie's not about to let him forget that one in a while.'

'Yeah well, perhaps you should have a word with your boyfriend just in case he thinks it's a good idea to be such a pain in the arse again. It's still put me behind. I'm doing jobs I didn't need to today. Plus, I've now got to go and replace the bacon at some point, or there won't be any for tomorrow.'

'He's not my boyfriend, Trixie.'

'Well, what is he then?' she replied, raising her eyebrows at the tone in Clara's voice.

'He's not anything, not yet… possibly not ever. We went for one drink, that's all, and a bite to eat.'

Clara was a little hurt by the comment that somehow what happened earlier had been Declan's fault; it really hadn't happened that way. As for the suggestion that she could influence him in any way…

She glanced at her watch, thinking that maybe the kitchen wasn't such a great place to be after all.

'If you like I'll go and get some more bacon. I'm not quite sure what's occurring out there, but no one seems to need me, and it doesn't look like they're going to be ready for ages yet. I can be there and back in just over half an hour.'

Trixie smiled for the first time since Clara had entered the room. 'Oh, would you really?' And then she grinned. 'You'd really be saving my bacon…' She groaned.

'I can get some more eggs as well if you like?'

'And sausages too, I'm sure they'll get used.' She continued kneading the bread. 'Are you really sure you don't mind?' She bit her lip. 'I'd be ever so grateful.'

Clara shook her head, acknowledging the unspoken apology. 'No, it's no problem. I feel like a spare part. I might as well go and do something useful.'

★

It was typical. On any other day mid-week, Clara could be guaranteed to find a parking space along the High Street with no trouble at all. Except of course today, on the one day she couldn't hang around. She tutted as she turned into the next street and grabbed the first space she could find.

By the time she had walked the entire length of the road, she had convinced herself that the butcher's would be busy too, but fortunately the queue was small and within a few minutes she was back out on the street again, clutching several packages and a tray of eggs to her chest. She had only gone a couple of steps when she realised it had begun to spit with rain and she picked up her speed.

Balancing the eggs on the roof of the car, she fumbled with her keys to get the driver's door open without dropping any of the bags. Once they were stowed safely on the back seat, she ducked back out of the car's rear door again and straightened up to lift down the eggs. As she did so she looked up into the window of the tearoom opposite.

With only the car's width and the pavement separating her from the building, she could see Liam very clearly. And he was not alone. Nor was he with Megan. Sitting opposite him was a very attractive blonde who, despite the relative cool of the day, was wearing a very low-cut tee shirt. It didn't leave much to the imagination and Liam was smiling broadly.

She looked away quickly in case they made eye contact, packing the eggs with as much speed as she could while still ensuring they would remain unbroken and hastily closing the car door. She climbed into the driver's seat looking resolutely ahead and within moments had pulled away from the kerb.

By the time she negotiated the tiny turning into the lane that led to Joy's Acre she had all but convinced herself that it was an entirely innocent meeting. The woman with Liam could have been anyone; a sister, an old friend, one of Megan's friends even. After all, they were sitting in the window seat of a popular tearoom in broad daylight, it was hardly likely to have been a clandestine meeting.

She hurried across the yard as a scuffle of leaves blew past her. Trixie would be able to put her mind at rest, with her no-nonsense appraisal of any situation, but when she got to the kitchen, it was empty. The table, however, was still strewn with flour and Clara could see that the dough had been left to rise in a bowl beside the range. She checked her watch before unpacking the shopping into the fridge. The trip had taken her forty minutes from start to finish, that was all.

The study was also empty and she wandered out of the back door and on into the gardens. Trixie was just coming down the path back to the house.

'Don't say a bloody word,' she said as she got closer. 'I look like a bad Andy Warhol painting.'

Clara had to smile; it was a very apt description. With her bright pink hair, and now bright red lips and heavily made-up eyes and cheeks, she did look very… colourful.

'It's not that bad,' she replied, but Trixie's rolling eyes told her that she could save her breath.

'Anyway, you're up next with the delightful Samantha,' added Trixie. 'For the full works, I believe, and you'd better get a move on, you've been missed, apparently…'

'Does that mean we might finally get to do something?' asked Clara. 'There seems to have been an awful lot of hanging around.'

'Tell me about it. Since you've been out, I've been over there three times to have something or other checked, and I'm still none the wiser. If they don't get a move on there'll be no point anyway.' She eyed the sky which showed rolling black clouds.

Clara made to move past her. 'I'll get going then,' she said. 'Although, remind me later – there's something I want to talk to you about…'

'Oh?'

She could already see Maddie waving at her from the top of the path. 'I'll tell you later,' she said, backing away. 'Don't smudge your mascara!'

Maddie's face was anxious as she joined her.

'Where did you get to?' she asked. 'Everyone's been looking for you.'

'Into town,' she replied, knowing full well that Trixie would have told her. 'And don't say anything because that was Seth's fault. Anyway, this lot were dithering about.'

Samantha came rushing towards her. 'Oh, thank goodness. Come on, let's get you sorted out. Declan will be having kittens otherwise…'

Clara resisted the arm that was trying to hurry her along. 'Really?' she said. 'Because he hasn't spoken a word to me all morning.'

The words were automatic, but they had come out a little stronger than she intended and as soon as she said them she realised she did feel a little miffed that Declan had said next to nothing to her, save for hello. She didn't expect him to fawn over her, or treat her differently from anyone else – in fact, nothing would be worse – but seeing as they had spent an evening together, he could have at least acknowledged her.

'He's always like this,' sighed Samantha. 'He can be a bit blinkered when he's on a shoot. Don't take it personally.' She shot another anxious glance towards the main garden. 'We haven't got long so, er…'

Clara let herself be subject to Samantha's ministrations, even though a part of her resented being 'sorted out'. She didn't consider herself to be particularly vain, but somehow that sentence seemed to imply that there was a considerable amount to improve upon. She chided herself for being quite so touchy; it was probably just a turn of phrase.

Finally, after another half an hour, she had her feet planted back in the strawberry bed where she had stood to film the last time. Essentially, they were reshooting what they had captured before, but for longer this time, and with a far greater attention to detail apparently. Clara would also need to have a chat with Fiona, the series advisor to discuss the format for each episode which would be based round a different theme each week. It was these themes which needed teasing out, and her input was 'paramount'. Today they would be concentrating on fruits, specifically berries, and all

Clara had to do was perform exactly as she had last week. Declan's smile was warm as he gave her the final directions and encouragement before the camera started rolling. She felt herself begin to relax.

But it was different from the minute she started.

Could you turn slightly further to your right?

And look up at that bit?

We need a pause between what you're saying and doing.

Cut!

Clara looked up, startled. Declan and the series advisor had their heads together again.

'I think Fiona's right, Clara,' said Declan. 'You're assuming too much. I think you need to explain what you're doing in much greater detail, as if the person you're describing it to has no idea what they're doing. So, really spell it out this time. Let's go again.'

It was hard to know what to say. What she was describing was hardly rocket science. She took a deep breath and began again.

Better!

And I want a zoom on that runner, focus on the cut…

No, not you, Clara, just carry on.

Samantha, come and fix the hair for goodness' sake.

'Right, and this last section now. I want to keep that part with you eating the strawberry but, Ed, back off this time and lose the close-up, we're not making a bloody porno… What I want is—'

She stared at him, fighting the colour that she knew was rising up her neck.

'Clara, what's the matter?'

He gave her a searching look.

'Nothing, I'm fine.' She swallowed. How could he say such a thing and embarrass her in front of everyone like that? She looked at Ed, but he just nodded, accepting Declan's directions. Then she looked at the strawberry in her hand, and put it back down on the ground. She would probably choke on it now.

'Right, everyone got that? Okay, Clara, we're good to go and remember, nice big smile now.'

Somehow, she got to the end, and was just about to heave a sigh of relief when a sudden squall of wind blew across the garden bringing a smattering of rain drops with it. A mass of black cloud had gathered over the field behind the Gardener's Cottage that Clara hadn't even noticed.

'Good work, everyone. But stay focused please. I want one last piece in the new strawberry bed that Clara has already prepared so that we can see one of the fledgling plants being transferred. I'm well aware that the weather is closing in, but we're still okay on the light, and until I'm told otherwise, we're good to go.'

Clara stood up, feeling the breeze more keenly now, and made her way back to the path. Seth and Maddie were still standing at the side and he was glancing anxiously up at the roof where Tom was working. She knew exactly what he was thinking. The table set up for Trixie to cook on was still covered in a red checked tablecloth which was now fluttering wildly. It didn't bode well.

She waited while everyone checked angles to get the perfect backdrop to the shot, trying to ignore the increasing number of rain droplets falling on her arms. She hugged them to her, beginning to feel quite cold. Eventually, everyone seemed satisfied and she was invited to take up position.

All she had to do was to dig a hole for the new strawberry plant and then remove it from the pot it had grown in and transplant it. Which was fine, except that as soon as she removed the plant and laid down the pot a gust of wind chased it away.

'Cut!'

She looked up. 'Sorry,' she called. 'There wasn't much I could do about that.' She had turned to look at Declan, who was standing slightly to her right and as she turned back into the wind she felt another barrage of droplets against the side of her face. She hesitated for a moment, unsure what to do, only to see Samantha rushing to her side with a cloth and a make-up brush. Someone else had retrieved the pot and handed it back to her.

'One more then,' said Declan. 'And this time if you think the pot is going to blow away again, place it behind you as you remove the plant… That way at least when it rolls it won't be in the damn shot.'

She gritted her teeth.

'And, action!'

A sudden piercing whistle broke the silence.

She looked up sharply in the direction of the sound. Tom was waving wildly.

'What the—'

She was aware of sudden movement, as Seth took off down the path, leaving Maddie with a helpless expression on her face. 'I'm sorry,' she shouted, 'but the roof!'

And then the heavens opened.

Chapter 17

Declan's face was as black as the sky.

'Would someone like to tell me what the—'

And then he stopped as Clara shot past him too, all thoughts of the filming forgotten.

She reached the cottage and looked up. A tarpaulin had already been set in place a couple of days ago in anticipation of the forecast rain, and covered the half of the roof yet to be re-thatched. Tom had anchored it down, rolling it back to expose the edge that he was currently working on, and she could see that the wind had ripped it loose from its binding and it was now flapping wildly. There was no way he would be able to secure it on his own.

Running around to the other side of the cottage from Tom and Seth, she began to climb the ladder already set up. Maddie was hot on her heels.

'Can you foot the ladder for me?' she called from a third of the way up. She didn't particularly have a problem with heights, but she would feel happier knowing that the base was secure.

The noise level increased the higher she got. The wind was now driving the rain onto the tarpaulin, and coupled with the sound it made as it flapped it was hard to hear. She ran a hand over her face to clear it as she reached the top.

It was instantly apparent what the problem was. Tom was frantically trying to secure the covering, but the direction of the wind meant that it was catching the outer edge and constantly ripping it free. Seth was already nearing the apex of the roof and, as she watched, he straddled it, leaning forward precariously to snatch at the tarpaulin, heaving it toward him and pulling it close to the roofline. She would need to do the same or Tom would never be able to get the fixings to hold.

She was lying almost flat against the slope of the roof now. The unfinished thatch at least meant that she had plenty to hold onto. She doubted very much if she would be up on the roof were it not for that, and she used it now to pull herself to the side, leaning out so that she could try to grab the tarpaulin as it flapped beside her. She inched her fingers forward.

Seth was only a couple of feet above her now, his mouth open, shouting something at her, but she struggled to hear. Her hair was whipping around her face and she had to keep shaking her head to see. She stretched out... and then she realised what Seth had been trying to tell her, because she was lying right on the very edge of the newly laid thatch. Next to her, where the old layers of straw had been removed to within a few inches of the roof itself, were the wooden rafters and not much else. If she were to put her weight on the gaps in between she would likely fall through.

A sudden lull in the storm brought the edge of the tarpaulin tantalisingly close and she managed to lock one finger and thumb around it, frantically feeling for the eyelets which would give her something to hang onto. The ladder was bouncing alarmingly but she clung on as the wind speed increased again, billowing the blue sheet away from her like a ship in full sail. It was pulling her further and further away...

And then a solid weight was upon her, holding her, pulling her back to safety. And an arm was snaking along hers, a hand brushing past, fingers moving on top of her own.

'Lie still, Clara, I've got you.' Declan's voice was close to her ear, his breath warm on her cheek, his muscles hard against her back, her legs...

His fingers grabbed at the tarpaulin, and she felt his arm tense as he prepared to heave it towards them. She dug her fingers in too and, as she felt the traction begin to have effect, she pulled with everything she had. The muscles were burning in her shoulder, but then all of a sudden the tension went slack as the cover was finally subdued, pinned beneath them.

She risked a glance upward, hardly able to move with Declan's weight pressing her against the roof, but she could see that Seth was virtually lying flat too, hanging on for grim death, and beside him was Tom, swiftly hammering in the stays now that the tarpaulin was no longer flapping. She closed her eyes, feeling the rain run down the back of her neck. The thatch was rough under her cheek but she didn't care, she couldn't move.

It could have been two minutes or half an hour before Tom finally managed to secure the tarpaulin and Clara felt Declan's weight slowly lift from her. A sudden chill raced across her wet back as the wind whipped between them.

'It's okay now, it's okay. Just slowly move back down, I've got you.'

And inch by inch they descended the ladder. It was all Clara could manage; her legs felt like jelly. By the time they reached the bottom she was shivering uncontrollably.

She felt a pair of strong arms go around her, but they were Tom's, not Declan's.

'Jesus, Clara, you scared me.'

'I scared myself,' she whispered back, looking up at the roof where the tarpaulin was now just rippling gently.

He held her head into his chest and she clutched at the back of his shirt, sopping wet, just as she was.

'Come on, let's get you inside.' And he picked her up as if she were a doll. Out of the corner of her eye she could see Declan and Seth, hugging fiercely, and then Maddie too. It was too much, and she closed her eyes again.

By the time they got back to the house, the crew, damp but no worse for wear, were already gathered in the kitchen. Trixie was nowhere to be seen. She appeared, moments later carrying an armful of blankets and, as Tom lowered her into a chair, Clara accepted a red fleecy one gratefully. It was the one from Trixie's bed. She shooed the crew out of the way. Declan, bringing up the rear, nodded.

'Guys, perhaps you could wait somewhere else... Is there somewhere?'

Trixie's mouth was set in a hard line. 'I'll show you.' She bustled out of the room as everyone trailed after her.

'I'll stay, shall I?' offered Samantha. 'I can help make drinks or something?'

Maddie gave her a tight smile. 'The kettle's boiled. Teapot's on the side.'

It was warm in the kitchen and Clara felt herself begin to relax a little. At least the shivering had stopped. She looked at everyone in turn, but they were all wearing the same shell-shocked expression she suspected she was.

'Will the roof be okay, Tom?' she managed. 'And the cottage?'

He looked up. 'It will be fine. The new thatch will do its job and I don't think too much rain got into the other sections. The ceilings will hold.'

No one needed to spell out quite what a close-run thing it had been. Or why it had even happened in the first place. They probably would at some point, but now was not the time.

Trixie came back into the room. She reached forward, taking something from the side, and turned, depositing it onto the middle of the table. It was a huge caramel apple cake, one of Clara's favourites. With its crumble topping, it was rich and gooey.

'Right, you all need a hot drink and some of this inside you. The sugar will do you good. Plus, you all need to get out of those wet clothes.' She looked at Clara. 'You especially.' She pulled the fleece around Tom, who was nearest to her.

'I can sort you out something, don't worry.' It was Maddie. 'And Tom and Declan, I'm sure Seth can find you something, even if it is just a dressing gown for now.'

'You should have hot showers too… or a bath… I could run one for you if you like.' It was Trixie again, her face full of concern.

Clara let their voices wash over her; she was suddenly so, so tired. She closed her eyes against the sound of the wind, the feel of the rain… How could she have been so stupid? She could have fallen… but then… and suddenly her head was filled with thoughts of Declan, holding her, protecting her, his body lying against hers… Her head began to swim…

'I think I want to go home,' she said, opening her eyes.

Declan's chair scraped backwards against the tiled floor. 'I'll take you,' he said.

'No, not yet.' Trixie's voice was firm. 'She needs dry clothes first, and a drink.' Samantha had just placed a full teapot down on the table, and Trixie pulled a mug towards her, dumping two sugars into it from a bowl on the table. She began to pour, adding milk from a jug.

Maddie got to her feet, still clutching her blanket around her. 'Come on,' she said. 'We'll take it upstairs.' She held out her hand to Clara, as if to usher her out of the room.

A few minutes later, and now dressed in leggings and a warm sweatshirt, Clara at least felt warmer. Having left Maddie to change her own clothes, she was about to re-join the others when the tone of Trixie's voice from the kitchen made her pause in the hallway. Low and grumbling, it was, nevertheless, perfectly clear.

'You might not feel you can say it, Seth, but I'm sorry, I'm going to. This could all have been prevented and you and everyone else around this table knows it... And don't look at me like that, Tom, you know it's true. I've spent the whole day running backwards and forwards, being told I'm needed one minute, only to find out I'm not. I've fetched and carried for everyone, made lunch – which incidentally is still on the side over there because no one bothered to come and eat it, or even tell me it wasn't required.'

Someone replied but Clara couldn't hear who it was.

'I'm happy to do this, but so far all that's happened has been a massive increase in my workload, and I didn't even get a whiff of a camera pointed at me.' She paused for a moment. 'All I'm saying is that there needs to be much better communication, and an understanding that what we do here is important too. Tom would have fastened the tarpaulin down way before he did under normal circumstances, but he put it off and put it off because everyone was too busy to listen to what he had to say. Any one of you could have fallen off the roof, and now Clara could get really sick—'

Clara had heard enough. She doubled back slightly to the head of the stairs and cleared her throat loudly as if she'd been coughing. By the time she entered the kitchen the conversation had changed direction.

'Could you pass me that knife from the side, Samantha?' said Trixie. 'I'll get this cake cut up so you can all have a piece.'

Clara smiled brightly, waving her mug. 'Thank you,' she said. 'That's much better.' She crossed to the sink to rinse it out, upending it on the draining board, and then returned to her seat.

'At least I'm not dripping on the floor now,' she said. 'And hopefully not as scary.' It hadn't been a pretty sight surveying herself in the mirror upstairs. Her mascara had run in rivulets down her face and her make-up was smudged, her lips blue with cold. She had removed what hair had been left in her bun and towel-dried it, but she still hadn't been able to drag a comb through it and was too tired to tussle with it. It hung in long damp tails almost to her waist.

Everyone was still staring at her, Seth wearing a guilty expression that she hadn't seen in a long time.

Tom was beginning to shiver. She pushed the plate that Trixie had just passed her across to him.

'Come on, you need to either eat this, or go and get changed… all of you,' she added.

Seth got to his feet. 'Come on, we'll go now.' He grimaced. Both of the other men were much taller than he was. 'This might be interesting…'

Maddie reappeared just as they were leaving. They sat in silence for a few moments, neither wishing to speak while there were still four of them in the room. Clara twiddled with the ends of her hair, Trixie stared straight ahead out of the window and Maddie inspected her fingernails.

Eventually Samantha made a nervous noise in her throat. 'I might just go and see what the others are up to,' she said.

'Good idea,' said Trixie, unabashed, watching as she walked from the room.

'What a stupid, ridiculous day,' she added, and Clara wondered for whose benefit it had been said, but then she turned to her, lowering her voice. 'Are you okay, Clara? Really… not just putting on a brave face?'

'I'm so sorry,' she replied, ignoring the question. 'I didn't even stop to think about what I was doing. It didn't occur to me it might be dangerous.'

'Well I guess that hardly matters now,' said Maddie. 'What matters is what we do next, and you're right, Trixie, today was a disaster on many levels. I don't think any of us got any work done, and now there's talk of each of you having to spend considerably more time with Fiona as well. I think we need some concrete assurances of how things will be, going forward.' She rubbed at her forehead. 'In fact, I think there's only one good thing that came out of today.'

Trixie sighed. 'Which is?'

'That Declan came to Clara's rescue.' She let the words hang in the air, but Clara didn't bite. It was the last thing she wanted to talk about. 'Although, he's hardly said a word since. I think he's feeling pretty bad about the whole thing.'

'And I was so looking forward to the filming as well,' admitted Trixie, 'but it wasn't how I thought it was going to be at all.'

Clara hung her head. 'Me neither. It seemed… different from last time. The way they talked about me, it felt like they'd forgotten I was even there half the time.' She felt embarrassed to be openly critical, but she wasn't sure how she did feel. Her head felt like it was stuffed full of cotton wool.

There was a bumping noise from the hallway as three pairs of feet jogged down the stairs. Clara swivelled to see Declan clad in a pair of forest green jogging bottoms that she couldn't even remember seeing

Seth wear. They finished several centimetres from Declan's ankles. He was followed by Tom wearing a dressing gown.

Trixie wolf whistled. 'Well, don't you two look nice…?'

Declan bowed.

'Folks, it doesn't get much better than this,' said Tom, 'although just in case you ladies are finding it hard to concentrate I have placed an emergency call to Isobel, who will be bringing dry clothes from home shortly.' He looked at Declan, pulling a sympathetic face. 'Well, for me at least.'

Clara smiled despite herself. 'Oh, but at least we'll get to see Isobel again. That will be lovely.'

Maddie shook her head. 'Nuh-uh, not for you, I'm afraid. Declan, you need to take her home now, before she falls off her chair.'

He looked around him, a little disorientated, before spotting his laptop and car keys on the dresser where presumably he had left them that morning.

'Yes, good idea.' He looked back at Seth. 'Paracetamol, bath and bed,' he added, nodding. 'No problem.'

Clara looked up at him, confused, before she saw the look that passed between him and Maddie. She was about to argue when she realised there was little point. Instead she nodded meekly, getting stiffly to her feet.

By the time she walked out to the car, every muscle in her body felt like it was on fire.

★

It was strange seeing a man walk around her kitchen and, in fact, since Clara had lived in her cottage, the only other man to do so had been Seth, on a couple of rare occasions not long after she had moved. Had she been able to think straight, she would have found Declan's awkwardness hysterically funny, or possibly rather endearing... As it was, she watched him with a rather odd detachment, as if she was seeing him but she couldn't quite decide whether he was a figment of her imagination.

She wondered vaguely whether it was just the combination of ridiculous clothes he was wearing that was making him feel uncomfortable, but as soon as he had placed another hot drink in front of her, he sat down, a serious expression on his face.

'Clara, I'm so sorry,' he began. 'I've behaved appallingly today, and I'm really not sure how to explain myself. I've got it all horribly wrong.'

She thought about his words for a minute, memories of the day flooding back. On any other occasion she would probably have been a little more generous, but her head hurt and she felt impossibly tired.

'Yes, you have. I'm not sure what you were trying to achieve today, but if you wanted to upset everyone, and make me feel an inch tall into the bargain, then I'd have to say you succeeded.'

He flinched, but held her gaze, nodding gently. 'I'm not going to argue,' he said. 'I think that's fair comment... but I would like to explain why I behaved the way I did.' His eyes were warm on hers. 'I have a good reason. At least I think it's a good reason.'

'Given that it's possible you also saved me from breaking my neck this afternoon, I guess I ought to hear you out.' She gave a weak smile.

He laid a hand across hers. 'Except that I'm really not sure that you're up to this...' His fingers closed over hers, sliding beneath them until he was holding her hand. 'Come on, I'll run you a bath and then I think you should sleep.'

Clara shook her head. 'No. I just want to go to bed.' There were too many things circling inside her head and all she wanted was to shut them out.

She felt herself being led up the narrow stairs of her cottage. 'It's to the left,' she murmured. Moments later she was sitting on the edge of the bed, aware that with the low ceilings upstairs, Declan seemed to be taking up a huge amount of space in the room.

'Do you have a hairdryer?' he asked.

She looked up, frowning.

'My mum used to moan at me never to go to bed with wet hair.'

He followed her gaze to the dressing table on the far side of the room. And then crossed over to it, pulling out the stool that stood in front of it.

'Come on, this won't take a minute. I don't want there to be any more risk of you catching a chill.'

She moved across the room and sat down as instructed, conscious thought moving further and further away from her. She closed her eyes as Declan scooped her hair around the back, his hands cool against her cheek. He stroked it down her back, switching on the dryer and playing it gently against her hair. The sensation was amazing. Her shoulders sagged as she gave in to his ministrations, waves of tiredness washing over her, and then a sudden thought… Her eyes flickered open – she still hadn't managed to speak to Trixie about seeing Liam with another woman. But, even as she fought to think beyond the sentence, her eyes drooped closed again.

Moments later she was in bed, her face turning against the cool smoothness of the pillow.

'I haven't been able to stop thinking about you, Clara…'

She registered a slight touch of his lips against her cheek, but that was all before sleep claimed her.

Chapter 18

She'd been having the loveliest dream, but even as she snuggled back under the duvet trying to lose herself in it again, she realised that the light in the room was too bright for it to be still night time. Clara opened a cautious eye and checked the clock on her bedside cabinet. She focused on it again, but it was still telling her the same thing. It was a little after ten in the morning. How on earth could that possibly be right? She never got up this late.

Throwing the cover back, she sat up, feeling the soreness in her neck and shoulders. She frowned and looked around her. Other than loudly protesting muscles she felt fine, and yet... She blinked, as memories came swimming back, faces mainly; Maddie and Seth... Declan, and someone she didn't recognise. And then she realised that she was wearing her pyjamas, except that when she went to bed she had still been in the sweatshirt and leggings that Maddie had lent to her...

It took Clara a couple more minutes to piece together what had happened the day before, but by the time she had, she had stood and found her slippers. She needed to get a move on, it was late enough as it was. She knew that Seth wouldn't mind her arriving at work at this time in the morning, but it wasn't fair to everyone else, not when there was so much to do.

She padded down the stairs which led directly to her kitchen and flicked the kettle on. She could drink her tea while she had a quick bath. It wouldn't take her long to get ready at all. She stared out the window while she waited for the water to boil. It was still raining, the street outside dark and gloomy. It was only as she turned away that she realised Declan's car was still in the driveway…

Her cottage wasn't very big. Two bedrooms, a small bathroom, the kitchen and her sitting room, the door of which led off the kitchen. She stared at it now, almost closed, and then slowly walked towards it. She pushed it open.

The first thing she saw was the enormous bowl of roses on the coffee table, deep red, like velvet, and sitting just the other side of it in her armchair was Declan. He had one leg crossed at the knee, reading. Gone were the hideous jogging bottoms; instead he was wearing pale jeans and a dark blue shirt.

He scrabbled to his feet the moment he saw her, placing the book down on the table. She recognised it instantly. It was the book about Joy's Acre which belonged to Seth.

'Good morning!' He looked delighted to see her. 'How are you feeling? You look much better.'

Her stomach gave a little flip before she could even think of a reply. God, he looked gorgeous. And then she realised she was still wearing her pyjamas.

'That wasn't me,' he said quickly, understanding the reason for her embarrassment. 'Maddie came over, when the doctor came, she—'

'The doctor?' Clara shook her head, vaguely remembering voices and having to sit up, having to… 'When did the doctor come?'

'Yesterday afternoon, but it's okay. No lasting harm done. You've been running a slight fever but he said the best thing was for you to sleep. Keep an eye on your temperature obviously, but other than that let your body do what it needed to.' He glanced at the coffee table where an empty mug stood. 'The others have visited… but, well, we thought someone should stay with you, just to be on the safe side. And that someone was me, I hope you don't mind? I slept in the spare room, obviously, and—'

Clara held up her hand, struggling to keep up with what he was saying. Something wasn't quite right about all of this.

'Wait a minute… how did the doctor come yesterday afternoon, when we didn't get back here until quite late?' She narrowed her eyes, re-running through the memories in her head. 'Besides which, I know I slept right through the night, but I…' She trailed off as Declan started to walk towards her.

'Clara, it's Thursday today? You haven't just been asleep overnight. You've been asleep a whole day and a night… two nights.'

She put a hand to her forehead. 'Thursday?' she repeated. She stared up at him as his arms reached out to her. 'Oh my God, that's… terrible.' She gave a sheepish smile. 'You mean I…'

He nodded. 'Yes, you have. Been in bed all this time.'

She let herself be pulled in close. 'And you've stayed here the whole time?'

'I have, looking after you…'

She pulled away suddenly, looking down. 'The flowers are beauti-ful…' She blushed slightly.

'I wasn't sure you'd like them?'

'But I do, thank you.'

'I wanted to do, something… and I thought they might be a nice surprise to wake up to.'

She had turned back to look at him. 'And they are, I—' She stopped suddenly at the look in his eyes.

'Clara?' And then his lips very gently brushed hers. 'I've been so worried about you.'

'I might have to sit down,' she murmured. 'Although I'm fine, honestly.' She grinned at him then. 'I just wasn't expecting... Is it really Thursday, you're not just having me on?'

He laughed. 'Swear on my life.'

They stared at one another for a minute, not knowing quite what to say. Clara was the first to speak.

'I need a cup of tea,' she said. 'I don't function without one first thing on the best of days, and today is definitely going to be a two-cup morning.'

Declan went ahead of her. 'Sit down,' he said, 'I'll make you one.'

Ignoring him, she followed him meekly into the kitchen, a hand touched to her lips which were curved upwards into a smile. The kiss was the last thing she had expected but she had to admit it had felt rather nice...

'Hang on a minute,' she said, still going over recent events in her head. 'I think I'm supposed to be cross with you...'

'Bugger.' Declan pursed his lips. 'I was hoping you wouldn't remember that.'

She had a sudden flashback to the day in the florist's shop. 'Ah... So they're *guilty* flowers then, are they?'

'Not at all.' He gave a rueful grin, remembering the same conversation. 'Although thinking about it now, I admit they might be what you could call dual-purpose.'

She took a seat at the small table in the kitchen. 'I might let you off anyway, I haven't decided yet. Although it would seem you have looked after me very well...'

His face took on a serious expression once more. 'I *was* worried about you, still am, in fact. Are you sure you feel okay?'

'I'm fine, honestly,' she replied, trying to separate her tangled hair with her fingers. She looked up at him through her lashes. 'You obviously know about my bone marrow transplant,' she said. There was no point beating about the bush. 'It doesn't normally cause a problem except when—'

'You get excessively tired, rundown or get an infection,' he finished for her. 'Although of course the three often work in conjunction.'

'I have a weakened immune system,' she replied, nodding, 'because of the drugs I have to take which stop the marrow from rejecting. But then I guess you know about that too. Who told you, Maddie or Seth?'

'Both of them actually... at great length, and in highly admonitory tones, which I deserved wholeheartedly of course.'

'I probably should have told you, but it's not something you really want to go into on a first date.'

'At least not until you've divulged the fact that you're married with three children at any rate.' He smiled across at her. 'It's not your fault at all, Clara... and for what it's worth I have admitted full responsibility for what happened on Tuesday.'

'But you didn't cause the storm—'

'No, but I should have been far more sensitive to what was going on at Joy's Acre, or rather what should have been going on. And I treated you very badly as well.' He swallowed. 'In my defence I *was* acting rather out of character... It would appear that a certain young lady completely overrode my ability to think of anything other than her and, given that it's not something I've ever experienced before, I wasn't being entirely rational.'

'Oh.' Her fingers stilled. 'That's rather a lovely thing to say... and very brave if I may say so. Particularly since I would imagine folk at Joy's Acre have given you a pretty hard time?'

'And rightly so.' He coloured slightly, and she could only imagine how much of an ear-bashing Seth and Tom would have given him. Maddie too, come to think of it, and Trixie...

'Fortunately for me, your friends are very generous, and we've agreed to say no more about it provided I don't behave like a total arse again...'

Clara nodded. 'Can't say fairer than that.' She grinned. 'Right, come on then, are you making this tea, or what? I need to get a move on or it will be Friday by the time I get to Joy's Acre.'

'You're not seriously going to work, are you?'

'Of course! Why shouldn't I?' She smiled at his horrified look. 'I am honestly fine, Declan, and given the weather I'm not likely to be doing any digging today. I shall take it easy, don't worry.' She accepted a mug from him. 'And I daresay you have a million and one things you need to be doing as well.'

He gave an easy smile. 'One or two,' he admitted. 'In fact, there's a lady called Fiona at Joy's Acre again today. She's my chief series consultant and has spent yesterday talking with Trixie about how the cookery side of things needs to work, gathering ideas, that kind of thing. If you're up to it, it would be great if you could spend some time with her too.'

She picked up her mug and got to her feet. 'No problem. Give me half an hour and I'll be ready to go.' She smiled, shaking her head. 'I still don't get how it's Thursday, that's completely weird.'

Up in her bedroom, she laid out her clothes on the bed ready to wear once she was out of the shower. She was about to take off her pyjamas, when she stopped for a moment, her cheeks suddenly hot. It was very sweet of Declan to let her know that Maddie had helped her get changed into her night clothes, but she only had the vaguest recollection of it. *What else had she done that she had no memory of...?*

★

If it hadn't still been pouring with rain, Maddie would have been out of the door and across the yard in a flash to greet her. As it was, Clara could see that she was practically hopping up and down as she waited for her. The parking arrangements were the only downside to Joy's Acre; the distance from the house necessitated a mad dash if the weather was bad. This time, however, despite the distinct feeling of déjà vu, Clara was well wrapped up against the elements.

She burst through the door laughing as Maddie jumped out of the way.

'Come on,' she urged, 'get your coat off, I need a hug!' She helped Clara to shrug out of her wet jacket and hung it on the hook in the hallway where it dripped onto the tiled floor. 'I couldn't believe it when Declan rang to say you were coming over.' She held Clara at arm's length, looking her up and down. 'Are you sure you're okay to be here?'

As soon as Clara nodded, she was wrapped in a tight hug that had her giggling. 'For goodness' sake, woman, I can't breathe.'

'You had us all so scared,' she replied. 'But at least Declan managed to redeem himself somewhat by looking after you.'

He had just entered the hallway behind them, taking off his own wet jacket. 'And I've already told her she's not to do too much for the next few days.'

'Hmm, well we might have to tie her to a chair or something,' said Maddie. 'I know what she's like.' She waggled her finger at Clara. 'Seriously though, you are to take it easy.'

Clara held up her hands. 'I will,' she surrendered, 'I promise.'

Declan touched a hand to her shoulder. 'Why don't you come and meet Fiona again. She's been working with Trixie over the last day or so, but will need some real input from you on the gardening side of things before we finalise the programme details. It's the perfect opportunity to help decide what goes in and what stays out.'

'She's in the study, Clara. Go on through. I need to brave the elements unfortunately – Tom and Seth are in the barn and I need a catch-up – but I'll see you in a bit. Trixie will be back soon as well; she's had to go into town for something this morning.'

Clara followed Declan down the hallway as the sound of voices floated out of the doorway. It wasn't until she reached the threshold that she realised they were hers and Trixie's, from the very first day's 'practice' filming. She took a tentative step forward.

'Ah, Clara.' The disembodied voice spoke from behind a PC screen. 'I was told you'd be coming today. Have a seat.'

Fiona rose from behind the table that usually stood against one wall. It had obviously been commandeered for her as a desk and, by the looks of things, she had made herself very much at home. Papers were strewn everywhere, atop of which was a huge ring-bound notebook, a pen resting on one page. A hand was extended towards her.

'We didn't have an opportunity to speak the other day, did we? But I'm Fiona,' she said, with a limp grasp of the ends of Clara's fingers. 'And it's lovely to meet you properly.' She sat back down, her head disappearing behind the screen once more.

Clara was somewhat lost for words. She hadn't really taken much notice of Fiona during the filming before, but somehow she had assumed that a series advisor for a media company would be a smart executive type with an overenthusiastic smile and a high-pitched laugh. Today though Fiona was dressed in a pair of jeans and a scruffy sweatshirt and would have looked more at home driving an old Land Rover and mucking out pigs.

Declan moved past her to stand beside Fiona. She caught a slight wink as he passed.

'Fiona, you're absolutely right, this is Clara. The one I've been telling you about… The one who might be feeling a little under the weather today, and to whom you are to be especially nice.'

'I'm always nice,' she grumbled, but the screen was pushed to one side and Clara received a nod and a perfunctory smile.

'And Clara, this is Fiona, whose bark, appearance, and general demeanour are a lot worse than her bite. She's actually quite a nice person underneath the resolutely hostile exterior she displays.'

Clara thought for a minute that Fiona was actually going to disagree, but instead she fixed Declan with a steely gaze.

'Yes, thank you, I think we're done here. Off you go.' She got to her feet and shooed Declan out of the door. 'Clara and I will be just fine, so no snooping. Go and be charming somewhere else.'

'I'll just be in the kitchen, Clara, in case you need me—' If he was about to say anything else it was lost as the door was firmly closed in his face.

She braced herself as Fiona returned to her seat.

'Right, that's better. Now, I think we've both managed to establish our identities, although goodness knows how we ever would have done so without Declan's help.' She rolled her eyes. 'So, let's make a start, shall we? First off, I know absolutely nothing about gardening or growing vegetables, which is entirely irrelevant, so please don't think that it is. My job is not to be enthusiastic or even interested in what you do, but, instead, to take my vast and virtually exhaustive knowledge of the viewing population and couple it with certain ideas to produce a series of programmes not only worth watching, but a hit with the ratings people as well. In short, I make things happen, Clara. Is all that understood?'

Clara nodded, too scared to say anything in reply.

'Excellent. I had a feeling it might be.' She gave a small smile, giving Clara a glance just long enough for her to see the twinkle in her eye before she looked back down to the papers on her desk.

'So, what I want to know first is what you want to get out of all of this?'

The question surprised her and, as the seconds ticked by, she realised that she had never even considered this. She looked up at Fiona, who was waiting for her response and searched her face for some clue to the answer. She was pretty sure Fiona had already made up her mind about Clara, unless it was a trick question of course…

'So, you're not looking to be famous then?' Fiona asked.

'God no.' That was something Clara was very definite about.

'I'm only checking, because that's a possibility, if you want to go down that route…'

Clara shook her head. 'No, definitely not… I'm not really sure why I want to do this. There's Joy's Acre of course… and what it will mean for Seth and Maddie. I want the business to be successful of course, for their sakes, but I suppose it's more about sharing the love of what I do, in a beautiful part of the country, and maybe hoping that other people can experience it also.'

Fiona made a note that Clara couldn't read. 'Pure motives then?' she asked.

'I… I don't know, are they pure? Is there something wrong with that?'

'Not at all. It just helps me to know what to consider, that's all.' She studied Clara intently. 'Your hair for one. How attached are you to that?'

A long plait currently hung over Clara's shoulder. She gave it an experimental tug. 'Yep, it's pretty attached…'

Nothing. Not a flicker.

'Sorry, I know that wasn't what you meant…' She cleared her throat. 'I won't be changing my hair, thanks.'

Fiona consulted her screen. 'And you've been wearing it up for the shooting, I see… down on one occasion. How is that working?'

Clara bit her lip. 'Erm… Fine, I think. I guess I thought it was up to Declan.'

'Yes, well he likes to think it is.' She made another quick note. 'Plaits can be a bit Pippi Longstocking… Nothing wrong with that either necessarily, but Joe Public can have funny ideas about plaits. If you want my opinion, I'd recommend up. Down is a bit try-hard.'

'Oh, right…' Clara had no idea what she was talking about.

'So, now we've got all that sorted, I think I know what I'm working with.' She pushed a sheet of paper across the desk. 'This is what I've come up with for possible episode guides, based on availability of produce, seasonal variations, and links in with Trixie's cookery spot. I've tried to cover as many different techniques as possible, and concentrate on those areas our feedback informs us are relevant to what people want to see.'

Clara nodded.

'Have a look and see what you think?'

The paper was covered in dense handwriting, and a quick scan of it confirmed Clara's thoughts.

'I thought you said you didn't know anything about gardening?'

'I don't, but it's my job to find out.' She got to her feet. 'Now sit and have a proper look at that and I'll go and see if there are any more of those cookies we had this morning. I don't normally eat biscuits, but those were extremely moreish.'

Clara was left sitting staring at the piece of paper in an almost trance-like state. She felt exhausted just keeping up with Fiona's trains of thought, and she took a calming breath, pushing the piece of paper away. She was finding it hard to concentrate. It wasn't until a couple of minutes later that she realised she could hear voices through the open door and a smile crossed her face. Trixie was back.

She hurried out of the study just as Trixie shot out of the kitchen door and the two of them met in the hallway, Clara skidding to a halt in shock. Her arms were outstretched for a hug, but instead one hand went to her mouth as the other hung redundant in mid-air.

'Oh my God, Trixie, what have you done?'

Chapter 19

'Don't you like it?'

Clara stared at her friend. The last time she had seen her she had bright pink hair. Now it was a rich chocolate brown.

'No, yes, I mean. It's just a shock, that's all. Crikey, you look really… grown up!'

'I know, great isn't it?' replied Trixie. 'I actually look like an adult, instead of an emotionally suppressed teenager…'

'Oh, Trixie, you were never that.'

'So, you don't like it then?' She frowned, but Clara smiled, shaking her head.

'I didn't say that… I'm surprised, and it's going to take some getting used to, but it suits you, and if you like it, that's all that matters, surely?'

'I just thought it was time to have a change, go back to my roots, if you'll excuse the pun.'

Clara held out her arms for the overdue hug. 'Then it's perfect.' And she'd lay money on the identity of the person who'd suggested it. 'And yes, I'm fine to be here before you ask.'

Trixie gave her a squeeze. 'Then that's perfect too.'

The two of them wandered back into the kitchen where Fiona was standing by the biscuit tin, unashamedly cramming a cookie into her mouth. She took another before replacing the lid. Declan watched her from the kitchen table with an amused expression on his face.

'Right then, ladies, we'd best make a start again. There's still an awful lot to be gone through.' A biscuit crumb was clinging to the side of Fiona's mouth and for some reason it made Clara want to giggle.

Trixie looked at Clara and then back at Fiona, uncertain. 'I hadn't realised the time,' she said. 'I'm sorry but I still have cakes to make for the farmers' market, plus the weekend. Then there's tea and—'

'Just give me an hour, Trixie. I don't want to leave things while the inspiration is still fresh in your head. Isn't Clara capable of taking your place for the time being?'

'Yes, very, but—'

'Then that's what I suggest we do and when you and I have finished you can relieve Clara and she can come to me in turn.'

Declan looked up from his laptop.

'Is that all right, Clara?'

'Yes, actually, that's fine. I'm not sure my head is quite up to being inspirational at the moment anyway. You go ahead, Trixie, I'm fine here.'

Trixie waved a hand towards the pantry. 'You'll see what I've already made… Apart from that, whatever you want to do will be fine…' And with that she disappeared back through the door in Fiona's wake, leaving Clara somewhat lost for words.

Declan chuckled. 'You'll get to like Fiona, honestly. I realise that she's blunt to the point of rudeness and can leave you gasping for breath, but she has an uncanny knack for putting together brilliant programmes, and more than that, ones which always hit the right spot in the market.'

'Well Trixie obviously doesn't have a problem with her.'

'Fiona responds well to… ambition.' He grinned at her. 'And before you go biting my head off, that's not a criticism of you, or her for that matter, merely an observation that the way Trixie views the prospect of being on television is different from yours.'

Which was exactly what was worrying Clara…

She began to roll up her sleeves and took down an apron from a hook by the pantry door.

'Are you sure I won't be in the way here?' asked Declan. He shuffled some of his papers together so that he occupied less room on the table.

'No, not at all. It will be nice to have some company while I work.' She went to inspect the pantry, returning with several packets of ingredients which she laid out on the counter top. Next to them lay the notebook where all Trixie's recipes were recorded, and she flicked through it to find the one she wanted. Blackberry and apple strudel cake was as good as any to start with.

Perhaps it was simply the act of making cakes but, by the time the first couple were in the oven, Clara's stomach was growling with hunger. It was hardly surprising given that she had probably had very little to eat over the last couple of days, but a quick glance at the clock confirmed that it was definitely lunchtime. She washed her hands and went through to find Trixie; the hour she was supposedly having with Fiona had long since gone.

The door to the study was still firmly closed, and she gave it a couple of quick taps before opening it and walking straight in. Trixie had moved her chair so that she was sitting on the same side of the table as Fiona, and their heads were bent together studying several sheets of paper laid out in a row. Fiona was in full flow and, although Trixie looked up, the conversation continued. After a couple of moments more during which it became clear that Fiona had no intention of even acknowledging her presence, Clara cleared her throat.

'Sorry to interrupt, but I was just wondering about lunch?'

Trixie had just picked up one of the pieces of paper and moved it in response to Fiona's suggestion. She laid it down again, looking back up.

'I really don't mind, Clara,' she said. 'Whatever is easiest? A sandwich will be fine.'

Fiona tapped on the keyboard beside her. 'Oh, absolutely. Although if there's any of that quiche left we had yesterday, I wouldn't say no.'

'Oh, did you like it?' asked Trixie. 'I wasn't sure myself, I thought I'd gone a bit overboard on the Stilton.' She turned back to Clara, smiling. 'Good job I made two then, the second is still in the fridge.'

Clara backed out of the room, feeling her cheeks begin to burn. The conversation hadn't gone at all how she had envisaged. She felt like the maid.

'Would you like a sandwich, Declan?' she asked, returning to the kitchen. 'It would seem I'm making lunch today. There's quiche too apparently.'

'I'd love to stay but I can't, I'm afraid, I have an early breakfast meeting in the morning, so I need to get on the road, back to London.'

'You're leaving?' Somehow she'd thought he would be staying.

He closed the lid of his laptop. 'That rather makes it sound as if you wish I weren't,' he said, with a soft smile. 'In which case, I hope you'll be glad to know I'll be back next week.' He got up and came around the side of the table. 'And in the meantime you are to promise that you'll look after yourself.' His eyes were warm on hers.

She nodded. 'I don't think there's much I'm going to be able to get up to,' she said. 'But yes, I promise not to overdo things…'

She hesitated slightly, an unformed question on her lips.

'Go on.'

'I was wondering about Fiona, I guess. Whether she's going to be here for a while. I thought perhaps that you…'

'I would stay if I could, Clara, but this is a meeting I can't put off, I'm afraid. But you and Fiona will be fine. She's here tomorrow and then that's it, certainly for the time being. I'll have a word with her before I go so that she knows the score, and if you have any problems, you contact me, okay?'

'Okay.'

He started to gather his things together and she crossed to the side, pulling a fresh loaf from the bread bin to hide her disappointment. She was just about to start cutting it when she felt a light touch on her shoulder. As she turned his hand came up to tip her chin and his lips brushed hers. 'I'll be back on Monday.' His voice was barely above a whisper.

As she nodded all she could think about was that Monday was four days away.

★

'Clara!' She spun around to see Tom and Seth in the kitchen doorway, Maddie just behind them.

The two men came across the room, arms outstretched.

'Crikey, anyone would think you hadn't seen me in weeks,' she said, but she grinned as both men hugged her in turn.

'It's felt like it,' replied Seth. 'Yesterday was weird without you. In fact, the whole week has seemed strange, like I've lost track of what day it is.'

It was a good analogy. It was exactly how Clara was feeling. 'I'm certainly having a hard time believing it's Thursday, but never mind, I suspect it will all get back to normal soon.'

'And it's the rain,' commented Tom, 'and the break in routine. This is the first day I haven't been up on the roof in ages. I feel a bit like a fish out of water.' She was aware that he was studying her. 'Are you honestly feeling okay?' he asked.

She had just finished making an enormous pile of sandwiches, and she picked up the bread knife again to cut them into triangles.

'I'm fine. Making lunch and cakes is hardly the same as digging in the garden. Don't worry, I shall ease myself back into things gently.'

Tom moved past her to collect the plates from the dresser. 'Do you need a hand with anything?' he asked. Two platefuls of sandwiches were already in the middle of the table. She had also put together a quick salad, and sliced the remaining quiche as suggested.

'Wait a minute, where's Trixie?' asked Maddie, before she could answer. 'How come you're making lunch?'

'Oh, she's still busy with Fiona,' she replied. 'Actually, Tom, you could give them both a shout for me if you wouldn't mind. Let them know that lunch is ready.'

Maddie gave her a sideways glance, but didn't comment other than to say that she would make some drinks.

'The kettle's boiled,' added Clara. 'Just water the teapot.'

By the time the pot was on the table, Tom had returned, muttering under his breath.

'Well she's a total charmer, isn't she? *Just bring us a selection if you wouldn't mind,* indeed. Who does she think she is?' He picked up a plate and began to add an assortment of sandwiches to it.

'Hang on, Tom,' said Maddie. 'What are you doing?'

He paused, staring at the plate he was holding.

'Yes, I know it's obvious, but who asked you to do that? Was it Fiona?'

He nodded, looking at Seth. There was a sharp note to Maddie's voice that they all knew well.

'Because we eat our lunch in here… together.' She looked at Clara. 'This was exactly why things went wrong before, and I'm sorry but I don't think we should be dictated to like this. Or spoken to the way you obviously have been, Tom.'

'I don't think Fiona means anything by it, Maddie. It's just her manner. Declan did say she comes across as rather abrupt, but to take no notice.'

'Then in that case, we won't. I'm sorry, but in my book if someone sounds like they're being rude, they usually are. If Fiona wants to eat then she can come in here with the rest of us, and the same goes for Trixie. She knows the score.'

Maddie sat down, signalling an end to the conversation. Tom still had the plate in his hand and he looked down at it for a moment, weighing up his options. Then he shrugged and sat down, adding a piece of quiche and taking the plate for himself.

Seth and Clara exchanged glances, but both of them knew there would be no dissuading Maddie once her mind was made up.

'Do we let them know?' asked Seth. 'Or…?'

'Up to you,' replied Maddie, pouring tea into mugs.

'I will then, I think,' he continued. 'Just in case we eat everything.'

Maddie waited until he was gone from the room. 'Coward,' she muttered.

It was a full ten minutes after Seth returned to the kitchen before either Trixie or Fiona appeared, Trixie with a face like thunder. She took a seat opposite Clara.

'Well, I must say this all looks marvellous,' said Fiona, beginning to fill a plate. 'And homemade bread too. I don't know how you do it, Trixie.'

'It takes a lot of constant hard work, doesn't it?' said Maddie. 'But that's why we're all so appreciative of the effort.'

'Oh absolutely,' replied Fiona.

Trixie nodded, and gave a slight smile, but said nothing. Clara's toes were beginning to curl. The atmosphere around the table was awful, although Fiona didn't seem to notice. Either that or she was a very good actress. She kept up a near constant stream of chatter which at least meant none of them had to sit in uncomfortable silence, but Clara knew she was not the only one who was relieved when the plates were cleared.

'That's me, utterly spoiled again,' said Fiona. 'But we really must crack on, Trixie, if you're ready. No point in not finishing now, not when things are coming together so nicely.'

'Have you any idea how long you'll be?' asked Maddie sweetly. 'Only I would imagine that Trixie has a million and one things to do, and must be getting quite anxious by now.'

Trixie had got to her feet, but said nothing, looking awkward, but a touch defiant too.

'I'm afraid I have no idea… except that it would be wise to finish this properly, especially as Clara is doing so well holding the fort meanwhile.'

Fiona breezed from the room with Trixie close behind, leaving Clara staring at their plates and mugs, which they had simply left on the table. She gritted her teeth, but held up her hand to Maddie.

'Don't say a word,' she said.

Tom and Seth excused themselves soon after, leaving Maddie and Clara looking at one another.

'It's not Trixie's fault,' said Clara, trying to lessen how cross she felt. 'Fiona is a bit of a force to be reckoned with and I don't suppose she feels she can say no. Besides, you can't really blame her, she's always been so excited about making this series. It is a bit of a dream come true.'

'And you've been poorly and shouldn't be lumbered with all of this either.'

Clara bit her lip. 'I know. But I don't really mind. It was my decision to come back to work and making cakes isn't exactly strenuous.'

'And what about tea?'

'Well if Trixie isn't finished by then, I'll just make some pasta or something. It won't be anything elaborate.'

Maddie checked her watch. 'I'll stay for a bit,' she said. 'But Seth and I need to go and sort out the new kitchen for the next cottage. If we don't get it ordered soon it won't arrive in time.'

'Then go,' replied Clara. 'Honestly, Maddie, I'll be fine.'

And she was, for about the first hour and a half but, shortly after that, she realised that she would need to sit down for a bit, her legs were beginning to feel wobbly. She poured herself a glass of lemonade and grabbed a cookie from the tin, hoping the sugar would give her a lift and, after a quick break, she ploughed on.

By the time Maddie reappeared at nearly five o'clock, the table was laden with another blackberry and apple cake, four lemon drizzle cakes, a tray of date and walnut slices and two dozen raspberry and white chocolate muffins. Clara was slumped at the kitchen table feeling worse than she had in a long while. The thought of having to start making everyone dinner was a very unwelcome one.

Maddie took one look at her and marched straight back out of the room again. Clara could hear her banging on the study door. She reappeared moments later.

'Right, Trixie will be here in a minute, and I've told Fiona that it's time to leave. I also know that you were supposed to be spending the day with her tomorrow, but I've told her that you're not well enough and that won't be possible.'

Clara looked up in horror, but didn't have the strength to argue. She would probably agonise over it in due course, but right now she didn't give a stuff.

'Now, would you like to stay for something to eat? Or I can get Seth to run you home now if you'd rather.'

The thought of her own quiet, undemanding space was suddenly very appealing. She was just about to answer when there were loud voices in the hall; laughing and somewhat gushing. Then Fiona's head appeared around the door.

'I'll be off now,' she said to Maddie, and then, looking at Clara, 'Goodness, you do look peaky. I'm quite glad we've decided to call off tomorrow – whatever it is you've got, I'm sure I don't want it.' She smiled, showing her teeth. 'I'll be in touch early next week anyway. Trixie and I have pretty much nailed the cookery side of things, so we're making excellent progress.'

She was about to duck back out again when something else occurred to her.

'Oh, and whilst I've obviously turned off my computer, I have left certain things still out on the desk, to ensure continuity when I return. So much easier than packing everything away again. I'd appreciate it if they are left exactly as they are now.'

Maddie's mouth was hanging open and Clara was sure hers was too, but neither of them said a word. The voices in the hallway continued for a moment before Trixie reappeared, having closed the door behind Fiona. She collapsed into a chair, groaning.

'I am so tired,' she said. 'Fiona is a bloody slave driver!' She was grinning from ear to ear. 'I'll tell you something though, what that woman doesn't know about television isn't worth knowing. I've learnt so much just from being with her for one afternoon, and I don't think

I realised before what an incredible opportunity we'd been given, but we really have.'

'Excellent,' replied Maddie. 'I'm sure that all makes us feel heaps better at having our day utterly disrupted and being spoken to like a piece of dirt on the floor.'

The grin dropped from Trixie's face.

'I'm sorry,' continued Maddie, 'but however good she is at her job, she really needs to work on her bedside manner. This isn't how we do things at Joy's Acre and, as someone who found that out the hard way, I'm not prepared to put up with it.'

'She's really not that bad,' argued Trixie. 'Not when you get to know her. But she's very competitive. I guess you have to be in this sort of industry and I don't think she realises how she comes across at times. I'm just glad she's fighting our corner, that's all.'

'Hmmm, well, we'll see. The jury's still out as far as I'm concerned.' Maddie looked across at Clara. 'Come on, let's get you home… unless you want to stay for tea?'

Clara shook her head. The kitchen had suddenly lost its charm. 'I'm not really hungry,' she said. 'I think I'd rather get going.'

Trixie looked around her as if suddenly noticing that the table was covered in cakes. 'Oh. You've made lemon drizzle…? Only there's a batch of these already in the freezer. I made some yesterday evening…'

A sudden rush of heat hit Clara. 'And how was I supposed to know that? For goodness' sake… You said to check the pantry, which I did. You didn't say anything about stuff being in the freezer, so if there are too many of one type of cake don't blame me because you didn't give proper instructions.'

The two women glared at one another for a moment, and then Trixie suddenly bowed her head.

'I'm sorry, Clara. I'm just knackered. I spoke without thinking.'

'So am I, Trixie!' Her voice came out louder than she wanted, and she probably ought to have lowered her tone, but she'd had enough for the day. 'Perhaps I shouldn't have come in today after all, but I thought I was okay. However, I have just spent the entire afternoon making cakes, plus lunch, I might add.'

'I do know that,' said Trixie. 'But you couldn't get in the garden with all the rain anyway, so what else were you going to do?'

Clara stared at her.

'That is hardly the point, and well you know it,' said Maddie.

'No? Well, what is the point then?' Trixie fired back. 'I thought we were supposed to help one another out, but it doesn't seem that way from where I'm standing. I've been busy too, you know, trying to put together something with Fiona that will really make this programme a success. I think we might have succeeded as well, not that anyone seems at all interested.' Her eyes flashed as she warmed to her theme.

'You're quite happy for me to do all the work to get this thing off the ground, because you don't want to do it at all, do you, Clara? That's what this is really all about. And yet, I'll still work my arse off to make this series something we can all be proud of, something that will benefit us all, but it won't be enough, will it? Because all you have to do is click your fingers and Declan will make sure you get all the best bits anyway. God, I am such an idiot!'

Clara's cheeks were burning. *How could Trixie say such a thing?* Just because Clara didn't love the whole idea of the filming, or the experience of it, didn't mean she wouldn't put in her fair share of work. For God's sake, she had even agreed to do it in the first place because of Trixie. And now she was having it all thrown back in her face.

'How dare you! I've done my best today, just like I do every day, even when I don't particularly feel like it. Today was one of those days, and yet I still helped as much as I could, *and* without so much as a please or thank you, I might add. Take a look around, Trixie, those cakes didn't get there by magic, even if they are the wrong bloody kind!' She got wearily to her feet.

'And don't you *ever* suggest that I'm calling in favours from Declan again. That's low, Trixie, even for you.'

Chapter 20

Megan blew on her hands to warm them.

It was the penultimate round of the blacksmithing competition, and they had started early. The last few days of rain had left the air damp and chill and, until she started work properly, Megan was feeling the cold. Perhaps it was nervous excitement, or just plain nerves.

The grounds of the Hall were thronged with people, even more than on the previous Saturdays, and there was a palpable air of expectation. Things were getting serious now; the competition was hotting up, even if the air temperature wasn't.

Megan took a hairband from the pocket of her dungarees and began to tie up her hair, her mind focused on what she needed to achieve during the day. Whatever else happened, she must not let her thoughts dwell on Julian and whatever he was up to. He'd been sniffing around already this morning, on the pretence of being friendly, but he didn't fool Megan; she knew him far too well to be taken in by his false charm. It was just a shame that Liam couldn't see it that way. She knew he hadn't believed her claims that Julian had pinched one of her pieces in the last round of the competition, and that was something else she was trying not to think about either. Even though she had understood his point of view, she couldn't help but feel let down…

'Morning!'

Megan looked up to see Clara's sunny smile and a very welcome mug of tea. She took it gratefully.

'It's a shame the weather is so rubbish, but how are you feeling today?'

'Nervous,' replied Megan, returning the smile. 'Even though this is the round that I've been most looking forward to. And I'm going to say it, although it will probably prove to be the kiss of death, but the one I think I'll do best in.' She cupped her hands around her mug trying to warm them.

'It's interpretive, you see, more of a freestyle round. It relies more on artistic and design skills, which is what I love about it.'

Clara nodded. 'I can see how that would suit you,' she said. 'The piece you showed me earlier is stunning.'

Megan blushed a little. 'Thank you,' she said, knowing that Clara was being honest. 'That's the second aspect to today's round, simply to showcase one of your original designs, something that you've already completed in your own time. I'm just waiting to hear what today's theme is and then I can get started on the first.'

'So you don't know what you're going to be making today?' Clara frowned. 'How can you prepare for that?'

'That's actually what I like about it,' said Megan, taking a sip of her tea. 'You have to think on your feet. All we get given is a theme... so in previous years that's been "dance" or "circles", for example, and you can make whatever you like as long as it fits the theme. You're awarded the highest number of marks for how well you interpret it.'

'But what if you can't think of anything?'

Megan smiled. 'Then I guess I'm going home,' she said.

'No, not you,' Clara replied. 'I've got a feeling you're going right to the top today. And if it's any comfort, Seth thinks so too.'

'Seth?'

'Yes. Don't tell him I said anything, but when you went to unload the rest of your things this morning, I dragged him over to look at what you've already made. His first comment was, *Wow*, and the second was, *I wonder if she'll sell it to us to have in the gardens at Joy's Acre?* So you see, I'm not the only one who thinks it's amazing.'

Megan nearly choked on her drink. 'Was he being serious?' she spluttered. 'He might really want it?'

'I don't think there's any "really" about it,' she replied. 'He definitely wasn't joking. So, whatever happens today, you remember that. You're brilliant at what you do even if things don't go as planned.'

'Aw…' It was such a lovely thing to say, Megan felt genuinely touched. She put down her mug and leaned forward to give Clara an impromptu hug. 'I shall be fine just as long as Julian keeps out of my way, although I struggle to see how even he can scupper today. There's no way he can pinch anything, which will make life a lot easier for Liam at least.'

She saw the momentary flicker of hesitation cross Clara's face, but then her expression changed to one of sympathy, and she knew that Clara wouldn't ignore her silent prompt.

'Don't be so hard on yourself, Megan,' she said. 'This competition means the world to you, anyone can see that. You're bound to feel emotional.'

'But I gave Liam such a hard time. He was only trying to help.' It was a tussle that Megan had had going with herself all week. On the one hand, she had been hurt that Liam couldn't just accept her word about Julian's guilt, but she also suspected that she had overreacted a little. She could be a moody cow at times.

Clara smiled. 'And he's a grown man, Megan, he'll cope. Besides, no one knows you better than Liam, I'm sure he understands how you were feeling.'

Megan ran a hand through her ponytail, wondering whether she had the guts to voice to Clara what was really worrying her.

'I'm worried he'll go off me.' There, she had said it. 'We're supposed to be thinking about moving in together and all we've done this week is bicker... I'm sure he's stayed out of my way because of it. It's only because I'm so stressed about this final design though. I've been working on it all week, chopping and changing bits, it's been driving me nuts. Then, last night, I thought I'd finally nailed it, and he came home really late and barely looked at it.' She bit her lip. 'Sorry, Clara... I'm probably just being melodramatic.'

She was studying Clara's face carefully to try and gauge her reaction and was surprised to see a rather wary expression appear. It disappeared in an instant, however, and Clara beamed a smile at her, pulling her in for another hug.

'What are you like?' she tutted. 'Liam is mad about you. He was having kittens last week he was so worried about you.' She pulled away to look at Megan. 'In fact, if you must know he did say that he would be glad when the competition is over, not because of anything you've done, but because he doesn't want to share you with anyone else and is looking forward to having more time with you.' She gave a satisfied nod. 'You can't get much clearer than that.'

Megan smiled gratefully. She knew she was being overly anxious, but she couldn't seem to help herself; this week was so important, for both of them, and their futures.

'Then I'll stop being stupid,' she said, pulling a face, 'and get on and win the thing.'

'That sounds like a good plan,' came a voice from somewhere behind Clara.

As she tried to peer past her, a man took a step to one side and came into the main area of the forge. It was the judge who had stood up for her during the first round of the competition. His big bushy beard made him instantly recognisable.

'Miss Forrester.' He nodded a greeting, smiling. 'We have a duty to inform all competitors of the theme for today's piece of work at exactly the same time, so if I might interrupt for a moment?'

Megan cleared her throat, glancing at Clara. 'Yes, of course.'

'You are required to produce a design today which complements the theme of "water". There is no restriction on the size of the piece, and it may be either functional or purely decorative, although it can of course be both. Marks will be awarded for the interpretation of the theme, the complexity of design elements and how well these have been executed. You may begin whenever you are ready.'

Megan stared after him as he flashed her a quick grin and left as suddenly as he had arrived. She felt a surge of excitement swell inside her.

'I don't believe it!' she whispered urgently. 'They couldn't have picked a better topic for me.'

Clara glanced around her before grinning broadly. 'I know! Oh, I'm so pleased for you.' She looked at her watch. 'Right, I'm going to leave you to it. You've got a watery masterpiece to create.'

*

Clara was pleased that her comments seemed to have had the desired effect. She'd hardly seen Megan since last week's competition; admittedly Clara hadn't been at Joy's Acre for some of the time, but she knew that Megan had been at Liam's for several days, working hard. With everything that had gone on this week, she had almost forgotten about seeing Liam with another woman, but this morning, back at the competition site, it had been hard to ignore.

This week was make or break for Megan and, knowing that, Clara had been determined that nothing should spoil her mood – which definitely meant there should be no mention of what Liam may or may not have been up to. She had nearly had a heart attack when Megan brought up the subject of their relationship out of the blue like that, but she was sure that her replies had been convincing enough. Megan's reaction had certainly seemed to suggest it. Clara hadn't lied to her, but it still felt awkward saying those things when there was still any degree of doubt in her own mind.

Megan beamed and drained the last of her tea. 'Right, I must go and get set up. I'll see you later.'

Thoughtfully, Clara watched her go before turning her attention to her own tasks.

'Penny for them...?'

'Morning, Maddie.' Clara sighed. 'Sorry, I was miles away. I'm just being silly again... overthinking things.'

She received a sympathetic smile. 'Are things no better?'

'I wasn't actually thinking about Trixie,' replied Clara, 'but no, they're not.' They were back in the refreshment tent, getting set up for the day, and she straightened a plate of cakes on the table in front of her. 'I barely got a hello when I collected these this morning. She was busy... but...'

'Not like her?'

Clara shook her head. 'And I don't know what I've done... not really. I know I got impatient and I probably shouldn't have taken offence over the stupid cake thing the other day but, something was off. I couldn't quite put my finger on it, whether it was just the whole

Fiona thing or not, but it didn't feel like that somehow. And then there was all that rubbish about Declan and me.'

'It's been a strange week, in lots of ways, and I think we all feel a bit out of sorts. I'm sure things will right themselves once we all settle down again.'

'I hope so… yes, I'm sure they will.' Clara bit her lip, wondering whether to continue and then deciding not to.

Maddie cocked her head. 'Anyway, if you weren't thinking about Trixie, what were you thinking?'

'Oh, I've really excelled myself this time.' She stared out of the marquee doorway as if a solution might magically make itself known. 'When the film crew first arrived on Tuesday and ate through our supplies of bacon, I popped into town to buy some more. Just as I was leaving I saw Liam sitting at a table in the window of the tearoom with another woman.' She picked up her apron and began to tie it around her waist. 'And I know I'm being stupid by reading anything into it, but the woman's cleavage was practically on the table, Maddie. It's been preying on my mind ever since.'

Maddie's eyes widened. 'Oh, I hate stuff like that. It's probably innocent enough…'

'I know, and ordinarily I would have told Trixie about it and she'd have told me not to be so bloody stupid and I'd have thought no more of it.'

'Except that you haven't told her.'

'No. And of course, Liam will be here today, although I haven't seen him yet. I'm terrified I'll give him a funny look or something, and he'll guess there's something up and there'll be an almighty row and—'

She stopped as Maddie touched her arm. 'And nothing…' she chastised gently. 'Except that you will tie yourself in even more knots thinking up ever more horrific scenarios, when in fact all that will happen is that we'll serve tea and cake the whole day. And you're probably only thinking this because you know that Megan feels uncertain about her relationship with Liam—'

'What?' Clara stared at her in astonishment. 'When did she tell you that? I didn't think it was anything serious. More just anxiety because she's been really stressed of late and taking it out on Liam.'

Maddie groaned. 'Oh, now I've gone and stuck my massive flipping foot in it too. I didn't mean that how it sounded.' She took a deep breath. 'All it was, was a passing remark Megan made the other week when we were talking about her winning the competition and what it would mean for her future. She happened to mention that in all the time she's been away, she's longed for nothing more than to be able to come back and set up home with Liam, but she wasn't sure he was ready for that yet.'

'But that's, that's…' Clara trailed off, unable to find the words.

'A massive assumption on my part,' said Maddie. 'Forget I even said anything. It was during the competition last weekend when Megan thought someone had pinched one of her pieces. She thought she was going out and was having bit of a meltdown. It was just one of those things you say when it seems as if everything is going wrong. I'm sure she didn't mean anything by it. And she was happy enough by the end of the day.'

Clara gave her a sideways glance. 'Even so, I'm not setting foot outside of this tent today. You can take all the teas round to the competitors this week. I'll just stay here and speak only when I'm spoken to. That way I can't possibly invent any other stupid dramas that aren't really dramas at all.'

She rolled her eyes at Maddie, implying she was joking of course, but both knew that her concerns over both Liam and Trixie were very real, and neither of them were about to go away any time soon.

★

As it was, Clara's request almost came true, for the morning at least. The stream of visitors to the refreshment tent was steady and she and Maddie hardly stepped foot out from behind the table. It wasn't until nearer lunchtime when Seth appeared that she managed to slip out for some fresh air, leaving him and Maddie to hold the fort for a few minutes.

She wanted to go and view the entrants' work which was already on display in the judges' tent, but instead, at the last minute, she carried on across the courtyard to the other side and headed into the walled garden where the huge greenhouse lay. The plants that were left over from making up the displays now decorating the Hall grounds were still there, and she slipped inside to collect a watering can to fill from the outside tap.

The day still carried a chill, but the gloomy morning had lifted, giving way to bright sunlight which now shone down, warming the walls of the garden and bringing a golden glow to the rich colours surrounding her. Inside the greenhouse it was warmer still and she spent a few happy minutes removing some of the spent blooms and giving the pots a much-needed drink.

Everything here was on a much grander scale than back at Joy's Acre, but it still held all the same allure that Clara felt back at the farm: the all-pervading sense of peace that was always present in the garden, a permanency – even though it was forever changing – and the singular feeling of rightness about a place which was abundant in nature.

Agatha's gardens might not yet be that familiar to her, but she could still feel their promise. She stood in the sunshine, but despite feeling the warmth she gave a sudden shiver. In all the time she had been at

Joy's Acre she had never given any thought to what might come *after*. She had never had to think of a time when things might be different for some reason, if she were no longer there… But, she realised, this week had given her a glimpse of what that could be like, and the thought of it was like a sudden pain through her heart. Without warning, tears filled her eyes, and she put out a hand on the bench to steady herself. Too much was changing, and Clara felt as if she were being carried downstream with nothing to cling onto to halt her passage. If she couldn't stop herself, she would end up in a place far from home…

She looked out through the windows of the greenhouse and into the space beyond, letting her thoughts settle. The garden was a place of nurture and growth, and of opportunity too. The plants and flowers it contained often found a way to flourish in the most unlikely situations, and this tenacity to survive even during the poorest of conditions always gave her hope that her life could be the same. Throughout her illness, she had gained huge strength from these qualities and had planted them deep inside of her. They remained there, dormant in the quiet dark until she had need of them, and then she would unearth them and feed them, exposing them to the sunlight and watch them grow. She rubbed her fingers together, which were slightly sticky from sap where she had pulled off the dying heads of some of the flowers. Now was one of those times, and with this realisation also came a clear conviction. Clara wasn't about to let her garden die, or anything else she cared about for that matter.

The water from the outside tap was cold, but she rinsed her fingers beneath it, drying them on her apron. Then she made her way purposefully towards the judging tent. She wanted to see all the competitors' artwork, but more than anything she wanted to see the piece that Megan had made again.

Designed to be the centrepiece for a fountain, it stood perhaps three feet tall, a stand of bulrushes waving in the breeze, wrought from solid iron. Tall leaves rippled around its side and here and there a fish leapt in a shower of droplets. On one side a tiny bird feasted on a seed head. The detail was intricate and exquisitely executed.

Close up, the piece was spectacular, but standing back to admire it from a slight distance, Clara could see Megan's true artistry and skill. The sculpture had movement and balance; it flowed, and came to life, no matter which angle you viewed it from. It was a very clever piece of design indeed.

Despite having been absent from the refreshment tent a little while, Clara took a few more minutes to look at the work from the other blacksmiths. They differed hugely; one was a bench, another a shield, while a third was merely decorative. It was hard to say which was better or worse than the next, but Clara wasn't really interested in that, she had simply wanted to satisfy her curiosity, and now that she had, she was certain that her instincts were right – whatever the result of the competition, she knew that Megan's future and that of Joy's Acre would touch at various points along the way. And if Seth wasn't already convinced of that fact, Clara would just have to make sure that he was.

She was about to leave the tent when she was practically forced to one side by five or six men who all entered at the same time, and were certainly not about to stop for anyone. They nearly all carried pints of beer and, judging by the rowdy nature of their conversation, had consumed several already. It wasn't this, however, that made Clara stare after them as they passed. The one closest to her was particularly strident.

'Yeah well, what can you expect? The whole thing is probably fixed so that she wins. It's bloody women's lib going one step too far, is what it is. Are they afraid she'll cry and stamp her foot if she loses?' There was a loud shout of laughter from the others.

There was only one person they could possibly be talking about, and as they made their way across the tent, sure enough they came to stand by Megan's work. Clara paused for a moment, unsure what to do until she spied one of the judges circling the room and keeping an eye on the exhibits. She could still hear the men's raised voices and it was unfortunate that they weren't able to keep their opinions to themselves, but as long as no actual harm befell the display, what could anyone do?

She hurried from the marquee and crossed the distance back to the refreshment tent, where she was rather disconcerted to find Liam standing right by their table talking to Seth.

'It's an out-and-out coincidence obviously, but whether folks will see it like that, I don't know.'

Seth shrugged. 'There's not much I can do about that.' His face looked anxious but he smiled when he saw her.

'Hi, Clara,' added Liam, and her smile in reply felt a little odd given the echoes of her earlier conversation with Maddie.

'Is everything okay?' she asked.

'Well Megan's having a brilliant day, but I have a horrible feeling it's going to end on a sour note,' said Liam. He took in Clara's raised eyebrows. 'There's a bunch of lads going around spreading a few rumours,' he explained. 'I've no idea who they are, but they're being very vocal about Megan. I think they've been on the booze all day too, which doesn't help. Their argument is not altogether reasoned.'

Clara shot a glance at Seth. 'I think I've just seen them,' she said. 'In the judging tent.'

Seth nodded. 'Yeah, they seem to be doing circuits.'

'So, what's their issue?' she asked.

Liam pulled a face. 'Long story short, they think Megan's been cheating – that she knew about today's theme in advance.'

Clara frowned. 'But why would they think that?'

'Because the theme the competitors have been given is "water"...'

'But I still don't...' And then the penny dropped as Clara remembered what the piece was that Clara had brought with her. 'She's not making another fountain though, surely? There wouldn't be time for that.'

Liam shook his head. 'No, an umbrella stand actually, but you can see how it looks. She isn't copying the motifs from her fountain exactly but she is using some of them – they're the perfect decoration for her design. Plus of course, once she's finished today, the two pieces when exhibited side by side will really complement one another when the final judging takes place.'

'Oh... I see what you mean.' She sighed. There always seemed to be something going wrong. 'It's still ridiculous to suggest that she's been cheating though. I was there when the judge came around to inform everyone of today's theme. He specifically said that they were telling everyone at the same time so there's no way she could have known in advance.'

'Well, yes it is ridiculous. Of course, it is,' added Seth. 'Except that when you factor in that Megan has been staying at Joy's Acre and that I'm involved with the organisation of the competition, you can begin to see where these idiots might have got their ideas from.'

Clara thought for a minute. 'But you said that Megan was having a good day, so presumably she's happy with what she's done today, and just doesn't care about the rest?'

'She doesn't know about it,' muttered Liam. 'I don't think the lads are really out to cause trouble, they're just obnoxious; got nothing better to do on a Saturday afternoon, so fortunately, as far as I know, nothing has been said in her vicinity. What worries me though is what might happen around judging time... When the other competitors will probably get wind of it.'

She exchanged a look with Seth. 'Can't you go and speak to the organisers?' she said.

'I'm just about to,' replied Seth. 'But the judges are nothing to do with the organisation, they're from the Worshipful Company of Blacksmiths. They judge numerous competitions across the country and throughout the year.'

'And speaking to them might give entirely the wrong impression,' said Liam.

Clara could see how that might be the case. 'For goodness' sake, this is stupid. Who would have thought that a competition like this could cause so much upset? First there was last week's problem when one of Megan's scrolls went missing and now this...'

'I guess it's what happens whenever passion for something is involved. Tensions are bound to run high.'

And that, thought Clara, *is at the heart of many a problem, not just Megan's...*

'It's just so frustrating,' added Liam. 'Megan has had such a good week. You should see my dining room table, it's littered with drawings and sketches, notes and plans. She's put so much effort into her final design for the gate, and biased I might be, but her overall idea is inspired. I can't believe she won't get the opportunity to put it into practice.'

'Then we have to trust that she will.'

Liam glanced at his watch. 'We'll find out soon enough.'

Chapter 21

'Declan, you really don't need to intervene. In fact, it's probably best if you didn't.'

It was now Monday and Clara had been trying to avoid him since he'd arrived about an hour ago, but now he had her cornered in the kitchen and there was nowhere for her to go.

'Why? Because you think this is about us? That I'm only picking this up because of how I feel about you...' He cleared his throat. 'I'd be lying if that wasn't a consideration, but it's not simply a question of intervening for that reason, it's also because of the wider implications. This *is* my show, and I do have a say over how it's put together.'

She looked at the floor, avoiding his gaze. 'Perhaps you misunderstood,' she said. 'I'm quite happy for Trixie to be filming today, and tomorrow, and the day after, so I don't actually want you to intervene. In any case this would seem to make more sense given the time that Trixie has spent with Fiona; they obviously have things well in hand.'

She looked up, wondering how best to phrase what she had to say next.

'And it was me who cancelled the day I was supposed to spend with Fiona, so in that regard my part in the show is far from being worked out. Fiona gave me a list of what she thought should be included in the gardening sections of each show, but there's been no discussion over it, nothing has been finalised. It's much more logical to concentrate on Trixie's role just now. I'm sure we'll get to mine... at some point.'

Declan took a step closer.

'Clara, this isn't the vision we had for this venture, and both of us know it. I'm not quite sure why...' He broke off, and she realised he was just as uncomfortable as she was. 'And I thought after last week, when I stayed at yours... that things were, moving in a certain direction... But now, well, you seem a little distant.'

She swallowed. 'I don't mean to be, it's just that I'm finding all of this a little hard to reconcile. How I feel about you, and how I feel about the filming...' She gave a rueful smile. 'And I'm absolutely rubbish at explaining it.'

He held her look for a moment and his expression changed to one of understanding.

'I think I would be as well,' he agreed. 'It's a strange thing for me too. In fact, I'm finding all this a little unnerving even. I'm a businessman first and foremost, I have absolutely no trouble speaking my mind, taking decisions and behaving in a forthright and no-nonsense manner. Except that when it comes to you, and how I think about you, I feel... a bit like a six-year-old, if I'm honest. I've never felt this way before, Clara.'

She gave a tiny nod of acknowledgment, the butterflies in her stomach suddenly taking flight.

'So why don't we take it one thing at a time?' continued Declan. 'And maybe start with the easiest thing... how you feel about the filming.'

'I'll do it,' she blurted out. 'It's not that. I'm not going to let anyone down or anything, but it's not me, Declan, it never has been. I realised that over the weekend and I also realised that it's different for Trixie. You've seen how she's been over the last few days, she's so excited by this, and she's a good friend. If this is what she wants to do, I can't stand in her way, and even though the thought of what this might lead to scares me if I'm honest, there's no point in worrying about that now. I'll fill in the gaps later on, I promise, and when the time comes I'll do my best, but for the time being I'm happy to let Trixie take the lead in the filming, I really am. I'm sorry, Declan, I know that's probably not what you wanted to hear.'

'It's not...' he sighed. 'But I do understand.' He screwed up his face. 'It's just that when I think how good both of you looked in that first rough video clip we saw, I can't help but want to keep all of that going.' He gave a sheepish smile. 'Sorry.'

Clara held out her hand. 'The trouble is, that isn't what we have now, is it? Things have changed in such a short space of time. Trixie's dyed her hair for one thing and, it's ridiculous, but it doesn't look like her any more, not the Trixie I know anyway. And then there's Fiona. I know you think she's good at her job, and I'm sure she is, but the balance has tilted somewhat.' She shook her head. 'Although, that's probably my fault, I think I let it... because of how I've been feeling about the whole thing, but now I feel awful because I'm not sure that you're even going to get the programme you wanted...'

She hung her head, but to her surprise Declan looked as if a lightbulb had just gone on over his. He smiled, and then entwining his fingers with hers, he pulled her closer. And closer still.

'Oh, Clara,' he murmured into her hair. 'I've had my eye well and truly taken off the ball, haven't I? Which is the most marvellous, wonderful and surprising thing that's ever happened to me, but I've been such an idiot...'

Clara felt relief wash over her as she relaxed into his arms. The way she'd been feeling had brought guilt too; but she couldn't have carried on without saying anything, that wasn't fair to anyone, least of all her, and now perhaps things between her and Trixie would get back to where they were before all this happened.

'I think we both have,' she murmured back, 'because I realised something else over the weekend too.'

He pulled away to look at her.

'I get scared of things changing and so my natural instinct is to push them away, even when it's something I want... The gardens here are a part of me, so I have to be honest and say that I don't think I could ever bear to be away from them. But, if someone else was okay with that...'

'Is this the bit where you tell me how you feel about me?'

She smiled. 'I think it might be.' And then she smiled again, feeling suddenly uplifted, but instead of continuing to speak she closed the gap between them, and her lips found his. Even though no words came out, she found she could convey exactly what she was feeling after all.

'Is that okay?' she whispered after a moment, 'because I'd very much like to let that other person into my life...'

'It's very okay,' he replied, kissing her back, and then almost immediately giving a slight groan. He pulled away, laughing, and ran a hand through his hair. 'Look at me, I'm a complete wreck... I have to go and have sensible conversations with people, and Fiona is going to take one look and make absolute mincemeat of me.'

Clara raised both hands, laughing. 'Then I'd better leave you alone,' she said.

They stared at one another for a moment, eyes dancing, and then Declan suddenly sobered, looking at his watch.

'Bugger, I need to go,' he said, reaching out to touch a finger to her cheek. 'But you are not to worry about things, under any circumstances.

I'll have a word with Fiona, and I promise we'll get it all sorted so that everyone is happy.'

He straightened his jacket, pulling his shoulders back slightly, before grinning and walking out of the room.

Clara watched him go, a huge smile on her face, and she stayed that way for several seconds, before standing up straight herself and looking around her as if wondering what to do first. *Goodness it's hot in here.*

*

It wasn't until Clara had wandered outside again that she remembered that she had originally gone into the kitchen to get the keys to the pick-up truck. Given the chaos over the catering arrangements the last time the film crew was on site, it had been agreed in advance of today's visit that neither Clara nor Trixie had time to attend to them as well. So, if they wanted food, they either brought it with them, or went out for it.

Therefore, as soon as breakfast was finished, Trixie had been whisked away to begin filming, leaving Clara with a free morning. The day was overcast, but dry, and there was one job which was becoming quite urgent. Doubling back to collect her keys, Clara was soon on the road, and moments later she turned in through the gates of Summersmeade Hall.

Parking in the rear courtyard as before, she could hear the rhythmic sound of wood being chopped as soon as she opened her car door. Seth was steadily working his way through a pile of wood in one corner of the courtyard and she went over to speak to him.

'That's a nice sight,' she said.

He looked up. 'What, a hot, sweaty bloke who looks completely knackered?' he asked, resting his axe on top on the chopping block.

'No.' She grinned. 'The firewood. I love the smell, and it's such an evocative image of the autumn, isn't it? The changing of the seasons… the coming of the colder weather, hot chocolate, big woolly sweaters, roaring fires of an evening…'

Seth regarded her as if she was deranged. 'If you say so…' he replied. 'Or possibly sore shoulders and arms, blisters, splinters…'

She tutted, knowing full well that Seth was only teasing her. He loved it just as much as she did.

'Time to build the fire pit at Joy's Acre too, don't forget about that.'

She nodded. 'How are things this morning?'

'Fine, I think,' he replied, straightening up. 'But there's a definite edge to the atmosphere. The competition was one thing, but this commission malarkey has taken it to a new level, and it's suddenly got very serious.'

Clara looked over to the archway which led through to where the blacksmiths would be busy with their final pieces. They had only a week to work on their gate, and so the Hall had been opened back up to them so that they could spend as much time as they wanted here. It was unlikely that they would finish but, whatever they had managed to produce at the end of this time, together with their detailed plans for the design, would be judged at the end of the week. She could only imagine the task that lay ahead of them all, and she wondered how Megan was feeling.

'I'm not sure whether to go and say hello, or not,' she said. 'I might be in the way.'

Seth nodded. 'I'm sure Megan would love to see you, but I don't think you'll get much conversation out of her to be honest. She had an extremely focused look on her face when I popped through earlier.'

She bit her lip. 'Perhaps I'll leave it. I wouldn't want to break her concentration.'

'I take it you've come for the plants?' said Seth. 'Only Agatha, bless her, is determined to do her bit for morale and has declared that elevenses will be served. I said I'd give her a hand to take them across to everyone so, if you're still here then, you can come with me and say hello.'

Clara nodded. 'Sounds like a plan,' she said.

She was about to go through into the garden when Seth spoke again. 'Will you be okay? Shifting everything, I mean.'

'I'll be *fine*,' she replied, smiling. 'Seth, I've been lugging plants around for years with no ill-effects.'

'I know, but…'

'But, nothing.' She touched his arm. 'Except thank you.'

He dipped his head in acknowledgment. Their friendship was such that neither of them needed to say any more. Seth would continue to look out for her, even when she was feeling fine, and she would continue to be grateful to him.

He glanced in the direction of the enormous pile of wood. 'Thank the Lord,' he said. 'I haven't got time to be running around after feeble girls…'

She stuck out her tongue before moving away towards the archway that led into the garden. When she looked back he was grinning, and she waved an airy hand.

It was really generous of Agatha to let her have some of the left-over plants for the garden at Joy's Acre. She had said it was the least she could do considering all the help that Clara had given her with the garden recently, but even so, Clara was well aware that they would have cost a considerable amount of money. They would, however, transform the front garden of the latest cottage that Tom was working on, and if she got a move on, she might even get the job finished today.

She wandered through the greenhouse to the store room at its rear and brought out the wheelbarrow, pushing it alongside the benches where the plants were sitting. It wouldn't take her long to select what she needed, as the planting plan for the garden had already been worked out in her head, but she took a few minutes to choose the right specimens before placing several of them into the barrow.

Backing out of the greenhouse carefully, she had only just manoeuvred through the door when she became aware of the sound of hurried footsteps from behind her. She dropped the handles down, and turned to see Megan running down the path towards her. Even from a distance Clara could see that she was upset.

'Megan, slow down,' she said, in response to her garbled greeting. 'I didn't understand a word of that. What on earth is the matter?'

'I didn't know where else to come,' said Megan again. 'Seth said you were in here.'

'Why, what's happened? Is someone hurt?'

She shook her head impatiently. 'No, nothing like that.'

She looked like she was about to burst into tears and Clara took her arm, leading her into the centre of the garden where the fountain stood, long since dry. She pulled her down onto the bench.

'Come on now, what's this all about, Megan?'

A sudden dread filled Clara. What if someone had told her about Liam? Or somehow she had found out by herself... Perhaps he had even confessed? She rooted up her sleeve for a clean tissue; she usually had one on her, and she had a feeling Megan was going to need it. But instead of the tears Clara expected, Megan drew herself up, jutting out her chin.

'The out-and-out bastard!' she spat. 'I don't know how he thinks he's going to get away with this. Not content with making my life a misery for years he has to resort to *cheating* now as well. I always knew he was an utter scumbag. I've got more talent in my little finger that he has in his—'

She stopped suddenly, her face crumpling. She stared at Clara in horror.

'What am I saying? Of course he's going to get away with it… who on earth is going to believe me? I'm just a stupid girl who should know better and they'll all be laughing at me, in fact, I bet they are already…' Tears were beginning to well up in earnest and, as Clara watched, one spilled over and ran down Megan's cheek. She dashed it away angrily.

Clara was confused. Why would Megan still be with Liam if he'd made her life a misery? And apart from that, why would anyone be laughing at her now? It didn't make any sense.

'I'm sure it's just a misunderstanding,' she said gently. 'Sometimes it's easy to see things that aren't really there and jump to the wrong conclusion.' She reached out her arm to touch Megan's sleeve again. 'Do you actually have any proof?' she asked.

'Yes, of course I have proof!' retaliated Megan. 'I know what he's planning. It was all there in black and white.'

Clara drew her eyebrows together. 'I'm not sure I follow…'

'Julian,' said Megan, her exasperation showing.

Clara felt relief wash over her. 'Oh, I see… Sorry, I thought you were talking about Liam for a moment. I got confused.'

'Why would I be talking about Liam?' asked Megan. It was her turn to look puzzled.

'No reason,' said Clara quickly, her heart beginning to beat a little faster. She had come very close to putting her foot in it. 'Just ignore me, I told you I was confused.' And then she realised what Megan had said.

'Hang on, Megan, I'm sorry. Did you just say that Julian has cheated? Why? What's he done?'

'Only bloody gone and stolen my design for the gate. And don't try and tell me that I'm imagining things, or that it's just a coincidence, because it's not.' She glared at Clara, defying her to argue.

Clara opened her mouth to speak, and then closed it again. Megan really did seem adamant, but Clara didn't understand how something like that could have happened in the first place.

'And you said you have proof…?'

'Yes, I've seen his design. He was that bloody cock-a-hoop about it, just like he always is, arrogant git. He wanted me to see it, didn't he? Just so that I'd know there was no point me even continuing with the competition.'

Despite not knowing a huge amount about Julian, Clara knew enough to know that this was quite possibly the case.

'But possibly it's just that it's similar. Don't gates all look a bit alike when they're sketched out?'

Megan's look was scathing, and Clara was left in no doubt how ridiculous her last statement was.

'His design isn't just similar to mine, it's *identical*… Okay, so it looks as if he's changed a couple of small things, but there's no way it's coincidence.'

It was obvious that Megan had already made up her mind about Julian's guilt, and no matter how many plausible alternatives Clara offered, none of them would be believed. But still, Clara felt the need to offer them because there was also something else to consider here…

'But did Julian actually show you his design? That wouldn't be normal, surely; I would have thought you'd all be quite anxious to keep what you were doing under wraps.'

'Well to some extent you can't help seeing what other people are doing, but usually no one's particularly interested, you're far too busy with your own creation to worry about someone else's. Julian likes to flaunt what he's doing, he always has, but today he seemed especially smug, even for him. He actually called me over as I walked past, saying his phone had died on him and he wanted to know the time. Of course, he had all the pages with his design sketches laid out beside him so I could clearly see them.'

Clara thought for a moment.

'But he didn't make any reference to them?'

'No, none. And I didn't say anything either, I'm not that daft. It still didn't stop him from boasting about how confident he was, and how he didn't think the standard of the competition was up to much this year.'

'But he only scraped through by the skin of his teeth in the round where your scroll went missing!'

'I know… but none of that will count in the final judging, Clara. It will be up to the National Trust judges to decide which design wins this commission. I might as well quit now.'

'Oh, no, you won't,' said Clara. 'Don't you dare give him the satisfaction. You have just as much chance of winning as he does, don't forget that.'

Megan pulled a face. 'I'd like to believe that, but faced with two identical designs, what are the judges going to think?' She heaved a sigh. 'Don't answer that because I already know – they'll think that either Julian or I have cheated… and they're far more likely to believe him over me. He comes from a well-respected local family, and has been a blacksmith for years. I'm just starting out, fresh from college, with hardly any experience to speak of.' She prodded a finger morosely at a spot on the wooden bench. 'Of course, they might just decide to disqualify us both.'

Clara didn't say anything, but the same thought had already crossed her mind.

She shook her head. 'In a way it's pointless even trying to surmise what the end result might be. It's what you do now that's important.' She gave Megan an encouraging smile. 'I can speak to Seth and let him know the score but I'm not sure what he can do to be honest, if anything. He'll be here every day this week though so at least he can keep an eye on things while we try and sort this out…' She squeezed Megan's hand. 'I know this isn't going to be easy, but you've got to grit your teeth, go back over there and carry on, no matter what. Otherwise it makes no difference who has designed what, Julian has as good as won.'

'Easy for you to say.'

'Yes, it is.' She held Megan's look, and then got to her feet, pulling Megan with her. She found a tissue and passed it to her, watching while she blew her nose, and wiped her eyes.

'That's it,' she said. 'Come on now. You haven't got time to be wasting here, you've got a competition to win, and you can't do that from the garden. I'll walk you back to the forge and that way if Julian wonders where you'd gone, he'll think you just popped out to say hello to me.'

She linked her arm through Megan's and began to walk back up the path towards the courtyard.

'And think about it for a minute… You're a brilliant blacksmith, and artist. Julian knows that and, while he might be those things too, what reason would he have to try to copy your design? He might be trying to force you to leave the competition, but that's a very risky game to be playing, as is cheating… I think the truth of the matter is that he knows your design is way better than anything he could have come up with and so, by allowing you to see his design, he's simply trying to unnerve you. Do you see what I mean?'

Megan sniffed, but she nodded.

'So, if the only thing standing between you and winning this competition is Julian's attempt at psyching you out, then it's up to you whether or not you let him. The very fact that he feels he has to try should tell you something. You've got him on the run, Megan, you intimidate him… enough that he feels he cannot win if pitted against you on equal terms. He's trying to unlevel the playing field. All you've got to do is level it again.'

Megan looked up, astonished as the realisation of what Clara had said hit her. 'Are you saying you honestly think I can win?'

Clara smiled. 'I'm saying, I think you already have.'

Chapter 22

By the time Clara had walked Megan back to the competition area and doubled back to the courtyard, Seth was already waiting for her, an anxious expression on his face.

'Is she okay?' he asked. 'I wasn't sure what was wrong.'

Clara indicated that they should move into the garden, not wishing to say anything where there was still a possibility someone might hear them. As soon as they reached the shelter of the walls, she quickly filled him in.

He stared at her incredulously.

'And she's absolutely sure?' he asked. 'That's a hell of an accusation to make.'

'I don't think there's any doubt in her mind, and it would be easy enough to check, I suppose, although I doubt Julian would be quite so blasé about leaving his design sketches around where other competitors are concerned. I think his little show was solely for Megan's benefit.'

Seth nodded. 'Yes, you're probably right, although only time is the real proof in all of this.'

'Well, whatever his reasoning it still doesn't explain the one thing that no one has addressed as yet.'

'Which is?'

'Well, we've all been trying to think what Julian intends to gain from all of this, but what really worries me is that he's been able to copy Megan's design in the first place. Where did he get it from, Seth?'

He ran a hand through his hair. 'Shit… I hadn't thought of that.'

And what was worse was, having already thought of it, Clara now had to accept one very real possibility…

Seth narrowed his eyes. 'You know, don't you?' he said, frowning when she shook her head quickly. 'Or at least you've a suspicion. I can see it on your face.'

She groaned. 'Seth, I don't know what to do. It's one of those horrible situations where you can't unknow something, and I really wish I could because the thought of what it means is just too much. I hate myself for even considering it.'

'But?'

'I guess I have to consider it, because right now I can't think of any other explanation.'

'Go on…'

They were walking back to the same bench she had sat on just moments ago, and she waited until they were seated again before continuing.

'Megan has told me a little about her design, but I haven't actually seen the detail. As far as I know, only one person has…'

She looked beseechingly at Seth, not wanting to be the one to say the name out loud.

'Liam,' he said quietly, and she nodded sadly.

'I might be wrong. I hope with all my heart I am, but…' She trailed off. 'I saw something else recently. Something which made me think he's not quite the person we thought he was. And again, it could all be entirely innocent, but somewhere along the line, in the absence of any other information, things stop being a coincidence.'

She thrust her hands under her legs, her body tense with anxiety as Seth sat motionless beside her waiting for her to speak. She took a deep breath.

'When I was in town the other day, I saw Liam with another woman. Nothing compromising, they were in the tearoom just round the corner from the High Street. It was broad daylight, and any number of people could have seen them…'

She didn't need to say any more. Seth could work it out.

'Does anyone else know about this?'

Clara nodded. 'Only Maddie… I had to tell someone, if only so that they could agree with me that there was nothing suspicious about it. But then Maddie mentioned that she thought Megan was a little uncertain about her relationship with Liam, and then worse, Megan said more or less the same thing to me too. I've been trying to put it out of my head ever since.'

She stared ahead of her, this time waiting for Seth to speak, to say anything that would put her mind at rest.

'It probably is nothing,' he said. 'And I can see why it's been troubling you, but what I can't understand is why Liam would do such a thing? What on earth would he stand to gain by having Megan lose the competition?'

But Clara had already thought about this. 'Only that if she wins, she's already said she'll set up her own business here. If she loses, I don't know, perhaps she'd go back to Lancashire. If you were having an affair, that's possibly what you'd hope for?' She tutted furiously. 'Oh, this is stupid, Liam loves Megan for goodness' sake. Just ignore me, I'm turning into a hideous, suspicious… cow!'

Seth leaned into her. 'No, you're not,' he said gently. 'You'd be crowing with delight if that were the case, and I can see how badly you feel about this. The trouble is that, however much we don't want to believe there's any truth in this, like you said, we have to acknowledge the possibility.'

'So what do we do now?'

'I'm not sure there's much we can do, or at least anything that's going to help Megan. We could confront Liam, or we could tell Megan… we could also confront Julian, but none of those things is going to help her win the competition…' He sighed. 'So perhaps the only other option is to do nothing, and just let it play out. And in the meantime we keep as close an eye on things as possible and see what we can find out.'

★

By the time Clara got back to Joy's Acre she was in desperate need of a few hours in the garden; a quiet, undemanding space where she could reconnect herself with everything that was important to her and let her troubling thoughts subside, for a little while at least. Plus, she could still feel the echoes of her conversation with Declan surrounding her and she wanted to pull them closer. She wasn't sure what there was between them yet, but this morning had resolved some of Clara's fears and she felt only warmth when she thought about their relationship now.

Climbing down from the truck, she made her way across the front yard to fetch her own wheelbarrow, ready to ferry the plants to their new home. In the end, Seth had given her a hand to load them up over at the Hall, and she was grateful for his help. Now, though, she would need to cart them quite some distance, which was irritating. The location of the filming in the garden meant that, instead of cutting through the garden as usual, she would have to wheel the barrow around the entire perimeter to the cottage at the far side. She pulled a face; there was no point moaning about it, she had just better get on and do it.

She was halfway across the yard when she realised she could hear raised voices coming from inside the house. Whoever was in the kitchen had probably chosen the location because it was the furthest point from the gardens at the rear. It was a good bet they wouldn't be overheard by those still outside, but here, at the front of the house, the voices were clear.

It wasn't any surprise that Fiona's voice was incredibly forceful when raised, but Declan was giving as good as he was getting, and Clara practically ducked as she walked past the window. She'd heard her name once already and that was enough, she really didn't want to hear it again. She ran around the side of the house and disappeared into one of the large sheds where she kept her tools and other equipment. Her iPod was on the bench where she had left it, and she picked it up, praying it was still charged. She rarely listened to music while she worked, preferring to hear the sounds of nature around her, but on occasion when she was tired or the weather inclement, it gave her just the pick-me-up she needed. Today, it was a necessity. She jammed the headphones into her ears and turned up the volume, slipping it into her pocket before grabbing hold of the wheelbarrow.

It took her eight separate journeys to transport all the plants to the site of their new home, and on all of the sixteen occasions that she passed by the kitchen window she kept her eyes straight ahead, concentrating on the music assailing her ears. She didn't remove her headphones until she was finally standing in the muddy border of the cottage where the plants were going to go. On the other side of the garden, the film crew were milling around looking busy. In the middle of it all was Trixie. Clara hoped that things were going well, but beyond that it was not something she wanted to think about just now. Resolutely turning her back on them, she knelt on the soft earth and plunged her hands into the warm soil, heaving a sigh of relief.

She worked solidly for quite some time, having first stood each of the potted shrubs on the ground where she wanted them. Then, she stood up and moved one or two of them around, checking their positions relative to each other and to the overall planting scheme, and once she was happy she began to systematically transfer them into the soil. The plants were of a good size and the space filled quickly, the results immediately pleasing. She rose from her knees having planted the final two hydrangea bushes, and moved on to the grassy area beside the bed to admire her handiwork.

'I love this, don't you?'

Clara turned to see Maddie only a few feet away, walking towards her.

'When it all starts to come together, I mean.' She squinted up at the roofline. 'In a few more weeks another cottage will be finished and then we'll be on to renovating our last one.'

Clara smiled, moving to stand beside her. 'I bet you didn't think any of this was possible when you first arrived, did you?'

'Oh God, don't. It makes me cringe now when I think about how dismissive I was of all of this, wanting to tear everything down and put up great glass edifices.'

'And turn my garden into a shrine to minimalism, don't forget that…' Clara laughed. 'Mind you, we converted you pretty quickly. I can't believe that was only six months ago.'

'We've come a long way since then…'

'We have,' agreed Clara.

Maddie turned back to look across the gardens where the film crew were still at work.

'It's weird though, isn't it? In that it's only when you look back you can see the journey you've been on and the distance you've travelled. While it's happening you don't get the same sense of it somehow.'

'Perhaps that's for the best… If we knew how far we still had to go we might never continue on our journey, or even start it in the first place.'

'Or know which passengers we might pick up along the way…'

With his jacket off and his sleeves rolled up, Declan was rather an arresting sight and Clara laid the back of her hand across her brow in a mock swoon.

'Hmm,' she murmured, 'just so long as we don't put any down either.'

Maddie tutted. 'Would you listen to yourself. Declan is not going anywhere, Clara. Anyone can see he's absolutely besotted by you. I know it's early days, but you're good together.' She gave her a warm smile. 'I can feel it in my waters.'

Clara returned the smile, following Maddie's line of sight across the garden.

'I'm not sure I was referring to Declan actually,' she said. 'But, thank you. I'm glad you think so.'

Maddie took her arm. 'It will be all right, you know,' she said. 'Things with Trixie will sort themselves out. We're all just going through a period of adjustment and that can be tricky for a while. Anyway, I came out to fetch you for lunch, so come on, let's go and grab Tom and we can put the world to rights while we're eating.'

Clara looked back at the flower bed she had just finished planting, and checked her watch. She was amazed to see that the morning had long since passed. Lunch suddenly seemed like a very good idea. She followed Maddie around to the rear of the cottage where they both stood waving like lunatics until Tom finally registered their presence. He waved back and moments later the three of them were walking back around the garden to the main house.

It didn't seem right to be doing so without Trixie, and Clara couldn't help but throw a backward glance towards the film crew. She had to hope that what Maddie had said was true, but the anxious feeling that was still in the pit of her stomach didn't feel like it was going to go away any time soon.

★

'I thought I might make toad in the hole for tea,' said Clara as soon as they were settled with their lunch. 'Is that all right with everyone? Only I happen to know it's one of Megan's favourites, and I think she might be grateful of it tonight.'

A dreamy look came over Tom's face. 'Absolute heaven,' he said. 'And with a ton of mashed potato and gravy as well?'

'Of course…'

'Perfect,' added Maddie. 'Don't forget that the new family staying in the Thatcher's Cottage are off out for a meal tonight, so there's only us and Megan to worry about.'

Clara nodded. 'Yes, Trixie said. Megan will probably be putting in some long hours today, so if it's okay, I'll make it for a bit later than usual.'

'Suits me,' replied Tom through a mouthful of sandwich. 'I need all the time I can get on that roof.'

Maddie watched him for a moment. 'And that still doesn't mean you have to eat your food at ninety miles an hour,' she admonished. 'Slow down a bit, Tom, and give yourself a proper break. You'll get indigestion otherwise.'

He grinned at her. 'Yes, Mum,' he said, winking. 'Just so long as you don't tell me off when the roof isn't finished on time.'

It was a light-hearted remark but Clara knew there was an element of truth in it. Tom had lost a lot of time to the rain over the last week and his schedule had been tight to begin with.

To her surprise though, instead of rising to his teasing challenge, Maddie grew serious.

'It hasn't helped that Seth has had to be over at the Hall so much either, has it?' she said. 'Particularly this week. But with the change in the final event of the competition it's meant he has no choice but to stay there when he could have been helping you instead.'

She took a bite of her own sandwich, but smiled at the same time too.

'Don't kill yourself getting it done, Tom. It will get finished when it's finished, and it's madness with everything else that's been going on to expect things to be as they have been. Something's got to give, and I'd really rather it wasn't one of us.'

Tom stared at her. 'It has been a bit mental of late, hasn't it?'

She nodded. 'Too mental. We're victims of our own success, and if we're not careful we're going to end up as exactly that, victims, and that's not a nice word. I suddenly realised when I was out in the garden just now, how much we have accomplished over the last six months, but we are also supposed to be enjoying it, and over the last couple of weeks I'm not sure that's been the case.'

Clara and Tom exchanged looks but neither of them said anything. To agree would lend weight to what she had just said and somehow that seemed like a step too far.

'Anyway,' said Maddie, brightening again. 'How is Megan getting on, she must be so excited at having got through to the final?'

The sandwich that was halfway to Clara's mouth suddenly halted mid-air. She lowered it to her plate with a sigh.

'How long have you got…?' she said.

★

It had been good to share her concerns about Megan and Liam with the others at lunch. Somehow it made it seem less scary and, although they could see the reasoning behind Clara's thoughts, both Tom and Maddie felt that it would be a mistake to do anything just yet. Julian could have been bluffing over his final design in an effort to make Megan lose her nerve, and Clara had done her best to counteract this by bolstering her confidence again, and it would seem she had largely succeeded. What was important was that Megan tackle the final part of this adventure in the right frame of mind, and understand that, whatever happened, she had absolutely done the best she could. It was only Monday after all, and jumping in now might cause more harm than good... And as for Liam, there was probably a very rational explanation for what Clara had seen and time would doubtless reveal all.

She had spent the afternoon in the quiet of the kitchen, baking bread and refilling both the biscuit and cake tins, and as the afternoon turned to early evening, Maddie had appeared to help with the preparation for dinner. Clara had just removed another tray of muffins from the oven.

'Are you going to be doing this all week?' asked Maddie, checking the pan of boiling potatoes to see if they were cooked.

'I'm honestly not sure,' answered Clara. 'I suppose it depends on how things go with the filming.' She bit her lip. 'And I don't really mind, after all, I've always helped Trixie when I could.'

'I know, but that's not really the point, is it? Nobody minds helping out when it's just for a day or so, or like with the competition when there was suddenly masses more to do than usual, but—'

'I miss her,' blurted out Clara, who was anxious not to let the conversation descend into a moaning session. 'I miss her being in the kitchen, her sunny good mornings, her rude jokes and scandalous gossip from the village.'

She put down the knives and forks she was holding on the table. 'But even though I miss her, most of all I'm scared… because what happens if she likes filming more than she likes us, Maddie? What if when all this is over she decides she doesn't want to be just a cook any more?'

'But she's not *just* a cook…' replied Maddie, coming over to put her arm around Clara. 'And I'm sure she knows that. She probably misses this too.'

'Does she though?' countered Clara. 'Does she know she's not *just* anything, or have we all been taking her horribly for granted?'

Maddie looked at her in astonishment.

'I've been wondering if that's why she's been a bit off with everyone lately,' added Clara. 'If that's the reason why the whole TV thing seems so appealing, because it's so much better than this… Looking after everyone day in day out is hard, cooking and clearing up practically every minute of the day. And then there's all the extra stuff as well.'

'But I thought she loved doing this? That it was a dream come true.'

'It is, at least I think it is. But you yourself said earlier that you didn't think things had been much fun lately.'

'You're a good friend,' Maddie replied, her eyes searching Clara's for a moment, concern written across her face. 'And perhaps you're right… In any case, even if she doesn't feel that way, it wouldn't hurt to make sure she knows how we feel about her, would it?' She glanced over at the cooker, then released her and began to lay the table.

'Come on, folks will be here any minute now. Let's get this lot dished up and have a proper meal; good food and good conversation, Joy's Acre style.'

★

At least they were trying, thought Clara halfway through their dinner. But, even with the best of intentions, it would seem that things didn't always go according to plan. Megan professed herself delighted with the toad in the hole and seemed genuinely touched that Clara had thought to make it for her, but everyone could see that she was plainly exhausted by the day's exertions. Although she ate steadily, she became quieter and quieter as the meal wore on. Trixie, on the other hand, was simply monosyllabic from the moment she entered the kitchen.

Clara had just exchanged another plaintive look with Maddie as Trixie pushed her fork aimlessly into her mashed potato when the back doorbell rang.

'I'll go,' sighed Maddie, getting up to answer it.

Seth looked up, giving her a questioning glance, but everyone else simply carried on eating. The film crew had gone home, and although Declan had been invited to stay for dinner, he too had declined, possibly on the grounds of giving them all some time together. With everyone else currently sitting around the table, the only people who could have rung the bell were the new guests from the Thatcher's Cottage.

Clara strained to hear what was being said, but the back door was right at the other end of the house. She didn't have long to wait, however, before Maddie returned to the table, red in the face and looking a little flustered. Clara caught her eye and was about to ask what had happened when she received a slight warning shake of her head in reply. Tom, however, obviously missed her signal.

'Everything okay, Mads?' he asked innocently.

Maddie picked up her glass of water. 'Yes, thanks, Tom,' she replied, 'nothing to worry about.'

But her voice sounded strained even to Clara, and Seth looked up immediately.

'Well, who was it?' he asked. 'The Bellinghams? What did they want?'

Maddie nodded. 'Oh, they just had a query, that's all. But it's all sorted.'

Clara willed Seth to leave it there, but although he didn't say anything, he was sitting next to Maddie, staring at her with his eyebrows raised, waiting for her to elaborate. And if she didn't, it was patently obvious that he would ask her. The silence stretched out, and Clara could feel her stomach begin to burble with anxiety.

'There was just a slight mix-up about dinner, that was all,' she said quietly.

Trixie's head snapped up. 'What mix-up about dinner?' she asked. 'They didn't want dinner tonight, they said they were going out…'

'Crossed wires, I expect,' said Maddie reasonably. 'That's tomorrow, apparently.'

'So do they want dinner or not then?' Trixie glared, her voice rising. 'Which is it?'

Maddie was doing her level best to keep her voice calm. 'It's a bit late for them now,' she said, 'so they've popped out to get some fish and chips.'

Trixie practically threw her fork down. 'Oh for goodness' sake. I wish they'd bloody make their minds up. It's bad enough we have to pander to their every whim, without them messing us around like that.'

Clara closed her eyes.

'I could remind you that we're here to pander to their every whim, Trixie. That is what they've paid for, after all.' There was an edge to Seth's voice that Clara knew well. 'And, correct me if I'm wrong, but you didn't actually cook dinner tonight, did you? So if anyone is being messed around, it certainly isn't you.'

There was a second or two when Clara thought Trixie might just take it on the chin and apologise, but to her surprise she turned and glared at Maddie.

'Well, you might at least back me up,' she said. 'You were there this morning when they said they were going out tonight. You heard them!'

Maddie flushed red. 'I wasn't, Trixie. Besides, it isn't about backing anyone up, it's—'

Tom cleared his throat. 'No, that was me, Trixie. The Bellinghams were just on their way out for the day when I arrived this morning if you remember, and I'm afraid they definitely said Tuesday…' He gave Maddie an apologetic look. 'They wanted to go to the buffet night at the local Indian, and that's only on Tuesday nights, which is tomorrow…'

There was a hideous scraping noise as Trixie's chair shot away from the table and she jumped to her feet.

'Well, thanks a lot, guys,' she snarled. 'Now I know exactly where I stand!'

And with that she stalked from the room.

Chapter 23

Clara must have replayed every syllable of last night's conversation over and over in her head a thousand times. It was no wonder she hadn't been able to sleep. And she had stared at her phone a thousand times too, thinking that she would call Declan, but somehow, each and every time, she had talked herself out of it. She would have loved to have seen him, or even just talked to him, but somehow he seemed too close to what was going on at Joy's Acre and Clara was anxious to keep the two apart.

She had never before heard Trixie speak the way she had yesterday, and a part of her wanted to give her a slap while the other part wanted to hug her. How could things have got so bad that they were reduced to snarling at one another and laying blame instead of helping?

Her alarm shrilled loudly beside her and she switched it off with a sigh. There was no longer any chance of sleep but, looking on the bright side, if she kept busy, at least no time to dwell on things either. But first, as soon as she arrived at Joy's Acre, she would need to run the gauntlet of breakfast time.

As it turned out, only Maddie was in the kitchen when she arrived, and she immediately came forward to give Clara a hug.

'You look like I feel,' she said, a pair of tongs in one hand. From behind her Clara could hear bacon sizzling gently.

Clara grimaced. 'Yeah, thanks for that,' she replied, looking around the kitchen.

'So what's still to do?' she asked, crossing to the pantry door and pulling an apron from the peg there.

'I'm just making Seth a sandwich. He wants to get over to the Hall early for a quick "shufti", as he called it, to see if he could find anything incriminating. But after that, it's two breakfasts for the Bellinghams. They'd like the full works this morning, and they're damn well going to get it if I have anything to do with it.' She pulled a face. 'I haven't seen Megan yet this morning, so I'm not sure what she'd like. Would you mind popping over for me to check?'

Clara nodded. 'No problem.' She paused in the doorway for a moment.

'And what about Trixie?' she asked.

'Not even put in an appearance,' Maddie replied. 'I am seriously unimpressed.'

'I would imagine she feels awful,' said Clara, feeling her heart sink.

Maddie weighed up her words for a moment. 'Yes, I suppose she does… but then I think we all do, so the least she could do is come and tell us how she feels. You're far too nice, Clara, but surely the rest of us are not so bad that she can't come and talk to us. Ignoring us isn't going to help in the slightest.'

There really was no answer to that.

'I'll be back in a minute,' said Clara.

By the time she returned, the film crew were all just arriving for the day and Clara hurried back inside.

'Another full works for Megan, please,' she said. 'She's just been out for a run and, although she's feeling "sick to the stomach" with nerves, she reckons a fry-up might help.'

'Righty-oh,' replied Maddie, turning back to the cooker. 'Is she coming over this morning?' she asked. 'Only I wondered whether Trixie's unpleasantness last night might have put her off.'

'Oh, I didn't think to ask her,' replied Clara, but then turned at the sound of footsteps.

'I wouldn't be at all surprised if it had, I—'

'Maddie!' hissed Clara in warning, but it was too late. Trixie was standing in the doorway.

She stared at Clara, her brown hair subdued from its usual spiky style and instead, much like the rest of her, looking like she hadn't had a very good night. Tears sprang into her eyes while Clara watched, helpless and unable to think of anything to say. A second later Trixie turned on her heels and marched out the front door, slamming it behind her.

'Shit,' said Maddie, vehemently.

'Oh, this is horrible,' said Clara, a trembling hand reaching to touch her mouth. 'Now what do we do?'

Maddie swallowed. 'I'm not sure there's anything we can do. Except let her calm down for now… I'll go and apologise later.' She pursed her lips. 'Mind you, she needs to apologise as well. She's at fault here too, don't forget.'

'I know,' replied Clara, 'but it's a horrible thing hearing people talk about you behind your back, particularly when we're all supposed to be friends.'

The sound of laughter drifted down the hallway from the direction of the back door, and Maddie straightened.

'Come on,' she said. 'Eyes front, and best foot forward. I'm not letting Megan suffer another awkward meal time, she's got enough on her plate.' She gave a sad smile. 'We'll fix this, Clara, I promise.'

Clara had just enough time to nod before Tom and Megan came into the kitchen.

'Do you know, I honestly think the smell of bacon frying could wake the dead,' quipped Tom, flashing a wide grin at the two women.

Oh, bless you, Tom, thought Clara, returning his look with a grateful smile.

★

Clara shooed Maddie out of the kitchen the moment everyone had finished breakfast. She wanted to pop over to the Hall as soon as possible to see whether Seth had managed to glean any information, but first, there was something else she needed to do. Everyone at Joy's Acre had a favourite cake and, without fail, Trixie had always tried to make it for them when she felt they needed it. If Tom had had a particularly long day, then he'd be rewarded with a Victoria sponge and if Seth had a bad headache then a huge lump of sticky gingerbread would wing its way in his direction. Trixie's absolute favourite was, of all things, jammy flapjack; intensely sweet, and incredibly sticky, and something she very rarely made for herself. Today, Clara was going to remedy that.

It wouldn't take very long to make and, once the film crew broke for elevenses, Clara could take it out to her. She was just melting the butter and sugar together in a pan when a distant thump heralded the sound of the back door slamming once again.

'Well, that's just bloody great, isn't it? Not content with moaning about everything I do and then talking about me behind my back, now you've gone and scuppered the only bloody chance I had of getting anywhere!'

The sudden outburst from behind her made Clara jump.

Trixie had obviously been crying. Her face was red and blotchy from her tears, but her eyes were flashing with anger.

'How could you, Clara? I thought we were friends!' The words were practically spat from across the room and Trixie's stance was anything but conciliatory.

The colour rose up Clara's cheeks in an instant, and with it came her own anger.

'How could I *what*, Trixie? Why don't you stop yelling at me for just a minute and tell me what all this is about, because I'm damned if I know.'

'Oh, don't come the innocent with me,' sneered Trixie. 'Of course you know, it's your bloody fault!'

'What is my fault?' shouted Clara. 'I haven't done anything!'

'No?' Trixie took several steps into the room. 'Oh, yes, Clara, no, Clara, three bags full, Clara…' Her voice had become sing-song, but there was an edge to it also, sarcastic and scathing.

Clara stared at her, seeing her face contorted in disgust, and then the penny dropped…

'You're jealous?' she asked incredulously. 'You're actually jealous… Of me, and Declan… I don't bloody believe this.' She shook her head furiously. 'Well, thanks a lot… First you tease me mercilessly about him, knowing how nervous I was about the whole thing and then, when I finally do decide, for the first time in years, that it's okay to let a man into my life, you throw a hissy fit! And what the hell has he got to do with anything, anyway?'

'The filming, *Clara*…' Trixie intoned, like she was talking to a two-year-old. 'Or the lack of it… You click your fingers and Declan does whatever you want him to…'

'He does not! Trixie, I'm not filming at the moment so they can concentrate on you for God's sake. In case it slipped your notice that that's what's been happening…'

'Except that it isn't, is it? I wouldn't be standing here now if it was. Jesus, how stupid can you get!'

Clara glared at her. 'Incredibly, it would seem, seeing as I haven't got the faintest clue what you're talking about. Why don't you do us both a favour and tell me, instead of just standing there spitting venom at me?'

From behind her, the pan on the cooker began to hiss. She turned to look at the boiling dark mess it now contained.

'Shit!' she said, snatching it off the heat and thrusting it into the sink. 'Well, that's flaming well ruined now as well.' She turned on Trixie. 'I haven't done anything to you, except to try and be a friend. I even thought I was helping you out over the TV thing, which *I hate* by the way, but which I've gone along with the whole time because I knew how important it was to you. And then you come in here, shouting and screaming about stuff when I haven't got a clue what you're talking about, and all I'm trying to do is cover for you and do your work—' She stopped suddenly, the words sticking in her throat. 'And even more stupidly, I'm making your favourite jammy flapjack to try and cheer you up. And congratulations, you've sodding well gone and spoiled that as well.' She stared at Trixie for a moment and then burst abruptly into tears.

She turned towards the sink, her hand over her mouth as she tried to contain her tears. Her emotions, which had peaked and troughed repeatedly over the last few days, finally gave way, and she stood that way for quite some minutes, not caring what she sounded like.

Apart from her sobs, the room prickled with silence around her, and Clara was so lost in her sadness that she was surprised to suddenly hear Trixie's voice again.

'I'm so sorry...'

There was the sound of a chair being drawn away from the table and, as Clara turned around, she saw Trixie lower herself into it, her face white and pinched. She was staring straight ahead, unseeing.

'You really have no idea what I'm talking about, do you?' She still wasn't looking at Clara.

'No,' she replied. 'I really don't.'

Finally, she turned her face toward Clara. 'I think they're going to cancel the show...'

Clara's mouth dropped open, and she closed it, sniffing. 'Oh no...' That was the last thing she'd expected to hear. 'But why would they do that? What's happened?'

'Fiona and Declan had this huge row... He took her off into the barn so none of us could hear what was going on, but when they came out, Fiona's face was like thunder, and Declan's wasn't much better. He went to speak to one or two of the crew, while she stomped off to sit on the bench in the middle of the garden, and then he came over to me. He didn't say a lot, just that there were some issues with the filming schedule they needed to resolve, and for the time being I was free to get on with something else.' She raised her eyebrows. 'Then he asked me where Maddie and Seth were.'

'Well Seth is over at the Hall.'

'I know. And Maddie is with Declan now. I fetched her just before I came in here.'

Clara frowned. 'But that doesn't necessarily mean they're going to cancel the filming, it might just be exactly what Declan said, that they need to rejig things. That must happen all the time, surely?'

Trixie shook her head glumly. 'I don't think so. All morning Declan has been stopping and starting things, changing what Fiona has said. It was a bit like that yesterday as well.'

It didn't sound good, Clara had to admit, but there was something else to consider.

'So, why is this my fault, Trixie?' she said quietly.

There was silence for a few moments until Clara saw a tear splash onto the table, and Trixie's head turned towards her. Her eyes were wet.

'Because I'm a cow,' she said. 'No other reason. It's not your fault at all. It's not anyone's fault. It's just that I wanted this so badly, Clara… I finally thought I had an opportunity to make something of myself.' She wiped a tear off the end of her nose.

'Oh, Trixie…' There was a huge lump in Clara's throat. 'You didn't need an opportunity to make something of yourself. You were already pretty special… are special.'

'But I've behaved appallingly.'

Clara remained silent. It would be just too cruel to agree with her.

'I've treated everyone like dirt. You've all been covering for me and I've never once said thank you, not properly… especially to you; Maddie's told me how much you've been sticking up for me.'

'You're my friend, Trixie. That's what friends do…'

'Huh, and I've made a right bloody mess of that too…'

Clara got up and crossed to the dresser where she pulled two tissues from a box. She handed one to Trixie and kept the other for herself, sitting back down and blowing her nose noisily.

'I think we've both made a mess of things… I should have been more honest about how I was feeling about the TV show, and instead I said nothing, letting things drift, convincing myself I was going along with everything for the right reasons, and that everything would be all right in the end. I should know by now that never works. It always comes back to bite you on the bum.'

Trixie gave a wan smile. 'I really am sorry,' she said.

'Me too…'

There was silence for a few moments, save for the occasional sniff.

'So, what do we do now?' asked Trixie.

Clara turned to look at her. 'Hug?' she suggested.

She was relieved when Trixie's face brightened slightly and she scrambled to her feet, but although her arms went around her, Clara could feel she was still holding back. She pulled away to look at her and was saddened to see her lip trembling again.

'I think I might have to leave,' she said.

'Leave?' replied Clara, startled. 'And go where?'

Trixie shrugged. 'Anywhere. Away. I don't know…'

'But why? I don't understand.'

'Because I live here, Clara, as part of my job. How can I possibly stay when I get the sack?'

'Who said anything about you getting the sack?' said Maddie, coming into the room. Clara could see how horrified she looked on hearing Trixie's words.

'But I'm an employee; that's what you do when employees behave the way I have.'

'Oh, Trixie, you're not an employee.' She glanced at Clara, obviously thinking of their recent conversation. 'I mean, you are… technically, but more than that, you're our friend… one that just happens to be paid for the things she does.'

She was about to speak again when the film crew began to walk past the kitchen window. They were followed by a knock on the front door.

'I think that might be for you,' said Maddie with a pointed look.

Clara suspected she knew exactly who would be standing there, and went to answer it with a sinking heart.

Declan looked uncomfortable to say the least and, even though Clara stepped back to let him into the hall, he remained where he was, a sheepish half smile on his face.

'I've come to say goodbye,' he said, 'just for the time being,' he hastened to add, 'but I think we all need to get out of your hair for a little while. Maddie will explain…'

'I think Trixie possibly just has,' replied Clara, searching his face for some clue to how he was feeling.

'Ah… I wondered if she'd come to you. She's a bit upset, I think.'

'*Really?*'

She grimaced as soon as the word had left her mouth. 'Sorry,' she said. 'I think we're all a bit… emotional today.'

Declan held her look for just a second before pulling her into his arms. 'I don't want to leave you like this,' he said, one hand stroking the back of her hair. It felt divine. 'I don't want to leave you at all…'

A small noise escaped Clara's throat as she burrowed herself deeper into his arms because she didn't want him to leave either, but that's what this felt like; an ending…

'I'll call you though, later… if that's all right? Maybe come and see you?'

Clara nodded. 'Please,' she managed, before reluctantly straightening a little. She didn't want things between them to finish like this – a rushed conversation in the hallway – but now wasn't the time to talk, there were other things to consider. 'I ought to get back…'

'I know,' he murmured.

They stayed that way for several more moments before Declan gently stepped away, pulling her back at the last moment for a lingering kiss.

'I'll see you later,' he murmured, before turning away.

Clara watched him go and touched a hand to her lips, wondering what she could taste there. Sadness? Regret? Longing? Hope, perhaps? Then, taking a deep breath, she stepped back into the kitchen.

Trixie and Maddie were sitting back at the table.

'Besides, we've all been out of sorts just lately,' Maddie was saying, 'and the decision to have a rethink over the filming has got nothing to do with you, or your abilities. But you have to admit it's caused problems. More importantly though, it's got in the way of what we do best... what *you* do best. I think we all need some time to remember what that is.'

Trixie nodded, but there were still tears sliding down her face.

'So I don't want any more talk of you or anyone else being sacked. We're a family here, and you are as much a part of that as everyone else. I've had a long chat with Declan this morning, and I won't lie to you, Trixie, I've been honest about how I see things but, so has he to be fair, and there's a surprising amount of common ground. I obviously need to have a chat to Seth later on, but I have a feeling he'll think the same way.'

She put her arm around Trixie. 'I'm sorry, but I think this might be the end of this particular adventure.'

'I know, I think I just... wanted... or hoped...' Her tears began in earnest again, her words hiccupping through her sobs. She dabbed a hand at her eyes. 'I'll apologise, to Seth... and Tom too.'

'Trixie, he does understand, they both do.'

She nodded again as she thought of something else.

'There's Megan as well. The competition is stressful enough, she should be able to come here at night to relax, not listen to me behaving like a spoiled brat.'

Emma Davies

Maddie exchanged a look with Clara. 'Megan is fine. And she has more pressing things on her mind right now than taking any notice of us, so don't go worrying on that score.'

She sniffed. 'How is she getting on? It all seems to have passed me by.'

Clara smiled, passing Trixie another tissue. 'She's doing really well – through to the final and hard at it working on the design for her gate. Of course, Julian got through too and is being his usual slime-ball self, but Seth is on the case, he'll get things sorted.'

'You'd have thought Julian would know when to give it a rest, wouldn't you? Seeing as they're both in the final; that he'd just grow up and get over himself.'

'You would, but now Megan's convinced he's cheating. That somehow he's got hold of her design and is going to try and pass it off as his own, discrediting her in the process.'

'But how has he managed to do that? Where on earth would he get the design from?'

'Ah, well that's just it,' replied Clara. 'We don't know, because the only people that have seen it are Megan... and Liam.'

Trixie caught the intonation in her voice. 'You think Liam might have something to do with this? I can't believe that...'

'No, I don't want to either, but...' Clara looked at Maddie. It didn't seem right to be continually repeating her suspicions.

Maddie sighed. 'You might as well tell her. I don't know if it has anything to do with it either, but under the circumstances, you have to admit it's a bit odd.'

Trixie's head swivelled from one to the other. 'Well, someone tell me!'

'I saw him with another woman...' said Clara, her face falling. 'That day when I went into town to buy more bacon. Blimey, that feels like a million years ago... He was sitting in the tearoom with her, and I know it's probably totally innocent, and it was in full view of the street in broad daylight, but it's been playing on mind, and—'

'She was probably just one of his customers…' said Trixie.

'What?'

'Say that again.'

Both Maddie and Clara spoke at the same time, exchanging astonished looks.

'One of his customers,' repeated Trixie. 'I think he sometimes goes to the tearoom for meetings. Megan said he hasn't got an office set up yet.'

'Why, what does he do?' asked Maddie.

'He's a financial advisor, didn't you know?'

Clara stared at her. 'No, I didn't…' She looked back at Maddie. 'Oh, but this could change everything… I can't tell you how relieved I am.'

'Well, he might still be having an affair,' replied Trixie, 'but I really don't think so. He's besotted with Megan. But some of his clients, particularly women it would seem, don't always want their partners to know about their personal finances, so they arrange to see Liam somewhere away from home.'

Clara grinned. 'Why on earth didn't I talk to you about this earlier, Trixie? I could have saved myself a whole heap of anxiety.'

'I don't know, why didn't you?' And then she looked at Clara. 'No, don't tell me. It was because I wasn't around, and then you got poorly, and then you didn't want to talk to me and… so it goes on,' she finished.

'Nuh-uh, none of that,' said Maddie. 'Let's focus on what happens now, not what's already been and gone because, although what you've just told us is good news as far as Megan and Liam are concerned, it still doesn't answer the question of how Julian got hold of Megan's designs.'

'No, it doesn't,' answered Clara.

'So then we just have to do a bit of detective work,' said Trixie. 'It can only have happened in one of two ways – either through some connection with Megan, or some connection with Liam, so we could ask Liam…'

'No, we can't do that.'

'Why not?' asked Trixie.

'Because…' She paused for a moment. 'Imagine how he'd feel if we as good as told him that he was somehow responsible for the leaked design, even if it was by accident. We have no proof that's how it happened—'

Clara flapped her hands as a sudden memory returned to her.

'Wait a minute,' she said. 'On Saturday when we were waiting for the judging over at the Hall, Liam mentioned that it would be unthinkable for Megan not to go through into the final. He said she'd had a brilliant week and that his dining room table was covered in her sketches and plans… What if a client of Liam's had been to the house, someone connected with Julian, and they had seen the design. Wouldn't that explain it?'

'Bloody hell, Clara, I think you're right.' Trixie sat forward in her chair. 'So now we really do need to find out who this woman is; check whether she knows Julian, and importantly whether she's ever been to Liam's house.' She pursed her lips. 'Although, realistically, I suppose any of his clients could have been there and seen Megan's design, not just this woman.'

Maddie nodded, sighing gently. 'That's true, but right now she's the only possible connection we have, and I still think we should start with her. If we draw a blank, then we'll have to ask Liam about his other clients as well. But don't forget there's still a possibility, however slight, that he could be having an affair. I don't want to think badly of Liam for any reason, any more than you do, but until we know otherwise we still have to consider it. For Megan's sake, if nothing else.'

Trixie nodded. 'Agreed,' she said. 'Now, it's about time I got back to work, and I'm sure I must need supplies of some sort. I think I might pop into town for a spot of shopping, and perhaps a spot of gossiping… Tell me exactly what this woman looked like, Clara.'

Chapter 24

By Friday evening the tension was unbearable. Following their discussion on Tuesday, Trixie had indeed gone into town and spoken to a few people who, she claimed, could always be relied upon to give her the lowdown. Except, as yet, nothing had been forthcoming.

Seth had done his best to check out Julian's design and Megan's suspicions had been confirmed. It was practically a carbon copy of hers and, if that were not enough, the evidence became clearer to see as the week wore on. There was now only one full day left before the competition was judged on Saturday, and it was rapidly looking like they were going to have to ask Liam who the mystery woman was. If they couldn't get any proof of Julian's wrongdoing before then, poor Megan would really be up against it.

Clara checked her watch and opened her oven door, peering at the beautiful lasagne inside. Trixie had baked it for her and she was anxious not to let it overcook. Declan would be arriving for dinner at any moment and, although she had been reticent about allowing this little subterfuge, Trixie had been quite matter-of-fact about it.

'It's been a stressful week,' she'd said, 'and you and I both know you can cook lasagne, but the truth of the matter is that you don't *need* to, so give yourself a break and let me come up with the goods.'

As it turned out, Clara was immensely grateful. She was nervous enough about Declan's visit as it was without having to worry about cooking as well.

Right on cue, her doorbell rang and she switched off the oven, leaving the food to take care of itself for a few minutes. Declan was almost hidden behind an enormous bouquet of blush pink peonies and dark voluptuous roses. She laughed when she saw them.

'Sorry,' she said, at his raised eyebrows, 'I'm just imagining the conversation you had with the florist.'

'I went into a great deal of detail, I can assure you,' he replied. 'And I have it on good authority that these are definitely not guilty flowers.' His smile lit the depths of his eyes. 'It's good to see you, Clara.'

She felt her stomach give a little flip. Keeping frantically busy all day was one thing, but even if it had distracted her from thinking about this evening, now Declan was standing in front of her and her thoughts could no longer be imagined.

He leaned forward, laughing as they only managed to brush lips around the enormous bouquet he held.

'I'll put them in some water,' she said, taking the blooms from him. 'Come in.'

She ran some water into the kitchen sink, not wanting to take the time to arrange the flowers properly just yet, and had just turned off the tap when she realised that Declan was standing very close behind her.

'Now that your hands are free,' he said, 'I'd quite like to do that again properly... if you don't mind.'

One hand slid around the back of her neck, the other around her waist, and Clara found that she didn't mind in the slightest. Her nerves evaporated as a new feeling slid over her, replacing the one that had worried her most about this evening; because the way that Declan was kissing her left her in no doubt that this was not an ending, but a beginning...

'I'm so glad you came,' she whispered, once they had drawn apart.

'I felt awful,' admitted Declan, 'leaving you like that the other day.' His face was inches from hers. 'But it would have been wrong to stay.'

She nodded quickly. 'I know. We all needed some time to get back to being who we were before this whole TV thing happened.'

'Before I happened...'

She put a finger on his lips. 'No,' she said. 'You're the only good thing that *has* come out of all this.' She thought for a moment. 'No, that's not strictly true, something else has—'

She broke off as her mobile phone trilled a tune from the table. 'Really?' she said. '*Now?*

Declan laughed, releasing her. 'There's no hiding, is there? You'd better answer it.'

She crossed to pick up the phone, thinking she'd be annoyed if it was someone selling something, but her heart beat a little faster when she saw who it was.

'Trixie?' she said. 'What is it? What's wrong?'

'We've got her,' came the reply. 'I've found our mystery woman, Clara.' She couldn't disguise the excitement in her voice.

'Where? Who is she?'

'Well, if you can meet me at the Frog and Wicket in about ten minutes, you can come and find out for yourself.' Almost as soon as she had finished speaking there was a groan. 'Oh, no, you can't, can you? You've got Declan coming. Bugger! That's the most awful timing.'

Clara glanced across the kitchen. 'He's here now actually,' she said.

Declan looked up at her words. 'What is it?' he mouthed.

She grimaced, torn. There always seemed to be something. For goodness' sake, when would they ever get a break? But on the other hand, this might be the only opportunity they got…

'Hang on,' she said to Trixie, and then turned the phone in to her chest so she wouldn't hear the reply. 'I don't suppose you fancy a quick trip down the pub, do you?' She paused for a moment. 'It's for a very good cause.'

Declan's look was quizzical, but he held up his hands in an affable gesture. 'Sure…' And then he grinned. 'Some things are worth waiting for.'

Clara eyed the oven; their lasagne was probably not going to be one of them. She turned her phone back around.

'We'll meet you in the car park, Trixie,' she said. 'Ten minutes.' She hung up and looked at Declan.

'That's the most spectacularly bad timing,' she said. 'I'm so sorry, but it is kind of important…'

Declan fished his car keys out of his pocket. 'You can explain on the way,' he said.

★

'Oh, yes, that's definitely her,' said Clara, looking over at the group of women who had taken one of the larger tables in the pub. 'The boobs on the table are a dead giveaway.' By the looks of things, they were already several drinks down and didn't have much intention of stopping either.

She, Declan and Trixie were sitting at a small table in the corner of the room and, although Trixie had her back to the party, Clara had a direct line of sight.

'So, now what do we do?' she asked.

'Drinks, I think, ladies,' said Declan. 'What are you having?'

Once Declan had returned from getting their orders in, Clara leaned forward.

'How did you know where to find her?' she asked.

Trixie picked up her glass, tapping the side of her nose. 'Ah, that's easy when you know the right people,' she said. 'Don't forget I used to work here, and trust me, if you want to know what's going on in a place, ask the local bar staff. They hear *everything*... Monica, that's the girl serving at the bar, hasn't been on shift since Tuesday so only just got the message tonight, but she lives in the same village as Donna, and certainly knows who she is. The Frog and Wicket isn't a place she usually frequents, so Monica was just about to call me when, lo and behold, she walks in with that lot.'

Clara shot another look across the room to where the raucous laughter was continuing.

'So that's her name, is it? Donna,' she asked. 'But who is she, Trixie?'

A knowing smile spread over Trixie's face.

'Julian's *girlfriend*,' she said. 'A prize bitch apparently.'

Declan spluttered into his drink. 'Remind me never to get on *your* wrong side,' he said.

'You already have,' she replied coolly, and for a moment Declan's smile faltered, but then she grinned. 'Just teasing,' she said. 'It gets better though,' she added, 'because rumour has it that Donna has set her heart on becoming Mrs Julian Happily-Ever-After, quite possibly because her prospective daddy-in-law is absolutely minted and Julian stands to inherit a substantial sum of money. That's without the massive house they already live in, of course.'

'Oh my God,' said Clara slowly, as the full implication of what Trixie had just said sank in.

'I don't get it though,' said Declan. 'If Julian's family are so well-off, why is he so desperate to win the competition?'

Trixie shrugged. 'There's nowt so queer as folk, but my guess is that Julian is actually what Megan said he is – an obnoxious chauvinist on the one hand, but also a pretty good blacksmith on the other, with a real love for what he does.'

Clara frowned. 'I don't follow…'

'He wants to win the competition for the same reason as the next man – the glory of winning. And from what I've picked up, his daddy isn't too smitten on his choice of career, so maybe Julian feels he has something to prove to dear old Dad. Winning a prestigious commission might be just the thing to convince him of its merits. Donna, on the other hand, probably views her handing Julian the winning ticket as a free pass down the aisle.'

Declan stared at them both. 'Is this really what rural village life is like?' he said. 'Because if it is, I'm definitely coming to live here. It's better than anything on the telly.'

'And this from the TV producer…' said Trixie in a deadpan voice.

'Are you really coming to live here?' asked Clara, ignoring Trixie's comment.

But Declan just smiled. 'Being serious for a minute though, what you've said makes perfect sense, but this is pretty heavy stuff. What on earth are we going to do about it?'

Trixie smiled. 'What we girls always do…' She winked at Clara. 'We wait until she goes to the loo… and then we take her down…'

Clara raised her eyebrows at Declan. 'A tad melodramatic, Trixie…'

'No, I'm serious. There's no point in messing around. We need to get proof of what's gone on or we're no use to Megan at all. And the only person who can give us that proof is Donna. We have to go and talk to her.'

'She's right, Clara,' said Declan. 'I'd volunteer myself, but I don't think I'd be welcome in the ladies'.'

Trixie was staring into space. 'No, but you might be able to do something else though… We need to get Donna away from her coven, and you know what women are like, Clara, they always go to the loo in packs, so somehow we need to get her on her own.'

Clara grinned. 'Well, that's simple,' she said. 'What self-respecting gold digger wouldn't want to talk to a TV producer?'

Trixie slapped her forehead. 'Of course! Oh, that's genius…'

Fortunately for them, the drinks were flowing fast, and it wasn't long before there were signs of movement from Donna's table.

'Okay, three of them are getting up,' said Clara. 'Which just leaves Donna plus one other.'

Trixie put her drink down purposefully. 'That's fine,' she replied. 'I'm quite happy to do this here. Let me know when they've gone.' She held out her hand towards Declan. 'Please tell me you have a business card on you,' she added.

As soon as Declan had fished one out of his wallet she sat up straight. 'Right, I'm your location scout, and Clara here is your PA.' She ruffled a hand through her hair. 'Have they gone yet?'

Clara nodded. 'Just.'

'Back in a sec,' she said, and with that she got up from the table and strode over to where Donna and her friend were still sitting. Clara saw her drop to a crouch beside Donna and whisper in her ear.

'What on earth is she doing?' muttered Declan.

'I have absolutely no idea…' she said, trying to look as confident as possible. 'Keep smiling…'

She saw Donna look over at them, and Clara dipped her head in acknowledgment. 'Shit, she's actually coming over...'

Clara watched in astonishment as Trixie led Donna over to their table. She was clutching an enormous bag and trying to pull her skirt down a little at the same time. She barely succeeded.

'Right then, sit there lovely. Donna, is it?' She waited until Donna had done as she asked before taking a seat herself.

'Now then, you know what they say about us TV people, don't you? Never off duty!' She trilled a little laugh. 'And lucky for you we're not, eh?' She paused to give Declan's business card to Donna. 'This is Declan Connolly, and his PA, Clara. Actually, it was Clara that spotted you first, but we wanted to talk to you about a little project we've got coming up, and Declan thought you'd be just the person to help with it.'

Donna beamed at them, not in the least self-conscious as her chest asserted its authority over the table.

'So, over to you, Declan.'

There was a look on his face as if he could quite cheerfully murder Trixie but he smiled nonetheless.

'We're making a series of programmes about local village life,' he began, 'the fetes, the shows, the competitions, all that jazz, but in particular focusing on the incidence of cheating, which sadly seems to be rife. I wondered if I might have your views on that.'

For a moment she nodded and smiled just as would be expected. She even opened her mouth to answer, but then flushed bright red and clamped her jaw shut. 'What the hell has any of that got to do with you?' she said.

Declan smiled again, unperturbed, and was about to carry on when Trixie crossed both arms on the table and leaned forward.

'You see, it's like this, Donna. We're very good friends with Megan and Liam. That's Megan the blacksmith, in case you were wondering; she's the one whose design you stole for Julian. Liam is her boyfriend by the way, and he's the one you stole the design from…'

Donna folded her leopard-skin-clad arms under her bosom. 'I'm not saying anything.' She glared at Trixie. 'And you've got no proof.' She sat back, a smug look on her face.

'Possibly, possibly not… but we know you've been to see Liam, and it doesn't take a genius to work out why. Looking forward to all that lovely money, are you, Donna? Julian might not be quite so keen to escort you down the aisle once the judges know what's been going on and he realises you're the reason he gets outed as a cheat.'

Clara saw the ripple of fear cross her face, but within seconds it had changed to something else. Women like Donna didn't get what they wanted by baking apple pie.

'You say anything and you'll be sorry,' she sneered. 'You're right, I have been to see Liam. I went to his house as it happens, to sign some papers, but it would be such a shame if someone made an allegation against him, wouldn't it? He might lose his business, his home… He'd certainly lose his reputation and possibly even the love of his life…'

Trixie narrowed her eyes. 'What are you playing at, Donna?' she asked.

'You snitch on me and Julian and I'll tell everyone Liam tried it on with me, it's as simple as that.' She got up from the table and threw Declan's card down. 'I think we're done here.'

Clara closed her eyes; it was all over. She heard Declan's hiss of anger from beside her.

'Yeah, fine, Donna, we're done,' said Trixie wearily. 'One last thing though… I used to work in this pub once upon a time and I got to meet some lovely people… One chap, in particular. You might know him

actually, his name's Roger. He lives out Welton way, big white house…
I was only thinking about him the other day, how we're a bit overdue
for a catch-up. I must mention you to him next time we meet up…'

Trixie turned to Declan and Clara. 'Time to go,' she said abruptly,
and with that she got to her feet and walked out the pub, leaving Clara
and Declan to trail after her.

Clara was the first to catch up with her.

'Bloody hell, Trixie!' she exclaimed. 'Who the hell is Roger?'

Trixie stood in the middle of the car park, her hands on her hips,
grinning. 'Oh yeah, nice bloke. Just happens to be Julian's dad…'

Chapter 25

'Are you really going to talk to Julian's dad?' asked Declan.

They were still standing in the car park of the Frog and Wicket.

'No way!' Trixie was appalled at the suggestion. 'I've no intention of sparing Julian from Donna's clutches, that scumbag deserves everything he gets. He can find out what she's really like at his leisure as far as I'm concerned. I only mentioned Roger because I wanted to have a bit of leverage of our own. I doubt that he'd think much of Donna's antics, enough perhaps to have a chat with his son about her suitability. If Donna really has set her sights on marrying Julian, she'd hate that, enough perhaps to persuade Julian not to go through with his plans…'

Clara nodded. 'You know, that's really clever…' She gave Trixie a warm smile. 'In fact, the whole thing was brilliant! I can't believe you just waltzed over there like that and let her have it.'

'Yeah, but it didn't go according to plan, did it? Donna's a bigger bitch than I realised and we're not really any further forward.'

'You were still amazing though. I would never have had the nerve to do what you did. And at least you tried.'

Trixie held her look for a moment. 'Isn't that what friends do?' she asked, an anxious look on her face.

She was asking for forgiveness and Clara responded in an instant, pulling Trixie into a fierce hug. 'Oh, you daft bat,' she said. 'I've missed you!'

The two women grinned at one another.

'I do still think you should be on the stage though,' admitted Clara. 'You looked like you rather enjoyed it back there in the pub.'

Trixie thought for a moment. 'Hmm, maybe,' she said. 'Although perhaps am-dram is more my style...'

Declan laughed. 'Well, I for one would certainly pay good money to come and see you,' he said, and then sniffing, turned to look at the street behind him. 'Can anyone smell vinegar?' he asked. 'Because I'm absolutely starving. Do either of you fancy some chips?'

Clara clutched her stomach. 'Ah, yes please. The smell is driving me mad, and sorry, Trixie, but I think your beautiful lasagne might be dry as a bone by now. We never got to eat it after all.' She clapped a hand over her mouth as soon as she realised what she had said, but Declan just laughed.

Trixie stared at them in horror. 'I've completely ruined your evening,' she said. 'I'm so sorry...'

Declan gave Clara a look which made her insides do peculiar things. 'There'll be other evenings, Trixie, don't worry. Clara and I can wait.' He gave an exaggerated sigh. 'Besides, there are other things which are important too. Not *as* important obviously, but still a teeny tiny bit important... Shall we take our chips back to Joy's Acre? I think we need to come up with a battle plan.'

★

Megan was white as a sheet. And Liam wasn't much better. He looked stunned, and if anything, Clara was more concerned about how he was taking the news.

'I'm really sorry, but we thought you should know, and as soon as possible.' Maddie handed them both a mug of tea, and then fetching the last one for herself sat back down at the kitchen table to join the others. The chips that Declan and Clara had bought in had long since been eaten and cleared away.

'I knew I was right,' said Megan, looking at Clara, her eyes welling with tears. 'But now that I know Julian really is a cheat, somehow, it doesn't make it any better.'

'In a way, it's still a massive compliment, don't forget that,' she said. 'Whatever Julian's hateful motives, by copying your design he's as good as told you he thinks you're better than him.'

'Except that none of that matters if he wins. That's my future, Clara. The chance to open my own forge, to follow my dreams in creating what *I* want, building a business and watching it grow.'

Liam swallowed and took her hand. 'You can still have all that, Megan, I promise you. Without the money it might take longer, but you'll get there… we'll get there.'

She snatched her hand away. 'How could you have been so stupid?' she cried. 'Didn't you stop and think for one minute what might happen?'

Liam flinched. 'No,' he said. 'I didn't think about it… Why would I? Megan, I try to live my life believing people to be decent human beings, and on the whole they are. If that makes me naive then…' He searched the air for the right words. 'Then that makes me naive,' he finished helplessly.

His face was searching hers for a clue that she might not hate him.

'I would give anything right now to turn back time so that none of this happened, but I can't, any more than I can change the way I am. I had no idea who Donna was. I see clients all the time and they come in all sorts of shapes and sizes, young and old, and generally I don't need to know their life history. How could I possibly have known that Donna is Julian's girlfriend when she's deliberately never been to the competition? Out of the dozens of people I see every month. And I certainly never thought that she would take photos of all your work the moment I stepped foot out of the room.'

'Megan,' said Seth gently, 'this is not Liam's fault. It's not about apportioning blame, it's about trying to make sure that the talent you have is recognised, and that the result on Saturday is the right one.'

'That's easy for you to say,' she retorted. 'It's not you that's worked your arse off over the last few weeks, and sunk everything you have into a project. How would you feel, knowing that you've still got a whole day's work ahead of you, and at the end of it someone will discount every ounce of effort you've put into it and call you a liar?'

Seth nodded, accepting her anguish. 'You're right, it is easy for me to say. But I say it knowing that every single person sitting around this table has known what it's felt like to lose a dream. At some point or another, we all have.' He glanced at Trixie. 'Some more recently than others.'

Trixie pushed forward a Victoria sponge she had made earlier that afternoon. 'And the thing is, Megan, sometimes you convince yourself that there's only one way to achieve your dream, and you become so blinkered in that view that you close your mind to possibility, or worse, think you've failed if something goes wrong.'

'She's right,' added Clara. 'Life's not like that. There's never just one path through the woods, and any number of them can lead you out the other side. Some paths may look better than others, but in the end they all take you to the same place. Whatever the outcome on Saturday, it doesn't change who you are, or what you're capable of, neither does it change your skill as a blacksmith. Now we can only tell you what we believe to be true, but you, Megan, you have to believe it.'

Liam nodded, looking like his heart was breaking. As Clara looked at everyone sitting around the table, she could see that same belief written on each of their faces, because in a way Megan's story was the same as their own. They had all come to Joy's Acre following a dream, and all had been sorely tested over time but, through all the trials and tribulations of life there, one thing still remained: even when they lost faith in themselves, they all still believed in each other.

The room was filled with an expectant silence which no one wanted to be the first to break, though all were secretly hoping it would be Megan.

In the end it was Liam who cleared his throat nervously, and tapped his fingers on the table a few times before reaching into the inside pocket of his coat. He extracted a white envelope and gently laid it on the table, where it sat looking rather like an unexploded bomb.

He stroked a finger across one eyebrow, frowning as he did so. There was a sharp, quick intake of breath.

'I've been waiting for this to arrive,' he said, 'and it came today.'

Megan looked up.

'And I had thought that I would wait until after you'd won on Saturday before I gave it to you. But now, with the outcome of the competition so uncertain, if I did that I have a feeling you might think I was offering it as a consolation prize… and I couldn't bear for you to think of it that way. It was never that, Megan. This is all I've ever wanted.'

He pushed the envelope towards her. 'Go on, open it, please…'

She fingered the edge of the white paper, her hand trembling slightly. Her eyes were full of questions but, although her lips moved, no words came out. And then, with a sudden swift movement, she slid the envelope towards her and pulled out several sheets of thick, creamy paper.

Clara could feel the breath collectively held around the table as Megan scanned first one sheet and then the next. She looked up, her eyes finding Liam's, and then looked down again. A hand strayed to her chest and then returned to clutch the paper once more. She sniffed.

'This is about your house,' she said, 'but I don't understand...'

'It's a transfer deed,' replied Liam, clearing his throat again. 'Because when my gran died and left me the house, it was obviously solely in my name. I had to have a bit of work done to sort out the electrics and whatnot, but now, apart from just the cosmetic stuff, all that's been done. It's essentially a blank canvas waiting to have a new stamp put on it, and I rather hoped we might do that together...'

He tapped the top sheet of paper that Megan was still holding. 'This is from my solicitor, and if you sign the bottom sheet next to my signature, half the house will become yours.'

Trixie let out an excited gasp.

'I wanted to wait until the work was finished before I discussed it with you...' he pulled a face, 'which is probably why you thought I didn't want you to move in with me.' He gently took the papers from her and then leaned forward to take her hand. 'You asked me about it once before and I sort of fudged the issue because I wanted to do this properly, Megan. I didn't want you to just come and live with me...'

He reached back inside his jacket pocket and placed a small red velvet box on top of the papers. 'Instead I wanted you to live there with me, as my wife...'

Megan's fingers closed over the box as the first tear slid down her face. 'Oh my God,' she breathed. Her lips were trembling.

Liam's chair scraped across the tiles as he pushed it back from the table and sank to one knee.

'Megan Forrester, would you do me the very great honour of becoming my wife?'

Chapter 26

Clara took the last of the cakes from Liam and laid them down on the table. As yet the marquee was empty but today was set to be their busiest of the competition yet, and they had come prepared. Trixie had really excelled herself this time and the table was groaning with sweet offerings.

'I still can't get over the fact that you asked Megan to marry you in front of everybody,' said Clara. 'You need a medal for bravery, I don't know about anything else.'

Liam rolled his eyes. 'It didn't occur to me until afterwards what would have happened if she had said no. I think I might have passed out. More bizarre than that though, at the time it felt like exactly the right moment to do it.'

Clara laughed. 'Less bizarre than you'd think. Stuff like that tends to happen at Joy's Acre. It probably earned you some brownie points though. Women usually appreciate grand gestures, and that was pretty big by anyone's standards.'

She gave him an impromptu hug. 'I am so happy for you though, both of you, and whatever happens today, just hang on tight to each other and you'll be fine. How is Megan this morning anyway?'

'Well, put it this way, when we walked into the forge this morning, Julian called a cheery good morning, which sounds nicer than it was.

He has the most peculiar way of making even a greeting sound smug. Megan walked past him, without so much as turning a hair in his direction and said, *I am so taking you down, you worthless piece of...* Well, I'm sure you can imagine the rest.'

Clara's eyes widened. 'Crikey... That's probably a good thing though, don't you think? Fighting talk and all that.'

'It is. Whatever happens, Megan is going to do her absolute best, she can't do any more. The rest lies in the hands of the judges.'

The three finalists had been hard at work for about three hours now and already the number of spectators far exceeded that of previous weeks. The representatives from the National Trust had just arrived and would spend the rest of day with the competition judges, perusing the entrants' past work, their designs and of course the work in progress. It would become obvious to them in a very short space of time that two of the entries were almost identical. And it was what happened after that which would be crucial.

The whole competition could just be halted then and there, declared null and void. Or possibly, the third entrant made the winner by default, but everyone had to hope for Megan's sake that the judges allowed the competition to run its course and leave the matter of any potential cheating for dealing with in the final decision-making process. Seth and Declan were quite prepared to petition for Megan at that point, but doing so in advance of any judging seemed like potential suicide. Even then, gaining the commission itself was another matter entirely. The judges from the Trust still reserved the right not to award it; after all, the resultant gate would be sitting on one of their properties and had to be worthy of their investment. But Clara couldn't see how they could possibly ignore what had gone on, and no one needed to spell out what that could mean.

Clara looked anxiously towards the entrance to the marquee, but there was still no sign of Seth. One thing was sure – it was going to be a very long day.

'Liam, could you do me a favour and keep an eye on things here for a few minutes? I usually take everyone a drink about this time, and I'm dying to see what has been going on.'

He nodded. 'Yeah, sure. I'm not sure what to do with myself anyway, I feel like a spare part.'

She gave him a sympathetic smile. 'Maddie will be here soon, and we're not open for refreshments yet so you shouldn't need to serve anyone, just make sure no one swipes the cakes.' She looked at Liam's anxious face. 'Have something yourself though, obviously… if it helps.'

With only three people now left in the competition, it took a matter of moments to load up a tray with drinks, and Clara carried them across the courtyard, her stomach in knots. She had grown used to the noise from the forges, the rhythmic striking of metal upon metal, but this morning, the place rang with an almost frenzied energy that could be heard in every note.

'Morning, Peter,' she called as she entered the first forge, setting down one of the mugs on a work table. The blacksmith looked up and smiled, nodding a thank you, but carried on without a word. Clara sighed. This was so hard for everyone.

Peter was probably the person to whom they had given the least thought, and seeing him now Clara felt awful for his predicament. He was a quiet man, a competent blacksmith, committed to his craft, who had worked solidly throughout the competition, but who was now about to become embroiled in something through no fault of his own. He had eyes in his head as much as the next man and, as Clara crossed to look at his display board showing his design, she knew he must have come to his own conclusions about what had been going on. Yet still he had not said one single word about it.

The boards had only just been put up today to enable the judges to view the design process of each competitor and, as she studied Peter's, she could see straight away the difference between him and Megan. Peter's work was solid, and traditional, but it was clear he didn't have the same artistic skill that Megan had. His sketches lacked detail and had none of the embellishment that hers did, favouring instead twists and scrollwork which, while giving his design a very stately, traditional feel, were rather lacking in originality.

She wished Peter good luck and crossed into the space next door. Julian was also hard at work although she was surprised to see how far his piece had progressed. He seemed to be much further ahead than Megan and, although she could see straight away that the design had been copied from hers, it was also very apparent that there were huge differences in the physical gate that had been made. Not differences down to the design, but instead the evolution of it due to the workmanship of two very different blacksmiths.

Placing Julian's drink down on the work bench, she was about to leave when he thrust the piece of metal he was working back into the forge and came to stand beside her. She tried to appear casual, as if she weren't really interested in what was taking place around her, but to her alarm he took up his mug, smiling broadly at her.

'You're Megan's friend, aren't you, from the farm?'

'I work there, yes,' she replied, determined to be as vague as possible.

'I thought so. You're also friends with the bloke that's been sniffing around here all week. The one that seems to think he can help out a certain competitor and no one will notice.'

Clara eyed him cautiously. 'If you mean Seth, then he's been around this week simply because it's his job to be here. You can hardly expect an elderly lady of eighty to organise things for the competition. Besides, Seth looks after a lot of the maintenance here, has done for years.'

'Yeah right. So him being so pally with the judges is just a coincidence then, is it?'

'Well, in so much as that they are also organisers of the competition, yes I guess it is.' She smiled sweetly.

'Or maybe it's that the old lady's house is not the only thing he's fixing?'

Clara held his look calmly. 'Goodness, that almost sounds as if you're accusing him of cheating. I can assure you Seth would never stoop to that level. You really would have to be a gutless, low-life scumbag to stoop so low, wouldn't you?'

The sickly smile fell from Julian's face, but Clara wasn't about to stick around to hear what he had to say next.

'Anyway, got to dash, sorry, I'd hate Megan's tea to get cold.'

There was at least some measure of truth in her statement and moments later Clara passed Megan her drink, watching anxiously as she wrapped her hands around the mug.

'I am so nervous,' she said. 'My mouth is dry as a bone.' She took a sip of her tea. 'And it doesn't help that the judges have been up and down several times already, asking questions. I could barely speak to them.'

'Hmm, Julian mentioned that they'd been around. That is what they should be doing though, Megan, don't forget that. It doesn't necessarily mean anything. What sort of questions were they asking?'

'Pretty general stuff really. Could I explain the reason why I chose the design I did? Where had my inspiration come from? Was my design based on work I've done previously?'

'So things you might expect them to ask?'

She nodded. 'I guess so.'

'Well then, all is well, for the moment at least.'

★

Clara didn't really become aware of the mumblings and gossiping until just after lunch. People had come and gone from the refreshment tent all morning and the atmosphere had been good-natured, with an air of excitement permeating the place. The comments had all been complimentary as far as she could tell, and it was hard to put a finger on exactly when that had begun to change, but slowly Clara became aware that the rustle of conversation had grown sharper in tone. Not only that, but Maddie had heard snippets of several conversations which would seem to confirm her fears. People were talking, and they were mostly talking about Megan.

Neither she nor Maddie had managed to get out of the tent for a while now, and Clara was relieved when, looking up from her latest customer, she saw Seth coming towards her.

'It's not good news, I'm afraid,' he said, as soon as they had moved away. 'The word is that Megan and Julian are both going to be disqualified. I don't know where that's come from, because I certainly haven't heard it from the judges – in fact, they've been exceptionally tight-lipped all day – but tongues are wagging big time.'

Clara's heart sank, even though she'd known this outcome was a distinct possibility. 'Oh no, that's so unfair.'

'It is, and I've just been to check with Megan. No one has asked her any questions about potential cheating so, if she's going to get any opportunity at all to defend herself, it's going to come right down to the wire. Liam is over with her now in case anyone does want to talk to her in advance of the judging but, as that's supposed to be at three o'clock, it doesn't give them much time.'

Clara checked her watch. It was nearly half past two.

'I'll text Trixie and get her to come over here now. We need everyone here who can possibly provide any evidence against Julian. Are you and Declan all set?'

Seth's expression was grim. 'As much as we can be.'

Clara was about to say something else when she became aware that the general milling about of people had turned into a steady exit from the tent and, as she looked towards the entrance, she spotted Declan waving furiously.

'You need to come over to the judging tent now,' he said, once he reached them. 'The judges are going to make an announcement.'

★

'If I could have quiet please…'

Clara felt Declan's fingers entwine with hers.

'Ladies and gentlemen, please… If I could have quiet so the judges can speak to you all.'

Two of the judges and the representatives from the Trust stood on a small stage at the top of the tent. The third judge was pacing back and forth, trying to be seen, and, more importantly, even though he held a microphone, to be heard. Megan was locked in Liam's arms, standing a little further forward than Clara was, but of Peter and Julian she could see no sign. The marquee was a crush of people, and it was impossible to see past the throng of bodies.

'Ladies and gentlemen, please.' His words were accompanied by a shrill whistle from one of the massed throng of spectators, and the loud hum of conversation dropped away to nothing.

'Thank you… As you know, today is the final round of competition and, after a full week working on their designs, the time is now up for our three blacksmiths.'

'Yeah, one of them at least!'

The voice from the crowd was loud in the hushed tent. There was a titter of amusement and Clara clenched her jaw. How could people possibly find this funny?

'Unfortunately, after several weeks of excellent competition, a rather serious matter has come to our attention today. I'm extremely saddened therefore to have to announce that as a result of this it has been decided that Julian Bamford and Megan Forrester both be disqualified from the competition.'

What?

A huge wall of noise rose up.

Clara swung her head to look at Declan. *Oh this was so unfair! Calling it off without any explanation of what had gone on at all…*

'And as a result… And as a result…' The judge was struggling to make himself heard above the noise. '… We have all agreed that Peter Fielding be declared as this year's winner!'

The crowd erupted into noisy shouts, clapping, catcalls, and whistles.

'If you would like to make your way to the front please, Peter.'

Clara struggled to see what was going on but it was impossible above the jostling heads. She pushed her way forward until she had reached Megan's side, and in seconds, Seth and Maddie were standing there too.

Liam had released Megan from his arms and to Clara's amazement she stood in their circle, a resigned but calm expression on her face.

'It's okay,' she said. 'Honestly, it's okay… It's what I guessed would happen.'

It broke Clara's heart to see that, despite her pain, Megan was determined to cling to the last shreds of her courage and dignity.

'But you haven't had a chance to even explain!'

Megan nodded. 'The rules of the competition are quite clear – if there is any sign that a blacksmith has tried to give themselves an advantage over any other in the competition then that person is disqualified. I can't expect them to be judge *and* jury. Their only course of action is to do exactly what they have.' She smiled at Liam. 'I'll get there,' she said. 'One day...'

A lump rose in Clara's throat that was a mixture of many things and, at that moment, the strongest of which was pride.

She stood back a little so that she was directly facing Megan. 'Then I applaud you,' she said. And with that she began to clap. And so did, Maddie, and Seth, and finally Liam, with a look on his face that she hoped Megan would always remember.

There was a shrill whistle as Peter, having made his way to the stage, took the microphone. In an instant the noise in the tent ceased.

Clara craned her neck to see.

'Hello...' he began. 'I'm sorry, you'll have to all bear with me, I'm not much used to being up in front of folks and talking.' He cleared his throat. 'I just wanted to say thank you... to the judges, to the other competitors, to Agatha for allowing us to use the Hall again and making us so welcome... and to everyone else for coming today...'

A huge round of applause broke out.

'It's been a tough competition, the third I've entered, and so it's pretty special to be standing up here, I can tell you...' He broke off for a moment to look at the judges to his right. 'But I'm sorry, I can't accept this prize.'

It took a couple of seconds for his words to gather meaning. Everyone was poised to start applauding again, and a couple of claps rang out before hands were suddenly stilled as what Peter had said sank in. A ripple of shock ran around the room, and Clara could see heads swivelling to look at one another in astonishment.

'You see, the simple fact of the matter is that mine is not the best design here today, nor is it the best gate by any means. I understand the judges have had a difficult decision to make, and I'm very grateful that they have declared me to be the winner, but I'd rather not accept it, if it's all the same. I think there's a worthier winner here today.'

The crowd erupted as Peter stepped down off the stage. Megan stared at everyone, her face echoing the same stunned expression as on those around her. Her hand went to her mouth in shock and she looked at Liam, silently asking him if he had also heard what she just had. Clara had no idea what would happen now.

The conversation around the room grew louder and louder and, although Clara couldn't see the judges, she could only imagine the disarray at the top of the tent. It continued for several minutes more, Clara's heart pounding in her chest as they waited to see what would happen.

A voice suddenly boomed out from the microphone.

'Ladies and gentlemen… could I please ask Miss Forrester and Mr Bamford to make their way to the staging area please… And if I could ask for your patience while the judges have some time to… er, consider what we do now.'

'Bloody hell,' said Seth. 'I bet they're having kittens.'

Liam was already beginning to lead Megan forward, and Clara immediately stepped into the space they had just moved from. There was no way she was getting left behind. She shot a glance at Declan and was relieved when he nodded and followed suit, as did Maddie and Seth. Megan would not be doing this on her own.

She had just reached the edge of the stage when Megan suddenly stopped, pulling at Liam's hand. Her face was contorted with emotion.

'I can't do this,' she whispered. 'They won't believe me.'

'Yes, you can,' he urged. 'Come on, we're all with you.'

But it was as if she was suddenly stuck, her feet rooted to the ground. It had taken nearly all of her strength to get her this far, and the effort of remaining dignified in the face of the huge hurt she must be feeling had sapped the last of it.

Liam pulled her to him and placed a soft kiss on her lips. Then he simply held both her hands and stood, holding her frightened look with one of love and encouragement. He let go of one hand, and fished in his pocket, withdrawing the same red box that they had seen the night before. In it was Megan's ring, a ring she had so desperately wanted to wear today but had taken off at the last minute in case it got lost or damaged. He slipped it back over her finger.

'You'll be needing this,' he said. 'Don't let today go, Megan. You are a strong resourceful woman, beautiful, incredibly talented, and the only woman I have ever loved. Ever since I was a small boy I looked at you and saw the stars, and when you looked back at me I felt your light shine through me too. I couldn't believe it when our friendship turned to something more... I still can't, but I do believe in us and, above all, I will always believe in you.'

A sudden rush of tears filled Clara's eyes, and she felt Declan's warm hand slip around her waist. His other hand found hers, holding it close to her heart.

Megan nodded, trembling, and took a deep breath. 'I love you,' she whispered. And then she moved forward to go and stand by Julian's side. Peter smiled and made room for her.

The head judge approached her first.

'Miss Forrester. I don't have to explain the seriousness of this matter, but under the circumstances it would appear that we have no choice but to allow you both to speak. Perhaps you might like to go first.'

She swallowed. 'I'm not a cheat,' she said. 'And I don't believe I should be disqualified when I've done nothing wrong. That would be tarring me with the same brush as Mr Bamford and that's not something I'm prepared to accept. By copying my design not only has he made a mockery of it, but he has also sought to make useless the incredible amount of hard work that I have put into this competition. I have done none of those things. I have simply done my best, and abided by all the competition rules. As a result, I wish for my work to be judged on the basis of my skill in fulfilling the design brief and also the execution of that design.'

'And you think that stealing the design from my car means you've done nothing wrong, do you?' Julian sneered at her. 'You're more delusional than I thought.'

The judge held up a hand. 'Mr Bamford, I don't believe I have asked you to speak yet, but now that you have, is that what you're saying happened?'

Julian nodded. 'Yes, I'm saying that's what happened. Everyone round here knows my car, and I'm often in town. It wouldn't have been difficult for her to swipe my stuff. I'd left the drawings in a folder on the passenger seat.'

'How convenient,' drawled Megan. 'Why would I possibly want to pinch your sketches, Julian? When my own were already fully developed.'

Clara looked at Liam. She knew that Julian wouldn't go down without a fight, but the threat of an allegation from Donna was still a real one and Megan needed to be careful. They had no idea whether Trixie's warning to Donna had been enough to keep her from telling

Julian about their questioning of her, but either way Megan needed to keep the details of how Julian obtained her design as scant as possible – if she could, that was. Julian had always taken great delight in goading her at every opportunity and he would be unlikely to stop now.

'Well, I would imagine because my design was better than yours,' he said. 'After all, you don't have many years under your belt, do you? Fresh out of college, no real experience of taking a design brief from a client, and you must be desperate to make your mark. It's a tough business to be in, Megan, especially for—'

'For what, Julian?'

'Someone so young,' he answered with a smug grin, knowing that he had just avoided the trap he could have so easily fallen into. Maybe he wasn't so stupid after all.

The judge held up his hand again.

'This really isn't getting us anywhere. You are both accusing each other of cheating, and discussing motives won't get us any further towards the truth. What I need is evidence, otherwise it's one person's word against the other's.'

Clara's heart sank as she looked at Liam's distraught face. The only evidence Megan could give might leave him open to allegation from Donna, and yet the truth of what had happened was the only thing that would save Megan right now. Unwittingly, Liam had put her in an impossible position.

'Mr Bamford, do you have anything to add?'

He shook his head angrily.

'Or you, Miss Forrester?'

Megan looked straight at Liam, and gave a small smile. 'No,' she said. 'I don't, I'm sorry.'

'Then I think we must accept that our original decision still stands. Gentlemen, do you agree?' He turned to look at his fellow judges.

'Oh, this is awful,' said Declan. 'There must be something that can prove it was Megan's design originally… Liam, can't you think of something, anything that might help? Something that Julian couldn't possibly know about Megan's design?'

Liam's eyes widened. 'Bloody hell, the photos! Christ, why didn't we think of that before?' He took several steps forward. 'Megan, your phone! Show them your phone, with the photos you took when we visited Powis. Tell them why your design works…'

It took a second for Megan to understand what Liam was saying but then she began to fish frantically in her pocket. 'Wait!' she shouted. 'I do have something…'

With shaking hands, she opened up the pictures on her phone and began to scroll through them, her face creased with concentration.

'See, look,' she said, passing it to one of the judges. 'These are how I got my inspiration for the design. If you take them over to my sketches you'll see what I mean.'

He did as he was asked, crossing to the display boards at the side of the stage where the designs had been pinned. He passed the phone between his colleagues, their heads bent together, and it felt like several decades passed before he returned.

'Miss Forrester, I can see that you have copied the elements from the photo quite carefully, but with respect, this is a picture of the original gate on the site at Powis Castle looking into the gardens beyond, and it's an aspect that is much photographed. I don't quite see how—'

'Then ask him,' she argued. 'Ask Julian how he came up with the design. I bet he can't tell you. Ask him what's special about it.'

Julian's face was like thunder. 'Well, it's like he said, isn't it? Everyone knows that photo. I looked at it just the same as you did, and decided it would make a great gate. With the trees in the centre and all the leaves and stuff. It's pretty obvious, Megan.'

'No, that wasn't what I asked you... I asked you what was special about it? Go on Julian, tell us!'

'Miss Forrester, I'm not sure that this is getting us anywhere, I—'

'Please,' she begged. 'This is important.'

Slowly, one of the other judges came forward, the tall man with the bushy brown beard. He looked first at her phone and then back at her sketches. 'I think I'd like to hear this,' he said. 'I'm beginning to understand what you mean.'

Megan took a deep breath. 'You see, I don't know that much about Powis Castle, but what I do know is that the gardens are renowned, and everywhere you look there are focal points, things that draw the eye, a bit like setting the scenery on a stage. I know that gardeners do this, because at the place where I'm staying, Joy's Acre, Clara does just the same thing. It's so that when you stand in certain places things come together in a perfect view...'

Clara felt Declan's gentle nudge on her arm.

'When I looked at the gate the day I took these photos, I saw the perfect frame of the garden behind it. You have the huge tree, just right of centre, with the sweep of the hills behind, and then in front of the tree the path leading off to one side, and the flowers... My design doesn't just copy the view; it exactly mirrors it. I scaled it in such a way that if you stand where I stood on that day the detail on the gate exactly matches what you can see behind, like it's superimposed. But you can only see that from one exact spot...'

She pointed to her phone, still in the judge's hand. 'Look again,' she said, 'and you'll see what I mean.'

There were astonished looks between them all, and then the bearded judge broke into a huge smile. 'Oh my word, that's clever,' he said.

Clara suddenly became aware of the swelling noise behind her. The last few minutes had felt like they were standing in a separate room, she had been so intent on what was happening, but now it was as if all the other sound had suddenly been let back in.

Liam broke away from the group and ran forward to scoop Megan up in a ferocious hug, swinging her off her feet. Peter stood back, a huge smile on his face, as a scarlet-faced Julian pushed past him and stormed out of the back flap of the marquee.

One of the judges touched Peter on the arm, and Clara saw the answer to the man's question on his face even before he nodded, looking straight at Megan. And then he began to clap. Within seconds everyone around them began to clap too, and Megan stood in the centre of them all, grinning from ear to ear, Liam holding her hand in the air.

Declan crushed Clara to him, kissing her with such an intensity it left her reeling for a moment. Then he pulled away, grinning, and crossed over to where Peter was standing, shaking his hand, and the two of them stayed there, clapping as loudly as they could.

All around them people were beginning to notice what was happening and the noise was becoming louder and louder. She almost jumped out of her skin when she felt a hand on her shoulder and turned around to see Trixie beside her, grinning like a Cheshire cat.

'Ladies and gentlemen…' began the judge into the microphone.

'She did it! She bloody well did it!' squealed Trixie in her ear, and then she threw her arms around Clara, hugging her tight.

'And we did it too! What a team!'

Clara stared at her, a fresh load of tears welling in her eyes, because Trixie was absolutely right. They *had* all done it, every single one of them.

Chapter 27

Seth threw another log on the fire and went to retake his position on the bench beside Maddie, his legs stretched out in front of him.

'I think we should make it a rule that every Sunday be like this,' he said.

From beside him Maddie raised her glass.

'Sounds good to me,' she said. 'I don't think you're going to get an argument from any of us.'

'That's because everyone's too knackered to argue with you,' quipped Tom.

And it was probably true, but they all laughed just the same. The only people missing from their group were Megan and Liam. Not surprisingly, Megan had gone home with Liam the night before and today they were being left alone to celebrate Megan's win in their own way. And, of course, to spend some much-needed time together, and perhaps, just maybe, make a start on planning their new life together.

For everyone else back at Joy's Acre it had been a day of getting back to normality, of catching up with sleep, and just enjoying doing what they did best, and that included a rather late, but nonetheless splendid, roast dinner of epic proportions.

Now they were sitting outside, each nursing a glass of wine, and enjoying a perfect autumn afternoon. The rays from the sun hit the garden at an angle now, and soon the days would shorten even more, but for now everyone was lapping up the golden glow, warmed even more by the flames from the fire pit.

This was a tradition that Seth had started a few years ago, and one that for Clara always brought a huge sense of peace to the garden as it began to settle itself for the winter. Her frantic days of activity were over for the year, and a more gentle rhythm would assert itself until the return of the spring next year. Every day the fire would be lit to be enjoyed by them all as they worked around the cottages, a place to sit and warm bones, to chat over a cuppa, or just to stare into space and relax.

'So, how long before the roof on the Blacksmith's Cottage is finished then, Tom?' asked Seth. 'Are we going to be up and running soon?'

'Aye, I reckon another week should see it done. Now that you're not sloping off to do other stuff every five minutes of course.'

Seth rolled his eyes. 'No, I'm happy to be back, I think we all are… It feels almost as if we've all come home. And even if we haven't been away, I think it's time to simply enjoy Joy's Acre and get back to where we used to be.'

It was an easy comment, with no barb to it, just a simple statement which encapsulated how everyone had been feeling.

'And just because I think we all need to hear it, are we all agreed that, as much as we love Declan, he's going to have to find someone else to star in his TV show, because none of us are going to be in it?'

There was a chorus of agreement, none more emphatic than from Trixie, who was lying on her back in the middle of a blanket.

Beside Clara, Declan squeezed her hand, and from the corner of her eye she could see the smile break over his face.

'No one is more relieved than me, I promise you,' he said. 'I'm happy to admit that filming here was the worst idea I've ever had… and that telling Fiona to retract her claws and let go was one of the best.'

Seth leaned forward so that he could see Declan better. 'I know I'm speaking for everyone when I say how much we appreciate your honesty, and your integrity. You put the needs of Joy's Acre above your own business interests and it's a rare man that has the courage to do that.'

'Some might call it stupidity,' he said, 'but in this case I'm very happy to have been proved wrong. I honestly thought that what I could bring to Joy's Acre would be perfect for you, but sometimes, despite what you long for, you have to acknowledge the reality of the situation and act accordingly. My being here was ironically tearing apart the very thing that I loved about this place. Had the filming continued, I fear there would have been nothing left of it, and I couldn't do that to you, however much I believed that Clara and Trixie would have been perfect for TV. I couldn't let it go ahead knowing how wrong for you all it was. And I'm very grateful to a very special person for helping me to see that.'

'Hear, hear!' said Trixie.

'Clara knew that Joy's Acre exists and thrives because of the people here, and removing even just one ingredient from that mix would be like Trixie leaving the toffee out of her sticky toffee pudding. Without it, it would be a very plain pudding indeed. Clara was always the one who could see how dangerous changing the recipe could be and, although she might not have the loudest voice here, she spoke volumes nonetheless.'

'But I've still ruined the plans for the barn,' said Clara. 'If there's no TV series, there's no barn, no accommodation, no dining space for our guests…'

'We were going to manage perfectly well before Declan's idea even came along, and we'll manage perfectly well now,' said Seth, waving a finger at her. 'So none of that.'

Declan cleared his throat. 'Erm, actually I might still be able to help with that… in a roundabout sort of way.' He stared across the garden towards a figure making their way along the path.

'That's Agatha,' said Maddie. 'I didn't know you had invited her over, Seth.'

'I didn't,' he replied, confused.

'Er, no. That was me, I'm afraid,' said Declan.

They waited until she reached them, Seth immediately standing so that she could have his seat.

'I'm not so ancient that I can't stand for a few minutes,' she said, 'although on second thoughts, perhaps I will sit.' She patted Maddie's knee. 'Hello, dear,' she said. 'I'm not stopping though. I know you young things have plenty to be doing, but in view of what happened yesterday I thought I had better come and tell you my own news.' She gave what almost sounded like a giggle. 'As if things weren't exciting enough,' she added, and then to everyone's enormous surprise she winked at Declan.

'Hello again, young man,' she said. 'You haven't told them yet, have you?'

'Agatha, would I?' replied Declan, looking shocked that she could even suggest such a thing.

Seth ignored the theatrics. 'Told us what, Agatha?'

She gave a triumphant smile. 'I am eighty years old now,' she said. 'And I think it's high time I took things easy for a change. I've been rattling around in that big old house on my own for far too long now and I rather think I'd enjoy being waited on for a change, before I get too old to enjoy it.'

'Oh, Agatha, you're priceless.'

'Thank you, dear.' She tutted at the interruption. 'Now, I have bought a rather splendid bungalow in the village, and have also engaged the services of a lovely young lady called Pauline who is going to help look after it for me, so that I can become extremely lazy in my very old age.'

Clara glanced at Declan. 'What?' she said, looking up at Seth. He shook his head.

'So that obviously leaves the rather pressing question of what to do with Summersmeade Hall, and I'm very pleased to say that this darling man here has agreed to buy it from me. Isn't that right, Declan?'

Trixie sat bolt upright. 'Oh my God, Clara, you're going to be the lady of the manor!'

'What…? Trixie, you can't say things like that!'

All heads swivelled in Clara's direction, including Declan's, who was grinning like he was fit to burst. 'I think she just has…'

Agatha clapped her hands together in delight. 'Oh, I knew this would all work out perfectly. Now, I've told Declan that he can't have the lower field or the woodland at the bottom, because I want you to have that, Seth. It makes much more sense for it to belong to Joy's Acre. And, because I'm going to be rolling in pots of money, I'm going to do what I should have done before I went a bit gaga when Maddie first came, and give you the money to get your cottages and the barn finished. I want to see this place properly on the map before I die.'

Maddie was so surprised that she nearly threw the contents of her glass down her jeans, and for moment there was a shocked silence.

'Well, isn't anyone going to say thank you?' said Agatha, staring at Seth.

He roared with laughter, and in that moment all became movement as everyone crowded around to give Agatha and each other a hug. Everyone, that was, except for Clara, who was still staring at Declan.

'Lady of the manor,' he said. 'I rather like the sound of that.'

His gaze pulled her in, and who knows how long their kiss might have lasted had Trixie not cleared her throat very loudly.

Clara looked up to see that Agatha was on her feet once more.

'Now, I'm going to go and catch up on all the scandal in *Emmerdale*. What with all the excitement these last couple of weeks, I've missed several episodes and haven't got a clue who's murdered who! I shall leave the rest to you, Declan.' And with that she bent to kiss both Maddie and Clara before moving off again down the path, as quickly as she had come down it in the first place.

'You mean there's more?' said Maddie weakly.

Declan grinned. 'Only that I've agreed that Megan sets up her business there once the house is mine. Can't have a good forge like that going to waste, can we? It rather seemed like the perfect solution all round.'

'I can't take it all in,' said Seth, sinking back down on the bench. 'What are we going to do now?'

'Live happily ever after?' suggested Tom.

A voice floated up from the rug to which Trixie had returned. 'Well, I don't know about you lot, but I'm going to dye my hair pink again. I look middle-aged for goodness' sake. How can I possibly act like a teenager without bright pink hair!'

The sound of laughter echoed around the garden for quite some time as smoke drifted up lazily from the fire. A wood pigeon cooed from a tree behind them and a gentle breeze stirred the stands of lavender which bordered the path. It really was a perfect Sunday afternoon.

A Letter from Emma

Thank you so much for your company again throughout *Return to the Little Cottage on the Hill*. If this was your first visit to Joy's Acre, I hope it's a place you have come to love as much as I have. If you'd like to stay updated on what's coming next then please sign up to my newsletter here:

www.bookouture.com/emma-davies

Of course, Seth, Maddie, Tom, Trixie and Clara first began to tell their story in *The Little Cottage on the Hill*, and I have loved seeing them grow and develop individually as I've written each successive book. I never know quite how they're going to turn out, and as characters they have managed to surprise me on more than one occasion, but I hope you'll join them again as winter brings new challenges, romance, and a few tough times as well. As with any community, life isn't always plain sailing, but with a little love, hope and friendship, plus copious amounts of cake, of course, many a storm can be weathered, and it's been an absolute joy to spend a year in their lives. I hope you think so too.

One of the things I love about being a writer is when readers take the time to get in touch, it really makes my day. The easiest way to do this is by finding me on Twitter and Facebook, or you could also pop by my website where you can read about my love of Pringles among other things…

I hope to see you again very soon, and in the meantime, if you've enjoyed your visit to Joy's Acre, I would really appreciate a few minutes of your time to leave a review or post on social media. Even a recommendation to anyone who'll listen at the hairdresser's is very much appreciated!

Until next time,
Love Emma x

Acknowledgements

Like a lot of authors, I find writing acknowledgments quite difficult. Who do you thank when there are so many people who have influenced both your life and your writing? What if you miss someone out? When I mentioned this to a friend, the response was that this time around maybe I should acknowledge the achievement I myself have made in the writing of this, my tenth book. Now, while the comment was made with tongue very firmly in cheek, it did set me thinking...

Even though I consider myself lucky and very grateful to have the best job in the world, writing isn't easy. There are days when the words flow effortlessly and others when every word has to be ground out of your very soul. It's an incredibly intense and personal experience, and can leave you feeling like nothing in the world or totally bereft, but – and it's a very big but – when I read a book that touches me, or moves me, makes me laugh or cry, inspires or comforts me, I understand my own drive to write, and write better. Books matter, words matter.

Every book I write is written under changing circumstances, my own life goes on alongside it, and sometimes there are good things and sometimes there are not so good things, but each book always seems to have its own zeitgeist, and for me, this time around, it has been marked by reading some incredible books and words that will stay with me for a very long time. The writing and poetry of David Whyte for one, and the works of the late John O'Donohue have had particular significance for me during the writing of this book and to them, and all the others, I am incredible grateful.

And so, my heartfelt thanks on this occasion of course go to my fabulous publishers, Bookouture, my brilliant and very lovely editor, Jessie Botterill, but also, importantly to readers everywhere who, like me, make what we writers do a possibility but also give our words meaning.

Made in the USA
Coppell, TX
08 July 2022

79723045R20175